FIRE ... HOT ... SMOKE ...
NO AIR ... THE HEAT ...
THE PAIN

Something in Brevelan's past brought on this terror. Something she dared not let him see. Jaylor stroked her cheek comfortingly and cupped her chin gently. "Brevelan, trust me. There is no fire. We can get out of this if you'll just call the dragon. That rogue Thorm still fears her."

"Bring the torches!" Old Thorm's voice carried on the evening breeze. "The thatch is damp, the smoke will drive her out."

"She's mine when she runs," the fisherman crowed.

"What gives you first right?" someone else challenged.

"Once we've had her, she won't be a witch anymore," Old Thorm chortled.

"What about the wolf?"

"I'll slit the devil dog's throat first, before he can protect his mistress; before he has the chance to drain the blood from another man's body."

Brevelan blanched. Jaylor pulled her, and the wolf she cradled, tight against his chest.

"I won't let them hurt you," he promised. Though how, he didn't know. There were at least ten of them, and his magic wasn't designed to hurt people. That was the first law of the Commune.

His answer came from overhead, as a roar that only a dragon throat could muster filled his mind and ears. . . .

Also by
Irene Radford

*Coming soon from DAW Books

THE GLASS DRAGON

IRENE RADFORD

DAW BOOKS, INC.

DONALD A. WOLLHEIM, FOUNDER

375 Hudson Street, New York, NY 10014

ELIZABETH R. WOLLHEIM
SHEILA E. GILBERT
PUBLISHERS

DAW TRADEMARK REGISTERED
U.S. PAT. OFF. AND FOREIGN COUNTRIES
—MARCA REGISTRADA
HECHO EN U.S.A.

PRINTED IN THE U.S.A.

This book is dedicated to
Karen, Judith, Laurie, and Barbara,
who taught me how to search for dragons.

PROLOGUE

Coronnan is dying. Isolation, imposed upon us by the magic border, is the cause. This kingdom needs to be jolted out of its lethargy. No one is willing to grasp the tremendous power of this land, save me.

Our king is spineless, incapable of decision. My father was just as useless. So I killed him. My brothers, too. I used the king as long as I could. But he is so weak he cannot act, even with my prompting. The time has come to eliminate him for good.

Only I have the resolution to save this land. The great winged god Simurgh shall guide me. I shall make a sacrifice to him. What shall it be? A spotted saber cat? A great gray bear? Or perhaps a Kahmsin eagle.

No. I shall offer up the greatest sacrifice of all. The last female dragon.

CHAPTER 1

"The only way to catch dragons is to hunt 'em when they're young. Still silvery, you know," said a one-eyed derelict.

A half dozen heads nodded in the dim, cavelike pub.

Jaylor sucked in his breath, as shock drained what little energy he had left from his thin spell of delusion. Didn't these people know that dragons provided everything that was good and safe and free in Coronnan?

He'd encountered suspicion and distrust of dragons before. But never out and out hatred. The University of Magicians needed to know about this strange little village.

"Yeah, if you wait 'til dragons're growed, there ain't no way you can see a *s'murghin'* one of them." The middle-aged man next to Jaylor smelled of stale fish and salt brine. "About ten years ago we had to root out a whole nest of the blasted monsters. They was eatin' all our fish."

Green smoke from the crude hearth burned Jaylor's eyes. He kept them half closed, avoiding direct eye contact with the half-drunken men who shared his table in this cave that served as the tavern. As long as these local gossips viewed his body and not his eyes, they would see only a long lost friend. A different friend to each man.

"Lord Krej has the right of it. Told us we didn't have t' provide nothin' for dragons. They can feed elsewhere. Can't afford a tithe to the dragons and another tithe to lord, too." The derelict's one eye glittered and probed from the depths of his grizzled and wrinkled mask of a face. Jaylor looked away nervously.

"We can't afford to anger the dragons though. The

witchwoman's in league with them," another man added. He was covered in wood dust and wore an apron with more pockets than Jaylor bothered to count.

"Netted a big male in the nets last time we hunted. Couldn't kill him, but after he escaped he never came back." The fisherman leaned across the table toward the carpenter. "The old witchwoman deserted us then, and we did fine without one for nigh on ten years. Then last summer a new one shows up, and the dragons came back. I say we burn 'em both out."

"Without a witchwoman we have to depend on University healers. Who among us can afford a healer? If we could even get one to leave the comfort of Lord Krej's castle to come all the way down here," the carpenter argued.

Shouts of agreement and argument rose around Jaylor. The noise covered his recitation of a strengthening spell.

"Young'uns are cunning hunters. Only feed at night." Old One-eye continued to stare at Jaylor's unkempt appearance.

Nervously the young magician finger-combed his unfamiliar growth of new beard and long hair. It was so unlike his habitually clean face and fashionably restrained queue, he wondered if he'd ever get used to it.

He halted the gesture in mid-comb, afraid to call attention to his discomfort. He wished he could see the old man's aura, but the delusion blocked his inner sight.

He turned his combing gesture into a signal to the man tending the cask of ale. Somewhere across the bleak cave, the barkeep caught his gesture for more ale.

Awful stuff. It tasted more like . . . Jaylor decided he didn't want to think about what it really tasted like. It slaked the thirst of weeks on the road. That was all he asked.

"Young dragons're the same color as moonlight, slip in and out of shadows like a dream. Make a more interesting hunt that way." Old One-eye's intense stare drew Jaylor's gaze once again. The spell of delusion slipped a little more.

Stargods, he was tired. Carefully, he reinforced the

spell. Just a little longer. He had to keep these provincials believing he was a local just a little longer, until he had the information he needed. Then he could slip away and rest his depleted body in preparation for the next stage of his quest.

"Sometimes you have to go after dragons at the source. Clear out all the juveniles and sucklings in the nest and the ma goes away, too." One-eye continued rubbing his grizzled jaw with a scarred hand. Jaylor's own chin itched in sympathy. He resisted running his fingers through the new growth again. "If you let'em get too big, they'll rob the whole province."

"Worse than Rovers stealin' our young'uns."

Jaylor sat up straight and listened closer. There hadn't been Rovers in Coronnan in, oh, three hundred years. At least. Not since the magic border had been established. So, why were these people familiar with Rover habits?

Jaylor willed the conversation back to dragons. He needed to hear about the dragons.

The barkeep finally wound his way around the darkness of the cave interior. "Heard tell of a new nest up in the mountains."

"Last year's little'uns ought to be coming out for their first hunt right about now." One-eye threw out that information as if it were bait. For Jaylor or the rabble-rousers beside him?

The fisherman grabbed it, like the voracious fish he snagged out of the cold, blue depths of the Great Bay. "If'n they start robbing our catch again, we'll have a merry hunt. Soon as the snow clears the pass. This time we'll get the *s'murghin'* beasts 'afore they starve us out!" the fisherman laughed.

Chills radiated out from a tired place where Jaylor stored his magic. He knew he didn't like the viciousness of his informants. The disturbance in his magic convinced him not to trust them either.

"Odd season for first sight of the young." Jaylor found his voice after coughing out the acrid taste of the ale. "Most animals birth in the spring and have the young weaned by fall."

"Not dragons." The natives of the place chorused.

The equinox had just passed, though it still felt like winter outside. The last of the snow was still crunchy in the shade. Mud mired the roads so badly the huge, splayed feet of sledge steeds sank up to their hocks. Now was the time for birthing not weaning.

Jaylor quaffed more of the hideous ale. It was starting to taste good. He'd had too much. Pretty soon he'd lead the dragon hunt with his drinking companions.

The king's magicians gathered magic generated by dragons, to be used only for the good of the kingdom. King Darcine ruled by Dragon-right. He sat upon the Dragon Throne and wore a crown of precious glass forged by dragon fire.

Yet, according to village sages Jaylor had encountered on his journey, no one in his right mind went to see a dragon with less than murderous intent.

Who ever said a journeyman magician on quest was in his right mind?

"Go see a dragon," Old Baamin, the senior magician had ordered Jaylor.

But how did one see an invisible creature.

"The dragon nimbus is dying," said Baamin, defining the quest. "During your search you must listen very carefully for clues to the cause."

Jaylor had his answer. These locals hunted dragons for fun and for protection of their livelihoods and their lives.

Jaylor was also to keep his eyes open for any youngsters with signs of magic talent. University recruits were fewer and fewer each year. Of course (his youthful wisdom dictated), with fewer dragons left to emit magic, there naturally were fewer men to gather that magic.

"The rest of Coronnan reveres the dragons," Jaylor prompted the men around him.

"More fools they. *S'murghin'* predators they are." The barkeep grumbled. "More'n enough dragons in the north to keep them *magicians* happy. They're as mean a predator as any dragon."

"But if we hunt dragons again, the witchwoman will go away. None of you are sick right now, but who'll help my

Maevra when her time comes?" the carpenter interjected. He looked as if he wanted to agree with his companions but didn't quite dare.

"Dragons used to fly over nearly every week during the summer, until we stopped planting the Tambootie for them. You could catch sight of their rainbows now and again. Too bad something so pretty belongs to a creature so evil."

"Rainbows?" This was the first Jaylor had heard of a dragon having anything to do with a rainbow; though ancient sources said good weather was the result of a strong nimbus of dragons.

"When the sun hits a dragon's wings just right, a rainbow arches out and touches the ground." The barkeep sat to join the conversation. He swilled a huge mouthful of the poisonous ale. "If we see more'n one or two a week, we know it's time to go on a hunt again."

"Prism effect." Jaylor mumbled.

"Whism effect?" The one-eyed drunk looked up from his cup. His left eyelid was permanently closed, but it twitched with an emotion Jaylor couldn't read. He wondered if the eye were really gone. Perhaps, behind the scars, it glittered with the same malice as its undamaged mate.

Just for a moment Jaylor's magic vision penetrated the eyelid. He caught a brief image of a tall vigorous man with bright red hair. University red hair. Then the image faded. At one time the old derelict might have been an apprentice magician at the University. If so, he'd know about precious glass and prisms.

"Prism," Jaylor explained, "when sunlight hits clear glass at a precise angle the light refracts into a rainbow." He twisted the crude pottery mug in the firelight. Had these villagers ever seen enough glass, even the muddy colored stuff that was common in the capital, to understand its properties?

"Glass? Do you suppose a dragon is made of glass?" the barkeep murmured with awe. No one from this village in the back of beyond had probably ever seen true glass.

But they might have seen a dragon.

Jaylor wondered what kind of reaction he'd get if he pulled his tiny shard of viewing glass from his pack. They'd probably hang him, or throw him into the deepest part of the Great Bay as fish bait. The glass was barely as large as two of his fingers pressed together. But the mere possession of it identified him as a magician.

"Glass?" the one-eyed drunk laughed maliciously. "Another privilege for the Twelve and their greedy magicians. Wouldn't surprise me if dragons and glass come from the same hell. We're expected to provide food and shelter and cursed Tambootie trees under their orders, for their profit. And what do we get from it? Poorer by the day. I say we kill 'em all, magicians and dragons."

The little bit of magic left in Jaylor quivered in reaction to the derelict.

"I need to find the road into the mountains." Jaylor started to push back his stool. He'd had enough of the smoke and the steed-piss ale. It was time to move on.

One-eye stopped Jaylor's retreat with a look. The undamaged organ gleamed black in the dim light. The smell of Tambootie smoke tickled Jaylor's nostrils and lifted the top of his head to the cave roof. He silently mumbled an armoring spell before the odor sent him into the void between the planes of existence.

This old man suddenly reeked of the aromatic smoke. The old books in the library cautioned, repeatedly, to beware the stench of burnt Tambootie wood. A rogue magician intent on evil usually lurked behind it.

Old One-eye cast off his semblance of inebriation. The stench of Tambootie smoke intensified.

Jaylor tasted copper on his tongue. Tambootie trees always grew near veins of copper. The smoke must be infiltrating his entire body!

He pushed away his natural panic while he reached into the well of magic within him. It was dry. He was too tired to think. Instead he blinked his eyes, shifted his feet to a stronger position, and found another source. He strengthened the spell with a silent image, more precise than the formula of words.

In his mind he clothed each portion of his body in armor. He began with his vulnerable torso, spreading the protection upward and outward. Iron could douse a Tambootie wood fire. Iron would smother the smoke. His head cleared. He felt stronger, more alert now that his protection was complete.

Not precisely a traditional answer to the problem, but the University needed any magician they could find, even one who used rogue methods to accomplish traditional quests.

"Someone's got to find the dragon nest, keep track of it until we see if we need to hunt them out." Jaylor sought desperately for an explanation for his actions.

"Can't find a dragon without the witchwoman. She guards the path into the mountains."

Silence greeted that statement. None of the villagers looked too happy, least of all the carpenter.

"What witchwoman?" Jaylor dismissed the concept of *witch*. Women just couldn't gather magic.

"Our witchwoman, the one who guards the dragons," One-eye explained.

"She'll sell you a potion for the coughing disease or help your woman get with child." The barkeep was looking into his mug rather than at Jaylor. "All she asks in return is some new thatch or help with the plowing."

"Or a piece of your soul."

Jaylor had seen plenty of old crones during his wandering, forgotten widows living on the outskirts of villages. Most did midwifery. Some were skilled herbalists. That was the extent of their so-called magic.

Inside his head he heard cackling laughter. The high-pitched mockery denied his University trained assumptions. Tambootie smoke drifted around him once more. Jaylor's magic armor shriveled. He slapped a patching spell into his protection. The holes spread, the metal dissolved.

He shifted his feet once more. Energy and power seeped upward through his body. Stability and sanity followed the renewed magic.

"I've dealt with witches before." He turned on his heel

to leave the cave before anything else stripped him of more magic.

"I'll bet you have, magician."

"What did you call me?" Jaylor swung back to face One-eye. The other men seemed frozen in time and space.

"I called you what you are. Magician. Watch out for the witch and her familiars. She has a wolf who will tear out your heart while she shreds your soul and leaves you living. You'd best kill the beast right off."

Noon sunshine shattered into a thousand bright colors around Brevelan. She looked up through the shade of a leafy tree into the brilliance. One hand sought the silky ears of the wolf at her heels while the other shaded her eyes. The huge canine sat blinking his yellow eyes in contentment as he eased his injured foot. Brevelan cuddled the weight of the animal against her side. Affectionately, he grasped her hand in his mouth. No tooth penetrated her skin.

"Good morning, Shayla," she called to the fleeting shadow that streaked across the blue sky.

'Tis past noon. The pragmatic words formed in Brevelan's mind, just as the magnificent image of the speaker did. A swirl of all colors, that were really no color at all, formed into a faint winged outline. Shayla might be as small as an insect or as large as Krej's castle. Brevelan had no idea which.

"Did you have a good hunt?" She spoke openly for her own benefit while she threw the thoughts to her friend.

The picture of a fat cow appeared in her mind.

"Oh, Shayla," she sighed. "Some farmer is going to be very upset when he finds the carcass."

We didn't leave enough for him to find.

"We? When did you hunt with other dragons? You've been alone longer than I have." Something akin to loneliness snaked through her. Her golden companion whined to remind her that she wasn't really alone.

"You're right, Puppy. I have more friends here in the forest than I ever did at home." She stooped to hug the wolf. "Still, it would be nice to talk to someone who talks back occasionally."

I talk back.

"Too much sometimes. Who joined your hunt?"

The image of three huge male dragons appeared. One had blue tips on his transparent wings, another was red-tipped, the third still had the silvery gloss of adolescence clinging to the delicate wing vanes. One day soon those silver vanes promised a green glow.

The images hovered in a background of erotic purple. "Shayla! You shameful thing. Three at once."

The more fathers, the larger and stronger the litter. There was no embarrassment in the dragon's thoughts. She merely communicated a fact.

Suddenly the clearing around Brevelan's hut filled with children. A gangling blond teenager stood by her side, a babe suckled her breast. She felt the tug of its tiny mouth relieve the aching pressure of heavy milk. Off by the door, twin girls, with mops of red curls, giggled while plaiting a basket of fragrant grasses. Another boy, also red-haired, chopped wood while his younger brother built stacks of kindling. Only the oldest was blond.

As blond as the golden wolf whining in distress.

Brevelan sagged with relief when the illusion vanished as quickly as it had come.

Did that ease the thing you call loneliness?

"No! It made it worse." Brevelan's entire body ached with grief for the babies she would never have. She looked up once more. She couldn't lie to Shayla.

"I thought we were too close friends for you to spin your dragon dreams on me. Haven't you led enough innocent wanderers astray?" Bevelan forced indignation. Inwardly she wept for the figure of a dead man she had found last fall. Shayla's illusion had danced him through the forest until his skin hung from him like rags.

Stargods, but the man's death-smile haunted her still.

Perhaps my visions prepared you for him.

"Who?"

The one who comes.

"The barkeep," she mused. "He promised me an ell of

good cloth for the infusion I prepared." She'd caught him sneaking a glimpse of her breasts as she bent over the hearth. That had probably helped him satisfy his wife more than the tea.

Not the swiller of poison. Shayla was emphatic. *You should have given him a tincture of wazool root.* The dragon named a powerful laxative. Her thoughts were bright pink with humor. Then, still in a lighthearted tone, the dragon added: *Prepare yourself for the one who comes. Him.*

The image of a tall man carrying a gnarled walking staff flashed through Brevelan's mind. He appeared in the distance with the sun behind him. The glowing light of sunset outlined his long frame while it hid the details of his features.

Brevelan forced herself not to tremble in memory of the same image waking her in a cold sweat from deep sleep.

"Him."

The one in your dreams.

"The one who brings destruction." The vision had come to her three times. Only terrible portents of the future came in that number.

Her mind was empty. Shayla was gone. Back to her lair to sleep off the exertions of mating and hunting.

CHAPTER 2

Taylor dumped a bucket of water from the village well over his head. Icy droplets penetrated his unkempt hair and beard. His eyes cleared as some of the smoky stink washed away. Removing the stench from his clothing and hair would be another matter.

He drank long from the next bucket, rinsing the rancid taste of ale from his mouth. The air around him was clean and cool after the closeness of the cave.

When he had arrived in this village, he was too relieved to find habitation with drink and hot food to pay much attention to the place. Slowly he turned to survey the homes of the men who'd been in the pub.

Hovels. All the dwellings were as poor and as ragged as the men. A scrawny pig rooted around the edges of the village. He'd never seen such a skinny creature!

Now he felt guilty for eating the hot pasty and drinking their horrid ale—even though he'd paid good money for them. He felt as if he'd robbed the villagers of basic sustenance.

It had been a hard winter for everyone. Food stores rotted from too much rain. Privation always brought out diseases that thrived in the cold damp. Yet the weather was never cold enough to kill the pestilence and stop the rot.

Surely this village was in a better situation than most. The Great Bay lapped the foot of the cliff below the village. Fishermen had easy access to the bounty of the bay that fed Coronnan. Heavily forested foothills rose behind the rooftrees of the cottages. Wood should be plentiful for fishing boats, housing, furniture, and heat. Behind the houses he spied extensive fields and pastures spreading out beyond the village.

In the center of the village stood the ceremonial Equinox Pylon. A cluster of five poles, sparsely decorated with oak branches and faded ribbons. Where were the fronds of everblue, bright with new life, the first shoots of grain and new garlands of ribbons to celebrate the coming of the most fruitful season?

This was the first village he had encountered where life was so tenuous they didn't sacrifice the best of the new for the equinox or even have garbage for a pig!

Was this the result of a dragon stealing their food supply, too heavy taxation, or evidence of a neglectful lord?

Krej, lord of this province, donated thousands of drageen every year to the poor, to the study of healing arts, and to the priests of the Stargods. The nobility in Coronnan City considered him a good and generous man. Perhaps he should have donated some of that money to his own province.

Jaylor put aside his questions. His quest came first. Where was he, and where should he go next? "Go find a dragon, indeed." He snorted. "As if they grow under rocks. More likely they roost on the top of the blasted Tambootie trees."

From memory he drew a map of the kingdom in the air before his eyes. Green lines glimmered in nothingness as he sketched the sweep of the Great Bay on the east, a long chain of mountains curving from northwest to southeast. Coronnan River wound from those mountains through the central plains to open out into a wide delta filled with islands and aits. Entrenched among the largest islands created by the river's merging with the bay, Coronnan City presided over all shipping and commerce in the kingdom. Twelve provinces, equal in resources if not area, radiated out from the capital.

He had started his quest at the University in Coronnan City. A blue dot appeared on the map at the head of the bay. A line wandered away from that dot on the map to track his journey east and south. At each stopping place, the blue line widened a tiny bit. He dredged from his capacious memory every detail of every village along the way, the size, wealth, location, and the number of poles in their Equinox Pylon. Most Pylons consisted of three poles, scrupulously maintained with flowers and fruits in due season.

Five poles denoted ancient prominence. So why wasn't this Pylon revered?

As Jaylor had wandered south through Faciar, the groups of dwellings had become farther apart. The trader-roads had been well maintained, and usually there was enough to feed a stranger. Especially if he had news from the capital.

A stranger wasn't turned away as long as he wasn't a magician. Distrust of that elite order of talented men ran rampant beyond city and castle walls. No wonder Baamin had ordered Jaylor to guard well the nature of his quest and his status as journeyman magician. The secretive old sot knew the mood of the country better than Jaylor had expected.

Conditions were worse here in the south. Hostility toward everything from the capital was so strong Jaylor could see waves of hatred almost without magic. No one cared about news from Coronnan City, the king's waning health, or their obviously absent lord—Krej, first cousin to the king.

Something was very wrong here. He hadn't even had to ask about local dragon lore. These people seethed with it. As if the winged creatures embodied all of their problems. Had they even seen enough of their lord to know that he should be taking care of them?

Rumors in Coronnan City said that Krej's latest philanthropy was sponsoring sculptors. He collected life-sized figures of rare creatures to display to deprived children who had no other way to view the wonders of Coronnan. Did Krej have a dragon? One made of precious glass perhaps? No. Even Lord Krej, second in line to the throne, couldn't afford an entire dragon made of glass.

"Stranger." A soft feminine voice broke his concentration.

With a word and a quick gesture the glowing map, evidence of his magic talent, disappeared. Only then did he turn to face the owner of the voice, the barmaid.

In the dark cave of the pub, the girl's dirty face and ragged clothes revealed little but too thin limbs, hollow cheeks and sunken eyes. The noon sun revealed a lush bosom.

"Stranger, my da sent a pasty and some ale to see you on your road." She arched her back so that her breasts threatened to burst through the threadbare homespun of her bodice.

This girl was so thin and bedraggled that all she roused in him was outrage that she had been reduced to such a level.

Women, girls, always they tempted him; with their loveliness, their scent, their generous curves. Their mere presence usually made him forget he was a magician born and bred, and as such forbidden to take any woman. If he gave into temptation, he would lose his magic. And because he was forbidden to lie with any woman, all of them became more desirable.

"Give my thanks to your da," he replied politely. It would probably be considered an insult to refuse, even though he knew they couldn't afford to be so generous.

"Must you leave so soon?" Her eyelashes fluttered.

"My journey is a long way from ending."

"It's festival tonight." Her finger traced the neckline of her garment.

Stargods! Last night, not tonight, had been festival. The girl was lying. For while he'd heard that some barbaric peoples celebrated on both the night of the equinox and the first full day of spring, no one in Coronnan followed that custom.

Slowly, she outlined the dip and curve of her breasts with a lingering fingertip. Her lips pouted prettily while her eyes wandered toward the sparse decorations on the Pylon.

"Aren't you celebrating a little late this year?" Jaylor asked through clenched teeth. Her invitation touched him with panic rather than desire. A close regard for the movements of stars and planets, sun and moon was among the most sacred duties of magicians and priests alike.

He had spent the night in the hills outside of town, determined to avoid the temptations of festival. If the celebration had gotten out of hand, he might have awakened in the morning to find his magic reduced or gone altogether just because he hadn't resisted what spring and the fertile women offered.

"Tonight is festival," the girl insisted. Her eyes traveled to the cave opening of the pub as if seeking answers. She avoided looking at the Pylon. She couldn't lie while her eyes rested on this ancient symbol of the movement of sun and moon and stars.

"Does your da think me so simple I can't read the skies? I learned to follow the passage of sun and moon as an infant. Either your priest is lax or the world spins in a different path here in the south." He glanced at the cave opening, too, with his mind. There was a shadow there his eyes couldn't see.

"You must stay." The girl's color rose and she twisted her hands in her skirt.

"Why?"

Her voice rose to a whine. "I . . . I was told you must stay." She swallowed and dropped her voice to a purr that might have been seductive in a whore less desperate, less pathetic. "I can make the evening quite pleasant."

Jaylor squinted in the first stage of a truth spell. Shock waves rolled back on him. Echoes of his own magic reverberated against his body. He gritted his teeth until his toes stopped tingling and he could stand upright without effort

The girl was armored!

Who in the village was powerful enough to throw such a strong spell? The same person who had ripped holes in his armor earlier. The person in the shadows of the cave. Was the one-eyed derelict a rogue magician?

He whirled to face his adversary but found only sunlight flooding the doorway. The shadow was gone. Where did it go?

The voice of his inner guidance hummed a warning. He

needed to get as far away from here as possible, and quickly.

A cloud of roiling, red-orange fog, that was trying to be green as well, erupted from the doorway of the cave. Gathering speed, the magic mist flowed over the ground. It passed the rooting pig. The animal stilled, its life frozen in time until the cloud moved away. Jaylor knew that if he were caught in the magic mist, he, too, would be imprisoned by it.

The ground beneath him reached out and grabbed his feet. Frantically he searched his memory for a spell of release. None of the spells he'd so painstakingly memorized came to him. In desperation he tried to picture the books in the library. There was one on the back shelf that should help. In his mind he saw the book float from its shelf. The cover opened, pages turned. They were all blank.

His body recoiled in fatigue. He'd held the delusion spell too long, then wasted more energy with his useless map.

The cloying clay mud thickened and threatened to solidify around his worn boots like fire-case pottery.

His brow and chest were clammy with cold sweat. He forced his mind into a meditative trance. Breathe in three counts, hold three, out three. Breathe in. His mind stilled. The fog appeared distant and unreal through his refocused eyes.

With a dragon-sized effort he pulled one foot free, then the other, shattering the images that bound him. One foot in front of the other, he measured his paces on the muddy road to the southern mountain pass.

One step further away from the evil that followed him. One step further on his quest. One step closer to his master's cloak of deep blue wool with the silver markings of the Stargods on the collar.

Jaylor quickened his pace.

Baamin gathered his bright magician's robes tightly around his rotund figure as he squeezed through the side door of the University to welcome the king. 'Twas the study hour. The time when the senior magician and his king took advantage of the quiet to engage in a brisk game of piquet.

But King Darcine hadn't been well enough to venture out of the palace for many, many moons.

Leave it to his rather perverse king to prefer a quiet entrance through this little-used passage rather than at the wide front door. As if his arrival in a steed-drawn litter with a full military escort could be kept quiet.

The soldiers ringed the courtyard. Baamin noticed that many of the men were developing a bit of a paunch. They didn't have enough to do.

"Have you heard anything about my son yet, Baamin?" The slight frame of the king trembled as he wheezed the words.

Baamin paused to allow his friend and ruler to catch up. The pace the monarch set these days was still woefully slow. It was a miracle he'd survived the miserable winter.

Perhaps he had some good news for King Darcine after all. "Last night I had a vision in the glass. The dragon, Shayla, has bred." The ruling monarch of Coronnan was magically linked to the nimbus of dragons. In return, the people of Coronnan were pledged to plant and maintain enough Tambootie trees to feed the dragons' needs and to provide a tithe of livestock. Shayla's vitality should impart some strength to this ailing king.

But the peasantry rebelled against obligations they no longer understood. Precious few of the magic trees, and fewer dragons, were left these days. It would take more than one litter of dragonets to restore Darcine's damaged lungs and weak heart.

"As for your son, the glass is clouded," he whispered. So far they had managed to keep the prince's disappearance a secret.

Darcine's tall shadow wavered against the stone walls of the little used passage. In his youth, the king had been as tall and as strong as any warrior in the kingdom. But his illness had wasted muscle and mind. A strong gust of wind, or the loss of one more dragon. . . .

"The men you sent on quest, do they know they are looking for the errant crown prince?" The king coughed.

Baamin placed a chubby hand on Darcine's shoulder. He could feel the king's bones sharply defined beneath the layers of rich fabric. King Darcine wouldn't notice the small strengthening spell he added to the touch.

"Each journeyman's task is designed to teach him the full use of his talents, and to overcome his weaknesses." As any quest should. "I was careful to word each assignment so my students would cover the entire kingdom while they seek new recruits and the source of distrust of magic." Baamin didn't add the report that yet another healer magician had been stoned out of a village when he failed to save the last of the dairy herd from a mysterious wasting disease. It was the third such incident in Lord Krej's province of Faciar this winter.

"My students will also cover the hunting grounds of every dragon left in the nimbus. The beasts will instinctively protect the prince.

"You're certain, then, that my son was kidnapped by magic. He isn't on some wild caper with Jaylor and his hooligans? He used to take great joy in slipping away from the palace when I needed him most, to indulge in mischief with his common friends. I thought he outgrew his base preferences. Perhaps my son has just wandered into the mountains following a dragon dream."

"Others might wander aimlessly while in dragon-thrall; wander until they starved to death or broke their necks. But a true dragon of the king would never harm one of the royal family," Baamin asserted. "We are certain of the kidnap, Your Grace. The glass tells us he is alive, but we cannot be sure where. His face, figure, and location are lost in a mist of colored magic. All we can see is the essence of his soul. We can't even pin down the color of the mist and thereby identify the magician," Baamin sighed. "But I do know Jaylor's magic isn't sophisticated enough to blur the glass so well."

He hoped. Jaylor's talent was so unpredictable he might be throwing delusions while he and the prince devised some practical joke.

"Do the people really believe my son is at a monastery reconsidering an inappropriate dalliance?"

"Of course." Baamin smiled reassuringly. "Each of the Twelve thinks the prince will eventually marry one of his daughters. So, naturally, they believe you disapprove of every other romantic entanglement." And there were many, if rumors were to be believed. Baamin didn't believe in rumors. He knew the truth behind the numerous ladies who claimed to have bedded the prince. Most of them lied.

The official pretense for the prince's absence must end soon. Some of the Twelve were grumbling about his lack of leadership. The crown prince should be leading an army to control raiders on the disintegrating western border.

"How many journeymen did you send?" The king seemed slightly recovered as they proceeded down the dark corridor to the main hallway.

"Every journeyman who was anywhere near ready." Seven young men. Every journeyman in residence. There should have been a hundred.

"Including Jaylor?"

"Even Jaylor."

"Was that wise?"

"He never got the hang of why a spell works. At best I hope he'll stir something into action so that a more accomplished magician can follow through. I had no choice but to send him. I don't have enough journeymen to cover the entire kingdom otherwise." The boy was creative and powerful, but there was no proof his methods would ever be reliable or repeatable. And his magic tended to slip beyond the control of the Commune of Magicians.

"Did Jaylor pass any of his exams?" They moved beyond the main hallway and into the residential wing. Baamin's private study was just around the next corner.

"A few. Master Maarklin devised a test that allowed Jaylor to qualify for his quest. But we of the Commune cannot accept that he is master material." *But we'll use his strange talent for our own purposes,* Baamin thought.

"I've heard Jaylor was drunk much of the last two

years. The families of his friends complained constantly that he was corrupting their sons." The king dodged a book that came flying down the corridor from library to dormitory.

"Your Grace, you and I both know there is only one way for a journeyman to get drunk." Baamin pointed to a mug gliding slowly toward them. Its progress was steady, about a finger's length above the stone floor and very close to the left-hand wall.

"Someone is making progress." The first day of class new apprentices were invited to drink their fill of the fine wine in the cellars. The catch to this license was the magically sealed door. The wine cups could pass through the seal, apprentices could not. When the students could levitate a full cup of wine from the cellar to their rooms, without spilling any, they could drink all they wanted. By the time they figured out how to do that, they were usually ready to become journeymen. "Have you had to change the spell on the door to the wine cellar yet."

Baamin chuckled. "Not since Jaylor left. He managed to break it with little or no effort. But then he didn't need to."

"He kept your potter working overtime for several weeks at first." King Darcine seemed to find the antics of the apprentices amusing. When he was well, everything in life was amusing to him.

"Only until he discovered he could make the cup appear in his hand." Another example of his imagery becoming magic. "Then he smashed the spell on the lock of the cellar door so his classmates could share his celebration. But since he couldn't tell his master how he had accomplished the feat, he was denied promotion."

"At least he didn't teach his classmates how he performed that little trick."

"I heard he tried. They were smart enough not to listen to him. Jaylor's magic is too unorthodox for anyone else to follow." And without being able to keep his spells within traditional parameters, Jaylor was of no use to the Commune.

"Shall we follow the cup to your next prodigy?" King

Darcine smiled at the wobbling cup, as it slowly neared
the dormitory wing. It was a weak smile that appeared
more like a grimace on his gaunt face.

"Perhaps we should. I need to know who will have a
hangover come morning." They watched a moment as the
traveling cup connected with the floor while the unknown
apprentice rested. He was a smart one. Most boys thought
their levitations at eye level where a mishap resulted in
shattering the mug and splashing the wine. On the other
hand, cups traveling as close to the ground as the one
they followed ran the risk of being kicked. Whoever
moved this cup had solved the problem by keeping it
close to the wall and out of the way.

The cup paused again by a closed door. It settled to the
floor while the door was opened for it.

"He hasn't figured out how to suspend it while he per-
forms another task, or to open the door before he begins
the spell. Still, he shows caution," Baamin whispered to
his companion.

The cup rose a few inches and slid through the opening. There was the ominous thud of pottery hitting the
floor and shattering, followed by a string of curses.
"*S'murgh* you, Marcus! You broke my concentration," an
apprentice yelled to his roommate.

Baamin sighed with relief. "That's one promotion I
don't need to worry about. Yet." Baamin reached into one
of his deep pockets for an ever-present flask. He downed
a swig and grimaced.

"Tsk, tsk, Baamin. You know you shouldn't drink so
much of your cordial." King Darcine shook his head.

"My sacroiliac is killing me today." Baamin deliberately screwed the cap back onto the flask and repocketed
it. In almost the same gesture he popped a mint into his
mouth to disguise the telltale odor of his medicine.

"I have put a terrible burden on you, my friend." The
king looked contrite. "You have enough worries keeping
the University under control."

"I am Senior Magician, Your Grace. It is my place to
help you in this dire adversity."

"I sincerely regret that you are the only person I can

fully trust. No one but you is in a position to coordinate the search for the prince in secret." Darcine slammed his fist into his open palm. "*S'murgh it*, Baamin, I need my son here to negotiate the new treaty with Rossemeyer. The palace budget has become a mess since he's been gone, and the servants have become lazy."

Baamin touched his king's arm, feeding him strength once more. *Stargods*, he wished he could give his king health and determination as well. He didn't need the healing talent to know Darcine was dying, along with the dragon nimbus. Shayla was the only breeding female left, and her lair was kept secret even from the king. Baamin hoped Jaylor wouldn't be the journeyman to find her. Who knew what kind of trouble he'd stir up if he did.

"Why do we have to be so devious? Why was my boy kidnapped in the first place?" Darcine moaned.

Baamin wouldn't tell him the reasons. The crown prince had already proved he would rule with strength and wisdom.

None of the Twelve or the Commune would tolerate a strong king after years of noninterference. Especially Baamin.

CHAPTER 3

*T*he journeyman knows nothing of real magic. He only plays with his spells. Still, he can be useful. I shall drive him forward, make him lead me to my dragon.

The witchwoman will help. Her wretched thirst for love will drive her to betray the dragon. My dragon. There is no lasting power in love. The love she relies on will drag her down. Maman taught me to purify my power with love for no one but myself and the power.

I am the only one who can save Coronnan. But to do it, I must keep those inferior lords and meddling magicians in their place. Their loyalty to Darcine and his son will be their undoing.

The day was late when Jaylor awoke from his nap under a sprawling oak tree. With an appeal for protection to the broom of mistletoe in its highest branches, he had decided to sleep off the effects of his magic duel in the village.

He also had to make up for his lack of sleep the night before. Even a league away in the hills he had heard the cries and shouts of festival ringing in his ears.

They'd called to him, urged him to join the revelry. The voices had torn at his sanity and swelled his body with desires he dared not explore.

He knew of ten young magicians who had lost their powers. All because they took a woman too early in their training. Jaylor wasn't willing to risk his magic for the temporary pleasures of a woman.

In the fading light he stretched and pushed stiff muscles. A nearby stream enticed his parched throat. The skin of ale given to him in the village bumped against his side as he stood again. Ale would taste better than plain water. If ale was all the girl had put into the skin. He sniffed the ale cautiously. No obvious poison or spell.

Better to be safe. He drank deeply from the crystal stream and thought of the fine wines in the University cellars.

If he were still within the walls of the University, one quick image would place a cup in his hands. Mischief brightened his mind. What if he could bring wine from the University cellars to this forgotten corner of nowhere? Old Baamin wouldn't miss one more cup. The current batch of apprentices was probably breaking several right now.

Magic wasn't suppose to traverse such great distances. Still, he'd never allowed someone else's limitations to stop him from trying—especially if his stunts would irk the drunken old coot at the head of the University. Eyes closed, with the magic already gathered in his body, he formed an image in his mind.

In the cellars, halfway across the kingdom, a cup slid off its shelf and glided to the barrel. The spigot turned. Wine flowed into the crude pottery. Dark red wine, full of fruit and light.

Jaylor's mouth watered again. Using the magic that flowed through his being, he re-formed the image of the now brimming cup. It appeared in his hand. He nearly dropped the cup in surprise, spilling some of the precious liquid.

His magic had crossed half the kingdom!

He took a gulp to soothe his confusion. Then he laughed out loud, long and hard. He couldn't pass any of the Commune's infernal exams, but he could transport a cup of wine across three rivers, two forests, and a small mountain, without spilling a drop.

He gulped again, then paused to savor the flavors. It was good wine. The University kept the best cellars as an incentive to the apprentices.

His second sip was more leisurely. Jumbled thoughts

crowded his mind. He used the process of sip and taste to sort them, just as he had in his student days.

He knew his magic was different from the ritual sort prescribed by the Commune, stronger, too. When it worked. Time and again Jaylor had proved that magic didn't have to be limited by convention and approved methods. He could accomplish any task the masters set for him, as long as he could work the spells his own way. It was only when they forced him to limit his work to traditional methods or join his magic to another's that he faltered. Over the years he'd learned to fake traditional spells. Most of the time he got away with it. The times he was caught had cost him promotions and the right to pursue his master's cloak.

But he was on quest now. All he had to do was figure out the riddle of Old Baamin's command. His master wouldn't have given a single task, no matter how farfetched. Something else was cloaked in the wording.

"Go see a dragon." A dragon was invisible, so he'd have to use his magic sight. What else was he supposed to see while looking for a dragon?

This quest was turning into one of those incredibly boring story problems that were cloaked in archaic symbolism. Jaylor hated those tests. He always failed because he couldn't blend traditional spells with ancient language, or he looked at the problem from a twisted angle and saw too much.

The wine finished, he sent the cup back to the University. Not to the cellars. To the kitchen, where it could be washed and returned to its proper place.

He wished he could see the faces of the scullery drudges when the cup appeared on the counter. Would they tell Baamin? Serve the old wire-puller right if they did. Let him stew over the whereabouts of his least favorite student.

Jaylor stretched again. His leather journey clothes creaked with dirt and hard use.

The sun was still above the horizon, though the air was not truly warm this early in the season. The creek burbled happily, swollen with snow melt. Jaylor shivered in the light breeze. Just perhaps he could wash off some of the travel dirt from his shirt and body.

Another sip of wine, perhaps, to help him decide. Wine. If he could transport the wine why not a tub of hot water? He stirred his brain into trance mode.

No, he was still tired and drained. He might need some strength when he confronted the witchwoman and her familiar. Those old crones knew non-magical tricks that could fool some of the best master magicians.

Perhaps just a basin of hot water and some oil to condition his boots and trews. From Baamin's private bathing chamber? The old man wouldn't be there now in the middle of the afternoon. So why not?

As soon as the thoughts formed, a basin of steaming water, perfumed with sweet stellar petals, appeared before him along with a small flask of oil from the pantry. He set them in the nest of tangled roots that had been his bed.

The wash worked wonders on his mind and body. He'd forgotten how light and free one felt when newly clean. The restorative power of a wash was worth the drain on his magic.

Invigorated, he sent the basin and the flask back—to the kitchens. In his mind he watched them settle onto the washing counter. Returning his used vessels to the kitchen was his signature. By tonight the entire University would know that Jaylor was alive and well. They'd think he was back in the capital instead of nearing the southern border.

Baamin had taught him to hide his tracks, if nothing else.

He chuckled and set his staff on the road. As soon as he stepped away from the protective branches of the oak, the hairs on the back of his neck stood straight up. They almost hummed with tension. Was someone from the village following him?

He extended his senses around him.

Nothing. Whatever followed him was gone, or just the product of his imagination. He shouldered his pack and set the staff back on the path of his quest.

* * *

"Is that where it hurts?" Brevelan gently probed the huge paw of the golden wolf. He whimpered slightly and tried to withdraw the limb she held. She had no fear of the long teeth he kept muzzled.

"It's never quite healed, has it, Puppy?" He whined again and rested his head on her knee. His golden eyes looked up in adoration. A low moan, the canine equivalent of a purr, erupted from the back of his throat.

Ever so gently, Brevelan continued to probe the paw while she hummed a little tune of her own making. Her song rooted out the sore spot and soothed it. The golden eyes drooped in contentment.

"You old faker!" she exclaimed, but continued to rub the paw. "You limped in here just so I would give you some attention. With her free hand she ruffled his ears. The energetic caress roused the wolf from his near slumber. His tongue caressed her healing hand in response. Then he grasped it gently with his mouth.

"Well, off with you, Puppy. Go find your dinner." The thought of lives ending to feed his vigorous appetite made her shudder in revulsion. Yet she knew he needed meat, just as Shayla did.

In the early days of her association with the wolf and the dragon, his injured paw and leg had prevented his hunting. Shayla had magnanimously dropped rabbits or a haunch of something larger for the wolf every day or two. Now, after most of the winter had passed, he was nearly healed and able to fend for himself.

Somewhere in the wild forest that spread around the mountains, he must have a mate about to whelp. He was an adult wolf in his prime. Yet he showed no inclination to assume his family duties, something inborn in wolves. They mated for life and were devoted parents. If he had come to her as a pup she could have understand his attachment to a human.

A squirrel chittered to the wolf from the doorway of the hut. He ignored the scolding and continued to beg caresses from Brevelan. She ran her hands through his winter-thick fur, drawing as much comfort from the touch as he did.

"That's enough for now. I have work to do. Didn't you just hear Mistress Squirrel? There are roots to be dug, and seeds to be started. The floor needs to be swept and Mistress Goat needs a milking." If she kept busy enough, she wouldn't think about her dreams of portent.

She stood to separate the wolf from her hand. The stool wobbled when relieved of her slight weight.

"Someone remind me to ask the carpenter to fix this chair when his wife needs help with her birthing," she called out to the various mice and birds that scurried around her bare feet. The only other response to her command was a petulant meow from Mica, the cat curled up beside the fire. She didn't like her nap being disturbed, even by such a simple request. For a brief moment Brevelan thought Mica's eyes appeared round and hazel, like a human's. Another blink and the illusion was gone. The cat's eyes were yellow, slashed vertically by a very feline pupil.

Brevelan stepped out of her one-room cottage into the bright clearing. Her eyes wandered to the pathway. No tall man carrying a pack and walking staff. She breathed a sigh of relief.

"I'm not going to tell you again, Puppy, go get your dinner." She swatted his behind lightly. He trotted off, tail high, nose low, to begin his hunt. "And don't bring any of it back. I don't want your bones cluttering up my house." She shuddered again at the loss of a tiny life to feed her friend. He'd dragged a carcass back only once. Every crunch of a bone felt like her own limbs breaking. His sensual pleasure at the noise stabbed her through the heart. Since then she reminded him to eat his hunt in the woods. He'd never disobeyed again.

"And if you get muddy again, you sleep outside tonight," she called after his retreating tail. "Shayla may have given you a princely name, Darville, but you get too dirty and disheveled to be a royal pet."

A flusterhen dashed out from the cover of saber ferns at the edge of the clearing. Her sisters followed. They pecked at Brevelan's feet, and she shooed them away. "I'll feed you later. When the sun sets," she promised them.

As she went about the mundane chores of digging and milking, feeding and soothing, Brevelan sang. Music flowed and swirled around her, reflecting the beauty and serenity she found in her isolated clearing. Trees and plants, ground and hut seemed to hum in harmony with her song. She lifted her voice a note higher into a descant to the natural sounds. As she reached the apex of her voice she sensed the clearing sealing itself against intruders.

Less than a year ago her life had been devoid of music, just as the solitude she craved had been denied her.

Households were large in her home village. Many generations lived in each house. Excessive noise, like singing, was banned, lest it disturb the elders or the babies, or the fathers concentrating on their work. Girls were married off early to make room for the brides of the younger men. Babies abounded everywhere.

She missed the babies. Memories of Shayla's dragon-dream returned. A compelling delusion. Once more she felt milk-heavy breasts ache for a baby's suck. She shook it off. If she hadn't run away last summer, she'd have a child of her own by now. A soft, small creature with her own ruddy hair and pale skin. Her imagination would never allow her to supply that unborn child with the coarse black hair and angry disposition of her husband.

Sometimes in the night, when she was alone and her body ached for contact with another human being, she wondered what her life would be like now if she had stayed.

That was the trouble with dragon-dreams. They seemed so real it was difficult to return to the light of day. A day when she must be alert to word from the village. Maevra was close to her time and might deliver early.

Brevelan just wished the villagers would accept her help without the frequent use of garlic and gestures meant to ward off evil. She had never told them how much she liked garlic.

Jaylor followed the road as it curved and dipped into a hollow. He jumped a narrow creek where it crossed his path. Green meadows spread out around the road in all directions. A little farther along the stream, away from the road, would be a good place to camp.

As if he'd conjured an encampment, Jaylor found several tents nestled beside the water. Traders usually welcomed strangers. This far south, the traders could come only from Rossemeyer. Those stalwart desert dwellers were even more suspicious and insular than Coronnites.

He paused behind another protective oak tree. From its shadows he surveyed the scene ahead of him. In the creeping twilight he should be invisible until he decided to be seen.

Sturdy pack steeds grazed behind a picket line. Wary dogs zigzagged around cook fires and brightly colored tents. Purple, red, black, and blue shelters for unseen campers.

Who but Rovers would live in such garish tents? Certainly not traders from Rossemeyer who sought to blend into their environment. Rovers were homeless wanderers who worked no honest trade, were beholden to no lord, and obeyed few man-made laws. And they fascinated Jaylor.

The Council of Provinces had outlawed Rovers when the Commune of Magicians established the magic border three hundred years ago. Jaylor had read every enticing word about their forbidden lifestyle.

No band of Rovers should be within the boundaries of Coronnan for any reason. Where had they learned the spells to open a hole in the magic wall? Or which magician had they bribed?

Jaylor knew from his secret reading that Rovers weren't above robbing travelers of their purses, packs, and clothes. Mercifully, they slit the throats of their victims so they wouldn't freeze to death or be attacked by wild animals.

He checked his appearance. Worn and dusty journey clothes, provincially uncombed hair and beard, small pack and walking staff. He could be any benighted traveler. Except that few people journeyed through the kingdom these days. The Twelve lords were supposed to provide homes for their dependents. Traditions and superstitious fears established during the Great Wars of Disruption kept almost everyone in those homes.

The Rover camp was suspiciously quiet. No voices called out. Dogs didn't bark. No person stirred the savory smelling stew cooking over the fire.

Jaylor pressed his back into the tree as he scanned the landscape. Whoever had been here was not long gone. He hoped no one stood ready to plunge a knife into his back.

CHAPTER 4

Brevelan interrupted her root digging. Her inner sight tingled a warning. Someone was on the back path that sometimes led to her clearing. She faded into the shadow of a tree. Mastering the urge to run from a pursuer, she forced absolute stillness into her body and her mind. Every wild creature of the forest knew that predators saw only movement and disruptions in the patterns of light and shadow.

"Brevelan?" Maevra, the carpenter's wife, called. She was in the last weeks of her pregnancy and frequently sought Brevelan's counsel as a midwife.

"Coming." Brevelan breathed deeply once more.

With a wish and a firm image in her mind, she opened the path to the clearing.

"Oh, there you are," Maevra sighed wearily. "I forget how steep the back path is." She rubbed her protruding belly.

"You shouldn't walk so far on a steep track so close to your time, Maevra." Brelevan urged the woman onto a convenient stump. She sat heavily and awkwardly.

"I needed to walk."

Brevelan masked her concern. This woman, so near her own age, had lost three babes before they were fully formed. Under Brevelan's careful guidance, this pregnancy looked as if it might run to term.

"Why?" Brelevan asked. She rested one hand on the swell of the child, the other upon the woman's shoulder.

"Because the house was stuffy, the sun is shining, and Garvin is away for the day."

Good. It was just boredom and loneliness, not the compulsion that forecast an early labor.

Energy flowed through Brevelan's fingers, seeking the child. A personality shifted beneath the heavy folds of the woman's clothing and the taut skin of the mother's belly. A strong and steady heartbeat tingled up Brevelan's fingers. The dark comfort of the womb enveloped her. A soothing world of water and nourishment rippled against her skin.

She curled her back and ducked her head. Just before her knees bent and drew her into the same posture as the unborn, the same awareness as the babe, she clutched at her own identity and withdrew.

"Bold and restless, strong, too. I think it's a boy." She shook her hand to free it of the lingering link with the child. Her back wanted to continue to curl, so she arched it in defiance. The utter loneliness of being only one person, where a moment ago she had been two, left her dizzy.

"He's strong, but not yet ready to come out and face daylight."

"How do you know from just a touch?" Maevra looked utterly amazed.

Brevelan shrugged. "I'm a witchwoman."

"Don't let the others hear you say that." Maevra looked over her shoulder anxiously. "They may not call you that to your face, but they still make a gesture of warding." She held her right hand tightly in her left preventing herself from initiating the cross of the Stargods.

Brevelan covered Maevra's hands with her own and smiled at her patient. "Give them time. They must learn to trust." Brevelan released her hold on her patient's hands.

Maevra opened and flexed her fingers. "Soon, I hope. I need you with me when little Garvin is born."

"I will be there. I promise." Brelevan hugged Maevra reassuringly. "Come, rest in my clearing. I've baked fresh oat cakes, and I think there's still a little cider left." She guided her guest a few paces. The path opened and revealed the entrance to the clearing.

"I'll never understand why this place is always hidden, unless you show the way," Maevra laughed nervously. Her hand twitched again.

"I don't know myself," Brevelan admitted. "The clearing was waiting for me when I came here last summer. It protects me and provides for me."

"That's good. Then the magician won't be able to surprise you."

"What magician?" Fear lumped in her throat. Had her family sent a magician to find her and take her back for judgment?

"A wandering one. He was in the pub earlier asking questions. He was disguised, but Old Thorm saw through it. I swear he sees more with that one eye than the rest of us do with two."

Old Thorm, the wandering, one-eyed drunk who was always nearby when there was trouble.

"What did Old Thorm do to the magician?" Brevelan listened to the clearing. No one came. She was safe for now.

"Oh, you know Old Thorm, filled him with dragon lore. Then he sent the young man on a wild lumbird chase. Told him to come by way of the road. He'll never find you."

"I hope you're right, Maevra. But magicians have a talent for dropping in when you least expect them." The dream image of a man approaching at sunset haunted her.

Suddenly she saw the clearing from a second set of eyes. Eyes that approached from the west, the image they saw overshadowing her own. Chill dizziness swamped her senses. Her gram used to say that kind of feeling was a hand from the grave reaching out to remind you that all in this life is temporary.

"Baamin always said I was more stubborn than smart," Jaylor mumbled to himself. "I want answers, and I intend to get them. Besides, I may never again have the chance to visit with a real Rover." The magic he'd gathered and stored as he walked quivered anxiously. He should avoid this place, these people.

He listened to the power growing inside him for a moment. The warning was stronger than ever. Jaylor moved forward anyway.

The lone figure of a tall middle-aged man, nearly as big as himself, appeared before him. Silver wings of hair at his temples made the black mane seem darker, oilier.

Jaylor caught a whiff of the man almost as soon as he saw him. Musky sweat, days old, with just the faintest hint of Tambootie underneath. His instinct was to recoil from the faint scent of evil. His armor snapped into place.

He sniffed again to make sure he had caught it correctly. Definitely Tambootie, but not unpleasant. Mixed with the other pungent smells of bruised grass, fragrant stew, evening dew-fall, the essence took on a haunting hint of exotic adventures rather than danger.

"Welcome, stranger." The Rover's voice boomed out over the camp. He held his arms open in greeting.

"Have you hospitality for a lonely traveler?" Jaylor asked. In ancient times when passage across the border was easy and the people of Coronnan chose to travel, there were traditions of hospitality. Jaylor presumed that Rovers still held to those old rules.

He leaned heavily on his staff, as if he needed the stout wood to bear much of his weight. Thus anchored to the ground, the staff channeled his extended magic as he continued to scan the area with the extra senses available to him. The staff vibrated and tried to twist away every time Jaylor looked directly at the Rover.

"The camp of Zolltarn is always open to fellow travelers." The Rover's loud voice filled the stream's hollow with camaraderie. "Come share our evening meal and rest your weary bones on soft furs. In the morning we leave. Perhaps we follow the same roads?"

"Perhaps." Still wary, Jaylor slung his pack to the ground in front of him, keeping one hand on the strap. The other clutched his staff.

A woman emerged from the tent. Tall and handsome, with blue-black hair, she carried a basin. She wore the tent colors, red and purple with black trim. Her skirt and petticoats swirled about her ankles. The colors drew

Jaylor's eyes upward to nearly bare shoulders and the sharp shadow of cleavage. She, too, carried the musky odor of Tambootie.

Jaylor felt himself drawn forward to see more of her, smell more of the enticing mixture. His gaze rested on the just noticeable swell of her belly. She carried a precious life there.

He took a step back lest his magic influence the unborn. One of the many superstitions he'd encountered on his journey claimed a magician could capture and command the soul of an infant. Jaylor knew he, personally, wouldn't do such an evil thing. Who knew what the rogues of old had done? Rural memories, he discovered, were long, much longer than in the fashion-conscious capital city.

His glance shifted to Zolltarn. Somewhat old to be the father. Yet the woman was none too young either.

"My wife." Zolltarn rested his arm about her shoulders possessively. He smiled into her upturned eyes with warmth and pride.

Other members of the tribe emerged from the security of the garish tents. Each woman carried a bowl of food for the evening meal. All were dressed in wild color combinations similar to Zolltarn's wife's. Many showed the same degree of pregnancy. Jaylor reeled in the tendrils of magic that fed his senses. No point in chancing that his personality might influence the unborn.

"From where do you hail, fellow traveler?" Zolltarn led Jaylor to a stump beside the largest fire.

Caution, Jaylor warned himself. Rovers had a talent for reading thoughts. He couldn't allow this barbaric chieftain to suspect he was a magician on quest. He'd come this far without violating any of the rules of secrecy that surrounded such tests.

Except that in the last village a one-eyed derelict had called him "magician" as he left the pub.

"Here and there. Over the next hill and beyond." It was the truth in a way, just not the whole truth. Another of the rules on this endless journey.

"Your accent speaks of education. Why is it you rove

when you could be usefully employed? Why is it you
bring with you no trading caravan when only merchants
follow the roads of Coronnan?"

"The only goods I have left are in my pack," Jaylor
said truthfully.

"Your hair is ruddy brown, not black, your eyes are
soft and your skin pink like that of a city dweller too long
in the sun. You have not the look of a Rover." Zolltarn's
eyes squinted in the smoke from the fire.

"One roves. One looks as one looks." Jaylor avoided
Zolltarn's probing gaze. "Was there no magician at the
border to grant or deny you entrance?" he parried
Zolltarn's question with another.

Several Rover men moved closer. Jaylor felt his armor
strengthen. His magic didn't trust these people.

"In this forgotten corner of Coronnan? No one bothers
with a border. Not since Lord Krej inherited the province,
anyway." The Rover snorted as he fingered the wicked
blade in his belt. "Your question tells me you did not
cross the border at this point. Perhaps you never crossed
it at all."

"The people of Coronnan do not rove, as you said.
Therefore, I must hail from elsewhere." Did that qualify
as a lie? He was concentrating so hard on keeping
Zolltarn at bay with words that he didn't care if he spoke
the truth or not.

"Magicians wander on quest." Zolltarn eased his body
closer to Jaylor. "Magicians whose hair almost always
shows traces of red." The smell of Tambootie now dominated the camp odors. "Your aura, too, bears the colors
of magic, traveler of Coronnan.

"If I were other than a weary wanderer, would I tell
you?"

"No answer tells me all, magician." He laughed loud
and long. The men joined him in the momentary revelry.

Jaylor stiffened his spine. He didn't see anything funny
about being a magician. It was a talent he held with pride.
Most of the time. As long as more adept magicians didn't
ridicule him because a traditional spell failed.

He scanned the hollow nervously. The women were

busy around the fires. He caught the eye of a girl just barely of marriageable age. She smiled and ducked her head flirtatiously. Her eyes continued to seek him through long lashes.

"It takes the strength of a sledge steed to become a magician." Zolltarn's mirth eased. "I imagine you need much food and wine to maintain your powers. We'll feed you well, magician."

Why did his statement seem unfinished?

"Are you going to share this handsome stranger, Papa?" The girl who had smiled at Jaylor stepped into the light of the fire. She was tall, like her mother, with a majestic carriage that showed her splendid bosom to advantage.

The men behind Jaylor moved back a half pace. Each man drew a knife from his belt and toyed with the overlong blade. Jaylor's spine tingled with expectation of a killing blow at any moment. But he couldn't concentrate on the men. The girl's presence drew his mind and emotions.

Shifting shadows enhanced her beauty. Jaylor's bones melted as his eyes traced the clean lines of cheek and nose, full mouth, snapping eyes. She had the blacker-than-black hair of her tribe, the wild-colored skirts and deeply dipping bodice of the other women. But she was younger, slimmer, more beautiful. Much more beautiful.

Suspicions faded from his mind, along with Zolltran, and the other men with their wickedly long knives.

Once again Jaylor caught the enticing smell of musk and Tambootie. He felt himself falling into the alluring spell of the girl's dark glance and blossoming womanhood.

"Ah, Maija, you find this stranger pretty?" Zolltarn laughed as he pounded Jaylor's back heartily.

Zolltarn shouldn't have been able to touch him! How had he penetrated the armor?

"Pretty enough." The girl slid onto the narrow piece of stump on the other side of Jaylor. Her bare arms brushed against him. The smoothness of her skin sent shivers to his groin. She, too, was touching him when her hand should have been repulsed. "And strong. He will breed sons with strong magic. We need strong men with stronger magic in the tribe."

This beauty presented a greater danger than any of the armed men. They could only deprive him of his life.

Stargods! She could deprive him of his magic.

Once more he scanned the scene, this time estimating his chance of escape. The men continued to ring the log where he sat.

He stood, separating himself from the girl and her hypnotic beauty. "My road is long. I cannot afford to linger with you." He stepped toward his pack and staff. When had he allowed them out of his grasp? A young Rover with broken teeth and a malicious grin stepped in front of the gear.

Maija edged closer to him. The heat of her body penetrated the worn leather of his journey clothes. He felt his neck and face grow equally warm. Her breath whispered across his nape. Desire for her masked the danger of the men and their knives.

He longed to enclose her in his arms, to fit her close against his body. Her womanly scent, heightened by Tambootie, clouded his senses.

When did a magician know if his magic was strong enough to withstand an encounter with a woman? Was it before or after he achieved his quest?

Did he dare take the chance?

Not yet! He was too close. With a tremendous effort Jaylor pushed her away. A knife blade across his throat stopped any further movement.

"Sit, magician. You will stay the night. You will provide us with what we need," Zolltarn hissed behind him.

But it was Maija who wielded the sharp blade that tickled the sensitive skin beneath his half-grown beard.

No wonder his armor had broken down. His own lust had lowered his defenses. Reluctantly, Jaylor sat. Maija's knife disappeared, but he had no doubt she could draw it again and slit his throat faster than he could escape.

Jaylor searched for idle conversation that would engage them all until his mind cleared. Something he could concentrate on other than Maija. "You've wandered far. Have you had any trouble with dragons?"

"Dragons! The curse of us all. Do not speak of them, lest they hear you and come again." Zolltarn and Maija both made a superstitious, and useless, gesture of protection, wrists crossed and hands fluttering like wings. A gesture that was older than the cross of the Stargods. Perverted magic was the only evil. Gestures couldn't help against a rogue magician.

"Come again? You've seen them?" Jaylor pressed. This was great news. He was closer to the end of his quest than he thought. The information gained during a night in Rover company could shorten his journey considerably. He'd learn what he could from these people, but he wouldn't give them what they demanded.

"Nay. Who ever sees a dragon. They toy with us instead, sending their *s'murghin'* dragon-dreams." Zolltarn shook his head in grief. Maija pouted.

"Dragon-dreams?" Old Baamin had evaded discussion of that undefined term with great dexterity. "Of what nature are these dreams? I presume they are dangerous."

"Dangerous! Nothing less than murderous. May the Gods who descended from the stars protect us." This time he crossed himself in the accepted manner.

Zolltarn's wife thrust bowls of stew into their hands, then gestured with her head for the girl to come away with her. "Wait until he has eaten," she whispered to her daughter.

Sad silence hovered around them. The older man stirred his dinner absently with a horn spoon. The other Rovers turned away from Jaylor and ate with grim determination. Their knives were still too lose in their sheaths for Jaylor to risk running.

Jaylor tasted his meal. The spices burned his tongue. A welcome discomfort if it kept his mind off Maija. She sat with the women, her back half turned to him. Restlessly, she shifted her position, hiking her bright skirt to her knees.

"Why are dragon-dreams so dangerous?" Jaylor spoke

softly, enticing an answer from a preoccupied Zolltarn. His eyes strayed to Maija's shapely calves and ankles.

"My clan is murdered and you ask why the dreams that delude are dangerous!" Zolltarn shouted again as he leaped to his feet. The others stared. He sank back to his seat heavily. "Six men and three boys, nearly men. One night after moonset they were caught in some grand vision of bliss and just wandered off. By the time we found them, some had fallen, their bodies crumpled at the bottom of a cliff. Others were lying facedown in small creeks too shallow to be a danger to anyone. They all died with beautiful smiles on their faces. Two men we never found. I hope they died before wild beasts got to them." The man looked older, his shoulders slumped.

"When? When did this happen?" Jaylor pressed while Zolltarn was still vulnerable.

"At the solstice, just after the big storm."

No wonder so many of the women were breeding. This Rover clan desperately needed to replace the lost men and boys.

As soon as he'd eaten he'd find a way to escape. He had a knife of his own tucked into his boot. Staying the night looked more dangerous than the value of their dragon lore.

He took another bite of stew, savoring the sizzling seasoning. A drum and a string-gamba sounded on the other side of the fire. Jaylor felt the vibrations of the primitive music through the ground against his thin boots. The hot spots on his tongue thrummed an answer to the beat.

Two huge gulps finished his meal. Its fire made his eyes and ears swell and throb in tempo with the rising music. He cast around for a place to put his empty bowl while he watched the camp celebrate the first full day of spring. Perhaps when they began drinking and singing, he could slip away. The bowl vanished into willing hands, the same hands that pushed him closer to the ring of fires.

Maija stood, swaying freely to the music. Her skirts swirled about her ankles and bare feet, her hips undulated in a rhythm suggestive of a more primitive, more intimate dance. Her feet stamped out the music as she circled the camp, once, twice, a third time.

Jaylor's teeth throbbed, his blood sang with her steps. Each spin lifted her skirts higher, revealing more and more of the length of her lovely legs, drawing his eyes and imagination into the secrets of her body. Her movements grew faster with the increasing tempo of the music. She circled and spun widdershins around the fire in a parody of a planet around the sun.

All thought of magic and defense drained from Jaylor. He could only think—feel the dance. When a slender, feminine hand reached for his, he needed to extend his arm, to touch her in order to complete the pattern of sun and moon and stars. He became the music, swirling, pounding, undulating. One more note, one more beat in the rhythm of time.

CHAPTER 5

"**Y**ou put too much timboor in his stew, Maman!" Jaylor heard Maija's strident complaint through the fog that numbed his tongue and made jelly of his limbs.

Timboor. The fruit of Tambootie was a dangerous drug avoided by all, even a master magician. It could calm an hysterical child, ease a racing heart, or put one to sleep—forever.

As part of his training Jaylor had had to spend a night and a day in a closed room with only a Tambootie wood fire for heat and light. It was a rite of passage as well as a test of his abilities to control his magic under the drugging effect of the smoke.

There had been only one door in that cold stone room. It, too, was stone and securely bolted from the other side.

He'd left that stone room dizzy, sick, hallucinating. In his delirium, his heart had beat irregularly for weeks afterward, while his newly awakened loins ached for release.

One obscure text in the University library claimed that in the right dosage, timboor gave a man the stamina of a wild steed in rut. Or at least enough to satisfy a small harem.

This band of Rovers must be very desperate for his seed if they'd dosed him with timboor.

As he puzzled over the implications of his predicament, Jaylor found a spell deep in his memory. If he could just lift his leaden hand to form the proper gesture with the murmured words of the traditional spell. Hair's widths at a time, he moved his hand into view. It was so heavy he needed the other hand just to lift it. But that hand was heavier still.

In the end, it was easier to roll onto his side and leave the weary hand resting on the pounded dirt beneath him.

He placed an image in his mind of his hand following the prescribed gesture.

"He's not dead," the voice of Maija's companion announced. "See, he rouses."

Jaylor froze in mid-thought.

"Rouses. Not rises." Maija spat. "He's useless!"

"Useless now, perhaps." The older woman cajoled. "Later, while he's still docile, he'll be more than ready to give you his seed, again and yet again." Her chuckle was rich with lusty possibilities. "He'll give us the child who will insure us a homeland at last. No magician's border will stop such a child. Fifteen years we've searched for a magician whose strength could overpower the Commune. Fifteen years since your sister was lost and her babe with her."

The women turned their backs on him once more.

He had a few moments, Jaylor mused. No more. He had to hurry the spell.

Smoke from the fires pierced his nostrils with unusual pungency. He could hear the pacing of one of the men outside the tent as if he were standing beside his head instead of yards away, outside this tent. If he thought about it, he could identify the man by his smell. Jaylor sorted through the odors—the rich spiciness of the stew, the dankness of wrinkled clothes, and bruised grass—to find the unique smell of the youngster with the malicious smile and broken teeth. Jaylor recalled the features of the last man to sheathe his blade after Maija had approached Jaylor. A man whose own lust for the young beauty was strong, even without timboor.

A second man joined the first, his footsteps loud on the moist grass. The passage of wind as he swatted at an insect sounded like the raging thunderstorm at the solstice that had flooded an already drenched Coronnan. His senses were magnified; why couldn't he move? He had to escape before Maija joined him on this crude pallet. If he waited much longer, his quest and his magic would end forever.

Slowly he manipulated his hand, mouthing the spell.

Feeling rushed with painful tingles back into his fingers. Each grain of dirt rasped against his sensitive palm. Concentrating on that hand, he reinforced the spell. His body responded.

He needed a focus. Something to channel the energy of his overactive mind to his limbs. His staff and pack lay nearby. Someone had moved them into the tent with his body when he blacked out. How long ago? Carefully, lest he alert the women, Jaylor reached for the staff. It was too far from the end of his fingers to grasp. He stretched as far as he could and only succeeded in pushing it farther away.

"Come here," he commanded as he strained to reach it again. The staff obeyed, appearing in his outstretched hand almost before it disappeared from its resting place.

Jaylor grabbed the instrument and tapped each foot as he whispered the proper words.

Again, control and strength returned with a painful rush. He flexed and twisted his muscles until the pricking subsided. Now if he could just sneak past the two waiting women without being seen.

He gathered his energy slowly and levered himself into a crouch. The women's conversation rose in distress. He froze in his uncomfortable position. They turned and stared at him.

"See how heavily he sleeps!" Maija wailed. "We're running out of time. We have to move again at dawn or risk discovery."

She didn't see him, saw only what she thought she should see. Or rather what Jaylor wanted her to see. How could that be? He hadn't thrown a delusion at her. He shouldn't have the energy for it. Any normal man would have been brought to the brink of death by that dose of timboor.

Cautiously, he stood. Maija continued her conversation as if nothing had changed. Jaylor summoned his pack. It thumped against his shoulder. He grabbed it with his left hand before it fell. Still the women saw nothing unusual.

He must be invisible! He looked back to the pallet. A shadowy form reclined there. In his need to escape he'd projected that shadow to delude the women.

Outside the canvas walls, pack steeds snorted, birds awoke, insect chirps faded. He smelled the dawn dampness and knew he must move quickly, before sunlight revealed his shadow and the women decided to investigate the form they thought they saw lying on the ground.

One bold step after another Jaylor paced to the tent flap. No one stopped him. He saluted the camp with his staff in relief as he silently slipped into the protection of the woods.

Large hands, callused, with splotches of dark hair on the back reached for Brevelan. They grasped her arms, cruelly. Bruises would form in the shape of his fingers. She screamed and screamed again. Desperately, she tried to wrench herself away from the hot breath of the black-haired man who held her. Each movement only tightened his grip, brought the heat of his body closer. One last scream and twist of her body. She was free!

She was awake.

Brevelan breathed deeply, trying to calm her racing heart. Cold sweat covered her face and back. She was so tangled in her blankets she couldn't break free to clear her mind and body of the nightmare. She rolled off the oversized bed onto the hard-packed earth of her own cottage deep in the woods.

The cat, Mica, lifted one round-pupiled eye in mild curiosity then settled back into a sleeping ball at the foot of the cot. The wolf by her side lifted his head. His warm tongue darted out to lick her hand.

"It's all right, Puppy. We're safe here. No one will find us and make me go back." Her pet caressed her again with his tongue. She scratched his ears and lay her head on his neck. The long winter-thick fur comforted her as his gentle warmth replaced the evil memory of her dream.

"It's almost dawn, Puppy. We might as well get up and

begin working the garden." The wolf responded by leaping up, his tail wagging so hard his hind end moved.

"You're too eager." She laughed at his antics. He stood by the door, waiting to be let out.

Mica mewed in protest. Her half-open eyes showed the vertical pupils of a cat again. She settled back into the warmth of the blankets.

Brevelan reached out with her mind and checked each of her charges. The rabbits emerged one by one from their holes for early grazing; the goat still slept. The flustercock stood and strutted for his first crow of the day. Somewhere above, Shayla circled.

You were frightened.

"Only a dream." Brevelan shivered as she shed her damp shift and pulled on a clean one. Her woolen overgown added warmth. She slipped her feet into thick stockings and clogs against the dawn chill. Later, when the sun found the clearing she would discard them.

More than a dream. A memory.

"From a long time ago, almost a year. I don't need to worry about it anymore."

You will.

"Now what is that supposed to mean, Shayla?" For the first time, Brevelan allowed anger to tinge her conversation with the dragon. Just once, she wished Shayla would explain her thoughts.

You will have to face that man again.

She didn't say mate or husband, just "that man." That told Brevelan something. In Shayla's mind the black-haired man was not her husband. The law said differently.

"That man is dead. Isn't he?"

Blankness. Shayla did not deign to respond.

Darville is well?

"Of course. The wolf thrives." She wondered why Shayla doted so on the wolf. Dragons usually hunted wolves and other creatures of similar size, rather than feed them and ask after their welfare.

You must protect him. Trust the one who comes to help you.

"Shayla?"

But the dragon was gone. Where, Brevelan had no idea. Somewhere up in the mountains to her lair probably. Someday she'd go up there and find the dragon's home. Then, when Shayla couldn't fly away, she'd ask all the questions she'd stored up all winter.

Like why Shayla had summoned her into a raging snowstorm to save an injured wolf. She'd never spoken to a dragon before that awful night. Never known it was possible for anyone outside the royal family to have any contact at all with the magical creatures. But then, if the rumors back home were true, she had royal blood in her veins.

Krej, lord of the castle next to her home village, was first cousin to King Darcine. Krej had the same bright red hair as herself and many children in his villages. The hair was a lingering legacy from the lord's outland mother.

That was all in the past. She had escaped her abusive husband and her village. Now there was work to be done. Brevelan stepped forward and set about her morning chores with her usual energy. The song she sang lightened her mind as well as the weight of the work.

The work was for herself and her animals, not some duty imposed by an elder.

As she sang, her clearing filled with light and joy. This protected place was hers, and all who resided there responded to the security her songs offered them.

Just beyond where the stream crossed the road Jaylor saw the first obscure markings on the rocks at the side of the road.

YOU APPROACH THE BORDER, said the first sign.

The next mark a few feet beyond was less obvious to the eye. This one was written in ancient runes. The magic rather than the visual image leaped out at Jaylor.

THE KING'S MAGIC CAN NO LONGER PROTECT YOU.

Not exactly the king's magic. The Commune maintained the border, repelled possible invasion, and kept the overly curious inside. King Darcine had no real magic, nor had any king before him. This king had very little of anything left—health, personality, power. All he did have of value was a son. And no one in the capital had seen the prince for weeks at the time of Jaylor's departure.

He pushed beyond the sign. The air thickened and resisted his efforts. Jaylor stopped and looked back.

A faint shimmer in the air marked the spot where the last rune rested. Only magic could produce that kind of distortion. Only a magician could see it, penetrate it.

Ordinary folk couldn't pass that border. The Rovers had. The villagers must if they sought the witchwoman.

The wrongness of the situation bothered him. He should consult with Baamin, and soon. He wasn't supposed to ask for help on a quest. But it wasn't help he sought. He needed to warn the Commune. About the border and Rovers entering the kingdom. Warn them of dragons starving out villages and leading large numbers of people astray.

A few feet farther on, a path wandered off to the east and south. This must be the way to the home of the witchwoman. Kind of far out for her to serve the village. Her home would be in the foothills, possibly near the dragon's lair.

The path narrowed. Trees closed in, darkening the way. Once more he had the sense of another presence—behind him. Closer this time. A whiff of Tambootie in the air.

The Rovers? He stretched his heightened senses once more and encountered a void. Not just the absence of a presence, the absence of everything. Someone, armored, was sending Jaylor's awareness around the space he occupied.

A magician. In the pub he had encountered an old derelict who carried an image of himself as a vigorous man in his prime. A man with hair as red as Lord Krej's.

Three years before Jaylor had entered the University, Krej, the youngest son of the Lord of Faciar had been a journeyman magician. His father and brothers had been killed in a senseless hunting accident. A wild tusker had charged. Arrows went astray. Grief stricken, the new lord renounced his magic and took a bride. He had to have

lost most, if not all of his magical powers on his wedding
night.

The magician who followed Jaylor could not be Krej
himself. Possibly a rogue hired by him, or a cousin from
his mother's country? But why play with outlaw rogues
when he'd been educated into the benefits, ethics, and
strengths of traditional magic? Jaylor slipped off the path
behind a tree. The rough bark was the same color as his
dusty cloak. He merged with the tree. Even a master magician would find only a tree.

The reek of burned Tambootie preceded the nearing
presence. Jaylor stilled his mind and his magic.

Just as Jaylor expected, it was the one-eyed man from
the pub who emerged from around the bend in the path.
Old Thorm, someone had called him. No longer drunk or
derelict, he walked fully upright with hands extended before him. He sniffed the air carefully as he walked.

Rough bark scraped Jaylor's face as he pressed closer
to the tree. With his mind, he sought the core of the tree,
identified with it, made it part of himself.

His pursuer moved forward, still seeking by sense and
by magic. He was abreast of Jaylor when he turned and
faced him. Jaylor stopped breathing.

"You there, magician," One-eye hissed, "you can't hide
from me. I can feel your magic."

Fear climbed Jaylor's back and brought moisture to his
skin. His mind deliberately closed off the seeking words
that were a spell in themselves. He thought nothing,
moved nothing, was aware only of the smell of Tambootie and the essence of timboor that lingered in his
mouth and groin.

The pursuer looked more closely. His head shifted right
and left, above and below, seeking and sniffing.

Jaylor's sheltering tree dissolved before his eyes. His
eyes locked with those of his pursuer.

"Whaour!" Some beast above him screamed.

One-eye jerked his eyes away from Jaylor, looking up
in fear. His arms flew above his head in protection. Piercing turquoise shafts of glasslike light became speeding arrows aimed at his one good eye. They made contact and

splintered into a thousand bright shards of brilliant color.
Rainbows arced and danced on every beam of light
through the tree branches.

"No! No!" One-eye backed down the path, his arms
still over his head and face. "Leave me alone. Go away.
Go away." He turned and ran back the way he had come.
His shrieks of pain and terror marked his path. He left behind a lingering aura of evil.

Relief washed over Jaylor's entire body in waves of
coolness. He looked up at the one small patch of visible
sky. The blue-green color shimmered with a magic distortion. Squinting with his extended sight, he could just see
the outline of a wing and a long, lashing tail.

The lilting, feminine voice came into his head unbid-
den. *You are safe for now. Hurry. They need you.*

Had he just seen and heard a dragon? Startled and bewildered, he grabbed a branch of his tree for support. He
jumped back, amazed that the tree hadn't really dissolved.
His hand came away with a clump of gray berries, dried
and desiccated from the long winter, clenched in is fist.

Timboor. He'd used a Tambootie tree for shelter. Had
the tree aided his magic sight or One-eye's? The reek he
had sensed was Tambootie smoke, not the crisp sap he
smelled now. He needed to stop and think about this. But
the dragon had urged him forward. He pulled off another
handful of the berries and stuffed them into his belt
pouch.

Jaylor pushed on. He pondered the significance of the
tree, of the man who'd followed him, and the dragon, and
how they were all related to the magic that came to him
with increasing ease. He hummed a strange little tune that
visited him on the wind, the vibration of the music swelling in his chest and tingling through his body.

Song burst from him in joy. Nonsense words flowed
through his mind as he tried to find their meaning. None
came. He just sang with uplifting cheerfulness over a narrow escape, a good quest before him, a firm road to tread,
and fresh air to breathe.

The song grew in him. He built a harmony to round it
out. His strides lengthened, his mind cleared. This grand

adventure was the best part of his training. He reaffirmed his determination to enjoy it.

The path rounded a bend to reveal a wide clearing bathed in glimmering sunlight. Near the center stood a neatly thatched cottage. Before the home stood a beautiful red-haired young woman. Her song lifted and swirled around and around her.

A robin perched on her shoulder, chirping his own version of the song, while a rabbit nibbled at her toes. Squirrels chased each other about the garden area in a joyful dance. A mouse peeped out from the thatch, its nose twitching in greeting.

Jaylor had found the witchwoman.

CHAPTER 6

Darville trotted into the undergrowth. Each step brought new and interesting smells to his active nose. He sorted through them with care and delight. Dominating all, was that of Brevelan, just as she dominated the existence of all the forest creatures. Underneath her human scent he detected the familiar traces of Mica, the goat, a pair of squirrels, the flustercock and his mates. Darville disregarded the odor left by anyone who shared the clearing with Brevelan. She would never forgive him if he killed any of her special friends.

He tested the air to right and left. Nothing new. He trotted farther, delighting in the spongy surface beneath his feet, the cool air on his tongue, and the sense of power in his frame.

A stream crossed the path. Exuberantly, he bounced into the chill water, rolling into an icy splash with a playful lunge. The cold couldn't penetrate his thick winter fur. His tongue lolled out in pure delight. He flexed his hind legs and bounded from the stream.

Instinctively, he shook water from his coat. The spray bounced back into his face. He wanted to share his joy in the shooting drops of water. Brevelan wasn't here. So the trees and ferns received the gift of his shaking. A little farther along Darville caught a new scent. Hare. He tasted and savored it. Just enough for a tasty meal, without any leftovers to distress Brevelan.

For a moment he wondered why the feelings of a woman should matter. They never had before. Brevelan's approval and goodwill were as essential to his being as was the dragon who flew the skies above. He'd never owed his life to a woman before. The least he could do was respect her wishes.

In the meantime he would take pleasure in the power of his body, the keenness of his senses, and the beauty of the day.

A short time later he licked the last morsel of hare from a bone just as a new sensation enveloped him.

Fear. The smell of it, taste of it, was thick in the air. It lapped at the pit of his belly.

Darville channeled all of his alerted senses into his search for the source of that mind-numbing fear. There. Into the wind, he found it. Brevelan was afraid. His muscles bunched and propelled him forward. Brevelan. He had to save her, just as she and the dragon had snatched him away from death last winter. Whatever threatened her would die. Shayla might help. But he no longer knew how to call her.

Darville raced along the path in the most direct route to the clearing, crashing through the undergrowth. His passage disturbed the homes of several creatures. He didn't care.

His breath came quick and sharp, his heart beat and beat, pumping blood to make him fast and strong. He had to protect Brevelan!

There at last was the clearing and Brevelan, his beloved.

She stood, hunted-still, staring at a man with a walking staff. Her fear beat around Darville in waves. It echoed and reverberated through his bones.

Darville could almost taste the hot blood from the man's throat as he cleared the last few strides. This man would die. Brevelan would be safe.

Instinctively, his front paws fought for traction while his hind legs bunched and coiled. Teeth bared, fur bristling, he leaped.

He hit a wall. Bounced. Fell. Pain. PAIN. Blackness.

A flying ball of fur crossed Jaylor's vision.

His arm came up, automatically, in a gesture of warding. The words of a spell rippled along his tongue.

"No!" the witchwoman screamed.

Time slowed. Jaylor could see only dripping fangs, sprouting from a gaping muzzle. Fangs meant for his throat. The wolf's body hit the height of its arc and kept coming toward him. He could see the anger, the hunger in the animal's eyes. And still it kept coming.

Jaylor looked into the golden, hate-filled eyes. He tasted the same hot blood, the same sense of urgency.

The wolf recoiled against Jaylor's armor and dropped to the ground. His huge golden body crumpled in the grass.

"No!" The witchwoman screamed again as she ran to the fallen beast. She knelt beside the wolf, hands gently probing the slack body.

"Get away. He's in pain. He'll bite anyone." Jaylor tried to pull her away from the head and lethal teeth. "He'll savage us both before he's fully conscious again."

"My Puppy would never bite me. Never."

"I don't know much about animals," he argued. Most of the last ten years he'd been isolated at the University. "But I do know wild animals can't be trusted, especially when they're in pain. Stay away from his teeth!"

She ignored him. Her hands caressed the wolf's fur and a soothing hum rose from her throat.

This beast must be very special to the woman. A companion. Or a familiar? One-eye's description came back to haunt him.

No. Women didn't have magic so they couldn't have a familiar, a focus for magic like his staff. This was probably just a pet raised by the woman from a pup. She'd called him "Puppy."

If that was the case, the wolf's health was important to her. The villagers had said, if they could be trusted to tell the truth, that he had to get past the witchwoman in order to find the dragon. Therefore, the woman's goodwill was important to Jaylor if he wanted to find out anything more about dragons.

"Let me see him. I think I just stunned him." Jaylor decided to try his few healing techniques.

"Get away. Haven't you hurt him enough?" Her despair

stopped him just short of contact with the wolf's body.
She probed at the front leg, which jutted at an awkward
angle. The hum at the back of her throat intensified as she
kneaded the thick fur.

Witchwomen had all kinds of tricks to make people believe they had magic. None of them really worked. His
own mental probe revealed the source of pain.

"I can help him. Get around behind and hold his head.
He might not bite you, but he will bite me," he grumbled.
She didn't move. "Trust me, please. I know what I'm
doing."

His eyes locked with hers. He looked away first.

"Do you?" Her tone froze any good feelings he'd been
having. This woman was beautiful. She had an aura that
invited confidence. But Jaylor wasn't tempted, not anymore. He'd seen her anger and despair when the wolf
dropped to the ground.

"Do you have the brute strength to reset a dislocated
shoulder?" He stepped back to allow her the distance she
had deliberately set between them. "Your herbal potions
and false chants won't do him any good. Magic won't
help either. Not even the University healers can set bones
that way."

She glared at him as if deeply insulted. Then, mutely,
she dipped her face deep into the animal's fur, dangerously close to the mouth and huge teeth. Teeth that had so
recently been aimed at Jaylor's throat. He pushed down
his instinctive fear.

"You're a magician," she said flatly. "I should have
known. The dreams were so detailed, I should have understood."

Stargods! What the *s'murghin* Tambootie did that
mean?

Silently, the girl shifted behind her pet. Her small
hands gathered the wolf's head onto her lap. The low
hum came again.

Jaylor felt the soothing effect of her music. He was
calm as he knelt beside the animal.

He shouldn't be. A wild wolf was unpredictable even
in the best of spirits.

He rested his right hand gently on the wolf's injured shoulder. His mind sought the source of the damage.

When his fingers tingled, he knew he'd found the proper place. He applied pressure while his strong left hand encircled the paw.

Golden eyes opened and looked up into his own, with perfect trust and understanding.

Something in those eyes was familiar. They spoke to Jaylor in sentiments he was too nervous to understand.

"Careful now. He's awake and this is going to hurt." He pulled on the paw slightly, testing the wolf's reaction.

Nothing. The animal just continued to stare, patient and controlled. More controlled than Jaylor felt under the influence of that golden stare.

Jaylor swallowed, clamped his teeth shut, and pulled. He felt the strain across his shoulders first, then his chest. Breathe. Must remember to breathe. He pulled harder. His other hand pushed with greater intensity. Sweat dampened his shirt and trickled down his nose.

"Move!" Jaylor grunted. He was tempted to stop and rest. He didn't dare. The wolf was awake. Pain glazed the yellow eyes. If Jaylor relaxed, the animal would attack. Fear increased the pressure he applied to the joint.

"Move!" He grunted again. This time he visualized the bone sliding into place again, much as he had seen the cup fill with wine in the University cellars. With his thoughts came the sound of grating, like a rasp on stone. The ground beneath him seemed to vibrate with the force of his efforts and the rhythm of the girl's tune.

The joint snapped into place.

Jaylor sagged in relief. But he didn't let go of either the paw or the joint. He had to see the joint with his mind to make sure it was reset properly. He'd do it in a moment, when his shoulders and arms ceased quivering from the strain he'd put on them.

"You did it!" Awe tinged the girl's voice. Her fingers reached underneath his and dug into the thick fur. A different tune filled the clearing. "He'll need a bandage for a few days to make sure it doesn't slip out again."

Jaylor nodded, too spent to speak just yet. He wasn't

sure how he knew, but he knew the woman spoke the truth.

He closed his eyes as he sank back onto his heels, his body and mind drained of energy. He'd used his magic once too often these last few days. Even with the nap yesterday and the drugged sleep last night, he could barely move his chest to breathe. His fingers reached for the timboor tucked into his pouch. He wasn't aware of the gray berry until it was halfway to his mouth.

Disgusted with himself, he shoved the magic fruit back into the darkness of the leather pouch. He wouldn't use the drugging effect of timboor to rebuild his store of magic. Nor would he allow himself the luxury of artificial strength.

"I need to get him inside, near the fire." The woman's soft words penetrated Jaylor's tired mind.

Inside! The wolf probably weighed more than she did. *Stargods!* How was she supposed to get him inside? He'd have to help. It was only a few steps, though it looked a league across the clearing.

Wearily, he opened his eyes again. "I'll help you." His voice came out as a croak. A little ale, or even water would sure help him right now. He hadn't performed that much magic. This aching fatigue could be a kind of hangover from the timboor. He firmed his resolve to avoid the berries even as he felt his fingers inching toward the pouch.

"No. You rest. I've done this before." She smiled. The sun shone with her happiness. He closed his eyes against the glare and laid his head next to the panting chest of the wolf.

"Stupid," he told himself. "This beast is still in pain and could lash out." His gaze lingered on the yellow eyes. Wolf and man continued to stare at each other, measuring and evaluating strengths and weaknesses.

The girl returned in just a moment with a blanket. Gingerly, while Jaylor cradled the injury, they rolled the beast onto the blanket. She rested briefly before dragging her burden inside.

For the first time, Jaylor looked at her. Really looked at

her. Her eyes were clear and sparkling blue, like the Great Bay in sunshine. Her skin was dusted with healthy freckles, already kissed by the sun at the equinox. A thick braid of University red hair hung down her back to below her waist.

It was rare to see hair that red outside the University. Rarer still on a woman. Not all magicians had true red hair, like hers. Jaylor's light brown locks only took on red lights in high summer when he spent most of his study hours outside. But it was more common to find red hair on a talented person than not.

Women had no talent, so they rarely if ever had red hair. He shuffled his numb body after her as she dragged the wolf toward the hut. "What is your name?" he finally asked. He didn't want to think of her as "The Witchwoman."

She was young for a witchwoman. Usually they were old and ugly, forgotten widows.

"Brevelan." The name floated over his tired consciousness like a soothing blanket.

"You are as beautiful as your name." Brevelan. Cool, calm meadows laced by quiet stream, sunshine and blue skies filled with rainbows. He reached for her hand and gathered it close against his chest. "I'm Jaylor." Peace. Sleep.

Brevelan placed a fresh bowl of water beside Puppy's sleeping body. She didn't want him moving any farther than necessary when he awoke. He would be thirsty from the herbs she had given him to ease the pain.

Jaylor, the magician, slept beside Puppy, next to the central hearth.

He could get to his own water when he awoke.

"Mrroww!" complained Mica. Jaylor slept in her place. Her back arched as she climbed onto his wide chest and settled in for a bath. Her multicolored fur already shone with cleanliness. Brevelan knew this was just a cat's way of testing a new sleeping place.

Cats had a way of probing a person's integrity. Mica seemed to trust this stranger. Brevelan wondered if she should. She didn't trust easily. If this man were indeed sent by her home village, she'd have to run again. But where? He stirred and mumbled something in his sleep. Mica braced herself against the movement then settled down as his big hand rubbed her soft fur.

Such strong hands. Strong enough to fix a wolf's dislocated shoulder as well as throw some nasty magic. His whole body looked as big and strong as his hands. Magicians had to be strong or they didn't last long at that University of theirs.

He wasn't bad looking either. Straight, clean lines to his nose and eyes. Beneath his untrimmed beard, his cheeks looked a little drawn, as if he hadn't been eating or sleeping properly. And that filthy, bedraggled hair and beard. Dusty brown now, but once washed and combed she was sure it would lighten up to a full head of auburn curls.

Some forgotten need in her wanted to smooth those unruly curls off his brow, feel the soft texture of his hair, ease some of the worry lines around his eyes.

"Forget it, Brevelan," she admonished herself. "He's a man. You won't get any tenderness or understanding out of the likes of him. So why try giving any?"

Would he never wake up? It was full dark, there was a thick soup of yampion root and beans ready for the eating. She was sure he'd need feeding when he finally did wake. Then she could ask him to go. Or sleep outside. Her own sleep would be much easier with him away from her bed. A bed that was more than wide enough for two.

"Well, Wolf, your mistress says there is a bathing pool upstream from here." Jaylor found himself addressing the pet in the same tone Brevelan used. He wondered if the girl had been alone so long she spoke to the animals just to hear her own voice.

The wolf turned his head to the right and whined. Jaylor followed his lead. Sure enough, they paced along a well-worn path beside the chuckling creek. Just beyond a slight curve in the path a fallen log and some well-placed stones created a small dam. Behind the blockage, the creek widened and deepened into a clear pool.

Jaylor tested the water with his hand. Still cool, but the frigid snow melt was warmed by an underground hot spring. He could shed his worn and dusty clothes for a real bath.

The wolf was not so cautious. He sprang from a low crouch directly into the center of the pool. For a moment his golden fur was lost in the splash of arching waves. Shimmering crystal drops caught the sunlight in a wonderful dance then fell back into their bed. The wolf opened his mouth in a grin. He whined again in a plea for company.

"I'm coming, Puppy," Jaylor answered the animal's plea. Right now the wolf appeared immature enough to deserve the name. Most of the time he was just "Wolf."

Quickly, Jaylor shed his tunic and trews, boots and loincloth. He dabbed his big toe in the cool water. He withdrew the cold toe then sank his entire foot into the pool.

Wolf whined again and paddled toward him. When he was knee-deep in the water he stopped and cocked his head toward Jaylor in question. Without waiting for an answer the wolf shook his fur clear of the drops that clung to the long guard hairs.

Jaylor couldn't retreat fast enough. Cold water sprayed over his naked body. Lumbird bumps rose on his arms and legs and the cold penetrated to his bones. Wolf looked as if he were ready to shake again. "At this rate, I might as well dive in." He resigned himself to the cold plunge.

The center of the pool was deep and clear, warmer than the shallows. The hot springs must concentrate here. He swam a few strokes before standing. He found he could just rest his toes in the mud and have his head break the surface of the water. But he had to keep his hands moving to maintain his balance. Air filled his lungs and he, too, shook his hair and beard free of excess water.

"You remind me of my misspent youth, Wolf." The beast was paddling around him in wide circles. "My friends and I used to splash each other a lot on stolen af-

ternoons along the river." That was the summer when
Jaylor had been twelve and his companions ranged from
eleven to fourteen. "There were four of us who used to
slip away from our studies for afternoons of adventure.
We had nothing in common except the urge to escape."

The many isolated islands in the delta of Coronnan
River offered the perfect playground for adolescent boys.

"All four of us schemed together, but Roy and I usually ended up paired."

It had been a surprise to Jaylor, who had grown up
along another smaller river in the north, to find any res-
ident of Coronnan City who had never learned to swim.
He thought all the population of a city totally surrounded
by water and many lesser islets would have learned to
master swimming early.

Roy had been so surrounded by adults—tutors, servants, guardians—he'd never been allowed to play in the
water and thus had never learned.

Jaylor taught him to swim that summer and earned
many a dunking in the years that followed.

"I met him in much the same manner I met you, too,
Wolf," he mused as he began to swim. His muscles
stretched with a new lightness as the water cleansed his
skin and his mind.

"We both claimed the same island for an afternoon of
freedom," he continued his reminiscence. "He arrived by
boat; I swam ashore about the same time. We challenged
each other. I didn't know enough magic then to defend
myself." He chuckled as he slowly made his way back to
the bank and his clothes.

"That time I lost. But the next fist fight I won."

Wolf bounced out of the pool and sprayed everything
around with water again. Jaylor didn't even bother to step
away from the shower.

"Shall we explore the paths, my friend?" The beast
grinned and cocked his head in a gesture so evocative of
Roy that Jaylor had to look twice to make sure a human
intelligence did not lurk behind those golden eyes.

Jaylor dressed hurriedly. Now that he was out of the

water, the air was rapidly chilling his damp body. He needed to keep moving to get warm again.

Wolf took a few steps back the way they had come. Jaylor started in the other direction. The wolf spun in place and bounded after him.

The path was not well traveled past the pool. Jaylor had to push giant calubra ferns out of the way. Each time he touched one, the fronds shook and gave out the faintest wisp of fragrance. By summer the scent would be druggingly powerful, a legendary aphrodisiac.

Wolf bent his nose to the faint trail. It was now no wider than a hand's breadth. No human foot had trod this way in many days. Jaylor watched the animal as he sniffed and played with the scents in the air and on the ground. With a sharp yip he bounded off the trail.

Curious, Jaylor also stepped off the trail in the same direction. He met an invisible wall. His hands pushed at the barrier. Inside him, the magic he had gathered strove to counteract the magic that tried to flow through his limbs from the outside. He stepped back onto the path. His magic stopped fighting the exterior forces.

The border should have been like this. Jaylor squinted his eyes, allowing his magic to see what hindered his movements. There! A shimmery distortion, like looking at the bottom of the pool through several arm's lengths of water. He pushed at it again, allowing the magic forces within him to meet the wall.

Nothing happened. He pushed again, using more strength and speaking the border release spell. His hand burned and pulsed, but the wall still did not give way.

He moved along the path a few more steps and tried again. If anything, the wall was stronger here.

Every few feet he pushed again, and again, until his hand was raw from the energy he'd expended.

"One more time. Then I'll circle back to the clearing again." He was getting tired. He needed rest and food to restore the magic in his body.

And not those meatless concoctions Brevelan served.

Using his eyes as well as both hands, Jaylor levered himself against the wall. It absorbed his strength then rebounded, pushing him back and back and farther back. He crashed through the underbrush, tumbling heels over head with the force of the thrust.

Brevelan stood next to his prone body.

"Did you have a nice bath?" she asked.

He was back in the clearing.

CHAPTER 7

"**D**ragon dung!" Baamin cursed. This was the third time a very simple spell had failed. He held his viewing glass to the light. There were no cracks, no flaws. Its smooth surface was perfect.

So why couldn't he make contact with any other magician? Several were waiting for his summons. They should be on the alert to answer through their own glasses.

He took a deep breath. In, three counts. Hold, three. Release, three. His mind was drawn out of his body and hovered just below the beckoning void of a deep magic trance. Magic flowed through him with velvet ease. Colors wavered and swirled in the glass.

At last!

He heard laughter, coarse and mocking. Alert to the spell going awry again, Baamin pushed the image closer to completion. Instead of the gaunt, lined face of the man he expected, a shaggy-headed monster with the body of a man looked back at him and sneered.

"With my head, and my heart, and the strength of my shoulders, I renounce this evil," Baamin recited the formula of the Stargods as he crossed himself. For good measure he completed the warding with the winged gesture of Simurgh.

"You didn't think I could do it, did you, Baamin?" The words floated about the room, followed by the image of Baamin's oldest enemy stepping out of the glass.

Baamin jerked back, throwing his armor in place as he sought answers to this abomination. This was the kind of prank he would expect of Jaylor. But how could a young man conjure up this manifestation of the red-haired beast/

man Baamin had fought during his trial with the Tambootie smoke? That nightmare existed only in the shadow world of Baamin's tortured dreams.

Eavesdropping on another's dreams was forbidden. To make doubly sure no one learned of his nightmares, Baamin had personally destroyed all records of his testing, all references to the beast, when he assumed leadership of the Commune.

His gnarled staff came to hand readily. He poked the vision, making certain the staff was as armored as he. Hard flesh and bone met the probe. The beast hadn't even bothered to cover his well-muscled body with clothing, other than a barely adequate loincloth. In Baamin's dreams, his nemesis had the decency to wear the same robes as Baamin did.

"Yes, Baamin, old friend. I'm real and I've come out of your dreams to haunt you." The mouth of the image worked but the words came from some other, indefinable direction. "I'm putting an end to the Commune." This time the image threw back his head and laughed long and loud. The gesture was familiar, belonging to a different man. Baamin was too befuddled by the presence of this monster to remember who.

"Every time you and your toadies throw the smallest spell, I'll be there to twist it round backward, sideways, or split it into good and evil twins. Dragon magic is finished, Old Baamin."

A knock on the door banished the image but not the voice. "Another time, Baamin. We'll finish this when I choose, and you'll not know ahead of time." The rolling laughter bounced around and around the room in decreasing spirals of sound until the glass absorbed it.

Rational thought deserted Baamin as he sat, stunned by the perversion. Had another magician read his dreams? Or had he gone insane and conjured up the beast again? The Commune had fought the monster back into another dimension after Baamin's adolescent testing with the Tambootie smoke had made him real.

Jaylor was the only other magician whose hallucinations had taken on three dimensions. But the red-haired beast had remained dormant at that time.

A second knock roused the senior magician from his stupor. He shook himself to mask the trembling that began deep inside him and radiated out to his hands and neck and knees. He couldn't allow anyone to suspect his own nightmares were interfering with his magic. Not yet, not until he had assured his supremacy over the Council as well as the Commune and University when Darcine passed on.

"Come," he called to the supplicant at his door. His voice broke. He was just tired. Perhaps he'd dreamed the beast/man. No magician in Coronnan could break apart one of Master Baamin's spells.

The door opened a crack. He could see one brown eye peering at him.

"Be you busy, master?" The voice was shy, hesitant about bothering a master magician.

"Not anymore. You disturbed my spell." Baamin growled. He reached for his flask and swallowed the last of the sugar water. Then he popped a mint into his mouth to hide the lack of alcohol smell. *Stargods*, he'd give a year of his life for a hearty swig of beta'arack, distilled from the monster treacle betas grown only in Rossemeyer. But he couldn't afford to befuddle any of his senses right now.

One of the kitchen boys crept into the room, wide-eyed and fearful. About ten or eleven years ago, the orphan, known only as "Boy," had been sent to the University from the poorhouse, one of many foundlings indentured each year. Boy was so late in developing that he couldn't be tested for magical talent. He was unusually slow at his lessons and undersized, but he worked hard and was willing to please, almost to a fault. He had his uses, especially when Baamin needed errands completed in secret.

"I needs to talk to someone, sir. Somethin' strange has been happening." An understatement to say the least.

Baamin sighed. The boy was proud of the trust Baamin seemingly had in him—trust only because the boy was

too stupid to disobey. Now Boy came to the master with
his troubles and triumphs, chattering freely when no one
else in the University dared approach. It was Baamin's
own fault.

"What sort of strange things? In the kitchen?" Probably
the only normal portion of the University. Apprentice magicians were encouraged to experiment with fledgling
powers anywhere but the kitchen. Cooking fires and carving knives were too dangerous for practice.

"Yes, sir. In the kitchen." The boy's eyes widened,
deep dark eyes whose innocence wormed into Baamin's
cynical heart.

Baamin nodded encouragement. This might be something he needed to know about. Boy had his uses.

"I'm used to the apprentices snitching deserts and such.
'Specially the brandied fruit when they can't get to the
wine. Some even try the cooking wine."

Baamin allowed himself a small laugh. Apprentices
only tried that trick once. Cooking wine was salted for a
very good reason.

The boy grinned back. For a moment, with that lopsided smile, he almost looked intelligent.

"Happens all the time. Sweets mostly. This mornin',
though, it was more than strange. Someone was magically
carving big hunks of meat off the spit, while it was still
cooking."

"Growing boys have big appetites. There have never
been restrictions on how much they eat. Magic takes a lot
out of a body. Probably some journeyman just finishing
an experiment." But not many journeymen were left. All
but the very newest were out on guest.

"That I know, sir. And I wouldn't question it, 'cept
when the plate was full it disappeared, just like that." He
snapped his fingers. His eyes looked straight into
Baamin's once more, begging for belief.

"It what?" Baamin sat up straight. "Has someone
learned Jaylor's trick?" Jaylor's talent hovered too close
to rogue manipulation of the elements. If another student
was developing this strange talent, Baamin needed to investigate and corral him.

With the decrease in the dragon nimbus, there wasn't as much magic in the air. Magicians trained in gathering magic could easily find rogue sources. The practice must be stopped until Baamin, the senior magician, had learned to direct and control those powers.

"That's what I thought, sir. Until the plate was returned to the scullery for washing. Only Jaylor does that. And he ain't here, hasn't been for moons."

And shouldn't be anywhere within magic range of the University either. *S'murgh* it, Baamin knew he shouldn't have allowed Jaylor out of his sight.

Baamin stared at his viewing glass. It was a big, master's glass, nearly as large as his hand. He could read the most obscure texts with it. Or contact someone anywhere in the kingdom when he was awake and alert. Jaylor's smaller glass couldn't provide enough power for a summons, let alone to transport food, unless . . .

"There's somethin' else, sir." The boy peered at him from under his forelock. "Several days ago a wine cup showed up in the scullery while I was washing up after dinner. Didn't hardly notice it. Guess I just forgot who was here and who was out. Then a few minutes later one of your washbasins shows up. It had to be Jaylor. No one else cares how much work they make for me. They just leave cups and dishes all over. In their rooms, the library, classrooms. Even in the stable, sir."

Warmed up, the boy might rattle on forever. Baamin had heard enough.

"I'm glad you came to me, Boy. I think one of the apprentices may have learned something from Jaylor and just taken his time perfecting it."

Baamin stared at his glass again. He dismissed the garrulous child quickly.

"More likely Jaylor knows more than you'll admit," Boy grumbled as he closed the door.

That was a possibility. And if Jaylor was transporting food and wine to some remote corner of the kingdom, was it because he was in trouble? Not if he was taking time to bathe.

What did it all mean? Those feats required more strength than Baamin had used in years.

"Tonight when the moon is full and can mask my spell, I'll call him." Baamin picked up the glass, fingering its lovely clearness. Its natural coolness calmed him "I've got to know what is happening out there. I'm not supposed to help on quest. Summoning isn't help. I'll just be monitoring his progress."

Meat! Brevelan could smell it. The contents of her stomach protested the odors. Her instincts for cleanliness forced her to hold it all back. She stumbled to the doorway. Where did that awful smell come from?

All the villagers knew she would not tolerate meat. They were wary enough of her not to violate this one rule of hers. Who would dare bring meat, cooked meat, to her clearing?

Darville emerged from the ferny undergrowth licking his chops with obvious relish. His golden fur glowed in the afternoon light.

Brevelan understood that the animal needed meat. It was part of his nature. But he couldn't cook it. Didn't need to.

Then her eyes caught sight of the broad back of the man. The magician. He was wiping his face with his sleeve.

"We don't need to tell her about the roast, Wolf. What she doesn't know won't hurt her. But a man needs a man's meal. All that mush and roots just can't fill an empty belly."

"They would fill your belly amply if you'd let them," Brevelan called to him across the clearing. "And what makes you think I wouldn't know about it. I feel the lives of every creature within the clearing, including yours." Sometimes. Many times she couldn't sense his presence, his emotions, nothing.

That man! He'd been here days and days, sleeping mostly, and eating up more of her supplies than she could consume in a moon or more. He claimed he needed shelter while he recouped his strength and power. In all that time she hadn't rested easily.

How could she, knowing he was so dangerously close? Most nights she lay awake waiting, wondering when he would demand what all men demanded.

When the darkness was so still she could hear her own heart beating, her bed yawned huge and empty. Lonely. She wasn't certain then that she really wanted to resist him.

She banished the image of the magician's long body stretched out, spilling over the ends of the double cot with his arm draped around her own slight form.

Puppy limped over to her side. He sat, as he always sat, leaning against her leg in affection, easing his weight off his injured leg. He looked up at her in a mute plea for attention. Her hand found his ears, scratched and tugged, automatically. He grasped her wrist in his teeth, then freed her hand so she could resume scratching.

"Your wolf needed food. I fed him. We didn't kill it either. It was already dead and cooked in the University kitchens," Jaylor defended himself. His stance was proud, unrepentant.

"A wolf might need meat. But you didn't have to indulge."

"No more work providing for two than one. That's one less meal you have to feed me from your stores."

"You could work at rebuilding my supply instead of sleeping so much."

"Now that I've had a decent meal, I might not need to sleep so much." He made to move into the cottage.

Brevelan blocked his way. "When you've cleaned the reek of dead flesh from your body and clothes, you can start turning the earth in my garden."

"Reek of dead flesh?" He stopped and looked at her as if he didn't comprehend her orders.

"Yes. Your body stinks of the meat. It will for a day or more. Perhaps it would be best if you made your bed outside." That way she wouldn't dream of him sharing hers. "The weather will be fair for a while."

"It's still glass cold at night."

"You've slept out when it was deep bay cold, as well as wet. You admitted as much just the other day."

"Yes, but then my body was strong, full of meat, not depleted by magic and a diet of gruel. I could tolerate the cold better then." He changed his expression to one of pleading innocence. His eyes opened wide. Their brown depths pulled at her heart.

Her resolve weakened.

He had recovered from his magic ordeal. He'd want more of her now, she reminded herself.

"Your body is full of meat. Your strength has been restored. You will sleep outside. And work for your keep." She finally broke eye contact. "Or perhaps it's time for you to leave. The way you came."

And how was that? No one but herself could enter or leave the clearing unless she opened the path. "I have no more hospitality for an uninvited guest."

"Uninvited?" His eyebrows rose in honest question. "If you didn't want me here, why did you open the path with your song? Why did you keep it closed when I sought to explore?"

"I didn't!" she gasped. "I was singing to keep the clearing inviolate."

"You sang, I harmonized, the path opened."

Aghast at the implication, she turned away from his probing eyes. "Gather your things and be gone."

"When the time is right."

"The time is always right for honesty. You seek the dragon. Then why do you stay here? I suspect you have no quest but me. Did someone in the village dare you, or bribe you, to seduce me?"

"Has any man from the village menaced you?" He sounded angry. At her or the villagers?

He was close now. Too close. She could feel the warmth of his body reach out to surround her.

With the warmth came the smell of meat. She backed away. "I refuse to be owned by any man." Her husband had tried. He died on their wedding night.

"You have no need to fear me, Brevelan," he whispered

warmly. His eyes turned cold and blank. She couldn't read any of his emotions.

"All men are alike," she accused. Her husband had needed to inflict pain in order to feel lust. The men who had crowded outside their door on the wedding night seemed to think the two went together as well.

"I'm different. I'm a journeyman magician. Women are forbidden to me." He looked hurt.

"That means nothing. You are still a man."

"My powers mean everything to me. I'll not risk them by taking a woman before I have my master's cloak." He raked a hand through his hair, a gesture she was coming to know. "I'm just beginning to understand the nature of my power, Brevelan. It's stronger than I ever imagined. But I'll never have enough magic to heal the hurt that is deep inside you. Only a man can do that. I can't be fully a man until I finish my quest."

He stooped through the doorway and gathered his blanket and pack. He held them to his chest almost as a talisman. "Until your hurt is banished or I can cure it, I'll make my bed outside."

"Good," she replied. When he was gone, she grabbed the broom made of stiff straw. Furiously, she swept his bedding of soft grasses off the packed dirt near the hearth. Soon, no trace of his presence remained.

Brevelan looked about her snug home in relief. Once more it was fully hers. Once more it was empty.

"Puppy," she called. Her pet was across the clearing, watching Jaylor set up his camp. The single room seemed to grow bigger, emptier, lonelier. She needed the comfort of her familiar companion.

The wolf looked toward her, then back toward the man, in indecision.

"Come, Puppy," she coaxed. She had to make the man realize he could not steal the affection of her pet.

Slowly the wolf rose to his four feet. He looked at Jaylor with interest, then made his way back to Brevelan. He seemed to be telling her the man was his friend, but his loyalty would always lie with her.

* * *

Women! Jaylor was mighty grateful there were none to contend with at the University. It was bad enough the king's court and capital abounded with women. Women with their beautiful bodies and seductive laughs. Because those women were forbidden, he was always tempted. Brevelan was more than a mere temptation. Could her University red hair be a sign of some subtle magic that made her irresistible?

How was he to fulfill his quest when all he could think about was Brevelan? He'd watched her for over a week as she went about her daily routine. The gentle songs she sang, the sight of her tightly controlled braid of unusual hair, even the way she spoke to each of her animal friends as if they could understand her, captured his imagination.

Good thing she'd kicked him out of the hut. Another night of sleeping so close to her might have been the end of his control. And her cot was not a small bed meant for solitary slumber. It was wide, more than wide enough for two. If he followed his natural instinct to love this woman, his quest and his powers would be terminated. Had the Commune of Magicians planted her to test him?

He had to leave this place, get away from the allure of the woman. And soon. Once he completed his quest, he could bed every attractive woman in the kingdom with no ill consequences, red hair or not. But in order to achieve that end, he had to get Brevelan to lead him to the dragon.

He'd been trying for days to find a path, any path that would lead him up the mountain. So far every path led straight back to Brevelan's clearing and nowhere else. He couldn't even get back to the village!

The still-limping wolf followed him everywhere, unless Brevelan called him. Jaylor had hoped the beast would lead him on one of his many hunts. Wolf came and went through the invisible barrier without notice or ill effect. He just lunged forward and was off on a chase. When he returned he grinned in that jaunty way of his, as if laughing at Jaylor's inability to follow.

Jaylor laughed in memory of some of the wolf's antics in the bathing pool or chasing down a scent. His enjoyment of life was very reminiscent of Roy's. They had fallen into an easy companionship, too, just as Jaylor had done with the young scion of royalty during their boyhood. The wolf's presence reminded Jaylor sharply of how distant he and Roy had grown in the last two years.

Most of Jaylor's teenage energy went into defying the strictures of the University rather than pursuing old friendships outside the institution of learning. Since Baamin wouldn't promote him, Jaylor had determined to make the old man's life miserable. Roy had his own problems with family, tutors, guardians, and growing responsibilities.

Mica cautiously stepped onto his blanket. Her tiny paws kneaded the texture of the fabric. She looked up with round hazel eyes. "Mrrrow." She was asking him to sit so she could sleep in his lap.

"Not soft enough for you, Mica?" He scratched the cat's silky ears. He was used to the changing shape of her eyes. "These soft ferns are a better mattress than some beds I've made in the last two moons."

"Mrrow." The cat purred in almost verbal agreement. If any of the creatures in the clearing were sentient, Mica was.

"But my cot back at the University would be better than this."

The cat blinked. Her eyes changed shape again.

"Why don't I bring the cot here?" He could almost swear the cat had asked him that question. Brevelan seemed to understand all of her pets, as if she had thrown a spell to grant the beasts communication. So why couldn't he understand them, too?

Why couldn't he? Bring the cot, that is. He'd transported wine and wash water. Just today he'd brought a wonderful meal from the University kitchens. Why not his cot?

No, not *his* cot. Before leaving, he'd armored his room in such a way that it might be dangerous to tamper with from this distance. But the storeroom was full of cots, folded in the corner.

He rearranged the magic deep within him so that it looked like the overstuffed storeroom. With his mind he plucked a cot out of the magic. Then he re-formed the image here in the clearing.

"MrrOW!" Mica protested and tried to climb his leg.

Jaylor opened his eyes, startled at the cat's frantic actions. There before him lay a cot, unfolded and ready for his blanket.

"Silly cat. You asked for a softer bed." He set her down so he could spread his blanket. "While we're at it, Mica, why not another blanket, and a pillow. We might as well be comfortable." He chuckled as the two items appeared.

"Mrrrrrew," Mica agreed as she circled, testing the bed, then settled in for a nap.

A cool breeze broke into the clearing, ruffling Mica's colorful fur and raising the hair on Jaylor's arms. "It might rain tonight. If we're going to stay dry, I'll need to build a cover."

Mica opened one cat-eye. She had no more ideas and just wanted to be left alone.

"Magic or brute strength?" No reply from the cat.

"Brute strength. It takes less energy than magic." He scanned the few dead limbs in the immediate vicinity. "Or does it?" The meat and the bed had been easy, barely taxing his powers at all now that he was rested and well fed—and the aftereffects of the timboor had drained out of him. He hadn't worked any magic in several days, so his store of power was full. How much harder would it be to gather some branches for a lean-to?

Jaylor closed his eyes and folded some magic into a rude shelter around three sides and over his bed. Nothing happened.

The spell needed more power. He lifted the cat long enough to slide under her and relax. Once more he formed the magic with an image of branches woven together around him. When he opened his eyes again, disappointment flooded him.

A soft chuckle brought his attention to the hut. Brevelan stood in the doorway. Her knowing smile mocked him. "I said you'd need to work for your keep. Letting your magic do it all isn't work."

CHAPTER 8

"What did you do to me?" Jaylor's voice quavered. "I did nothing." Brevelan backed away from him. His huge body stalked her across the clearing.

"If you did nothing, then where is my magic?" His hand reached toward her to stay her backward movement.

"It is still there." She eluded his grasp. The haven of her hut beckoned.

"No, it isn't. I tried a simple thing—twice. Nothing happened." There was panic in his eyes. "No wonder there are no women at the University. All I did was dream of you. I never saw or touched your body outside my imagination. And still you have robbed me of my powers." His hands shook. He placed them in his pockets to still the jittering.

"This clearing is mine." The ground beneath her feet tingled in response to her words.

"Yours? How? No woman owns anything."

"No. They are owned. But this place is mine. I control it. Everything in it obeys me." Except for the time when Jaylor had broken the magic barriers and found her.

Had she really invited him by singing a song to which he could harmonize?

"Not me. I obey only the guide within me that forms my magic. I don't even obey my master all the time. So how can I . . . Why am I . . .?" His voice rose. He swallowed deeply. "Don't you understand I am nothing without my magic?"

"I understand that you are a man who would bend me to your will, rob me of myself."

"You robbed me of my magic. I see that as a fair

trade." His hands darted from the protective pockets to capture her face. "If I can no longer work magic, there is nothing to keep me away from you."

Caught by the strength of his hands she could only stare into his eyes. There was anger there, bewilderment, even a little fear. He was as frightened as she.

A measure of control returned to Brevelan. He was as frightened as she!

"I've kissed girls before. At the king's court. I've kissed them senseless." His lips caught hers in a light teasing caress.

The sensation was pleasant, undemanding. A niggle of an emotion she couldn't describe fluttered in her stomach.

"Women sought me out. Experienced women, who liked the idea of a tall young man with the strength of a sledge steed for their lover." This time his lips held hers a little longer, enticing her with their gentleness.

The cold lump of pain deep inside her melted a little to be replaced with warmth.

Any semblance of control she had in his presence vanished.

"Please. . . ."

"Please what? Please do, or please don't?" His thumbs caressed her cheekbones.

His touch was light, tender, almost as if he cared for her. But he couldn't care for her if he had kissed so many other women.

"I always stopped at kisses before." He molded his lips to hers, seeking a response.

She felt her mouth soften. A quiver began at the base of her spine, a sensation so new, so lovely she didn't know if she liked it or feared it. "Why should I stop with just a kiss now?" He nuzzled her neck.

"Because your magic is intact." Even the weight of her pet wolf leaning against her in adoration could not match the fullness she felt at Jaylor's touch. She'd never known such tenderness, such wonderfulness.

"Why should I believe you? The spell didn't work."

"I did nothing to your magic."

"Then why didn't the spell work?" He withdrew

enough to look at her while his hands continued to hold
her face gently. She could escape if she wanted to.

If she wanted to.

"The clearing is mine. I don't know why. But when I
first came here last summer, it called to me, sheltered me,
obeyed me and no one else until you came. You are the
only one who has found me against my will." She tried to
explain the special attachment she had for this small
home.

"Even the deadwood I would use to build a shelter
obeys you? And what about the paths into the mountains?
They all lead back here, nowhere else. That is magic, and
women have no talent." His hands dropped as if burned
by her skin. He began pacing, his hands combing his
beard and untamed hair.

"Women are too worn out with bearing and raising
men's brats to have any strength left over for magic.
What talent I have has not been impaired by a man's interference."

Jaylor's mouth moved, but no words came forth. She
could see in his eyes that her words troubled him.

"Interference. Strength. Yes. Yes, that is why magicians must avoid women until their powers are full and
settled. Women drain their strength. Just as wifely duties
drain a woman."

She waited while that idea sank into his brain.

"If your father had an undeveloped talent you could
have inherited something from him." His eyes probed
hers. "There is a way to know." He hesitated as if embarrassed. "I could look into your mind. I have followed
other men's dreams before with just a touch." Again his
hands reached for her face.

"No." She backed away from those wonderfully gentle,
probing hands. "No." Panic tinged her voice. She forced
mastery over her mind and trembling body.

See into her mind! Never. He might see what had
driven her here to this remote clearing, so far away from
her family and the husband she had killed.

The image of her husband stretched across their marriage bed, eyes bulging, tongue protruding, limbs rigid in

death, flashed across her vision. The terror of that night visited her again. The terror and the relief. No one would look for the new bride early the next morning. She'd had nearly twelve hours to escape the prison of her marriage. Twelve hours to find the sanctuary of this clearing.

It had taken longer, closer to a full moon to walk the length of the province. A moon's cycle in which she moved closer and closer to the nameless thing that called her. She'd known the calling since early childhood. Back then she had thought it a yearning for peace and quiet, away from the noisy family home. Now she knew it was the empty clearing needing a new witchwoman.

But Jaylor must not see any of that. He would know then that she was hunted, blamed for a man's death. By law her life was forfeit. He must return her to her father's village for judgment and punishment. She wouldn't think what form that hideous punishment would take.

"To touch me that way is more intimate than if I allowed you into my body." She stalled his forward movement. Doubt clouded his eyes. She pressed her advantage. "You can't dare to look into my mind."

Jaylor's hand dropped again in agreement. "You're right. I can't take that chance."

"You still have your magic. But here in my clearing you must use your hands to move things."

My head aches with magic gone wrong. The glass is dark, obscured by another. More of the Tambootie removes the pain. I can see clearly again.

The wolf! Injured. Good.

He would have died, except for the cursed dragon.

He must die this time. Then I can get on with the rest of my plans.

The witchwoman and her lover will seek the dragon, and I will follow. Soon, very soon, all will be in place. I can set right three hundred years of mismanagement by the inept, so-called magicians!

Brevelan paced in front of the door of her cottage. If only Jaylor would hurry. He always headed for the bath-

ing pool first thing in the morning. So why was he daw-
dling over his morning routine? At last he stretched and
scratched, ran his hands through his hair and beard then
turned toward the creek.

"Shayla?" Brevelan called to her dragon friend as soon
as Jaylor had disappeared among the ferns.

Hm? The dragon replied sleepily.

"What am I going to do with that man?" Brevelan had
never had a friend before, someone close enough to discuss this sort of thing. Shayla seemed to be the only one
who could understand her dilemma.

Trust him. Came the succinct reply.

"Trust him? I don't even know why he is here." Partial
answers and dragon riddles weren't enough this time. She
wanted the truth, all of it and right now.

He is the only one who can save the Darville.

"I don't understand your obsession with a wolf. Why is
he so important to you?"

He must be protected. That seemed to be enough explanation for the dragon. Brevelan could feel her friend sliding once more into drowsy oblivion.

"Every creature has a name." The cat had told
Brevelan her true name. Every hare, squirrel, bird, goat,
and chicken within the clearing had names for themselves. But the wolf was notably silent on the issue.
Shayla had given him the name of a prince—Darville,
from the city of dragons.

"You tell me nothing new. You are a very logical and
practical creature. So why did you drag me out into that
storm when you had not concerned yourself with any human for ten years?" Five breeding cycles Shayla had
called the time. She had neither sought a mate nor concerned herself with people in all that time because the villagers had killed two of her litters. Why she stayed in
Coronnan was a mystery.

*Protect the golden wolf. The man is the only one who
can save him.*

"Why rescue the miserable beast? If you'd had him for
supper, your life would have been simpler."

And Brevelan would have been even more lonely

throughout the long winter months. Now that spring was in the air and Jaylor lingered, she didn't feel the empty ache quite so desperately.

Her thoughts stopped. Jaylor. She wasn't lonely with Jaylor nearby. She couldn't dwell on those impossible ideas. She had to press Shayla for information. "Why did you give the wolf a royal name? Is he the leader of his pack?"

What else should I call him?

"You could call him Wolf, or Puppy like I do, or any one of countless other names. You could name him Lord Krej or even call him Simurgh."

No! Shayla's roar of protest almost shattered Brevelan's mental ears. The roar continued, echoing in her head and around the foothills. *Never. Never consider the evil one. Do not even think of him.*

A wind rose and whirled about the clearing. It whipped the trees into a fury and drove all the small creatures toward shelter. A huge shadow passed overhead. Shayla was gone.

Brevelan stood her ground, not even bothering to subdue her swirling skirts. She might have known the ancient god of evil was at the heart of this puzzle. This wouldn't be the first time Brevelan had suspected his followers lurked within the kingdom. Even Lord Krej was rumored to have had dealings with a coven.

Three summers ago she had served at his castle for a banquet. All the girls from her village were bound to assist when extra servants were needed. Before the meal, while Brevelan spread fresh rushes on the floor, she had watched Krej in his Great Hall. He touched with fondness each of the six statues he kept there.

Most of the sculptures were of animals Brevelan had never seen before, did not know the names of. There was one huge cat, bigger than a pack steed, with teeth as long as a saber fern.

Krej talked to each of the statues. He sounded as though he were reminiscing about the capture of each. When he came to the cat she heard him say: "You led me quite a chase through that forest, special one. The trees hid you for a time. But you could not know they were all Tambootie and so they aided my search instead."

Then the cat blinked. Brevelan was sure of it because Krej cursed and waved his hands and the cat was still once more; captured in a prison of bronze.

"Behave, cat," Krej admonished the beast. "You have been granted the privilege of being sacrificed to Simurgh. You should be happy to serve the winged one."

This was worse than killing an animal for food! That at least had a purpose, sustained life in a way. Krej had imprisoned these beautiful creatures in stone and wood, metal and clay. Imprisoned their bright spirits for all time. She knew instinctively that each animal was still aware of that prison, not sleeping, not dead, but not alive either.

She had backed away, silently. By the time the banquet was served, Brevelan was at home, physically ill, unfit to be seen at the castle of one of the Twelve members of the Council of Provinces.

Wolf trotted up behind Jaylor. The beast had enjoyed splashing in the water almost as much as Jaylor had. Together they wandered the path back to the clearing in silent companionship.

"Whaoaar!" the dragon roared above them.

Strong trees bent with the wind of her passing. A mighty tail lashed across the sky. New leaves and old branches crashed to the ground around them.

Jaylor covered suddenly numbed ears with his hands. The sound of the dragon's anger echoed again and again through his mind.

Wolf merely stopped with one ear cocked as if listening. He showed no fear of the noise, and the unnatural wind did not so much as ruffle his fur.

When the dragon had passed overhead, her fury diminished, the wolf looked up to Jaylor as if to say, "Shall we go on home?" With his head tilted just so, his chin lifted and his golden eyes blinking up at Jaylor, Wolf looked so intelligent, almost as if a human soul resided within his body.

The Rovers had never found two of their missing men.

Jaylor had the sudden urge to talk to Baamin. He
needed to know more about dragon-dreams leading men
astray. Dragons were the essence of magic. Could their il-
lusions transform a man into a wild creature? And what
of his friend back in Coronnan City? Jaylor desperately
wanted reassurance that Roy had returned to the capital.

*Stargods! I need to end this farce soon. I can't tolerate
any more delays. Time is running short. I have eliminated
or bribed more than one old fool in the Commune. Some
of the students have talent. But they are gone, dispersed,
chasing wild lumbirds. Even this one, who has found the
wolf is only pretending to do magic.*

*I am the only one in Coronnan who can use the real
power. Throwing dragon magic is child's play, a child size
power.*

*Tomorrow I will finish the job. I must push the journey-
man and the witchwoman to lead me to the dragon. The
witchwoman is elusive. But I think I know her secret now.
The wolf and the cat, even the rabbits and squirrels return to the clearing easily. Only people are kept out.
There is a trick I must try.*

*First, I must take something for this headache. A little
Tambootie ought to do the job. It will also prepare me for
the task at hand.*

CHAPTER 9

Jaylor fed another branch into the fire. His lean-to was in place. The physical labor had acted as a release for the questions that churned in his mind.

He clutched Mica to his chest for warmth against the chill of his purpose. She purred in rhythm with his agitated pulse. Was summoning a master while on quest in violation of the complex rules?

Jaylor moved his staff within easy reach of his hand. The plaited grain of the once smooth oak offered reassurance. In these uncertain times, he might need the stronger focus for his magic even though the moon was full.

When he'd cut the staff in the heart of the sacred grove, just before beginning his quest, the branch had called to him, claiming him as its owner. At the time, the wood had been straight and smooth. Every time he used this tool the grain bent and coiled, taking on a pattern similar to a loose braid. The more often he used the staff the stronger the communication between them grew. He needed to use the staff. The staff needed to be used by him.

He folded his long legs underneath him and sat facing the blaze. There was enough fuel to keep it burning for quite a while without attention. He extracted from his pack a small oblong of glass not much larger than Brevelan's tiny palm. This was his first viewer, given to him as an apprentice, much more portable than the slightly larger, brass-framed glass he had earned as a journeyman.

One of Brevelan's soothing songs drifted across the

cool evening air. He allowed it to wrap his mind in comfort and relax his body.

Mica purred louder, harmonizing with the wordless tune. She butted her head against his chin. He stroked the cat's unusual fur in rhythm with his breathing. Her warmth settled him.

Jaylor focused on the seething green center of a flame. The glass brought it closer, enlarged it until the fire filled his vision. Gradually, he drew the flame into his consciousness.

The part of him that was aware of the night—listening to Brevelan's song, chilling in the rustling wind, feeling the hard ground beneath his butt—separated from his magic. The rest of him hovered near the void and knew only the flame. He breathed deeper, deeper. The flame in the glass grew cool and distant. It jumped to the edge of the clearing. There it paused, hesitant to break the armor. Jaylor pushed it onward.

A tiny flicker of magic fire climbed hills, skimmed over the bay, seeking, always seeking. Through the forests and down the broad highway to the capital, it drew ever closer to a familiar mind. When it found the barrier of the mighty Coronnan River, it paused to gather strength, then jumped the channels twisting around the city and wound its way through the alleyways with growing urgency until it found the University and the one window that faced the courtyard. Light flowed from the window, drawing the tiny flame. Like seeking like.

It slid up the stone walls and glided through the opening to merge with a candle flame. Into Jaylor's glass came the image of Baamin. Like the journeyman, the senior magician held a glass, though his was much larger and rimmed with gold.

"Jaylor?" The old man murmured from his own trance.

"Sir," he replied. Had his master really been that old and worn two moons ago when Jaylor left him?

"Finally, I've gotten through to you!"

Surprise wound its way into Jaylor's consciousness. He thought he had done the summoning. "You have need of me, sir?"

"Trouble is brewing in Coronnan. Strange reports come to me from all quarters. What is happening in your sector?" The old man's image wavered in the glass. Jaylor strengthened his contact.

"Baamin, I have seen a dragon. Twice. Yet I do not believe I have finished my quest."

"Which dragon? Is it well? Are you alone or have you been followed. Have you encountered anything or anyone strange on your quest?" The magician's questions came out in an anxious rush.

Some of Baamin's emotions reached Jaylor through the spell. Jaylor's disquiet grew. Which strange event should he relate first? "I believe a rogue magician frequents the southern mountains. He disguises himself as a one-eyed drunk, but he looks upon himself as a younger red-haired man."

"We must beware of anyone is disguise, Jaylor. I, too, have encountered a rogue in a different guise." An impression of a shaggy-headed monster, very like a spotted saber cat but with bright red hair, superimposed upon Baamin's features then vanished before Jaylor was certain of what he had seen.

The lines of worry deepened on the old man's face.

"I encountered Rovers inside Coronnan. The border is nearly gone and no magician guards it," Jaylor continued.

"Dragon dung! Lord Krej swore to me, two days ago, that Journeyman Tomalin was stationed there. Have you seen the boy?"

"No. I have seen no one from the University." Jaylor sensed the summons diffusing. The spell wasn't weaker, just more spread out. As if someone were eavesdropping. He tightened his control of the flames and pressed on with his report. "I have found a great golden wolf that a dragon protects."

"*Stargods* guard us all! Jaylor, anything to do with the dragons is important. There are very few of them left. If a dragon protects a wolf, then the wolf is important."

"He was injured but is healing. He appears more intelligent than a beast should be."

"Stay with the wolf and the dragon. We need more information before you return to the capital." This time the magician's agitation nearly broke the contact.

Jaylor forced his mind back into the flame. It burned brighter, the image steadied. Wasn't Baamin doing anything to maintain this spell? Again he sensed that this conversation was not private. He had to phrase his next comments very carefully. "I am told the dragon saved the creature from some kind of trouble at the solstice." More than a moon before Jaylor began his journey.

"A number of the Rovers went missing about the same time. Could the soul of a missing man have been trapped within the wolf's body? Any missing man? Someone we know perhaps?"

Baamin's image drew away from the glass. The swirling colors in the border of the spell faded to blinding white. "If that is the case, after so many moons he will still think himself a wolf when the spell breaks. Beware, Jaylor. Beware of attack when you least expect it."

The danger was clear. Jaylor remembered the dripping fangs aimed at his throat. But how was he to break the spell? Baamin clearly expected him to. He didn't know who had thrown that particular piece of magic. Each magician left a trademark in the colored aura of his spells. That trademark made it possible to trace the path of the magic and then reverse it.

But Jaylor was useless at following traditional magic forms, and this didn't smell like a University spell.

"Sir, has my friend returned to the capital?"

"Your friend?" Baamin looked distracted and uneasy. "Oh, um, your friend, of course."

Jaylor breathed a little easier. Roy had been absent from Coronnan City for several weeks before Jaylor was sent on his quest. Not unusual. But always before, Roy had left a secret message for Jaylor regarding his destination and expected return. Just one small precaution against assassination.

"Sir, I need some books from the library on shape change spells if I am to finish this quest."

He could almost see the volume he needed. But it was

an ancient tome, too fragile to leave the stasis spell placed on it for more than a few moments.

"Books are off limits on quest, my boy. You must continue alone." The old man looked more sad than querulous. "Befriend the dragon. Do whatever it asks. The dragon is our only hope. You must find a way to secure the border in your sector. I will work on the other points that have been breached."

The border breached at other points as well? What did one say in the face of such a tragedy. Without the magic border, Coronnan would be open to attack from foreign armies as well as outlandish cultures. Chaos—or growth—would soon result. The people of Coronnan weren't ready for either.

"There is other news as well," Baamin continued. "Two ambassadors are on their way to Coronnan. The kingdom of Rossemeyer seeks to marry their princess to our prince. Refusal will be considered a declaration of war. Their enemy, SeLenicca, claims any alliance with Rossemeyer will require retribution from them."

"*Stargods!* How long before I can expect raiders on the border?" Both SeLenicca and Rossemeyer claimed the mountains southwest of here. No one controlled the passes and hidden valleys, except possibly the Rovers. Sudden blizzards sprang up at all times of the year. Armies from either country could cross the pass in two days—weather permitting—and simply walk across the dissolving border.

"By the dark of the next moon both armies will wish to remind us of our trade-treaty obligations. If the dragons would give me enough magic, I could summon a storm to detain the ambassadors and delay a decision. I fear you are on your own. You must seal the border and discover why the dragon protects the wolf before then."

"If you had enough magic? What is happening, sir?" Jaylor forced himself to maintain the spell. The questions raised occupied too much of his concentration.

"The rogue in disguise is perverting my spells. I can't maintain this summons much longer."

He wasn't doing much to hold it together as it was.

"Are you certain the man is a foreign rogue, sir?" Silly question. The Commune had too much control over their members for one to step outside the bounds of University training. Masters of dragon magic could combine and thereby increase their powers to overcome any individual magician. All of the rogues who couldn't or wouldn't gather dragon magic had sought more agreeable locations three hundred years ago, when the Commune established the border.

"A rogue of great power, Jaylor. I know not his origins. He or his accomplice stalks you even now, since you are so close to the last breeding female dragon."

"I don't think the one who stalks me is from some other country." Jaylor allowed an image of the one-eyed derelict to form on the glass. The image shifted and changed to a red-haired man in his prime, broad shouldered, lean of hip. He dared not risk giving the image a name or full details of his face. That could summon him into the spell, allow him to eavesdrop or, worse yet, interrupt the communication.

But the vivid color of his hair should give his identity away.

"Then his magic is of a nature totally alien to us. I know not its source, nor its potential." The image wavered. "Even now he pulls this spell away from me. I dare work no magic at all, for it just makes him stronger and me weaker." The sound of his voice faded. "Be careful, Jaylor. Be careful."

The spell dissolved from both ends.

Darville stirred. As usual, he was curled up on the hearth. From there he could open one eye and observe all of the hut, as well as the door. Not much passed his notice.

His body would not settle. The usual comfortable positions pulled his muscles wrong, twisted his bones. He stretched out, resting his head on his paws.

Something was wrong. He could sense it, feel it, taste it.

He couldn't see as much in this position, but he felt

better. Brevelan was fully in his sight. That was important.

He smelled disquiet in her. Something to do with the
man. The man he now knew must be protected along with
Brevelan. The dragon had told him so.

Perhaps he should be out there with the man. Then he
could keep both his people under his eye. He yawned and
stretched up to a sitting position. One hind foot twitched.
He bent his head so he could scratch his ears. He didn't
really itch. It was just something to do while he puzzled
out his next move.

"What, Puppy?" Brevelan's voice washed over him
with love.

His tail thumped. He knew it did and wondered why. It
was as out of place as he was. Something was definitely
wrong. He wasn't sure if it was outside himself or inside.
He just knew he had to move, had to seek the source of
his upset.

"Out?" Brevelan asked. She rose and shook her head.
There was love in her voice. He thumped his tail again
and rose to all of his feet. He needed to be higher, to view
things from a different position. He jumped up and placed
his front paws on the wall beside the door.

His back stretched. He savored the tight pleasure of
that stretch. Better. But still not right.

"Oh, all right." Her hand pulled the leather thong on
the door and it swung outward. He slid through the narrow opening. His nose twitched.

Ahead was the scent of the man's fire. It burned hot
and strange, but he sensed no danger. He smelled the rich
warmth of the flusterhens, roosting for the night. The
goat was there as well. He found Mica's scent mingled
with the man's. That was fine. She would alert him to any
danger.

His head swung from side to side as he trotted around
the edge of the clearing. All was in order. Everyone who
should be there was in place. No one who should not be
there intruded.

Instinctively he lifted his outside leg and left his mark.
The action seemed out of place as well. His scent was

strong. No one threatened his territory. So why was he so restless? What was wrong?

The opening of the door brought a chill to Brevelan's shoulders. She should be used to the wolf's comings and goings by now. He wanted out at the strangest times.

How odd, she mused. She'd never had to housebreak him as she would a puppy or a feral animal. Darville knew not to soil her house.

When she opened the door, she saw the glow from Jaylor's fire. That banished her questions about the wolf and brought images of the man to mind. Images of his hands on her face, his mouth hot and seeking on her own. She should fear the man and the lust that drove him. Instead she wanted once more to experience the gentle warmth in her belly when his hands caressed her hair. She wasn't used to gentleness. If he'd beaten her, she could have resisted him.

She returned to her stool by the hearth with a sigh. The pot of herbs bubbling on the grate required a stir. It was something of her own invention to ease the birthing pains of the carpenter's wife. It would also dull the pain of severe injury. Puppy might need it again. Twice now he'd been injured. Twice she'd nursed him back to health.

He was just a wolf. What was so extraordinary about him?

She heard the wind stirring her thatch. A song rose to her lips in response. With the tune she secured her home and protected her clearing.

"Puppy!" she called the wolf from the doorway. It was time she slept. She didn't need the animal's restless wanderings to disturb her.

"Awroooo . . ." he howled mournfully in the distance. "Awroooo."

"Puppy!" Brevelan ran toward the sound. Jaylor's strong arm about her waist stayed her headlong plunge into the undergrowth. "Puppy, what's wrong," she cried, struggling against the pinioning arm.

"Stay here." Jaylor commanded.

"He needs me," she insisted.

"Awroooo. . . ." Brevelan shuddered at the distress in the call.

"Stay here," Jaylor said again. He released her. "There's magic in the air, too much magic." He swung his staff above his head in an arc. An eerie glow filled the clearing. "I can find him by this light, but no intruder can use it to find us."

"Awroooo . . ." Darville was silhouetted against the dark trees. He stood facing the back path to the village, neck fur bristling, tail erect.

"We are being watched," Jaylor whispered. His arms redescribed the arc and the light vanished. "Get inside."

Brevelan resisted the pressure of his hand on her back. Darville's call was full of pain. He needed her.

"Go! I will see to the animal." He shoved her in the direction of the hut even as his long legs took him across the open space.

"Puppy," she called as Jaylor's hand came down on the wolf's neck.

The wail ended abruptly. Wolf and man turned and loped back to the hut together.

"Who is it?" she asked as Jaylor leaned heavily against the closed door. He seemed out of breath from his brief exertion.

"Which village do you hail from?" he returned.

She was silent.

"Don't bother." His eyes closed in weariness. "With that hair I can only guess that Krej's castle was very close to your home."

"How did you know?" She was too shocked to be defensive.

"Rumors of strange happenings, his neglect of his responsibilities. There's a rogue magician in this village. He obeys a man with hair as bright as Lord Krej's."

"You bring that man," she spat, "here?" She allowed her disgust for the man who had probably fathered her, as well as a half dozen other bastards, to color her voice.

"He'd have found you sooner or later. I am not his quest." Jaylor turned to peer out the door. "The clearing is armored. I don't know if it will hold against this rogue."

"Could Krej's rogue capture rare animals and imprison them as sculptures?" She needed to talk, to keep her mind occupied so she wouldn't remember how empty her home had felt until Jaylor once more filled the room.

"Who knows what powers a rogue can tap. Perhaps they seek to add a dragon to the collection. Or a golden wolf." He sank down to the floor, back still against the door. Fatigue rimmed his eyes. He'd been working magic again. Strong magic.

Silence surrounded them. Brevelan, too, sank to the floor. Her arms reached for her pet. She buried her face in his fur and clung to him. He filled her arms with warmth. But he wasn't Jaylor.

"Light the torches! Let's burn her out." Men's voices, angry, insulting, broke the silence.

Jaylor's head rose in alarm. Brevelan's chest tightened.

"If we kill the witch the path to the dragon will open," one of the fishermen yelled.

"We should 'a run the woman off last summer. Then there wouldn't be no dragon up there now," the barkeep sneered.

"I lost another cow this morning to the blasted dragon. I want that monster dead any way it takes to do it," screamed a farmer who had sought Brevelan's help when he'd nearly severed his foot with an ax. She'd saved the foot, but the man would limp for the rest of his life.

There were other comments from men she didn't know. But the one in command, that one chilled her bones.

"Let's smoke her out!" Old Thorm's voice, and yet it was stronger, better educated than the drunken trouble-maker's.

"Witches can't fight a good fire."

She pulled Puppy closer, to still her shaking. She could face magic, or dragons, or even wild wolves. But fire? FIRE!

Jaylor's gaze darted about the hut, peering into the shadows. "Can you call Shayla?"

She wasn't sure whether she heard the words with her ears or her mind.

"Shayla?"

"She is the only thing he," Jaylor nodded toward the outside to indicate who he meant, "still fears."

"But they want to kill her!" She'd heard that much in the muffled sounds outside.

"Not when she flies. They want you to show them her lair. Call the dragon, Brevelan. You've got to call Shayla."

CHAPTER 10

L ight and music flooded the bridge between the University and Palace Reveta Tristile. Baamin made his slow, observant way toward the banquet hall and the festivities being prepared for the arrival of two, rival, ambassadors. The emissaries from SeLenicca and Rossemeyer each sought to secure an exclusive alliance with Coronnan. The two kingdoms had been at each other's throats for generations. Coronnan traded with both.

Baamin wondered if he could convince his frail king that the pattern of the future that the magicians saw in the glass was the same pattern of entrapment represented by the two rival ambassadors.

Tonight the senior magician's responsibilities in matters magical weighed as heavily on his shoulders as the diplomatic chores.

Master Fraandalor, assigned to the court of Lord Krej, had just reported the discovery of Journeyman Tomalin's body on the shores of the Great Bay. Death by drowning, five leagues away from his post.

"My Lord Baamin." A minor courtier bowed low to the magician.

Baamin touched the man's bowed head briefly, then jerked away as if in surprise. "What have we here, Bruce? A flower? Why are you growing flowers in your ears?" He handed the posy to the smiling man.

"Flowers today, coins yesterday." Bruce lowered his eyes, unwilling to meet the magician's glance. His hands fluttered in front of him, almost seeking a warding gesture. "When you honor us with your presence, who knows what will be found in unlikely places."

Tricks. Simple tricks that didn't even require magic. Still, the court expected this sort of thing.

And feared it.

"How fares the king?" Baamin prodded the sharp-eyed, sharp-nosed ferret of a man. Bruce was a notorious gossip. He was also master of the king's shoes and in a position to observe King Darcine in private.

Bruce of the Shoes shrugged, then leaned closer to whisper in Baamin's ear. "Good thing that foreign ambassador with the unpronounceable name sent a cask of beta'arack from Rossemeyer. Liquor perks him up like nothing else lately. A good strong dose of the stuff first thing in the morning works wonders on the king's spirits and constitution."

The liquor wasn't the only cause of the king's high spirits these days. Shayla was well and gravid. Therefore, Baamin knew, the king gained in strength. Today.

Baamin nodded sagely. They'd seen Darcine's spells of near manic strength before. But every day of good health was followed by longer and longer periods of depression and weakness.

If anything happened to the dragon or her dragonets. . . .

Anxiously, Baamin looked around for signs of the forces that interfered with his magic and the dragons.

He straightened his shoulders and stretched to his full height, slight as it was. There were appearances to be kept up. While the king felt so well and strong, Baamin would attend banquets and balls day and night. There had been precious few celebrations in the last ten years.

"Ah, Baamin." Darcine waved for the magician to approach him.

Brightly gowned ladies and richly jeweled men filled the Great Hall with shrill laughter. All were masked for the event, except the king. Baamin sensed the tension in the posture and rapidly darting eyes of the nobility. They must know this gaiety was only temporary.

"Your Grace." Baamin bowed to his monarch.

As he straightened, he took the opportunity to carefully survey the tall figure of his friend. New tunic and trews

of golden brocade, padded to disguise too thin limbs and
slumping shoulders. A small replica of the Coraurlia, the
glass dragon-crown, rested on his head. The token of his
kingship contained hardly any heavy glass at all.
Darcine's neck couldn't support the full weight of the
crown.

The king didn't need to mask his face. His entire body
was cloaked in the guise of health.

"You're late, my friend. But the night is still young.
There is plenty of time to sample the delicacies the cook
has provided." The usual feverish flush on King
Darcine's face was now replaced with a more even and
natural coloring.

Paint or healing?

"Have you seen aught of my cousin? Krej promised to
attend this little gathering." King Darcine snagged a gob-
let of wine from a passing servant. "He is so very enter-
taining."

"Nay, Your Grace. Lord Krej has not privileged me
with news of his activities." Baamin wanted to discount
Jaylor's theories that the rogue magician operating in the
south answered to Krej. The king's cousin, with his reputation as a fierce negotiator, was their only hope of
avoiding war if the prince could not be found soon.

"We can enjoy ourselves without Krej. He does tell
such outrageous stories though. When the ambassadors
come, his wit will charm then into a favorable marriage
settlement." The king made to move back to his guests.

"Your Grace, have you forgotten the most important element in the negotiations? Your son." He paused while
the king turned back, his face and posture slumped under
the strain of dealing with that matter.

Laughter rose and surged toward the entrance. Newcomers stood there waiting for all to acknowledge their
presence before entering. Baamin peered toward the bubble of excitement. Too many people crowded too close to
the masked lord and lady for him to see more than a swirl
of bronze and ebony lamé fabric. Costly stuff.

"Perhaps this is your cousin, Your Grace, and his
lady." Baamin gestured toward the brilliant figures.

"If not his lady, then another beautiful companion. Krej does have wonderful luck with women." Darcine winked knowingly. "Lady Rhodia is still recovering from her latest confinement. Yet another daughter. Very disappointing. I wonder who replaces her in my cousin's affections, and his bed, this time?"

"I don't think Lord Krej will keep her long enough for anyone to find out. Even your bold cousin won't risk another of Lady Rhodia's temper tantrums." The last time Lady Rhodia had caught Krej with a courtesan, she had nearly destroyed their costly suite in the royal palace as well as her rival's beautiful face.

Baamin turned away from the object of their discussion. He'd never liked Krej's arrogance, nor the look of disdain that always clouded his bay blue eyes. The soul within the man was as frigid as the depths of the Great Bay.

"Welcome, cousin." Darcine gestured toward the newcomer. In a complete departure from protocol, Darcine wandered away from his post on the dais toward Krej and the lady. The court flocked to them, currying favor and notice. Baamin held back, taking the opportunity to observe the entire banquet hall

Every muscle in his body froze with fear. Icy sweat popped out on his brow and his back. In the center of the huge hall stood the monster of his nightmares, clothed in bronze lamé.

"What kind of joke is this?" he whispered.

Just then, Lord Krej lifted his masked face and stared directly at the Senior Magician, as if he had heard the frantic question. Beneath the mask of a spotted saber cat, Krej's eyes glinted with malice. Baamin mentally shook himself free of the dread that rooted him to the spot. There was a glamour about the masked figure. He needed to move closer and examine the nature of that magic distortion.

His private fears stopped him cold.

"Can you call Shayla?" Jaylor raised his voice. Brevelan clung to the wolf with fierce intensity. Her eyes were huge in the dim light from the hearth.

"Call Shayla?" she asked into the wolf's fur.

"Yes. Call the dragon," he pressed. His hand reached out to stroke her hair, to draw her attention to his words. He didn't need magic to see the terror on her face. The lightest touch and the source of her panic flooded through his fingers to his mind.

Fire. Hot. Smoke. No air. The heat. The pain.

Something in the girl's past brought on this terror. Something she dared not let him see.

Jaylor allowed his touch to become comforting. He stroked her cheek and cupped her chin gently. "Brevelan, trust me. There is no fire. We can get out of this if you'll just call the dragon. The rogue still fears her."

Tender warmth filled the gap between them. Jaylor wanted to wrap the girl in his arms and hold her. He was aware of her, but for once desire didn't overwhelm him. He needed more than physical union with her. Their one kiss had taught him that. If only the wolf were not between them, he would reach over and hold her tightly against his chest and treasure the completeness she offered.

"Bring the torches!" Old Thorm's voice carried on the evening breeze. "The thatch is damp, the smoke will drive her out."

"She's mine when she runs," the fisherman crowed.

"What gives you first right?" someone else challenged.

"Once we've had her, she won't be a witch anymore," Old Thorm chortled.

"What about the wolf?"

"I'll slit the devil dog's throat first, before he can protect his mistress, before he has the chance to drain the blood from another man's body."

Brevelan blanched. Jaylor pulled her, and the wolf she cradled, tight against his chest.

"I won't let them hurt you," he promised. Though how, he didn't know. There were at least ten of them. His magic wasn't designed to hurt people. That was the first law of the Commune.

His answer came from overhead. A roar that only a dragon throat could muster filled his mind and ears. Both he and Brevelan sagged in relief. Wolf looked up, his mouth open in a doggy grin.

Seek me, you impudent puppet of evil! The dragon's thoughts flooded the clearing. As if from a dizzying height, Jaylor saw the object of Shayla's wrath. He was disguised as a one-eyed beggar, dressed in rags. But Jaylor/Shayla knew him now, knew a powerful magician hid behind a glamour. Once revealed, this enemy could never again hide behind this flimsy disguise.

The vision pulled back, and Jaylor knew Shayla flew higher. Then, as she tucked her wings back and dove, the ground rushed up at him with frightening speed. Nine men hovered near the rogue—a vigorous, red-haired man in his prime. But dragon eyes weren't meant to focus on the details of human faces. Nine white blurs looked up. Only the fear in their eyes shone through.

Jaylor felt the roar of triumph pelt from the dragon's throat, and his own. The first flicker of flame erupted, with a roar dredged up from the roots of the mountains.

The hut shook and trembled with the rocking ground beneath it. Jaylor plummeted back into his own senses. He heard shouts and screams from the villagers outside. Through Shayla's eyes, but his own body, he could see them running from the fingers of flame licking their heels. One man rested while flames tickled another's backside. Then, before he could contemplate safety in another's pain, the first man felt the heat of Shayla's wrath again.

"Why does she just toy with them? She should flame them and be done with the menace." Jaylor spoke to thin air.

Brevelan opened her mouth to answer. Her voice cracked with a giggle that bordered on hysteria.

"Are you seeing this, too?" Wonder flooded his senses. For a moment they had all been linked into the mind of a dragon.

She nodded. Her eyes were still huge in the firelight.

"Shayla will never harm a man, even though these are the same ones who slaughtered her litters. Dragon pride compels her to honor the pact."

"The pact with Nimbulan—three hundred years ago?" Jaylor asked.

Brevelan shrugged her shoulders. "Shayla only said there was a pact, made with all of Coronnan. She can send dragon-dreams to lead the dangerous ones astray. But to her, our lives are sacred and must be preserved."

Superstition in the village had become perverted over the generations. That perversion now endangered all of Coronnan. Had it been directed by a single man—a lord with red hair?

"I'll get you yet, you monstrous beast from hell! My magic will defeat you." A loud voice boomed across the clearing in defiance.

Cleared of disguise, the educated accent and condescending drawl became very distinctive to Jaylor's ears.

Through Shayla's eyes once more they saw the faceless rogue at the edge of the clearing. Gone were the trappings of the one-eyed beggar. They watched him gather a ball of dark red and green magic energy in his hands. With a mighty effort of broad shoulders and strong arms, he hurled it toward the sky.

Shayla sent forth a magnificent burst of bright green dragon fire. Flames engulfed the magic ball, then shattered it into myriad starry sparks. The pinpoints of light drifted harmlessly to the ground.

Puny man. Shayla dismissed him with another lick of flame. The rogue disappeared into the sheltering trees. One last lashing of flames followed him away from the clearing.

"Thank you, Shayla." Jaylor formed the words in his head as he spoke. Brevelan's eyes were closed and he sensed her joining her gratitude to his.

We must settle this. Bring the golden wolf to my lair.

"Can't you just land in the clearing?" Brevelan asked.

The evil one may return. I am not safe on the ground. Bring the wolf to me. Close the path behind you.

"How will we find you? The mountain is huge, the trails difficult." Brevelan's voice shook.

Follow the path that only you can find. Blur your trail

so he does not follow. Shayla's imagery disappeared from both their heads.

Jaylor looked to Brevelan and the wolf. She still clutched the animal to her. Wolf seemed perfectly happy there, his head nestling between her breasts.

If only she could learn to love Jaylor as much as she did this scruffy beast.

"Call your journeymen home, Baamin." King Darcine basked in his flower garden the morning after the ball. The spring sunshine flooded the bench he had chosen for this interview with his magician.

"Is that wise, Your Grace?" Baamin hedged.

"The dragons are protecting my son. They will return him when the time is right. I am well now and have the kingdom under control." The king closed his eyes as he turned his face to the source of the warmth. He looked like a contented cat napping in the sunshine. He'd gained a little weight this past week, lost a little of the gauntness.

"When did you learn that your son would be returned by the dragons?" Baamin mistrusted any predictions that didn't come from his own glass. A glass that had been dark and silent since the appearance of the beast-headed monster. The monster couldn't be the same rogue who plagued Jaylor's footsteps. No magician, no matter how powerful, could traverse such distances so quickly. Nimbulan had bewailed his inability to transport himself after he'd had to exile his own wife.

How much of the king's "control" was mere illusion created by the rogue?

Baamin's magic faded more each day. He could probably summon enough magic to throw a truth spell at the king. If he dared.

Long years of friendship and respect, as well as fear of the monster, stilled his desire to use magic.

"My cousin, Krej, told me in a dream last night. He assured me Darville is safe. The dragons need him for a while. We are not in a position to question the dragons." The king seemed once more a regal monarch instead of an ailing old man.

"How does Krej know so much about dragons? He is not the keeper of their lore."

"You forget, he carries the same royal blood in his veins as I do!"

"His mother is an outland princess, from SeLenicca with ties to Hanassa. Your mother, Your Grace, was a noble lady of Coronnan. The royal blood is purer in you." Baamin took a step away from his king. He didn't have to throw a truth spell to see an aura. But he did need space. The king's colors fluctuated and shimmered in and out of visibility. Darcine was not in control of his own emotions, let alone the kingdom. His health and resolve came from somewhere else.

"Does Lord Krej speak to you often in your dreams?"

"Lately he comes to me almost every night." The aura flared red with anger, then settled into a mild rainbow dominated by shades of green and red, the colors of Krej's crest.

"Lately?" Since dragon magic was on the wane and a rogue wandered Krej's province freely. "What about before?" Baamin prodded.

The king looked sharply at his magician. The aura flared once more, this time with the yellow of uncertainty. Clearly he had not thought about this often. "Ever since Krej was a teenager at the University he has advised me through my dreams. Never often. Just when I really needed his wisdom."

"Your Grace, with the prince gone, your cousin Krej is the next heir. He is ambitious. Can you trust him so completely?" Baamin offered in his mild way. He had learned long ago it was not wise to be aggressive with Darcine. He tended to resent the trait in others when he had so little aggression in his own soul.

"Krej has only the welfare of the kingdom in his heart. He will do what is best. He tells me the truth."

"But perhaps not all of the truth."

"You defame a member of the royal family, magician." The king's back straightened indignantly. The aura faded, as if masked.

Or armored.

"I am sworn to defend the kingdom, Your Grace."
Baamin swallowed deeply. Who had armored the king's
aura? Was the monster eavesdropping on Baamin's very
thoughts? "Our best defense now lies with your son. I
cannot order my journeymen home until the prince is returned."

"You speak of defense. The border will do that. You
need only obey your king." Darcine's meager strength
seemed to wane a little as the sun slid behind a fluffy
cloud.

"There are not enough dragons left to maintain the border."

"Explain," the king demanded.

"Shayla has bred. She is strong and healthy, so there is
more magic this week than last. But she is the only breeding female left. There is just not enough magic left for us
to hold the border inviolate. I have suspected this for a
long time. But the change was so gradual that no one noticed until the border refused to stay in place." Sadness
weighed his eyelids down to near closing.

So much good came from dragon magic, and not just
the border. Now they would be left vulnerable to rogue
magic as well as invading armies. Unless they took dras-
tic diplomatic measures immediately. Was the marriage of
Darville to the princess of Rossemeyer the answer?

That action would cause a war with SeLenicca. But if
no alliance was formed, Rossemeyer promised to invade.
And if Coronnan stalled, the borders would be vulnerable
to both countries.

"Lord Krej has said nothing of the border to me." Once
more the king was alert and concerned. Just as he had
been in his youth. "I cannot believe my cousin would not
inform me of such a dire mishap."

"Rovers have been sighted at nearly all the border
crossings."

"Rovers! Thieves and degenerates. Their women have
no morals. The men will steal anything without compunc-
tion." Outrage radiated from the king. "Have they stolen
any babies yet?" He half rose, as if to commence battle
with these menaces out of history.

"Not yet." Baamin hid his concern at Darcine's agitation. The king wasn't strong enough to withstand such strong emotional upsets. "The few dragons left to us are doing what they can to defend against the Rovers with their dragon-dreams." But that could work against the kingdom if the Rovers decided to replace their lost men with babies born to Coronnan.

"Have the marketplaces watched. Rovers are adept at hiding. But their wares are unique. If you see some of their distinctive metalwork, then you know a Rover is lurking nearby."

"Their crafts are indeed distinctive, creative, and in many ways superior to ours. If we alert the populace to beware, perhaps we can learn something from these strange tribes."

"At what cost, magician?"

"The border was established for a reason, Your Grace. Perhaps those reasons were shortsighted. Have we really benefited from three hundred years of isolation?"

"We trade with friends. We have avoided invasion. What more can we want?"

"Stimulation, creativity. Sometimes security leads to complacency. That has left us ill-prepared now that danger threatens." And the magic faded. They had no knowledge of the rogues who had been banished and might seek revenge.

"We still have armies. We can fight off any invasion."

"A very small number of troops who have grown soft with easy living. They are more concerned with the color of their uniforms than with how to wield a sword."

Fashions hadn't changed; artisans still held to traditional forms, good in their way but lacking imagination. Even at the University there had been no exploration of new techniques, not even new medicines. The secret technology of the Stargods had revealed nothing new in the heavens for generations.

Young people lacked the stimulation to grow beyond their parents. Without that growth there was only stagnation, decay, and death. Now that he thought about it,

Baamin saw all the symptoms clearly. He was as guilty of complacency as everyone else.

"Baamin, bring your journeymen home this very day. I would question them on the things they have seen. We must right the wrongs immediately, before our jealous neighbors steal our bounty." Darcine delivered his royal speech as if reciting instructions. "You will reestablish the border, or I will have to replace you at the University. Lord Krej has recommended someone."

CHAPTER 11

B revelan couldn't delay much longer.
 "It's time." Jaylor's words cut through Brevelan's
tumbled thoughts. Dawn crept above the treetops. Birds
greeted the sunlight with raucous song.

The sun was high enough for her to see the path up the
mountain. "I must . . . I must . . ." She sought an excuse
to remain. There was nothing left to do except leave. She
had packed enough food for the two of them for three
days. Their bedding was neatly rolled into Jaylor's pack.
Her house and the clearing were in order.

"You can't stay, Brevelan. It's no longer safe. The villagers followed Old Thorm and broke through the clearing's magic. They found you once. Shayla won't stop
them next time." His hand was gentle on her arm, urging
her out of the hut.

"If I leave, nothing will be the same when I return,"
she protested.

"Already things change. A rogue magician has altered
the path of all our futures. We must leave." This time
Jaylor's tone was firmer.

"My animals. I must see to them." She hesitated as a
lop-eared rabbit appeared among the ferns. Its nose wiggled in greeting.

"You have already told them to disperse. The clearing's
magic can no longer shelter them."

He was right. She had sent each of her pets an image
appropriate to its understanding. They must fend for
themselves, take their chances in the wild, until she returned.

If she returned.

"Why must I go with you? Without you here the rogue will pass me by."

"You heard Old One-eye last night. He wants to kill Wolf as much as he wants to burn you alive." Jaylor allowed that thought to sink in. "Besides, Shayla said you are the only one who can find the path."

"Shayla." She started to smile at the mention of her friend. The usual warmth and closeness she felt with the dragon faded with the memory of flames flickering through the clearing last night. Deep inside she had felt not only her own relief and Shayla's battle lust but also the real terror of the villagers, her villagers. It was not unlike the sensation of pain and death she felt every time one of her animals lost its life to a predator. "She seems to be demanding a lot."

"She protects you and the wolf." Jaylor's tone was insistent.

"From stray rogue magicians? Why?" They had both been reluctant to discuss the strange attack on the clearing last night. She felt as if words would bring the men back with their torches.

"Think about it while we walk." He set his jaw firmly. Brevelan's stubbornness waned in the face of his determination.

"Come, Puppy." Brevelan called the wolf to her. Happily, he bounced to her side. As usual, he sat on her foot, leaning his weight into her. She ruffled his ears, cradled his large head in her hands, and briefly nuzzled him. "We have to go see Shayla now," she explained to him.

Her reluctance to leave the shelter of her clearing made her pack heavier. "I'm not sure he's healed enough to make this journey." Her words came out sharp and ill-tempered. Puppy's enthusiasm for the journey grated on her nerves.

Jaylor didn't reply as he stooped to lift his own pack to his shoulders. His long walking staff was already in his other hand. He fingered the interesting grain of the wood that ran down the length of the staff in a twisting plait.

"Maybe we should wait another day." She looked up at him with hope. The set of his jaw told her they couldn't.

"Mrrew?" Mica sat in the doorway. Her plaintive voice echoed around the hut that suddenly seemed empty, devoid of life.

"She's asking to go with us." Brevelan smiled for the first time. "She belongs here, more than I do. She was waiting for me when I found the clearing. Now she's demanding to leave with us."

"I can't keep her from following." Jaylor stared at the cat.

"Mrrow!" This time the cat's voice was emphatic, her eyes very round and humanlike.

"She won't be left behind." Brevelan looked from cat to man. There was a special bond there. Yet she didn't feel jealousy, not the way she did when Puppy showed a preference for the magician.

"Mrrow." Mica rubbed her face against Jaylor's leg. Her purr was loud, meant to gratify.

Jaylor bent to scratch her ears. Her fur rippled with different colors in different lights, as did slivers of mica. She was rightly named.

"It's a long trip, kitty. Maybe you'd better stay here."

"Niow!" Mica protested. This time she reached up with her claws to cling to his shirtsleeve. A quick scramble and she was perched on his shoulder.

"But, Mica . . ." Jaylor protested. He tried to dislodge the animal.

"It appears she is coming with us whether we like it or not." Brevelan smiled in earnest this time.

"How does it feel to be a cat's scratching post?" Brevelan giggled, just a little, at the sight of tiny Mica kneading Jaylor's broad shoulder.

Arching calubra ferns made a shaded aisle of the path. Their feet trod soundlessly on the thick bed of rose-lichen. The elusive scent of aromatic elf-leaves touched their nostrils and disappeared again, like fairies flitting past their senses.

Mica's twitching tail brushed a fragrant everblue tree that dipped long needles into their pathway. The pollen filled Brevelan's nose with its clean fragrance, banishing all other scents.

"Perhaps your cat would be happier in your arms," he muttered even as he smiled and reached to pet the now purring Mica.

"But your shoulders are so much broader and more comfortable. She can see all around and not tire her tiny body."

Most of the last several hours they had endured the broken pathway in grim silence. Jaylor pushed the pace with an urgency Brevelan absorbed to lend speed to her own feet. She had used the time to memorize the landmarks of trees and rocks as she picked her way among them. As Shayla had said, there was a path visible, but only when she drew a song through her as if she were seeking a healing path through an ailing body.

"Jaylor, I have got to stop for a few moments," Brevelan protested. A steep incline loomed ahead of them. The stitch in her side needed time to unknot before she tackled the slope.

"Oh, all right." Jaylor paused beside a rock large enough to sit upon. Brevelan eased onto the worn surface. "We can't waste time though."

"Replenishing my body's reserves is not a waste of time." She stared at him until he, too, sat on the rock.

"Did Mica tell you she prefers my shoulders to yours?" he asked, eyebrows drawn together in puzzlement.

"Yes, she did." Brevelan had always listened to the animals. She'd been quite shocked as a small child to learn that others could not hear them.

"How? How do you hear them?" Jaylor seemed merely curious, not accusing as the man she'd called Father had been.

"It's not words." Only Shayla was verbal in her communications. "They look at me. I see into their eyes and feel what they need me to know." It was difficult to explain the sensation. She'd never found anyone willing to attempt an understanding. A tiny swell of affection for this strange man blossomed inside her. He'd invaded her life and made a place for himself there. Looking back toward her clearing, she tried imagining her home without him filling it. The image eluded her.

She touched her fingertips to her lips. The memory of his gently persuasive kisses brought a new flush to her face. He had been so tender with her. So unlike the man she had been forced to marry. Her husband had needed her terrified and in pain in order to become aroused.

"I've never heard of any magic that works like yours." Jaylor headed back to the path with long strides. "When did this start?"

"I don't remember." Brevelan skipped a little to catch up with him. She had trailed behind him for long enough. "Maybe I should say I can't remember not being able to talk to animals." Animals didn't lie and cheat. Only people did that.

"My magic began like that. I just did it. No one taught me how." They walked side by side a moment in silence. "Most magicians can't do much at all until they are twelve or fourteen," he continued. "Even then they have to be taught to gather magic." He reached back to help her over a fallen log. Her fingers entwined with his so naturally she left them there.

"The first animal that called out to me in need was a sheep." She allowed her thoughts to drift back to her home. For once she didn't recoil from the pain. Jaylor's touch kept it at bay. "She was birthing and in trouble. It was late at night and the shepherd was asleep. I never questioned why I got out of a warm bed and trudged through the mud to help her." In her mind she relived the experience. She hadn't been much more than a toddler. "My da followed me and did the work. I was much too little."

"Was he very angry?" Jaylor stopped again. This time his hand touched her cheek solicitously.

"Only because he didn't understand." She tried to explain. Her mind knew that. Still, she felt the hurt of her da's rejection every time she worked her healing.

"My da did the same thing." Jaylor continued to stroke her cheek. "But I was lucky. We had a full-time priest in our village, not a circuit-cleric. He helped me gain entrance to the University early. At the University, everyone expects you to throw spells to steal apples or turn the letters upside down in a book." The memory of a smile tugged at his lips.

She felt that smile all the way to her toes. His hand dropped from her face to her arm and lingered.

"But my magic is different. I don't use traditional formulas. Other magicians can't follow or copy my spells. Nor can they join their magic with mine to amplify our powers." The smile disappeared to be replaced by a shrug of his shoulders. He started walking again at a furious pace. "Once the masters realized that, they didn't encourage me much. They wanted me to give up and go home. One of them became so angry he suggested there must have been a rogue among my ancestors. There is no greater insult at the University."

"Why is one magician acceptable and another a rogue? As long as the result is for the good of Coronnan, I don't see the difference." She wanted to reach out and smooth the lines of tension from his brow.

"There are two kinds of magic." Jaylor closed his eyes as if trying to remember a lesson by rote. "The magic taught to me at the University is provided by the dragons. It's in the air and ground around us. We learn to still and prepare a special place within ourselves. It's almost as if we have an extra belly, put there for the sole purpose of gathering this magic. We then form it into proper spells and throw it out again."

He didn't have to tell her that women could not have that "extra belly."

They continued walking. As the path grew steeper, she became more thoughtful.

"I can't say I work my healing that way. I mean, I don't consciously gather it and then form it. It's just there." Brevelan searched his eyes for an explanation. Every time she tried to analyze her ability to heal, her mind went blank. She didn't know how she did it. People in pain or despair drew the healing from her.

"Traditional magic is bound to Coronnan and can only be worked for the benefit of the kingdom. The dragons see to that." He pushed aside one of the overhanging ferns. Once again the scent of elf-leaves whispered across their senses. "Magicians can combine and build stronger magic, but again only to make the kingdom safe. That is how the magic border was established and maintained. And how the rogues were exiled. A rogue works on his own, for his own benefit. I don't know where they find the magic. But each one must work as an individual. No one magician is stronger than the Commune and the ethics enforced by it."

"My magic works for the good of the kingdom."

"So does mine. But whoever hired Old One-eye wants something other than the best for Coronnan." He allowed the silence to fill the space between them.

"I'm not a member of the Commune, I can't 'gather' magic. Does that make me a rogue?"

Jaylor opened his eyes and looked deeply into hers. "I prefer the word 'solitary' as opposed to communal."

They stared at each other, and, slowly, she reached out to clasp his hand again. Stillness settled around them, isolating them from the sounds of birds and insects. Even Mica and Puppy seemed far away.

"My magic comes from deep within me. I don't have to follow exact formulas to keep it in line with everyone else's. If Old One-eye's magic forms inside him like that, then his only limitation is his own physical strength. I don't think he'll allow himself to be stopped by honor or integrity." Jaylor warned her.

"You face the same physical limits and you are much younger and stronger than he."

"But not as practiced. I've wasted most of the last twelve years trying to work the other kind of magic. I can do it. But it's harder for me."

This time Brevelan lifted her free hand to draw a finger along Jaylor's bearded cheek. The curling hair around his mouth tickled her palm, inviting a deeper caress. A contented sense of completeness filled her, gave her the courage to ask her next question. "Why is it so hard for you? If you have that extra belly, then you should be able to gather and throw magic."

A rough chuckle rumbled from his throat. "Traditional magic requires an inner peace and stillness. My insides are too restless to be still long enough to gather the proper amounts of magic."

She knew the feeling. There was always something more to do. Her body never wanted to be still. Until now. Standing here in the wilderness of the southern mountains, touching him, she felt as if everything in her life had a proper place. Her restlessness evaporated. "Perhaps we can join our magic, as we did to heal Puppy."

"That was no magic on my part," he protested vehemently. His eyes snapped open, but he didn't withdraw his hand.

"Wasn't it?"

"I merely pushed the bones back into place. You healed the muscles around them."

As if to prove his statement the wolf bounded back along the trail toward them. His step was strong and sure.

"Are you sure, Jaylor? Think back on it. How much of the effort you put into helping Puppy was brute strength and how much was magic sight?" She allowed her hand to drop just enough to clasp his.

"Oof!" The wolf jumped against Jaylor, muddy paws soiling his shirt. He dropped Brevelan's hand to fend off the animal. Puppy grinned in his special way and bounced back to the trail. "Your manners need a great deal of improvement, Wolf," Jaylor scolded him. He reached for Brevelan's hand once more.

Adventure! Darville raised his face to the sun and trotted along the path in front of his people. His instincts told him this journey was incredibly important. It was a return to a way of life that had been interrupted by his injury.

Already his nose felt keener. He was aware of much more than just the familiar scents back in Brevelan's clearing. His sight, too, was brighter. He was strong and eager for whatever the trail might bring.

A whiff of Tambootie drifted on the wind, an odor he associated with the dragon. Shayla had come last night, outlined in the moonlight, flaming Old One-eye. Just as she had that other time when Darville had fallen over the cliff. Only the enemy wasn't One-eye then. He was something else.

Deep in this throat Darville growled at the memory of the man responsible. The one-eyed man meant pain and changes Darville couldn't comprehend.

That man smelled of Tambootie. Shayla did, too, but the dragon smelled good. One-eye smelled evil.

There, on the wind, he caught again the elusive sent of Shayla. He savored it and proceeded forward, ahead of Jaylor and Brevelan. He'd go back soon and let them know the trail was safe.

He felt a need to stretch up again on his hind legs. This time he would linger against Jaylor's chest, make sure the man petted his ears instead of Brevelan's hand. Maybe he'd walk between them for a while, basking in their affection for him. He wasn't sure he approved of their affection for each other.

But first he would hunt.

CHAPTER 12

Jaylor's fingers suddenly felt empty and cold as Brevelan yanked her own hand free of his friendly grasp. She reached for her throat, her skin deathly pale.

"Aiyeeee!"

The shrill scream of a small animal broke the peace of a quiet mountain meadow. Delicate wildflowers swayed restlessly amidst the grass.

Jaylor looked to the source of the scream on their left. Wolf pounced and tore at the throat of a squirrel—his latest meal. He shrugged at the natural event. At least he would not have to worry about feeding the beast on the journey.

"No," Brevelan whispered through tight lips. She held her stomach and throat as if in deep pain, bent nearly double. Her face was drained of all color. She had pulled her hand free of his an instant before the scream.

"Brevelan!" Jaylor jumped to help her. "What ails you?" Tenderly, he cradled her against his side. He gave her what strength he could as he guided her to a rock where she could sit. His hands slipped against her cold, almost clammy skin. A shot of fear pierced his heart.

"Easy now. Rest a moment while I fetch some water."

"I must leave this place." She started to look over her shoulder toward the spot where Darville noisily ate his kill. Then she hastily averted her eyes.

"You're in no condition to move anywhere."

"It is the place that ails me."

"The animal Darville just killed." The truth dawned on him. "You felt it die, just as you felt an ewe's troubled labor when you were a tot." A chill knot formed in his stomach. "No wonder you couldn't stay with your own people. A village full of meat eaters would destroy you at every meal."

She nodded.

He was amazed she'd managed as long as she had.

"I soon learned to be elsewhere on slaughter days. It helps if I've never communicated with the animal, or if I'm not too close. Back home I couldn't separate myself from the herds. They needed me too often."

Jaylor helped her to stand. She leaned against him heavily as they walked away from the scene of the recent death. At the streambed he helped her onto the mossy bank.

"Drink. Then we'll be on our way. Wolf will catch up when he's ready." He looked back toward the animal just as the wolf looked up and grinned. "You don't have to enjoy it quite so much!" he called.

That grin. So like the young prince when he escaped his tutors and sought freedom among the apprentice magicians. Roy had enjoyed his pranks then, too, without a thought to the torment his guardians received at the king's hand for losing their prince.

Mica scampered back to the wolf. With an imperious paw she batted the wolf's muzzle away and grabbed her share of the meal.

"Not you, too, Mica. Don't you know you're hurting Brevelan?" Jaylor admonished the animals.

"Please, Jaylor. Let's just move on a little." Brevelan tugged at his sleeve. Her eyes were huge in her pale face. They were dark blue now, the color of the bay at sunset, almost black. He caught a fragment of her pain.

"Yes, of course." He eased her back onto the path. For a moment she leaned against him, gathering strength. His arms tightened around her slender body. She felt so good, nestled there against his shoulder. Tenderness filled him. He didn't want to move. But he had to.

"It is part of the nature of things for them to eat meat. I cannot begrudge them that. I can only ask them to keep their kill away from me." She took one slow step. Then another.

"Lean on me." He urged her forward. "We'll get you farther along before we have some fruit and another drink." He continued to hold her as they moved. She didn't pull away.

"How did Old Thorm break through our armor?" Brevelan's question disturbed Jaylor.

"I don't know." He rose from his crouched position before the campfire. Wolf had found this sheltered overhang for them long after the sun had set. The almost-cave was dry and vacant and should be a safe place to spend the night, safe from predators and conventional attack. But how did he protect them from a magic he couldn't understand?

"How are you feeling now?" He turned to face the girl. Her face was pale and her eyes shadowed. Still, she looked steadier than she had on the trail. Her sudden pain at the death of the squirrel bothered him. He knew he couldn't live with that kind of emotional pain day after day. No wonder she chose to live in isolation.

"Better," she said quietly.

"You felt that squirrel's death as sharply as a knife to your own throat." He shook his head at the memory. She had known the exact instant Wolf found his meal.

"I often do." This time he felt the sadness in her. She was throwing her own magic at him to help him understand. Jaylor was finding it more and more difficult to armor himself against her.

Uneasy, he cast the twig he had been chewing into the fire, then strode to the opening. He hated being so vulnerable. Aware that he was pacing restlessly from the fire to the cliff edge, he paused to think. Wolf matched him stride for stride.

"Did you know that squirrel?" He whirled to face her. The wolf whined at the abrupt movement. Strange that Brevelan put no blame on the animal as the source of today's pain. The bond between them was strong.

"No. But he was close. I had felt his presence. He was very happy to be out in the spring sunshine after a long cold winter. And Puppy was unusually triumphant." She

smiled then, dotingly. Her love for the wolf swamped
Jaylor. He felt a sudden surge of jealously that such a
wonderful emotion was being wasted on a wild beast.

A breeze shifted the brush outside their shelter. Wolf
shuddered against his leg. They both felt questing eyes
out there, watching them from behind trees and shadows.

Jaylor sniffed the air outside the camp. The wolf mimicked him. They both tensed just before Jaylor's personal
armor slid into place. There was something out there.
Something magical.

Doubt filled him. He wanted to armor the camp. But if
he could smell magic out there, then whoever, or whatever, watched them could sense his spell and be drawn to
it, like iron to a lodestone.

"Can we protect ourselves from Old Thorm if he
should come again tonight?" Brevelan's question left no
doubt that she too sensed the magic presence out there.

The image of Old One-eye following on the trail to her
clearing filled his mind. He'd been pressed against a
Tambootie tree then, and the rogue magician had not seen
him. Oh, he'd sensed where Jaylor had left the trail, but
not where he hid. At the time, he'd thought it important
to gather a handful of timboor berries.

He'd walked through the Rover camp, invisible to his
captors while timboor filled his blood. He seemed to be
made of magic for several hours after that. And was totally exhausted for days when the drug wore off.

"Maybe." Jaylor swung back to face her. The hope that
filled her eyes gave him new purpose. "Have you ever
eaten timboor?"

"The fruit of the Tambootie?" She wrapped her arms
around herself and shrank away from him. Mica climbed
into her lap and butted her head against the girl's chin, as
if offering comfort. "It's poison." Brevelan's tone was
evasive.

"I thought so, too. Now I'm not sure. Have you ever
eaten of that tree?" He concentrated his gaze on her.
There was no need to use magic to pull the information
from her. It would come if he could just stare her down.
He'd proved that often enough with his tutors. He was

amazed how disconcerted people became under a long stare. They usually began to babble within moments.

"Once." She barely whispered as she buried her face into the cat's fur. Mica didn't protest the attention.

"Once," he repeated. "When?"

"When I was running away from home."

"Why did you eat it?" Wolf sat on Jaylor's foot and leaned heavily against his leg. His hand reached for the animal's ears.

Brevelan fussed with the cat and refused to look at him.

"Why, Brevelan? What induced you to eat a fruit you thought to be poison?"

Finally she looked him directly in the eye. He felt something akin to what she must feel when she communicated with animals. Her fear and desperation were as strong as his own when he was in the Rover camp.

"I was running for my life. I dared not stay on the roads, so I made my way through the forest. There was no one I trusted to help me. The animals gave me shelter."

Jaylor couldn't see the specific images she remembered. Her emotions became his own, though.

"Which animal gave you the knowledge about eating timboor?" The berries usually grew on higher branches, seeking the sun. Her helper couldn't be a ground feeder like the timid deer or rabbit.

"A gray bear." A smile touched her lips.

He felt her humor touch him as well.

"Most sane people would run from a gray bear."

"Especially a female protecting her young."

Jaylor grew colder from his core outward. Gray bears had a reputation for being particularly nasty, vicious even, when in the best of humor. A protective mother bear could rend a strong man limb from limb. Trees were no protection from the beasts. They could climb better than most cats.

"Next you'll be telling me she protected and fed you like her own cub." He stared at her, wanting to disbelieve. No one should be so powerful as to tame a gray bear. Or was it her gentleness that undermined overt strength? The power of this kind of magic awed him.

"What did the timboor do to you?"

She hesitated. Her eyes sought the dark corners of their shelter. When she looked back at him, he stretched out a hand to shield her from her own bewilderment.

"I could hear everything, the tiniest rustle among the ferns, the faintest bird song. I could even hear the tug and chomp of rabbits feeding." She looked away again when she mentioned the most silent of all animals. "The most astonishing sounds were the thoughts of the people I encountered. But I was safe then because I could tell if they recognized me, knew of those who pursued me."

Jaylor nodded in agreement. This sounded like his own experience. "Were your other senses affected: sight, smell?"

"Yes." There was more. He could tell from the way she refused to hold his eyes with her own.

"When you didn't want to be seen . . ." he prompted.

"How did you know?" She looked up, startled.

"The same thing happened to me," he reassured her. "I have some timboor in my pack. If we each take a berry, I don't think we could be found."

She nodded, then hid her face again in the cat's fur. "Puppy and Mica?"

"They are not creatures of magic. The berries will poison them." She looked up in dismay at his words. He felt a tug at his heart. He wanted, and needed, to put the sparkle of well-being back into her eyes. "I think our aura of invisibility will extend to those we love." He was the only one who needed to eat of the timboor. He realized at that moment that his love should surround Brevelan with protection for the rest of his days.

Why had she told him so much about her past? Brevelan had revealed more to this strange man in a few days than to anyone else in her entire life.

Too many people misunderstood her magic. They reacted with fear, or cruelty bred from fear. So she hid her innermost thoughts and feelings. Her family and acquaintances had known only as much about her as they could guess from her actions.

After the death of her husband, she knew she had to flee her home or be burned as a witch. She scooted away from the warmth of the flames.

Mica protested the movement.

Brevelan soothed her with a few distracted strokes. Her mind refused to move from the images she had dragged out of her memory.

Another woman accused of witchcraft. An old woman who had taught Brevelan much about the nature of plants, which healed and how, as well as which killed. Lord Krej sitting in judgment, not allowing the poor woman to speak any defense. Then the punishment. All in the district had been required to watch.

Death by fire. Clouds of oily black smoke.

Her mother whispering in her ear that this would be Brevelan's fate if Krej heard of her healing ability.

Heat, pain. No air.

Her breaths were sharp and difficult. Heat seared her throat with each gulp of air. And when it was all over and the ashes scattered across the bay, a triumphant Krej had taken four virgins back to his castle.

"Brevelan!" Jaylor's hand on her shoulder broke the images. "Brevelan, what happened? What did you see in the flames?" He shook her free of her memories with anxious hands.

"Nothing," she lied. The look in his eyes told her he knew it was not the truth. "I was just thinking."

"Or remembering," he stated flatly.

She refused to answer. Whatever she said, he would see the truth in her eyes.

Puppy wiggled closer to her. He pushed under her arm with his muzzle. She drew him close, along with the cat. She didn't question that these two animals tolerated each other's presence.

"Here. Eat this." Jaylor held out his hand. In his palm rested some dry berries that had once been deep red with yellow bands. Now they were dull gray.

"Will the essential oils still be there?" she questioned

as she picked up one berry, about the size of her thumbnail.

"I think so. When I was given timboor, my captors had no access to fresh. They must have used dried."

She raised an eyebrow in question. It was safer to let him talk rather than question her past.

Jaylor recounted his experience with the Rover tribe while he petted each of the animals in turn.

"Modern magic texts proclaim everything about the Tambootie is evil. I can see how it might be abused. But evil? I wonder how much of our knowledge is carefully edited to avoid misuse rather than full understanding. I think I need to explore the effects of the berry more fully." His words floated over her.

She knew she would remember and understand what he said in the morning. For now she needed only to feel the smooth rhythm of his voice.

The fire came into sharp focus. In the heart of the flames she saw the wind stirring the treetops outside. Her body took on a new lightness, drifting upward and out into the forest. She was no longer a part of the cozy camp scene below her.

From her elevated position, she watched a man and a woman settle for the night. Their blankets were rough homespun. The dying fire grew pungent. The huge golden wolf crawled between them. A multicolored cat sought the wolf's back for warmth. In the darkness of night the silent thoughts of Brevelan drifted through the forest. Watching. Waiting.

CHAPTER 13

They think to trick me with my own tricks. I needn't see them to know where they are. My magic, the magic of the Tambootie, guides me. Tonight I will spin my dreams by my blessed Tambootie wood fire. I shall sleep safe and warm, while they lie wakeful and wondering.

They shall have nothing—no king, no prince, no magic. Tomorrow I will press them harder. Tomorrow I will find the dragon. After I secure the monster, I shall kill the wolf once and for all. And then all will be mine.

And I shall have the dragon!

Warm, sweet-smelling hair tickled Jaylor's nose. He breathed deeply of the lovely scent. Then he snuggled closer to the source. A soft, feminine body filled his arms. He could tell it was a woman by the curves that molded to his hand.

A woman?

No! He sat up abruptly. A woman in his arms, before dawn could only mean one thing. He'd lain with her and lost his magic.

Sleep-befuddled panic engulfed him. Sweat, cold and clammy, broke out on his back. His breaths came short and sharp until the cold morning air chased the fog of sleep from his mind.

Slowly his breathing returned to normal, and he thought in logical patterns once more. The woman he'd held most of the night was Brevelan. He had slept by her side in the rough shelter of the almost-cave. He had dreamed of her, but they had not lain together as a man and a woman.

The blasted wolf had seen to that. The beast had slept between them most of the night; Mica curled up with him. Any lustful thoughts Jaylor might have had were successfully squashed by the fuzzy barrier represented by the animals. Jaylor wasn't sure when Wolf and Mica had wandered off to their own morning pursuits.

Cautiously, Jaylor worked a small spell. He lifted a few spare twigs into the embers of the fire and reignited them. His magic was intact!

He lay back down on the hard ground, grateful that his natural lusts had not overcome his good sense. His arm automatically stretched to bring Brevelan's sleeping body closer.

He pulled the rough blanket up to cover them both more fully. Her warmth relaxed him while her natural scent filled him with more energetic ideas.

It was morning and he was at his most susceptible. He really should move away from her—and soon. After watching her rise one morning in the hut, he had always made sure he was well on his way to the bathing pool before she slid from the protective warmth of her enticingly large bed. Her shift covered her entire body, but it was old and thin. The nearly sheer muslin couldn't hide the delectable shapes and shadows of her petite form.

Brevelan stirred in her sleep. She turned toward him, seeking his warmth in the chill morning air. Jaylor groaned. He had to move away . . . now!

"Mhmmm," she murmured. Her small hand slipped across his chest.

The gesture brought her breasts snug against his side. Excited tingles spread out from the point of contact. "Ah . . . good morning, Brevelan." Jaylor sought to rouse her before her innocent attentions drove him beyond control. Good thing they were both fully clothed.

"Mhmm. Cold." Her eyes remained closed.

"Let me build up the fire." He slid his arm from under her head reluctantly.

"Fire," She mumbled again. Then her eyes opened in panic. "Fire?" She sat up abruptly. The blankets fell away and she shivered.

"Wake up, Brevelan," he commanded. Instinct told him to go to her, hold her until the morning fogginess cleared her mind of the nightmare that haunted her. Disastrous idea. She was much too tempting with her soft, innocent beauty. Russet locks tumbled about her face. He needed to push them out of her eyes, caress her cheek, kiss her soft mouth. He also needed all of his magic, intact, to safely confront the dragon. He didn't know how much more magic he would need to shore up the border once they found Shayla.

Thoughts of their quest brought to mind the absent wolf and cat. He couldn't count on being alone with Brevelan long enough to fulfill what his body demanded.

"Where ... where is Puppy? And Mica?" The panic had not quite left her voice as she scanned the shadows of the recess with troubled blue eyes.

"I don't know. They wandered off sometime in the night; probably to eat," he replied, keeping his back to her. It was best if he busied himself with feeding the fire. If he looked at her again, he would not be able to resist.

"How long ago?"

"I don't know. They were gone when I awoke." *And you were in my arms, where you belong.*

That thought startled him. She did belong with him. But she couldn't belong at his side night and day until he was a master magician.

"I'm going down to the creek for water." He stood as rapidly as his morning stiff body would allow. He stretched, easing his back. He turned to make sure Brevelan was awake and well. Another part of his body stretched and didn't ease. He took off for the creek at a near run.

"Mrrow." Mica greeted Brevelan.

"Did you have a good morning, Mica?" She watched the small cat sit next to the now glowing fire and wash her face.

Mica didn't deign to reply until she was finished with her face. "Mrrow."

Of course. Mica always had a good morning. It was her

favorite time of day. The cat's emotions, which were almost words, pressed into Brevelan's chest with joyful energy.

Brevelan chuckled. This was her favorite time of day as well. With each new dawn came the chance to move her life forward, an opportunity to leave the troublesome past farther behind.

"Where is Puppy?" she asked the cat.

No reply. Either Mica didn't know or, more likely, didn't care. Mica reminded Brevelan that Darville could take care of himself.

"Are you sure about that?" Brevelan asked. There were times when the wolf acted as if he'd never lived in the wild before. He needed her help and companionship too often. He also needed her healing. Sometimes he seemed terribly clumsy for a wolf.

Mica blinked. Her yellow cat-eyes changed to rounded hazel-green. She blinked again and the cat was once more inside those strange eyes.

Brevelan tested the water in the small pot she had brought along. It was nearly bubbling, time to add the handful of grains. By the time Jaylor returned from the creek it should be ready.

A little tune came to her. She hummed it quietly. When it was set in her mind, she sang it a little louder. The notes sought out the dark shadows behind her, then swirled forward to reach across the forest. Contentment filled the recesses of the overhang.

Mica butted her head against Brevelan's knee. She scratched the cat's ears to keep her out of her lap. "I'm sorry there is no milk for you, Mica. We left Mistress Goat behind."

A loud purr was the cat's response. She didn't mind as long as her ears were rubbed just precisely there.

"Grrower!"

"What a nasty thing to say!" Brevelan sat straighter. She shivered at the intensity of the protest.

"Grrower!"

That wasn't Mica!

* * *

At the edge of the cliff Jaylor looked out at the scene he had not seen the night before. Morning mist clung to the valleys and ravines while the mountain peaks soared above to pierce a cloudless sky. Below, the forest stretched, seemingly forever. Vibrant greens and blues of early spring shimmered in the sunrise.

The last of the winter browns faded beneath the new growth. He picked out the bright and dark pattern of new growth on the everblues. Nestled here and there among them were the flat-topped Tambootie. This far up the mountain the trees of magic hadn't been destroyed by superstition and the need for more pasturage. The area was even too remote for the greedy copper miners who sought the veins of ore beneath the roots.

His body tingled as he caught a whiff of the pungent bark. Clean and crisp. A healthy smell, totally different from the reek of the evil associated with the Tambootie smoke.

Jaylor gasped a lungful of cold air. The beauty of Coronnan lay before him, as he had never seen it before.

Old-timers called this dragon weather: a little rain in the night, sunshine and beauty during the day.

The weight of his guest settled upon his shoulders. Baamin said the dragons were ill, needing a magic medicine to bring the nimbus up to strength. Were they merely ill, or were they being killed?

The embankment was steep and slippery from the rain. Saber ferns grew in profusion here, but they offered no handhold. He dug in his heels to keep from sliding headlong into the briskly flowing water of the creek. His boots stirred the damp earth. He smelled the cloying sweetness of crushed rose-lichen where his boots slipped in the mud. A nubby-berry bush snagged his leather shirt. These hazards were familiar.

He splashed a handful of cold water over his face, carefully at first. His ablutions became more lavish after the initial shock of the icy creek, restoring his natural assurance and good humor.

Wolf was not as cautious with the embankment or the

cold water. He dashed down the bank to plunge into the water. He emerged with a gleeful grin on his face, water dripping from his coat.

Jaylor was reminded of the youthful prankster he had known several years ago. Roy's tutors had driven the boy to become more serious, pushing responsibility onto his young shoulders.

Jaylor hadn't seen much of his friend in the last two years. He didn't slip away from his duties to explore life in the city anymore.

Instead, he took to riding his steeds long and hard. Always, there was a cohort of soldiers to guard him.

No wonder he organized long hunts at every opportunity. During a chase he could escape the suffocating presence of others and forget his responsibilities for a while.

Cold water splashed across Jaylor's leather trews. He stepped back, laughing. Wolf looked up, an entreating gleam in his eye. "Sorry, fellow. There isn't time today for a romp in the water. We have to find ourselves a dragon."

Wolf cocked his head, as if trying to understand. He splashed again, then bounded out of the water, spreading almost as much liquid in his path as he left in the creek. He shook a few of the clinging drops from his fur.

Jaylor could almost see the wolf's thoughts. He didn't feel right, so he took a step closer to Jaylor before shaking again.

In his haste to step away from the cascade Jaylor slipped in the mud. *"S'murgh it!"* he cursed as he landed on his backside. "You had to do that, you miserable beast."

Once again Wolf cocked his head in curiosity. The movement brought another small spray of water across Jaylor's shirt.

"Watch it, Wolf. You'd feel cold without all that fuzz. Spray me again and I'll shave you bald," he threatened with a laugh.

Jaylor anchored his awareness in the reality of his surroundings. There was the damp earth and fresh leaves of the growing trees. Birds were awake and chirping now. Below him the creek danced over rocks on its downhill journey. Above him was just the faintest trace of wood-smoke. Brevelan must have stoked the fire.

She would be cooking breakfast. Grains with a wild nutty flavor. If it were later in the season, he could gather some nubby-berries to sweeten their morning meal. Perhaps Brevelan would throw some dried fruit into the pot. A hot drink would taste good, too. Jaylor's mouth watered in anticipation. A proper meal would go a long way toward giving him the strength to confront a magic dragon.

"Come, Puppy. We need to get back to Brevelan." He started up the hill again.

"Grrrr," Wolf replied. His fur stood up on the back of his neck.

"Grrower!" Another animal answered, louder.

"Spotted saber cat," he whispered into the wind. The largest, meanest, hungriest wild beast in Coronnan. An adult male could grow as large as a gray bear. Its elongated front teeth equaled those of a wild tusker in length. And the beast sounded as though it stood in the opening of the cave where Brevelan was preparing breakfast!

"Come, Wolf. Now. Brevelan needs us," Jaylor urged.

"Grroowower," Wolf replied as he bounded toward the menace.

Waves of anger washed over Brevelan. Pressure built behind her neck and eyes, pressure to move. Her eyes glazed under the impact of the anger and outrage bombarding her senses. The pressure increased. Air inside her lungs fought with the weight of the atmosphere outside her body. The compulsion to move weighed heavily on her limbs. *Move.*

But where?

She was encased in a red cage of emotion. Walls of suffocating red marched closer and closer. She couldn't breathe. The walls threatened to wrap her in hot, airless, burning hatred. *Block it out.*

I must turn my mind away. She forced a separation

from the red walls. Gradually her eyes focused. She sought the source of the emotional upheaval and wished she hadn't.

In the opening of the overhang, between her and escape, stood a spotted saber cat. The beast could be the twin or littermate of the only other one of its kind she had ever seen. The bronze statue that had blinked at her in Krej's hall. Its long teeth gleamed wetly in the early sunlight. Malevolence flashed deep within its eyes. That cat wanted nothing more than to use those huge teeth to rip her flesh open and taste her blood.

CHAPTER 14

Darkness dwelt within the cavern. The campfire glowed near the entrance. Behind it no shadow moved. Jaylor couldn't see Brevelan. Sweat clung to his brow and back. What if the cat had already killed her? Panic threatened to shatter him from the inside out.

The huge cat stood in the entrance to the overhang, its eerie roar echoing about the hillside. Jaylor took one silent step closer. Orange and gray fur gleamed in the early sunlight, temporarily blinding him with its brilliance.

"Grrower," the cat snarled again. Claws fully extended, one huge front paw reached up to strike at something in the shadows.

Each one of those claws was nearly as long as one of Jaylor's fingers.

One more step and he would be able to see if the cat's intended prey was Brevelan. A tiny pebble rolled under his boot. It struck another, larger stone. The sound drew the cat's eyes, eyes that were slitted with malice. The huge body remained between Jaylor and the cavern interior.

He crouched to ease his rapid breathing. He had to get Brevelan out of the way.

"Grrower." Once more the cat turned his attention toward the shadowy movement in the dark recess.

A rock that just fit Jaylor's palm came to his hand. Without bothering to stand straight again, he flung the stone. It bounced off the largest gray spot just behind the cat's ribs.

"Yeehowl!" The beast protested as it moved sideways and deeper into the recess.

"S'murgh!" Jaylor cursed.

Another growl filled the overhang. Wolf stood beside him, fur on end, ears upright. He too was ready to do battle.

Wolf bared his fangs and approached the cat. *We must save Brevelan.* His growls came close to words, their meaning clear in Jaylor's mind. Yellow wolf eyes narrowed to glittering slits.

There wasn't time to puzzle out that moment of coherent communication. The cat slunk beyond the campfire toward Brevelan's hiding place. Where was she anyway?

"We need a weapon, Wolf." His pack and staff were between the cat and Brevelan. He needed the staff as a focus for a blast of magic fire.

Jaylor gathered the magic necessary for the spell. Which spell? He'd never used magic for offense, only as armor for defense. "I'll think of something." His mind drifted away from his body, watched himself from afar.

Breathe in slowly, he told the body he was watching. *Feel the magic essence roll and form into a tangible shape. An arrow of light and energy. Like lightning.*

Breathe out. Let the magic grow in power. Say the words and watch the spell emerge from the body.

Nothing happened. He gulped back the panic. Once more he hadn't been able to throw the proper spell. He could hear his teachers grumbling, the other apprentices laughing at his clumsiness.

Maybe he had said the wrong spell. He rolled the words back across his visual memory. No, the words were right, the spell was proper. So what went wrong?

"Grrower!" The cat spat again as it took another step forward.

Movement caught his eye. Up there, on the small ledge at the back. Brevelan crouched, knees under her chin, Mica clutched to her breast. Even from the opening he could see her shaking. Some of her distress spilled out to him. For a moment he was shaken by the intensity.

Without thinking, Jaylor brought his staff to his hand with an image. "I won't let it hurt you," he declared. The words cleared his mind even as his body sent forth the first shot of red and blue flame.

A pitiful little bolt of fire, it barely reached the cat's thick fur. Its tail twitched in annoyance at the tiny pinprick against its flank.

"We'll have to do better this time," he muttered to no one in particular. He calmed his pounding heartbeat and evened his ragged breathing. That was supposed to be the simple part. Still, his mind echoed with the fear that was palpitating against the walls.

He had to forget the deeply ingrained limitations and restrictions on magic as taught at the University. The Commune working in concert could use magic as a weapon—for the good of the kingdom. Individuals couldn't throw those spells alone. But that was traditional magic. He was Jaylor, the solitary. If One-eye could use personal magic for his own greed, then surely Jaylor could summon enough to save a life.

Breathe in three, out three. In, one, two, three. Out, one, two, three. Again, two, three.

His vision cleared as he shifted his feet to a better position. Sound ceased, and time slowed. The rock walls glowed with silver light. He isolated the cat from its surroundings. The sun and fog of its fur filled his mind. He raised his staff with one hand, then grasped it with the other. His mind focused on the twisting grain of the wood, long fingers of magic braided along its fibers.

With a mighty effort he sent forth chains of fire. They pulsed, then merged into one huge ball. The dark recesses were filled with heat and light as bright as noon in the clearing.

"Yeeowl!" The cat looked him in the eyes, startled.

Jaylor held its gaze. He allowed his eyes to tell the beast he was serious this time. Another burst of his signature blue and red flame braided along the staff.

The cat jumped back toward the cave entrance to avoid the magic fire.

"Grrow." It spat one last comment before turning and bounding past Jaylor and away through the forest.

"Arrooff," Wolf howled in triumph. He chased the

beast away from the entrance, baying in triumph, his fur still stiff and teeth bared.

"You can come down now, Brevelan." Jaylor turned to her once he was sure the cat was gone. Brevelan didn't move. Mica began squirming away from her clenched hands now that the danger was gone.

Wolf trotted to a spot just beneath the ledge and whined.

"You're safe now, Brevelan." Jaylor coaxed. He reached up a hand to help her down.

Mica used it to reach the ground. Brevelan maintained her fearful crouch, eyes fixed, body trembling.

"Brevelan!" Jaylor spoke as sharply as he dared. "That cat may come back. We have to leave. Now!"

She whimpered slightly. At least she was responding.

"Come now, take my hand. I won't let anything hurt you." He reached up his hand again.

She didn't move. "*S'murgh* it, Brevelan. You have to come down. Now." This time he grabbed her arm and shook her.

Finally she looked at him. "I felt its need to kill. For a moment I needed to kill."

"I have failed, Your Grace." Baamin bowed his head before King Darcine in the royal family's private solar. He was careful to add a touch of humility to the carriage of his shoulders. It wouldn't do for the king to see how happy he was that he had failed.

"You dare to come to me, your mission incomplete?" The king's eyes narrowed in speculation. For a moment Baamin was reminded of the younger Darcine, strong and eager for battle.

"I am sorry, Your Grace. The magic has failed me. I tried to reach my journeymen. Something, or someone, interfered. The kingdom's magic has faded beyond my ability to gather it."

"Impossible." The king pulled himself up to his full height. It was a stance he had not assumed much in the past few years. His subjects had almost forgotten how imposing he could be when necessary.

"Nothing is impossible, Your Grace." Baamin straightened too. The top of his head barely reached the king's nose. He had to rely on his bearing and bulk to claim the respect due his position as Senior Magician, Chancellor of the University, and adviser to the king.

"Dragon magic is woven into the very fiber of this kingdom. It cannot fail. I am stronger, therefore the magic must be strong."

"Shayla has mated. You are stronger because she carries young. But she is the only breeding female dragon left. The nimbus of dragons is pitifully small, Your Grace. All the others in my records are too old, or dead, or they have left," Baamin argued.

"Left? Dragons can't leave Coronnan. They are bound to us." Darcine's shoulders caved in a little. He seemed to lose the strength to hold them back.

"The bonds of magic and Tambootie are not enough to hold the creatures when they are driven out by superstition and slaughter. Uneducated villagers have stopped planting the Tambootie. They no longer tithe their livestock to the dragons. Indeed, many have killed dragons rather than worship them. Shayla's last two litters were slaughtered in the nest. We are lucky she stayed. You are alive today only because she mated again."

"When did this outrage occur? And why was I not told? There is no greater crime in this kingdom than murdering a dragon and I was not told!" Grief and anger gripped Darcine's features. "Those responsible must be punished."

"The first time, I learned of it even as the lung disease gripped you. We feared for your life, Your Grace." Baamin swallowed deeply. He searched his king's face for signs of the weakness that had gripped him ever since.

"And the second time?"

"Shayla bred again, as soon as she could, so we . . . I felt it best to let you heal without that knowledge. The next litter was killed as well."

"That would have been two years later, when my heart failed." Deep sadness drained the straightness from his shoulders. "Was there no one who would lift a finger against the murderers?"

Baamin rested a comforting hand against Darcine's back. "The healers said the news of the second tragedy would kill you for certain."

"Where were the lords when this slaughter took place? Surely they would seek out and destroy anyone who dared harm the nimbus?" Darcine found his padded chair with shaking knees.

Baamin thought about assisting his king to the chair. In spite of his new vigor, Darcine's body was still painfully thin, and so frail he looked as if the slight breeze from the open window would crumble him to dust. Baamin decided he'd done too much assisting in the past. They had all, counselors and lords alike, allowed the king to become weak and uninvolved over the years. At the time it had seemed logical to ease his burdens as his health failed. Darville had been around then, young and strong, eager to take responsibility onto his broad shoulders.

Now Darville was missing. They could no longer rely on him. That left Krej, the king's cousin, as the logical person to consult. But it was that lord's tenants who had laid the traps for Shayla's mates and her brood.

"Your lords have become lax in their duties. You have not taken the time to keep track of them." Baamin hated to say it, but it might be the only way to force the king to take some responsibility for his inattention.

"Darville will see to it . . ." The command died on the king's lips. "My son is missing."

"You must use your strength, now, while you have it, to delegate authority to those you can trust—those you know have the best interests of Coronnan in their hearts."

"I shall handle this myself, Baamin. I dare not trust even you with this chore. Call the lords. I will meet them this evening."

"I can't."

"What?" Darcine roared with some of his lost power.

"I don't have enough magic to summon them. You must send messengers." Baamin assumed an attitude of defeat.

He must have time to convince Darcine to give the Commune authority over the lords.

"Messengers will take time. Three days at least."

"It is necessary. What little magic I can summon drains away as fast as I gather it. Something, or someone, is interfering with the very fiber of magic."

"Then send the messengers within the hour. You may commandeer the fastest steeds in my stable."

Three days. Was it long enough to find a way around the fading magic? Though his soul recoiled from it, Baamin knew he must seek out a source of rogue magic. It was the only way to counter the actions of a foreign rogue and find out who employed him.

"You didn't kill the cat." Brevelan's weak voice sounded more a question than a statement. She cleared her throat and tried again.

"You could have killed it. But you didn't." That was better.

"I didn't have to," Jaylor replied. His voice was a little strained. After all, he was carrying her, and uphill at that.

She felt strange moving over the terrain without the physical effort of her own limbs. Strange in a very nice way. She couldn't remember being carried since she had learned to walk.

She shivered again in memory of why Jaylor found it necessary to carry her. The cat's mind had been so filled with hatred that it had refused the touch of her empathy.

Jaylor's arms tightened and chased away her chill of emptiness. For a few moments she soaked up the nice feeling of his comfort, his care. Then she leaned back just enough to see his face when she spoke. "Why did you spare the beast? Most men would have killed it anyway, just to prove they could. Then they would excuse the slaughter by saying they had to, to make sure it couldn't come back."

She watched a gamut of emotions cross his face before he settled into a smile.

"There was no need." He held her eyes with his own for a moment.

She felt his gaze warm her all the way through to the

cold, empty place in her belly. It seemed only natural for her to rest her head once more on his shoulder.

Jaylor adjusted his hold to grasp her more securely. "Besides, you were shaken enough by the encounter. If I had killed something that large and close, you would've been useless for the rest of the day."

He was deliberately containing some very strong emotions. She could tell by the tremor in the pulse of his neck. She snuggled just a little closer. The beat of his heart echoed against her ear. Her own heart beat in the same rhythm.

"I've never before encountered an animal who refused the touch of my mind."

"I wondered about that. A gray bear is bigger, and just as mean. But one sheltered you. Why not the cat?"

She clung a little tighter as she recounted the story of the cat in Krej's great hall. "I think it might be the same cat."

"If so, it would associate Krej's cruelty with all people. No wonder it fought your magic."

The ground was becoming rough, strewn with loose pebbles and larger rocks. Behind them, Puppy whined. He trotted closer, brushing his body against Jaylor's leg.

"We'll stop in a moment. There's a fairly level boulder top just ahead."

Something akin to disappointment washed over Brevelan. As soon as they reached that broken boulder he would set her down. The wonderful security of his arms would be withdrawn.

"Here we are." All too soon she felt him lowering her to the stone surface, not so much a boulder as a ledge jutting out from the hillside beside the path.

Puppy didn't wait for him to step away before he butted his head between them. He licked Brevelan's face and whined again.

"I'm fine, Puppy," she reassured the wolf. As Jaylor straightened, she continued clinging to his neck with one hand. Puppy's wiggling body pushed farther into her lap. Mica chose that moment to scamper onto her outstretched legs. For a moment all four friends were caught in one hug. Brevelan wanted to cry with relief and happiness.

"I think we should find something to eat," she said to mask the depth of the emotion she felt. "Too bad we left the packs and our breakfast in the cave."

"No problem." Jaylor's grin was infectious. She found herself matching it.

Her back tingled where his hand still rested. She felt a tremor course through his body to her own.

The packs appeared beside her and his staff, more gnarled than before, came to his hand. With another blink of his eyes the campfire and breakfast pot appeared.

"Doesn't that tire you?" She looked up concerned.

"Not nearly as much as going without food," Jaylor replied.

CHAPTER 15

Baamin leaned all of his bulk into the ancient door. Oak panels, aged to the stiffness of iron, creaked open slowly, held back as much by disuse as by the spell that had sealed them for so many years. Three centuries of dust assaulted his nose. Minute particles tickled and irritated until he sneezed loudly. The cloud swirled faster.

"Dragon bones!" he cursed, and sneezed again.

At one time the corridor running past this room had led to a tunnel connecting the University with the Palace Reveta Tristile. Many generations ago, a spring flood had damaged the tunnel. Repairs had been deemed too costly, and this long hallway and its rooms had been abandoned, nearly forgotten.

"What is this room, master?" the kitchen boy asked. His eyes grew huge with wonder.

Baamin sneezed before he could reply. Some of the dust and mold had settled, but not all. A large swirl of it still filled his nose with another itch. He held his breath to stop the next sneeze.

"You know the value of books, Boy?" he finally managed to choke past the gathering tickle.

"Yes, master. Books are the storage place of knowledge. Without knowledge we are not better than the animals." The boy recited dutifully. His eyes held enough intelligence that he just might understand the words he quoted, in spite of his teacher's reports on his limitations.

"Very true. Unfortunately, some of my predecessors decided knowledge of some subjects is dangerous." Baamin shook his head in dismay. So many of the precious books were in a terrible state of decay, despite the spell that had sealed the room for so long.

His search for the room had lasted five years. He wasted another three in breaking the protective seal. Now he had found the key, apparently just in time. He didn't like secrets. Abandoned and forgotten books bothered him.

Lords secretly employing rogue magicians bothered him more.

"How can any knowledge be dangerous, master? The teachers insist that we must learn all we can to make us stronger." The lad gently ran a finger along the spine of a large tome. His hand came away grimy, leaving the gold letters of the title glittering in the dim light of their lantern.

"Has your history tutor told you of the Great Wars of Disruption?"

The dark-eyed boy nodded.

"When the rogue magicians refused to join the Commune, they were cast out of Coronnan." With good reason. The selfish interests of the rogues were responsible for prolonging the war.

Baamin continued, "Indeed, many could not join the Commune because their magic would not link up with other magicians. The kind of magic they performed was banned. And their books were burned."

"Someone hid these books to save them from the fire?" Fear tinged the boy's eyes.

"Yes, they did. I don't know who. It could have been a rogue who hoped to come back some day—the records say many magicians thought the Commune could not last. More likely it was one of our own who loved books for themselves rather than hating them because of their content." Baamin would have done the same thing.

He sighed in anguish as he plucked a small book from its shelf. The dust that covered it was all that held it together. Leather binding and vellum pages crumbled in his hands.

The protective spell had not done its job properly. It had kept intruders out but not stopped the ravages of time. It was evidence of the haste in which the spell had been constructed. Baamin suspected the book burners had turned rabid. Whoever secreted these books away would have had little time and a great deal of fear hindering him.

"Why do we need these books now, master?" The boy was puzzled. His eyes wandered over the vast number of the volumes; his hands remained carefully at his sides.

"Because the magic is changing. The Commune is no longer strong," Baamin sighed. So much good came from the Commune. If only the King and Council looked more to the Commune for guidance rather than for power and communication. Maybe the Commune was a little rigid in its traditionalism, but the wars of lord against lord, prompted by power-hungry magicians, had ended. The kingdom was at peace. "We need this rogue magic to negate a growing threat to the kingdom." Baamin needed rogue magic to summon his magicians back to the University before the lords gathered. The boy didn't need to know that. His only purpose was to carefully clean the books and note their titles.

Baamin must also keep this room a secret. He had no doubt the boy would keep his mouth shut. He had already proven his ability this last week. No one else at the University knew of Jaylor's antics with the wine cups and the sliced meat. Then, too, there was the matter of the cot and blankets missing from the storage room.

What would Jaylor's next stunt be? Very likely he would borrow a larger viewing glass or maybe a book of spells from the library. Or possibly a book from this very room?

Baamin shook his head, partly in dismay, partly in amazement. How had he reared a rogue magician in these very halls without noticing? All the evidence was there, in the very early manifestation of power, in the wine cups and wildly distorted spells. Maybe it was a good thing the tutors had thought young Jaylor merely inept at throwing magic. If they had realized he was a rogue at work, they would have banished him long ago.

'Twas Jaylor who had discovered the rogue inciting

dragon murder in Lord Krej's province. 'Twas Jaylor who had been the first of the journeymen to see a dragon. Perhaps he would learn the importance of the wolf the dragon protected, too.

Baamin almost hoped not. He needed to know what prompted the dragon before anyone else did. He needed knowledge and information to deal with the unexpected and unexplained. He began searching through the books in earnest.

Closer and closer they lead me. I must push them to move faster. Soon they will pass the place where I removed Darville from my path. And shall again. It is as close to Shayla as I have come on my own.

On the first dragon hunt, blind luck led us to follow a man in dragon-thrall. The next time, the old witchwoman was tricked into showing the way. I had to kill the old crone. Then the dragon changed her lair, relaid the path. She became smart, as smart as Maman. Almost, I lost the desire to pursue. But the Tambootie gave me the will to persevere.

My patience has been rewarded. I set everything else in place. Now, the girl will lead me. Once beyond this cliff top, nothing can keep me from my dragon.

At last, all the years of planning, the murder of my father and older brothers, the destruction of the nimbus, and Darville's enchantment, are coming to fruition.

No one in the kingdom will resist me. I will no longer have to steal my Tambootie. Dragons will bring it to me.

Brevelan's path up the mountain narrowed as it curved around a steep cliffside. An ancient landslide had left a wild scree above the narrow ledge they traversed. Occasional tufts of grass clung to the thin soil, telling Brevelan the age of the slide.

Below them, a sheer cliff dropped to a cluster of trees and a swift stream. In the rarefied air, Brevelan could see the details of the scene very clearly. She felt a moment of disorientation as she looked over the edge. The height was dizzying. Puppy whined and pressed closer to

Brevelan. His body trembled against her. She reached to
give him the comfort he craved.

"What's his problem?" Jaylor turned back from the
steep path to check on his companions.

"This place bothers him." Brevelan crouched down to
wrap her arms completely around the distressed wolf.

"Why?"

She sensed the man's armor falling into place. He was
nearly as wary as the wolf. There was a presence behind
them again. She felt it the moment she stopped concentrating on her footing. The spotted saber cat or Old
Thorm? She didn't like the thought of either one creeping
up behind them.

"I don't know," Brevelan replied. She crooned a soothing tune to the wolf. They needed to continue on, put
more distance between themselves and whatever matched
their movements. The follower had also stopped but had
not turned away.

"Mrrow?" Mica added her own questions to the conversation. The fur on her back stood upright. Her tail
swished in agitation.

Brevelan saw Jaylor wince as the little cat dug her
claws into his shoulder. He batted the offending claws
lightly. In response Mica butted her head into his shoulder. Her fur smoothed a little.

"Has Wolf ever been here before?" Jaylor peered
around the ridge they were climbing. They were very
high now. Shayla's lair couldn't be far.

Cautiously, Brevelan looked around, without releasing
her gentling hand on Puppy. Her gaze was drawn to the
valley below. It seemed familiar. She looked closer.

The height distorted her vision and balance. She knew
the terrifying urge to throw herself into the warm air rising from the valley floor. She closed her eyes as she
backed up, attempting to break the almost familiar need
to launch into flight.

Behind her squeezed eyelids she saw a winter storm
threatening the gray sky and the crumpled body of a
golden wolf at the foot of the ancient landslide. She re-

membered feeling panic, followed by the overwhelming
need to save that wolf. She needed help.

"The last time I saw this place was through Shayla's
eyes." She gulped in an effort to return to her own body,
her own emotions. "Darville was below, injured, and she
couldn't get to him to help him." She opened her eyes
again and looked at Jaylor. Just as Puppy was drawing
support from her, she needed the magician's calming
presence to relate the rest of the story.

"That was the first time Shayla spoke to me. She
needed my help. At her prodding, I was compelled to follow her lead and take Darville back to my hut." She relived the moment when another mind had invaded her
own. She was used to animals calling to her in their time
of need. But never before had an empathic link been so
verbal, so intelligent and overwhelming.

Always before, and since, she'd had the choice to refuse the animal. But not that one time.

Not until she had dragged the wolf on a blanket, through
the growing blizzard to the safety and warmth of her own
hearth, had Shayla released her from the compulsion.

"And the dragon checked on him daily, told you his
name? Are you certain Darville is the name she gave
him?" Jaylor touched her shoulder. His brown eyes widened. Worry creased his brow as confusion clouded his
emotions.

Brevelan nodded. "I've never understood why she protected him so fiercely. It would have been easier for her
to make a meal of him. I'm glad she didn't." She hugged
Puppy close again. "The winter was long and lonely. He
kept me busy, kept me company. Shayla was someone to
talk to when I craved the sound of words. They are my
family now."

"And you never questioned the name Shayla gave the
wolf?" He paced back and forth in front of her, dangerously close to the edge of the cliff. He seemed oblivious
to the crumbling rocks in his agitation.

"Yes, I questioned Shayla," Brevelan defended herself.
"The only answer I received was, 'That is his name.'"

Jaylor stopped his pacing abruptly. "Darville is his

name," he echoed her words. "*Darville* is his name. *Stargods!* It can't be. It just can't be." He rubbed his hand across his eyes then looked more closely at the wolf.

"What can't be, Jaylor?" Brevelan held tighter to her pet, filling her hands with his long fur.

"Why didn't you tell me this before? I could have consulted Baamin and found out for sure." He fumbled in the packs. Clothing and provisions went flying as he sought some object of dire importance.

"Found out what, Jaylor?" Brevelan refolded his spare shirt and gathered her packets of grain and dried fruit.

"You don't know?" He sat back on his heels and stared at her openmouthed.

"Know what?" she demanded, exasperated at his thick male understanding.

"When I left Coronnan City a few weeks after the solstice, Prince Darville had been missing almost a full moon. We were friends. When I asked to see him, to say good-bye, I was told he was in a monastery contemplating an unfortunate dalliance with a lady. The Darville I grew up with never regretted any of his encounters with ladies. The Darville I knew had no time for quiet contemplation and far too much energy for cloistered celibacy."

"So?"

"So, I believe the tale was a cover-up. The king and my master are close friends. They are hiding the fact that Darville is missing."

"Are you suggesting that this animal is our prince? Don't be ridiculous."

"Dragons and the royal family are connected by tradition, honor, and blood. Shayla is bound by instinct and magic to protect those with royal blood. Do you have any other explanation for her ties to a scruffy golden wolf named Darville?"

Jaylor's words chilled her.

"Are you telling me that my wolf is part of the royal family?" Disbelief and understanding warred within her.

"He is not just a wolf. Look at him. Really look at him. Do you see the intelligence in his eyes." He held an oblong of glass between her and the wolf. "Look through the glass and tell me he is just a wolf!"

Brevelan clung to Puppy's thick fur. He smelled of dog, and fresh air, and the plants he had brushed along the way. His tongue panted in the slight breeze, radiating heat. He swallowed, then licked her cheek in affection.

Darville had become a part of her life, a very important part. She had told him things she would not confide to another human, shared her home, her food, her love with a beast. She refused to believe he was anything other than wolf.

"And yet . . . ? There were times when he seemed so very intelligent, listening to her with comprehension in his eyes. And there was Shayla's almost reverent protection of him.

When she thought about the situation, it seemed very likely indeed that her pet was more than he appeared to be.

"How?" she asked. If Jaylor's words were too unbelievable, she would reject them and not allow him to take Darville away from her.

"I don't know. I can only presume Old One-eye is behind this. The prince has been missing since just before the winter solstice. I believe I was sent to find a dragon in hopes the dragon would know something of the prince's location."

"Instead you found a witchwoman with a wolf for a familiar. A wolf with a princely name and a dragon guardian," she breathed. It could be true, it was all so logical. And yet . . . and yet her heart did not want to release the wolf who had been her constant companion for months. Tears gathered in her eyes.

She remembered the saber cat trapped in bronze. Its anguish had made her ill at the time. Did the wolf at her side know he was trapped inside an alien body? Would he remember and carry the hatred as the cat did?

If Darville was indeed a man, then he must be restored to his true form, and soon. But when that happened, he would cease to be her companion, her confidant, her

friend. She hadn't been able to trust any man in a long
time. Would she allow herself to continue trusting *him?*

The answers lay with Shayla. Blindly, Brevelan began
walking again. Up the narrow pathway.

"I won't believe you are truly a man and not a wolf until I see it with my own eyes. Until then we belong together. Come with me, Puppy."

Darville lay down on the path, muzzle on his paws, and
whined. His eyes pleaded with her.

"It's obvious he won't pass this spot." Jaylor looked
around for a solution. "We've got to get moving. Our follower is getting closer."

"Come, Puppy," she coaxed, catching some of his
urgency. She, too, felt the threat. It was like a snake
climbing her back, tightening its coils around her neck.

Darville whined pitifully, scooting farther away from
the cliffside.

"Come with me." She put every ounce of command
available into her voice. Darville's golden eyes widened
then closed, effectively severing the channel of communication.

"He's not going to come willingly," Jaylor huffed.
"Here, take Mica. I'll carry Darville." He handed the cat
to Brevelan.

"Isn't he too heavy for you?" Brevelan cradled Mica
close to her chest.

"I'm big enough to manage, for a short while anyway."
The wolf was bigger and heavier than most of his kind.
"He should be fine once we pass the ridge." He stooped
to gather Darville.

A few small rocks bounced off the cliff, almost striking
Darville's head. The wolf backed up again, his paws
scrabbling on the stony path.

Brevelan and Jaylor both looked up toward the source
of the disturbance. They could see nothing unusual.

"You probably don't remember the summer you were
sixteen, Roy, but I carried you home the night of the mid-
summer fair." Jaylor bent to persuade the reluctant member of their company. "Even if you weren't a wolf right
now, you wouldn't remember that night. We'd both had

too much to drink and one too many fistfights with the local bullies."

Darville cocked one ear as he listened to the soothing cadence of Jaylor's voice. This time he didn't protest when strong arms gathered him up. "You wouldn't allow me to use your real name because you didn't want to be different from the others in our gang. So I called you 'Roy,' short for Royal." He scooped up the wolf, arms around his legs so he couldn't break free. "Now let's get out of here before the entire cliff gives way.

Following his words a larger stream of dirt and rocks broke free. Brevelan scanned the cliff once more. A flicker of movement caught her eye. Something was up there, disturbing the precarious balance of the hillside.

Brevelan ducked under the veil of dirt that lingered after the initial shock. "Quickly, get around the corner!" she called to Jaylor.

He bent into a sprint to follow her. The heavy burden in his arms slowed his progress. Another rock struck Jaylor's shoulder, bounced, and landed on Darville's back. The wolf yelped and wriggled, desperately seeking escape.

Jaylor stumbled on the loose rocks and went down on one knee. Puppy twisted free and ran up the path toward the unknown.

Beneath the roar of the rockfall came the hideous, maniac laughter of a man she knew. Not Old Thorm, or a foreign rogue magician. But her father—Lord Krej.

CHAPTER 16

"Jaylor!" Brevelan ducked beneath the barrage of cascading rock. Above her, the distinctive roar of a rockfall grew louder, closer.

Another rock struck Jaylor on the back. His eyes glazed in a disorientation. Stunned and bewildered by the blow, he seemed incapable of making the lifesaving decision to move.

All thoughts of Darville and his true nature fled from Brevelan. The man she loved was in danger.

Brevelan grabbed Jaylor's arm and heaved him upright by shear force of will. He stumbled and lurched along beside her, too dazed to choose a direction.

"Come on," she ordered through gritted teeth. "You have to move. Now."

The roar grew louder yet. She had to get him out of there quickly. Upward she propelled him, in the wake of the howling wolf.

Jaylor wiped blood that dripped into his eyes from a cut on his forehead and stared around him. A rock as large as Brevelan's clenched fist bounced off his boot. The new pain seemed to jolt him back to reality.

"*S'murgh* it." He stopped and looked around. "This isn't a natural avalanche. We've got to catch up to the wolf before One-eye finds him!" He reached his hands backward and his staff sprang to him. A single wave of his tool and a dome of shimmering blue and red light protected them from the increasing flow of soil and debris from the hillside.

Together they dashed along what was left of the path. "Mica? Where is Mica?" Brevelan turned back to search for the cat. In all this dust and turmoil Mica's coloring would be impossible to discern.

"Forget the cat. We have to protect Darville." Jaylor spun her back toward their path.

"I can't. She's my friend," she shouted over the roar of the collapsing scree. Half the mountain seemed to be raining down on them. Her heart lurched to think of Mica buried underneath all that weight. Desperate to find her pet, Brevelan yanked her arm free of Jaylor's grasp and dashed back toward the spot where they had stopped with Darville.

"Look with your heart, not your eyes," Jaylor commanded right behind her. "You've got about five heart-beats before the whole hillside goes."

"There!" A flutter of her heart directed her gaze toward glistening movement in the dust. Brevelan dove toward the spot. Dust filled her eyes and choked her. "Mica," she squeaked. "Come, Mica."

Jaylor's arms locked around her waist. Her body flew backward, not forward.

"Mrew," Mica pleaded for release.

"You can't save her, Brevelan," Jaylor pulled her backward. "I can't hold back the rockfall with magic anymore."

"I can't not save her. Please, let me go to her," she wept, still reaching.

"I can't let you hurt yourself to save a cat."

Brevelan went limp in his arms. His grip slackened. She lunged out of his grasp toward the tiny bit of overhang that still protected Mica from the rocks.

A tree crashed beside her, not three arm's lengths away. The mighty trunk bounced and rolled, caught a moment on the lip of the path then careened on down the steep slope.

Brevelan's fingers closed on a handful of dirty fur just as Jaylor hauled her backward once more.

Again the wolf has escaped me. We are too near the dragon. Shayla's aura grants him luck. Not much longer. The magician must die. Torture? Drowning? Something

deliciously hideous will occur to me. Perhaps he will be-
come an ivory statue in my collection. I've never had a
human before.

Yes. Yes. New statues. The wolf is already gold. He only
needs gilding. I shall make the girl watch and know the
horror of their undeath. Then it will be her turn to die.
Her death will infuse me with power.

The cat can escape. She is useless.

"Stupid, fool woman. You could have been killed."
Jaylor shook Brevelan, forcing his fear into her. Without
thinking, he clutched her tightly against his chest. His
arms enfolded her and the filthy cat in a cocoon of safety
and love.

"*Stargods,* Brevelan, what would I do without you?" he
whispered, awestruck at the implication.

Her eyes lost their sparkle. Something haunted her ex-
pressionless face, but no empathic emotions radiated from
her. Jaylor looked more closely at Brevelan.

He felt as empty as she looked. Surely they could find
something more than a blue cloak for him and a secluded
clearing for her!

"I can take Mica again." He reached for the little cat
hiding her head in the crook of Brevelan's arm and shivering.

"No." A spark of emotion lit Brevelan's eyes again.
She clutched Mica tighter as she pulled out of his reach.

"Fine. You carry her, or let her walk by herself."
Stargods! He'd been carrying one or another of his companions the entire journey. He felt like a nanny, not a magician within moments of completing his master's quest.

There was nothing left to do but trudge on up this endless mountain in search of a mythological dragon. Stub-
bornly he set one foot in front of the other. He'd find that
dragon if it killed him, and he'd drag the others with him
whether they liked it or not.

It was the resolution they both wanted. Wasn't it?

"Arroof!" Darville barked and bounded forward.

"Darville!" Brevelan called.

In two leaps the wolf was around a bend and out of sight.

The cloud came back into Brevelan's eyes. "Come back, Darville!" Her whisper was plaintive, almost desperate. "Come back to me."

The only reply was another sharp bark.

"You've got to catch him, Jaylor. It's not safe for him to be separated from us." She clutched his sleeve anxiously.

Her touch spread warmth up his arm. He wanted to grasp it and hold her close until her eyes sparked with enthusiasm again.

"Please, Jaylor. You've got to catch him," she implored.

"Yes." Briefly he clasped her hand then set off in pursuit. "You can hide in that clump of bushes until we come back for you."

His shoulders were tight from carrying first Brevelan and then Darville. She was so small, so special, he'd hardly noticed her weight. Darville, on the other hand, had been heavier than Jaylor thought possible. He knew the beast was big for a wolf, but he'd weighed as much as a man.

Darville is a man. He only appears to be a wolf, Jaylor reminded himself.

"Arroo, arroo, arroo, roo roo." Darville's concentrated bay announced his excitement.

Energy surged through Jaylor's limbs, his heart pounded faster. The wolf would only howl like that if he encountered another being.

"Darville!" he called.

"Darville!" Brevelan echoed just behind.

He turned to prevent her from rushing forward. A few tendrils of bright red hair sprang from her once neat braid. Her eyes looked as huge as the Great Bay and sparked with an intense glow of protectiveness.

"Wait." Jaylor stopped long enough to halt her headlong dash around the next bend. A large everblue with needles as long as his hand obscured his view. Beyond it a Tambootie soared, blocking the sun. In its shadow anything could lurk unseen.

He swallowed deeply to clear his mind of the wonderful vision of Brevelan. Her lips pursed in determination, and there was a light of battle in her eyes. As she hurried, her breasts strained the fabric of her bodice while her skirt was kilted up to allow her legs freedom. Would she ever dash to his rescue in such an immodest manner?

"Wait, Brevelan."

"But. . . ."

"Let me see what awaits us first." He didn't pause for an answer, or another protest.

Tambootie! Hot and sharp. A wave of pure magic assaulted him as he rounded the bend. He walked into a palpitating miasma of the stuff. His eyes watered, his skin tingled. Power invaded his entire body. All of a sudden his tongue was too big for his mouth and seemed to fill his ears as well. Even his hair itched.

Memories surged through him with each straining heartbeat.

He was back in that stone room filled with cloying smoke. Ogres and snakes assaulted him and dispersed with a word. His pulse pounded, then stuttered. He fought to draw air into his belabored lungs.

Sharp mountain breezes stung him back to reality. This time there were no walls to close in on him. He was out in fresh air with companions to help, if he needed them. He thought he was prepared for whatever the smoke could make him see. The reality in front of him was no match for delusion.

Shayla dipped her head in greeting.

"Master," the kitchen boy peeked over a pile of books, "I think I've found somethin'." He sat cross-legged on the cold stone floor of the hidden room.

Baamin looked across the waist-high stacks of discarded volumes piled between them. Not all of the books in the sealed room were as fragile as the first one he had touched. Many, especially those hidden behind the first layer, were in pristine condition. Evidence of the power of the original spell despite the haste of its construction. The outer row were mostly history chronicles, familiar and of no particular value. Behind them were books he had never seen.

"What, Boy. What have you found?" He breathed in a mouthful of mold and began to cough again, even as he reached across the lopsided stack to grasp whatever the boy held. The cold and dust crept into his old body, making his movement stiff and awkward.

"An old book, sir. Real old. I don't even recognize the writin', sir." He held up his treasure, open to the title page.

The strange script wiggled across the page like so many snakes. Words and images started to form in Baamin's mind but would not take hold. This was definitely a book of magic, very old magic. He doubted he could make writing confuse a reader like that. His discomforts were forgotten in his growing excitement.

Out of habit, Baamin calmed his mind and stilled his body, as if gathering magic. When he opened his eyes the letters held their place and formed words.

> *PRIVATE JOURNAL OF NIMBULAN:*
> *MAGICIAN TO THE KINGS*
> *FATHER OF DRAGONS*
> *VICTIM OF THE WARS OF DISRUPTION*

The last line was written in the same but an older and shakier hand, in a different ink. It appeared to be almost a postscript.

"Nimbulan!" Baamin breathed his excitement outward this time.

"Founder of the University. He's the greatest magician known." The boy's eyes widened in wonder. "Do you think his journal will tell you how to summon your magicians?"

Baamin felt much the same sense of awe. Nimbulan was remembered with reverence. His ideas and experiments had led to the development of the Commune. Without him the border would never have become reality.

Coronnan would have been consumed by civil war and left as easy pickings for greedy neighbors.

"If he doesn't tell us in his journal, perhaps he will mention a book that will." As he took the slender volume from the boy, he allowed his hands to caress the smooth leather of the binding.

Nimbulan was mighty in the annals of magic, not just for his achievements but for his loyalty and compassion as well. He was a man whom all his successors tried to emulate.

Baamin felt humble in the face of such greatness. He'd never be able to wrestle the kingdom through this current crisis. How could he possibly hope to live up to the legacy of such a magnificent predecessor?

"I'll take this to my private chambers, Boy. Keep looking." He stumbled to the door, consumed by his need to read the journal without interruption.

"Sir?" The boy disturbed his train of thought.

"Yes?" he replied absently.

"What if I find something else?" There was hope as well as a tinge of bewilderment in his voice.

"Then bring it to me. But do so quietly. We don't want anyone else to suspect the existence of this room." The boy would obey. He wasn't intelligent enough to do anything else.

Shayla defied Jaylor's attempts to describe her. Beautiful beyond words. All colors. And yet no color. Light reflected back and around the viewer. She was as translucent as an opal yet as glistening as a diamond.

The dragon dipped her steedlike muzzle to his level. He felt speared by the large multicolored eyes that scanned him, one at a time. Above the eyes, a ridge tapered up into a wicked horn, as long as his arm. That horn was repeated in spines parading down her long neck and back.

With majestic dignity, the huge dragon propped her short forelegs on a fallen log, resting her weight on her powerful haunches. From each foot sprouted a set of long colorless claws, matching the spines in shape and texture.

Behind her, a thick tail tapered to a sharp arrowhead

point. It looked as lethal as its counterpart. Her wings, too, could be considered weapons. At the end of each rainbowed vein lay a wicked hook. Jaylor revised his preconception of her size. Two sledge steeds together would match her width. Two more would be needed to fill the height of this magnificent dragon.

But her best defense was her shimmering opalescence. In flight she would be invisible.

Jaylor should have felt intimidated by her. Instead, he was filled with a glowing sense of affection. The great eye that scrutinized every bit of him—inside as well as out?—held only curiosity, no malice or greed. And, thankfully, no hunger.

You may touch, Shayla responded to his unspoken desire. The words were as clear in his mind as if the immense creature had spoken.

He reached a tentative hand to her velvet-soft muzzle. When he would have pulled his hand back she butted into his outstretched palm, just as any tame steed would nuzzle for attention or treats. The smooth fur that covered her body invited an extended caress. He reached around to her cheek bulge and scratched.

Ahh! He felt her sigh of delight.

"Awroof," Darville begged for his share of attention. He stood with his front paws on the same log as the dragon. He seemed taller, closer to his true height as a man. But he still held the form of a wolf. Jaylor gave the wolf his requested scratch while keeping his other hand on the dragon. Now that he was touching her, communicating with her, he couldn't bear to lose contact.

"Oh, my!" Brevelan gasped.

Jaylor turned to look at her and smiled. He extended his hand, inviting her to share the wonderful experience of tactile contact with Shayla. His arm came around her shoulders quite naturally. For a moment the image of family flooded him. He shrugged it off, but it returned.

You did well. You all came. Shayla rotated her eyes to see both of them at once.

"We were followed," Jaylor explained.

I know. He used timboor to hear your footsteps. We

must hurry. The dragon indulged in one last caress and then reared up and turned. Her movements were graceful and precise. None of her dangerous claws, or wing hooks, or sharp tail spines touched her guests. Instead the massive tail seemed to encircle them and guide them toward an opening in the cliff.

You must remove Darville's enchantment now.

"Me?" Jaylor stopped and clasped his hands behind his back in uncertainty. "You're the magic dragon. I'll need your help."

Only you can save him from degenerating into a wild beast.

"I can't do it alone."

The air is full of magic. For a brief time I can give you more. It must be enough.

They have found her! I can feel it. The core of magic has expanded to include them.

They seek to reverse my spell. But they can't. They never will. It is a special spell, a secret. When the magician tries to unravel the magic around the wolf, they will both be forever frozen in undeath.

I will rejoice with Simurgh to add them to my collection.

CHAPTER 17

Baamin lit a small oil lamp in the dim recess of his inner study. The day had suddenly gone dark. Chill dampness promised rain. He shrugged off the sudden iciness climbing his spine and returned to the fascinating book on his desk.

As much as he would have liked to dwell on the early life of the great Nimbulan, there wasn't time now. He had to skip large sections of the magician's private journal.

He paused and read a paragraph here and there. The painful Great Wars of Disruption were retold in heart-wrenching detail. Each contender for the throne, in that long ago civil war, had brought to his cause a different magician. When armies failed, sorcerers fought. Many died.

The words recounting each death tore at Baamin three hundred years later. He knew what it was like to lose a friend and compatriot. As long-lived as magicians tended to be, very few of his contemporaries still survived. He remembered the agonizing sense of loss at each death and felt again the reduction in magic caused by their passing.

Dragon magic needed numbers of men working together. It grew and expanded like a living being under the careful cultivation of the Commune. A strong Commune was the direct result of a strong nimbus of dragons. And there were so few dragons or magicians left! The fate of the kingdom hinged on the dragons.

Now Baamin faced the need for strong magic and a strong king without the means to provide either.

Darcine might appear to be reviving. But Baamin suspected it was only temporary and dependent on Shayla's

gravid condition. The last two times Shayla had bred, the
normally indecisive king had undergone similar periods of
renewed strength and determination. Each time the baby
dragons had been slaughtered, King Darcine had fallen
gravely ill. If anything should happen to the dragon or her
litter this time, the king would not survive.

A sentence caught Baamin's eye.

The pattern has become clear. Lord. . . .

The name was smudged and unreadable. Perhaps
Nimbulan had deliberately obscured the name to avoid
calling its owner and thus giving him power.

*Lord . . . has been gathering an alliance among the
other lords for many years. He has carefully arranged
marriages for his numerous children into the homes of his
strongest enemies. Through these children he has formed
a network for coercion and extortion. Few noble families
dare contest his bid for power.*

Was history repeating itself? Krej had at least seven legitimate children and untold numbers of bastards. Even
those too young for marriage had been betrothed in rites
as binding as a wedding. Nearly every noble family was
allied to him in some way. His network was in place.

And there was a rogue magician within the boundaries
of Krej's province.

Baamin longed for proof that Krej had hired the rogue
to work mischief among the dragons.

Krej's right to the throne was strong. If Darcine should
die before Darville was found, there was no one else
strong enough to hold this country together.

Was that Krej's plan, too? Had he arranged the slaughter of the dragons to weaken the king and make his own
leadership seem essential to the welfare of Coronnan? It
seemed logical until you considered young Darville. He
was a prince of character and wisdom, in spite of his high
spirits and preference for long, solitary, and dangerous
hunts.

Where was the boy?

Shayla protected a golden wolf in the southern mountains. What was the connection?

Baamin turned several more pages. This history was

compelling in its parallels to modern times. But he needed information about magic, not politics.

I must break the habits of a lifetime. No more can I dip deep within myself for the source of my magic. Now I must take the time to locate an outside source, gather it, change it, and throw it back out. Inefficient as this method seems, it is necessary.

Magic was so much easier when I could close my eyes and find the power beneath my feet. With my own magic, the words of a spell were changed by that power into deeds. It seemed I need only open my eyes again and find the deed accomplished.

I only wish my beloved Myrilandel could share in this new force. Alas, women and children no longer have the ability to work with us. Since we must banish the old form of magic, we must also exclude them from the joys of this new force and the intimate ties of those who join together with it.

"So I must delve deep within myself for the source of personal magic," Baamin mused. "Not so different from dipping into the reserves of magic I have gathered.

He closed his eyes. Nothing came to mind. What should he try? Something simple to begin with. Perhaps Jaylor's old trick. From memory he recited the words that would form the image of a cup filled with cool wine. At first he saw it in the cellar. Then he put the cup on his desk.

The crash of broken crockery startled him out of his reverie. On the floor, beside him, lay a broken wine cup; one just like those reserved for students. He had brought the cup through the sealed doors and into his study! Only the cup had slipped to the floor and crashed. He had forgotten the slope of the reading surface.

"I'm as bad as the apprentices!" Baamin's eyes watered from his near hysterical mirth. "Imagine me, Senior Magician and University Chancellor back among the rawest of students."

Never, in her dreams or in her conversations with Shayla, had Brevelan imagined a dragon could be so wonderful. She had seen vague images of the dragon and her consorts, but never this full, splendid view of power and iridescent light.

A bubble of joy replaced the weight of dread in her midsection. She wanted to laugh and sing with her companions. Shayla's magic already encircled them, bound them all together. Brevelan need only enrich the bonds with her own magic song.

The weight of Jaylor's arm about her shoulders made the circle of her love complete. Together they strode into the cool depths of the cave Shayla called home.

The entrance was just large enough for the dragon to spread her wings in preparation for flight. Deeper into the mountain it opened into a massive room, dry and cool. In one corner was a nest of dried leaves and everblue needles, with some feathers and bits of raw wool for softness.

Brevelan refused to think about where those bits came from. The bowl of the nest was wide and sheltered from the wind. Perfect for Shayla's brood.

"When will the babies come?" she asked timidly.

Winter Solstice. The dragon yawned. *Before long I will not be able to fly.*

"How will you eat?" Jaylor asked as he poked among the piles of loose rock that had been cleared from the center of the cave.

The fathers will share.

"Fathers?" he asked.

Brevelan smiled. Her magician had not been privy to the images of the mating flight. He had no way of knowing Shayla's preference for multiple fathers for her litter.

"Fathers," Brevelan answered. " 'The more fathers, the larger and stronger the litter,' " she quoted.

His mouth lifted in a long lazy smile. The line of his thoughts was clear.

Sit, my friends. Shayla curled her tail around her haunches. Once more she dipped her elegant neck so that her eyes were level with Jaylor and Brevelan. In the dim light of the cave interior the irises appeared quite red, slashed by a long, horizontal pupil. Deep inside the dark slash were all of the colors reflected by Shayla's soft iridescent fur.

Brevelan stared lovingly at the dragon, entranced by the penetrating gaze of her hostess. Shayla seemed to read her soul, strip it bare, and judge her mettle. Brevelan quivered a little as she adjusted her body and mind to that friendly but intimidating stare. Jaylor mimicked the gesture.

Drained by the dragon's scrutiny, Brevelan accepted the invitation to sit. A pile of leaves, without feathers and fur, near a large rock looked made for her. She sank into it, grateful for this small comfort. Her light pack made a wonderful pillow for her head against the rock. The minor injuries inflicted by the rockfall hadn't bothered her until she thought about resting. Now stiff muscles and aching bruises surged to the surface. She eased herself into a more comfortable position.

As usual, Puppy sat, leaning his weight against her. His head tipped and rubbed her shoulder. Mica scampered into her lap and commenced an overdue bath.

Brevelan accepted as natural that Jaylor chose to pace rather than sit. While his mind worked, his body needed to keep moving. His restless energy brought to mind why they were here and the dangers that awaited them.

There is not much time. The evil one comes.

Inside Brevelan's head appeared the image of the one-eyed derelict. A second image appeared of the spotted saber cat's head perched atop the powerful body of a man. Brevelan didn't need Shayla's mental pictures. She would know her enemy anywhere, in any disguise, by his insane laughter.

"Why can't you just change Darville back to his normal form?" Jaylor stopped prowling long enough to address Shayla directly. As tall as he was, head and shoulders above Brevelan, he barely reached Shayla's shoulder. Above him towered the dragon's long neck and graceful head. "For that matter, why did you allow it to happen in the first place?"

Brevelan pulled the wolf closer, cherishing the last few

moments of their companionship. Once the spell was
thrown from him, he would be a prince and no longer her
familiar.

*By the vows that were taken many years ago, I grant
him protection. The same vows limited my powers.*

"What?" Now Jaylor sat, suddenly and not altogether
gracefully, on a nearby rock. "Isn't that why we came?
So you could transform him."

*I make the magic for you to gather. I do not force it to
bend to my will as mortals do.*

"I'm not very good at gathering magic. I work better
with my own brand." Once more he put his hands behind
his back.

*For this you will need both my magic and your own. I
shall guide you.*

"For this I need to know how it was done. I can't reverse an unknown spell."

Was that truly panic in his eyes? Brevelan sent a small
amount of courage toward him.

"For this spell, you need only watch a master and weep
that you will never be able to do it yourself." A new
voice announced from the cave entrance.

Brevelan didn't need to face her enemy to know he was
disguised in the second image Shayla had sent her. The
bronze and gray fur of the spotted saber cat head gleamed
in the sunlight at the entrance to the cave. Oiled human
muscles rippled along the magician's strong arms and
bare torso. His sturdy legs anchored his barely clothed
body in a broad stance.

On another man, a man less evil, his naked splendor
could have been compelling. Brevelan nearly gagged
with fear and remembered pain. The last naked man
she had seen had tried to rape her on their marriage
bed.

A stream of red and blue flame erupted from Jaylor's
staff, aimed at the intruder. The plait of fire sped toward its
target almost faster than the eye could follow. An arrow
point formed at the end of the magic spear. The monster's
eyes narrowed and he waved his own staff—straight grained

with lumps at irregular intervals down its length—in a wide arc.

Jaylor stood frozen in place, arm still raised, staff in hand. His red and blue arrow melted to mist.

Darville growled and gathered his hind legs beneath him for a lunge. Saliva dripped from his fangs in his eagerness to taste the magician's blood.

Thorm raised his staff again.

Brevelan leaped in front of her pet. She had to protect Darville from any further hurt at the hands of 'his monster.

Darville swung around Brevelan and lunged for the enemy's throat. A reddish haze spread over and around Thorm as he laughed once more. A wall of magic stopped Darville's lunge. He tore at it with teeth and claws.

Jaylor broke free of his paralysis. A second braid of fire erupted from his staff and met the same fate as the first. His intended victim only laughed, that taunting, high-pitched laugh he'd heard at the rockfall.

"I penetrated your style of magic long ago, University man." Thorm sneered. He made it sound as if the hallowed institution of learning were merely a refuse pile, its students so much dirt and offal. "I can stop any spell you throw. Dragon magic is useless against a true magician!" he crowed.

Jaylor stepped toward Thorm, staff raised, and stopped, frozen in place again. A hazy green bell pulsed and swallowed him.

"NO!" Brevelan screamed. The force of Jaylor's mental pain at the paralysis nearly knocked her from her feet. She launched herself toward him to break through the magic. "Stop him, Shayla. Stop him before he hurts someone." Another pain assaulted her. From behind her she felt a crippling agony in her legs and arms. Shayla! Her beautiful, wonderful dragon was hurt.

Instinctively, she sent forth all of her strength and courage to support the dragon. Another wave of despair rocked her. She matched it with a high piercing note of healing song.

"Shayla!" The music echoed and reverberated back to her. "Fight for your life, Shayla!" The notes died in the vast emptiness of the cave. There was no mind or soul there to receive her healing.

CHAPTER 18

Brevelan turned to look for Shayla with her eyes when she could no longer find the dragon in the place within her heart.

Her movement must have attracted Thorm's attention. The air crackled with energy. She could smell it, taste it, almost wade through the thick wall. A haze of green magic enveloped her, just as it had Jaylor.

The confines of that nasty bell of red and green shimmering lights held her body frozen. Trapped with her was the reek of Tambootie smoke.

"Jaylor!" she called. The words echoed within her mind, for no sound erupted from her body. She called again with her magic, pouring as much emotion as she had left into her cry.

Just a faint tickle of responding fury reached her through the spell. Jaylor lived!

"Puppy?" If the wolf were still free, perhaps he could divert the magician's attention long enough for Jaylor's magic to release them.

The wolf's response was stronger, but still masked. She forced her eyes to move to her right where she had last seen him.

Teeth bared, neck fur on end, he was crouched to spring for Thorm's throat. She could hear his deep, menacing growl, muffled by yet another magic barrier.

"Think you can wreak revenge on me, Wolf?" Thorm sneered with Krej's voice. "You'll have to be faster and stronger than that." He laughed. The irritating waves of his cackles echoed around and around the cave.

Brevelan sought Shayla again. Her mind reached nothing. Her eyes found only a dim outline of the magnificent body. The dragon, too, was captured in the web of magic, unable to move. But unlike the others, her mind was as frozen as her body. Horror gripped Brevelan. She tried again and again to find a glimmer of the dragon, in her mind or in her heart.

Nothing.

Something within her died. She went limp, no longer resisting the magic. The disguised rogue was too strong. He held their defeat within the sweep of his knobby staff.

A forceful personality intruded on her despair. Mica clawed her way into her awareness. *Stay with us, Sister!* The command came along with a large dose of courage and strength.

What was this? Mica, her sweet little kitty, was supporting her, Brevelan, with words and empathy. The cat had never spoken to her before. But then, she hadn't needed to. The bonds of communication were strong enough without words.

With the cat's help, Brevelan reinforced her emotional tie to Jaylor and Darville. The channels opened, their thoughts mingled. Together they must fight the source of the magic, drain it, and then break free.

"Oh, what a splendid addition you will make to my collection," Thorm gloated. His hands ran lovingly over Shayla's flank, his caress almost that of a lover.

Brevelan swallowed her revulsion. How could they allow him to touch Shayla with his slimy hands and filthy mind?

"You do remember my collection, pretty one," he stated rather than asked of Brevelan. "You are from Krej's village, aren't you?" He looked up from his fondling of Shayla's front horn.

Brevelan couldn't respond, even if she'd wanted to.

"With hair like that," he reached through the haze to lift a bright lock off her cheek, "I would almost think you one of his get." His eyes widened.

"Of course! You're his oldest daughter." He laughed, nearly hysterical with his own humor. Cruelly he pulled the strand of hair just before releasing it. "Pretty as you

are, I can't spare the time to take you. Next time, sweet-
heart. Next time." He blew a kiss through the confining
haze.

The lascivious caress left a wet imprint on her cheek.
She longed to wipe her skin free of the rogue's touch.

Jaylor's jealous rage pounded against his bell. The haze
thickened and grew, feeding on the energy of his emotions.

"You're the one the villagers want to burn for witchcraft. Seems you murdered your husband on your wedding night." Thorm looked directly at Jaylor now, fueling
the younger man's anger and the magic that confined him.

"Didn't she tell you about that, boy? She wouldn't
want to broadcast her past to those gullible fisher-folk.
They might decide to burn her, too. But you, you're her
lover. Surely she would confide in you."

The blast of emotion from both Darville and Jaylor
shook the red-haired monster. He shivered once, but his
mask did not slip. Then he turned his attention from
Brevelan to the wolf and the magician. "I can see you
both have strong feelings for the chit. Perhaps I shall tell
the elders of the village where to find her. You would be
forced to watch her burn, before they fed you to the fish
in the center of the Bay."

His eyes narrowed in evil speculation. "You know, of
course, they blame her for the rainy summer that caused
their crops to rot in the fields last year. They also think
she is responsible for the very hard winter that took the
lives of all the old ones and some babies, too."

Not the babies! A huge emptiness settled inside
Brevelan. Babies she had helped bring into this world
were gone before they'd had a chance to live.

Tears of pain and grief worked their way through the
magic. They slid down her cheeks and dropped to her
breast. But she couldn't feel the moisture, only the pain
of death for infants who had become a part of her as she
brought them to life.

"May all the foul spirits of Simurgh's hell and beyond
take you!" Jaylor cursed as loud as his mind could

scream. "How could you betray your king and cousin, the kingdom, and the Commune with this abomination?"

"Still spouting ethics, boy? You of all people should have no qualm about ethics. Where do you think I found this wonderful creature to do my bidding?" The monster gestured to his naked torso and mask. "I read your thoughts, boy. Thoughts you stole from Old Baamin's dreams. I'm surprised you didn't recognize me sooner," he taunted.

"I recognize only your corruption." Desperately Jaylor sought contact with Brevelan and Darville.

Jaylor railed against his own ineffectiveness and the rogue's audacity. His accusations against Brevelan were just too preposterous to contemplate. Brevelan couldn't murder anyone. Least of all her husband on her wedding night! And this monster had accused Jaylor of being her lover and still having the strength of magic to throw those braids of flame. If the situation weren't so serious, he'd laugh himself silly.

"The day progresses, and I do want to be out of this cave before moonrise." The rogue shrugged his naked shoulders in dismissal of his prisoners as he returned his attention to Shayla.

Jaylor carefully watched each gesture the man made. Whatever happened, Jaylor would need to undo it later.

"Watch all you want, University man," Thorm laughed. "Your false magic won't be able to negate my powers. If I allow you to live long enough to try your puny spell, that is."

Could the man read his mind? If so, Jaylor had to bury, very deeply, all thought of his rogue powers. Thorm mustn't know that Jaylor might be able to counteract any spell that was thrown.

"What substance best suits a life-sized sculpture of a dragon?" Thorm mused rhetorically. "My gray bear is pewter, and the spotted saber cat was bronze. But then I had to let the cat go as bait for Darville." He whirled to face his captives. "Nice touch that, turning the prince into a wolf. It suits his personality."

Jaylor felt Darville's growl echo through his body. Was

it possible some sentience was returning to the prince now that he was confronting his enchanter? Jaylor hoped so. The wolf's cooperation would make escape and the spell reversal easier.

"But for a dragon," Thorm continued his gleeful monologue, "I think glass would be proper." He snapped his fingers in delight. "Yes, glass. You can see through dragons as well as the best glass, and only those of Lord Krej's rank deserve that wondrous substance. Glass, smooth, clear, and yet it reflects light in a myriad of colors. Wonderful glass." He almost sang it.

As the words took on a lilting quality, the air became heavier, filled with the stench of rotten Tambootie. Magic filled the confines of the cave. Clear and colored eddies swirled around the silent figures, over the piles of rock, and through the carefully constructed nest. Waves and waves of thick magic combined, pulled apart, and flowed with the rhythm of the spell-driving music.

A blue vortex grew and swirled into a tower of wind. Lightning flashed within the artificial tornado. It grew taller and broader, filling more and more of the cave. Then it moved around the perimeter of the cave in one huge circle.

A second vortex of green sprang up and circled the cave in a tighter circumference. Green combined with the blue and they twisted faster. Red, yellow, and purples joined in turn. With each new color the violent storm of whirling magic flew faster, higher, wider.

The magic wind sucked leaves and bits of fur from the nest into its central vacuum. Small pebbles lifted and darted about with more and more debris. Faster and faster yet, the eerie winds circled the cave.

Magic engulfed the figure of the dragon. Shayla's hide took on the color of the Bay in sunlight as the first unnatural storm swirled around her. Then she absorbed each color in turn until all the colors of the spectrum glowed together. All colors became no color. Blinding, piercing opalescent glass.

Jaylor watched in awe as the spell matched the chanting words in intensity and speed. Everything in the cave was sucked into the magic, even the existing magic. The green in the haze engulfing Jaylor thinned. His eyes cleared and he saw the same thinning around Brevelan and Darville. He tried to move his hand. His finger twitched, barely.

Concentrate, fool! he admonished himself. *Use the Tambootie in the air to shatter this immobility just as I used the timboor in my blood to remove myself from the Rover camp.*

His eyelids closed with effort. He turned his thoughts inward, gathering strength. A coil of stored dragon magic was ready for release. He pushed it aside and sought a different source. It was hiding where he had put it when he banished all thoughts of rogue magic.

Jaylor drew the thin line of magic upward to his eyes. His mouth wouldn't move enough to speak the words, so he created them in the front of his mind, for his imagination to read. The line sped from his eyes to the imagined letters, wrapped around them and then shot, like a barbed arrow, straight for the enemy's heart.

Darville couldn't move. Panic filled his body. He tried to growl in response to what he could not understand. The deep rumble vibrated in his chest, but he couldn't hear it as he should. This curious fog surrounded him, blocking his view of Brevelan and Jaylor. The evil one remained in his sight.

His ears heard the other noises about him with their usual keenness. His nose worked, too. He associated the curious smoky smell with the evil one. He growled again.

The faintest of sounds reached his ears. His fur bristled again, the way it should. Brevelan looked closer than just a moment ago, clearer. Jaylor, too.

"Glass! My pretty dragon is made of glass," the evil one chanted.

His words penetrated all of Darville's senses. He understood every sound the cat-headed man uttered. Anger and revulsion filled his suddenly cold body.

Even as he understood the entire scene, the rest of his senses dimmed. He felt as if his ears and nose were filled, like the times he had a winter cold. And his suddenly bald limbs ached. His back and thighs felt as if he had ridden his steed far too long.

Curious, Darville allowed his blurry eyes to look upon his body, to find the problem.

Vertigo engulfed him. He was a man. A naked man. He felt his skin hen-bump in response to the cold and his embarrassment at having been caught in the presence of strangers without his clothes. And not just any strangers.

The ball of multicolored fur that he presumed was a cat grew and uncoiled into the most beautiful woman he had ever seen. She, too, was naked except for the enveloping wave of hair that shimmered to her hips and below. As the woman turned, light reflected off the lustrous curtain, now blonde, then brunette, with a touch of red and deep sable brown.

She lifted her arms in joy. From her lips sprang a clear and sweet song. The most glorious song of freedom he had ever heard.

All too soon the woman shrank back into her cat persona. Just as he had shrunk to the size of a wolf on that fateful afternoon.

His past engulfed him in a wave. He saw again his betrayal on the ridge. . . .

The spotted saber cat tracks he followed disappeared in the rocky scree. Snowflakes drifted lazily into the crevices of the path. He turned to speak to his cousin and hunting companion. Krej was nowhere in sight. Darville drew his sword. Waning winter light made the weapon appear black and dull.

The snow increased in intensity. Through the heavy veil of flakes stalked the saber cat. Coming toward him.

He shifted his feet for better defensive balance. The uneven ground tilted his balance. The cat came closer.

No, it wasn't a saber cat at all, but a man with the cat's head. Had Krej killed the creature already? If so, why was Krej wearing only a loin cloth in freezing weather?

A slight shift of wind cleared the snow away for a moment. The man who stalked him wasn't a man at all, but some kind of monster with a beast's head.

"Krej, save yourself!" he called to his cousin.

"I am, Darville, I am saving myself," the beast spoke with Krej's voice. "With your death I am only one heartbeat away from the throne. Soon, very soon, I shall rule and my magic will grant me supremacy over all kingdoms!"

Fury filled Darville's eyes. Krej, his own cousin, had betrayed him. He had to kill the man before the snow froze them both.

Magic flame hit him in the chest, robbing him of breath. He thought it was his own anger.

As he had been taught in countless arms classes, he separated his mind from his body. He needed all of his wits, cool and alert, to divert the next blast of magic.

He succeeded in catching a ball of green flame with his sword. It bounced off the polished steel and hit a rock as big as a dog. The stone shattered. Dust and gravel filled the air.

Momentarily blinded, Darville didn't see the next blast. It struck his head, blinding him, shattering his control. His balance failed. The air around him shuddered and parted.

He was falling, falling into nothing. Cold vanished from his aching body. Fur covered him. His nose told him he had fallen into a snowdrift deep within the forest. . . .

Part of Darville rejoiced that the enchantment was broken. He was no longer a wolf, but a man once more. Even then, he mourned the loss of his keen wolf vision and sense of smell.

Then, just as suddenly, blackness swamped his awareness. But he was warm again. His fur coat was back. The stinking smoke filled his nose and he growled.

CHAPTER 19

A shriek beyond physical hearing tore a great rent in the air surrounding Baamin. The gaping difference in air pressure made the hair on his arms and neck stand up. Even his three-day-old beard bristled and cracked. His wine cup shattered in midair.

What was wrong? The air smelled different. Something was missing.

The magic was gone!

"Where is it?" He sniffed fruitlessly for a faint whiff of the ever-present—so easily ignored—spicy aroma of magic, something akin to Tambootie but not quite. His eyes widened as he sought every corner of his study for some clue to what was happening.

No magic anywhere. He couldn't smell it, taste it, feel it. And he certainly couldn't gather it. The only other time that had happened was when a dragon died.

"Shayla!" he whispered into the blankness. "What has happened?" Panic engulfed him. His breath came in short quick pants. He felt dizzy and heavy. "SHAYLA!" he wailed.

Darkness tried to enclose his vision even as the back of his neck threatened to separate from his body.

"Darcine?" he whispered.

By feel alone, he groped his way to his desk. He must run to the palace. He must summon the Commune.

He must contact Jaylor. The journeyman was near the dragon. He would know what transpired.

Where was his glass? He needed the glass and a candle to call Jaylor. Where the *s'murghing* Tambootie was his glass! The desktop was empty. He couldn't find the glass, his most precious tool. Sweat dripped into his eyes, darkness encroached. He had to find the glass.

It slid into his hand, summoned by his thoughts and rogue powers he didn't realize he had tapped.

His vision cleared instantly.

With shaking fingers, he struck the flame rock with a rough metal rod. A spark leaped from the rock to the wick. It wavered, nearly died, then caught. His breathing calmed.

Baamin held the glass in front of the candle with still trembling fingers and began his spell. For a moment nothing happened. Then he remembered again to seek his magic in a different place. Now that he knew where to look, it was there, waiting, full of life and ready to spring forth at his calling.

He reduced the aching pace of his lungs. Air swept deeply into his body. He held it the required three heart-beats and released it on the same count. Tension flowed from his muscles as the air escaped. His eyes focused on the leaping green flame, found its hot core, and sent it on its journey.

In his mind Baamin saw the tiny flame skip across the river boundary of Coronnan City, over the tilled fields, southward beyond the Great Bay. At a tiny hamlet in the foothills the tiny flame paused, seeking direction. Then upward it climbed into the mountains. Baamin followed.

He saw a hut, burned and abandoned. Forest creatures cowered at the edges of a clearing, equally forlorn and abandoned. The flame moved on.

Upward, ever upward, Baamin followed the seeking green morsel of magic. Finally it lingered on a small pla-teau. It hovered a moment, then recoiled in a straight shot back into Baamin's eyes.

The beast-headed monster twisted his torso into an im-possible angle. He reached out and caught Jaylor's magic arrow between two fingers. Playfully he lifted the weapon to his lips and blew on it. The blue and red magic with-ered and died.

"You'll have to work harder than that, University man.

I saw your attack coming. Your impudence just earned you a longer, slower death. My coven will delight in your screams. We'll have an orgy at your feet as Simurgh rips your soul from your body."

Brevelan's hope sank to the cave floor along with the attack.

"Well, my pretty little witch, I'm finished here." Thorm reached through the bell of magic to tug at Brevelan's hair one more time.

From any other man the gesture might have seemed affectionate. She knew that no such emotion ever entered this man's breast.

"Under other circumstances, I might consider training you to be my successor." The rogue magician quirked one eyebrow. "But circumstances dictate differently. As soon as I have settled my glass dragon in her new home, I'll be back to finish with you and the University man." He laughed. There was a weakness in his mirth—fatigue. He had worked some very strong magic in the past half hour.

Brevelan watched Thorm marshal his energies once more. With a mighty upward heave of his shoulders and arms, he commanded the glass figure that had once been Shayla to levitate an arm's length above the floor of the cave. The dragon had been reduced in size to little more than an extremely large sledge steed.

Thorm hovered the statue briefly, then gestured for it to follow him. He exited with a salute to the entrapped companions. The statue followed, drifting on a pillow of air.

A flash of muted colors streaked across Brevelan's limited vision.

"Yeowwll!" Mica screeched as she landed on Thorm's bare shoulder. Her fully extended claws and teeth drew blood.

"Aiyee!" Thorm hunched and whirled, trying to dislodge the cat from his back. He lost control of the statue.

Tons of clear glass dropped to the ground, rocked and titled. On the edge of one hind leg and tail the sculpture that had once been Shayla teetered and threatened to crash.

Pain washed back into Brevelan from the rogue magician. His spotted saber cat features blurred and faded for just a moment. His familiar face and hair as red as her own burst through the disguise.

Recognition tore at Brevelan's consciousness.

"Enough!" Thorm shook his arm, flinging Mica to the ground. With the same gesture he righted the statue with a magic tether. His feline mask reasserted firm control over his appearance.

"Mica!" Brevelan's scream echoed around the cave, bounced against the walls, and crashed back to the bells of magic isolation.

No response. The little cat lay limp where she had fallen.

"The same fate awaits you, little witch," Thorm—and yet not Thorm—sneered. "I'll be back for you and your lover. Only your deaths won't be as quick." With one last hate-filled glare, the beast-headed monster stalked out of the cave, his glass prize in tow.

Brevelan's anguish slammed into the green and red hazes. Now that Thorm was no longer present to maintain the magic, they shattered under the violence of her revulsion and grief.

Brevelan ran across the cave. Her hand brushed against Mica, checking for damage. Mica breathed in a painful wheeze, but there were no broken bones. She scooped up the cat and moved onto Darville. With a heart full of love, she gathered the quaking wolf and the little cat into her arms. A soothing melody sprang from her heart to theirs as she rocked gently in time with her song.

Slowly the animals' pain and confusion drained into her. She absorbed it, contained it, then dispersed it outward. Mica stirred and snuggled deeper into Brevelan's lap. She butted her head against Brevelan's hand, urging her to examine the wolf more carefully.

Brevelan's fingers sought deep into Darville's fur for hurt, while she searched his eyes for understanding.

"To be a man, trapped in this other body. Do you know of your entrapment, Darville, or has he taken away your mind?" A confusion of emotions disrupted the flow of her magic. She paused in her litany of grief to rub her face in his fur. Her tears dampened his neck.

"Brevelan." Jaylor's hand touched her shoulder.

She gathered its warmth and strength so she could pour more of herself into the wolf.

"Brevelan." Jaylor's voice was stronger, more demanding. "Dear heart, let me take care of this."

The endearment passed over her understanding. She heard only the insistent tone. Jaylor could take care of the problem. "What? How?" she stammered.

"I saw what happened. Thorm didn't have enough magic to transform Shayla and maintain Darville as a wolf while keeping us trapped as well. He had to pull some magic away from Darville to complete his spell." He looked about the cave, as if searching for clues. "I think I can break the enchantment."

Relief flooded through her.

"Please, Brevelan, step away. I need a clear field to work." His hands pulled her up and away from the wolf.

Golden eyes marked her movements with questions. The wolf clearly didn't understand what was happening, had happened, to him. But Brevelan knew that during the time the magic was pulled away from him he had suffered through the entire experience again.

Jaylor stepped between her and Darville. She moved aside to watch. He glared at her. For some reason he didn't want her to know how he did it.

She glared back. Darville had been her constant companion since last winter. She had nursed him through injury and illness. He had comforted her in her loneliness and despair. They both needed to be a part of this transformation.

"This won't be pretty," Jaylor warned even as he began the deep breathing she knew was the beginning of his spells.

"Not very much in this life is."

His eyes pleaded with her to step behind him again. She refused.

"Then make yourself useful. Get my cloak out of my pack." Even as he spoke, his breathing deepened further.

She fetched the cloak. When she returned to his side, his attention was beyond her, turned deeply within himself.

The staff snapped into his hand. He angled it so that it pointed at the wolf's heart. Darville looked up. Expectantly?

A low hum issued from the twisted wooden fibers of the staff. It echoed the tune Thorm had chanted while he danced magic around the cave. Jaylor, too, began to hum. His hands trembled on the staff. He gripped it tighter to control his focus. The staff shook and jerked away from Darville.

Jaylor fought the staff back to his target. It jerked away again just as braided lights of red and blue, green and yellow, with a strand of purple down the center, sprang from the tip. Magic light encircled the bewildered animal in a loose spiral. The magic widened to include Jaylor and Brevelan. Shock waves rippled through the magician. Jaylor broke off the spell before it went any farther awry. Pain clamped around his chest.

It was a good thing this was a solitary spell rather than a traditional one. He had ended it with a thought rather than a lengthy recitation of formulae.

"He laid a trap in the spell," he whispered. "The staff knew it and refused to direct the magic where I aimed it."

Brevelan sent him strength. He stood straighter, but not to his full height. His eyes squinted with the effort to keep them open.

"But now that I've found the trap, I can go around it." He began his work again. Magic plaited around the staff in vivid colors. It sprang backward through Jaylor, around the cave and over to Darville, twisting in the opposite direction from before. A single arrow of multicolored magic pierced the wolf's thick fur. Darville took on the colored glow as the power grew and brightened. He shed his fur, grew longer, paler. His legs and arms straightened. His head reared up and his eyes became aware.

The magic retreated from Darville and surrounded Jaylor. For a moment the magician donned a mantle of golden fur, shot with the red and brown of his own coloring. Then the hair broke free and fell from him in a shower of pinpoint lights.

Jaylor sagged. His skin took on the tinge of gray exhaustion. Each breath rattled in his chest.

Instinctively Brevelan reached her arms to hold him up. He clutched the cloak she held against his chest. "If I could sit a moment. I'm so cold," he whispered. She eased him onto a boulder. When his breathing slowed, she turned her attention to Darville.

Quickly she assessed the long clean limbs and golden hair of a tall man, crouched on the ground. One long foot lifted to scratch his ear in a parody of a wolf's gesture. He looked puzzled that the foot didn't fit, his back didn't twist, his head hung too high.

Only then was Brevelan aware that Darville, her prince, was naked. She turned her eyes away even as she held the cloak out to him. Jaylor had known this would happen. That was why he had asked for the cloak, why he had tried to block her vision.

"You'll need this, Your Grace." She held out the garment. He didn't take it.

"Darville!" He looked up at her. Understanding began to glimmer in his eyes. Still he crouched on the ground, looking as if he wanted to wag a tail that was no longer there.

"I was afraid this might happen," Jaylor said.

Brevelan looked at him as she spread the woolen cloak over Darville's now shivering form.

"He's been a wolf for many moons. It's going to take some time for him to remember what it means to be fully human." Jaylor's voice gained a little strength. The pulse in his neck still beat in irregular tattoo.

"Will he remember the time he spent as a . . . as . . . under my care." Heat crept up her face. During that time she'd had no need for modesty. Darville had been just another animal. Why should she hide her body from him?

"I don't know."

She turned from her embarrassment to practical matters. "We need to find a place to camp for tonight. I know you are both exhausted, and Mica still hurts, but Old

Thorm will come back. Soon. We must hide from his wrath until we are all rested and stronger."

"We have to go after that man," Darville croaked. He stretched his legs and stood slowly. She could see discomfort cross his face as he adjusted to his new posture.

"We'd waste more time than we'd save," she asserted, then looked away. She'd forgotten who he was. One didn't address the prince of the realm in that tone. She should have shown him more respect. That was hard to remember when she had been coaxing and ordering him around for moons.

"She's right," Jaylor groaned. His eyes were shadowed and his skin still had that gray tinge. "I have to rest, to eat. There is no more magic in me and not enough strength to gather more." He sniffed the air and frowned. "If there's any magic left."

Darville surveyed the cave. His eyes sought every crevice, assessing it as if it were a military encampment. "Very well." He strode to the entrance. His back was straight now, his step firm. "We might as well stay here. It's sheltered. There's wood for a fire and a spring at the back of the cave."

"What about . . . what about our enemy?" She couldn't bring herself to name him.

"I doubt he'll be back for several days. He's wounded, thanks to Mica. He's fatigued from throwing too much magic, and he must continue the spell to transport Shayla. We're safe here for tonight." Jaylor yawned and seemed to shrink within himself.

"I'll scout the perimeter," Darville announced. At the cave entrance he started to lift his left leg, just as the other Darville, the wolf, would have done to mark the edge of the camp. Face flaming, he stood straighter. "I don't suppose you have an extra pair of trews in your pack, old friend?"

Baamin guided his seeking flame back up the mountain. Slowly, warily, it crept toward the cave entrance. He pushed beyond aching eyes and throbbing head to make the flame go where he sent it.

He met no resistance at the cave mouth this time. The

weakened spark of green flame hovered and tried to retreat again. Apprehension grew in the old magician's breast. Never before had a spell fought him like this. Drawing on his newly found reserves of magic, he forced the tiny flicker of light to move onward, deep into the mountain.

There, finally, it found its like, another fire maintained but shielded by a magician's stare.

"Jaylor, at last!" Baamin breathed a sigh of relief. "What is happening? Where is Shayla?"

"Baamin?" The boy's startlement relieved the older magician's subtle fears. They were back to their normal relationship of master and journeyman. Last time they had talked, Jaylor had been in control of the magic as well as the interview, a man fully grown and worthy of his master's cloak.

"Who else would call in this manner?" Baamin almost chuckled. But his errand was too vital to linger in polite conversation. "Answer me. I fear that time is of the essence. Where is Shayla?"

"Gone, sir."

"Gone! She can't leave. She is tied to this kingdom by instinct and by magic."

"Perhaps I should say stolen and enthralled. The rogue transformed her into glass."

The image of a giant crystal, reflecting back the light of a hundred moons flooded Baamin's mind. "How? Why?" He stammered.

"To gain a kingdom."

"And the wolf?" Defeat dragged at his shoulders. With Shayla enchanted so, too, would the king be. If the golden wolf were indeed the missing prince, as Baamin had suspected all along, he had to be restored and returned to Coronnan City. Now.

"Nearly his old self, sir."

The boy didn't elaborate. No image of the wolf or his restored form came through the flame. Something was wrong.

"There was a man beneath the glamour of golden fur, wasn't there?"

Jaylor nodded wearily.

"Can you do anything about him?"

"I did."

The image of Darville riding through the woods on a spirited steed flashed across Baamin's mind's eye. Darville as he had been last autumn, before his disappearance.

"Wonderful, boy. Wonderful." For the first time in weeks, Baamin knew relief. "We need him in Coronnan City immediately."

"Weeks of travel at best, sir. And, sir, there are . . . um . . . complications." Jaylor stalled.

"What am I to tell the Council of Provinces and the king?" If the king were still alive.

"As little as possible. We follow the rogue at dawn."

"To what purpose?" The candle flame leaped higher. An ember of hope glimmered from Jaylor's end of the summons.

"To rescue a glass dragon." Jaylor hadn't used that flippant tone since he'd broken the spell on the wine cellar door and replaced it with one even the masters couldn't reverse. His inebriated, taunting laugh had haunted them for weeks. "Are you drunk, journeyman?" Baamin forced sternness into his voice.

"No, sir." His reply was slightly subdued. "Just fatigued beyond caring."

A sense of the great magic the boy had worked that day washed over Baamin. He understood. He gulped. If Jaylor had truly fought Krej's rogue that hard and then found enough strength to restore the prince, his magical prowess was greater than anyone had believed possible. He was a master already, without the talisman of the cloak.

Baamin was talking to a stronger magician than the entire Commune combined. He needed more information.

CHAPTER 20

Fatigue pulled Jaylor's eyes closed. The campfire Brevelan had built at the rear of the cave gave him enough warmth to still his trembling muscles. His stomach was pleasantly filled with one of her rooty stews. Already the nutrition had begun to replenish his body. An herbal tea soothed his body's aches. Mica purred gently in his lap. He should be able to sleep.

Yet the image of Lord Krej's face slipping through the mask of the beast-headed monster disturbed him almost as much as his own exhaustion. He had to put a stop to the man's treachery. But who would believe him? To accuse a member of the Council of Provinces, without physical evidence, invited trouble. The evidence of his eyes and ears while ensorcelled by a rogue magician was no proof a mundane man could accept.

His mind tumbled and spun with the day's events and the conversation on the other side of the fire.

"I feel as if I know you." Darville nursed a cup of the same herbal tea.

"You do," Brevelan's soft lilting voice replied in even tones. Yet Jaylor could hear the tension behind her words.

"No. I'd remember you if I did. You're too beautiful to forget." The prince's voice became lilting in flirtation.

Jaylor knew how the patterns of Darville's speech changed when he spoke to women—whether he wanted the woman or not. It was his nature to flirt with all of them, old or young, beautiful or plain.

Jealousy gnawed at Jaylor's innards like a hunger.

"Why were you in the wild mountains with Krej last

winter?" Jaylor found himself interrupting their quiet conversation.

"He wanted to hunt a spotted saber cat." Darville replied. "I needed to get away. It seemed like the ideal recreation." His eyes never left Brevelan. He reached to touch a tiny curl at her temple but stopped short of touching her.

Mica ceased purring. Her head lifted, ears back, eyes narrowing suspiciously. She watched the prince through rounded pupils. She knew what was happening, even if Brevelan did not. Jaylor willed the cat to distract her mistress.

"We encountered a saber on our journey here," Brevelan said. Subtly she shifted away from Darville.

Jaylor breathed a little easier. As much as he liked his royal friend, enjoyed his company, he didn't trust him around women. Their teenage escapades were more legend than truth. Still, Darville had never been forced to curb his natural curiosity and hunger for women as Jaylor had.

"Perhaps it was the same saber cat. Krej said it had escaped from his nets and he'd tracked it this far." Darville gave up watching Brevelan.

"The only saber reported within the kingdom in the last generation was the sculpted one in Krej's hall."

Darville looked from Jaylor to Brevelan and back again in obvious question.

Brevelan turned her gaze away from both of them. "Krej, or his magician, captures rare animals and changes them into precious metals. Didn't you hear him say his spotted saber cat was bronze, but he had to let it go?" Now her eyes sought Jaylor's, seeking confirmation.

"I wasn't paying much attention. I was too busy fighting his magic." But he had heard other, more disturbing things.

"That makes sense," Darville mused. "I saw the saber cat. We were tracking it. Then Krej disappeared and that monster attacked me with magic." His voice rose in anger.

"Krej led you into a trap," Jaylor asserted. "You are all that stands between him and the throne."

"My father. . .?"

"Your father is ailing. He has never been strong. Your disappearance and supposed death could very well kill him. He may be dead already."

"And this traitor of a cousin," Darville spat the word, "has been hiding his pet rogue for years. That is the only way he could hope to defeat me. A conventional attack by a warrior would not have succeeded." He stood up and began to pace.

His borrowed trews were too short and too loose. He looked less than majestic as he prowled the perimeter of their camp. "What will happen to the kingdom now that Shayla has been enchanted?" He whirled to face Jaylor directly.

"I don't know."

"Can the Commune of Magicians maintain the border without the dragons?"

"Doubtful. It was breaking down weeks ago when I passed through it."

The prince paced again. "We have neighbors who envy our peace and need our resources. As soon as they discover the open border, we are vulnerable to invasion." He sat again, not on a rock, but on the ground, crouched. His head tilted and one foot came up to scratch. But his body no longer twisted in that manner.

His face and neck flamed in embarrassment.

"What am I, magician, a man or a wolf?"

"You are a man now. You were a wolf for many moons. Some of those instincts linger. It may take a few weeks to forget." Jaylor looked into the fire, hoping to find some solutions in its green flames.

"I can't wait that long!"

"There is nothing more I can do. You alone must overcome those . . . memories." What else could he call them?

"But I don't remember being a wolf, other than those last few minutes before you restored me."

"Nevertheless, you were a wolf. Brevelan cared for you in that guise all winter."

"Brevelan?" He turned toward her, eyes wide. He started to lean against her leg, as he used to. "Brevelan. I do know you. You wouldn't let me hunt near you." He reached for her hand. His long fingers stroked the palm.

"Aye" she whispered in reply. But she didn't try to pull her hand away.

"Will you care for me again? Will you come with me to Coronnan City? I need you to guide me until I am fully me again." Darville kissed the back of her hand, as he would the hand of any court lady.

"No," Jaylor found himself answering instead. "I need her with me. I have to restore Shayla. She will be one very angry dragon when she comes out of the spell. Brevelan is the only one she trusts. Only Brevelan can keep Shayla from flaming the entire kingdom in revenge for the actions of your cousin." Mica butted her head against his hand in agreement.

"Then I must go with you, too. Without Shayla the male dragons will desert the kingdom. They must honor their bonds to me and stay." As he had many times in past months, Darville curved his jaws around Brevelan's delicate wrist in wolf greeting.

I have my beautiful dragon. She is crystal and light. Sunshine will refract from her into a million rainbows. The false Stargods could not produce a miracle so beautiful as my dragon.

Only Simurgh has the power to change my dragon into glass.

I have used all of my Tambootie. I must have more to get me back to the capital before the Council knows I have been gone.

The illusion of my visage on the body of young Lord Marnak cannot last much longer. If the boy wishes to consummate his marriage to my Rejiia, he will follow my orders and retire from court. Disaster will follow if his pockmarked face emerges through my illusion.

These mountains are full of my trees of magic. In the village there is one who owes me his soul. He will face the dangers and gather the leaves willingly.

With a fresh supply, this headache will leave me once and for all. I will have the strength to finish what has been ordained by Simurgh. I have my dragon.

So, now she knew for sure. Krej, her natural father, hadn't hired a rogue magician. *He* was the rogue. She'd know his evil laugh anywhere. Brevelan pondered yesterday's events while she busied herself with preparations for the journey back down the mountain.

Jaylor already suspected her true parentage. Had he seen through the monster mask as well?

If he hadn't, she dare not speak that truth. Jaylor might believe her, but no one else would. She was Krej's bastard, accused of witchcraft, and a runaway from justice. To accuse a member of the Council of rogue magic promised dire consequences for herself.

She must keep her own counsel.

Did Jaylor remember Krej's comments? He had given no indication that he had heard the magician accuse them of being lovers. If he had heard, he hadn't acted upon it. Most men she knew would have taken Krej's assumption as permission from a father to proceed.

She shook her head and roused herself from her thoughts. The day beckoned with a myriad of tasks.

Brevelan watched Darville draw lines in the dirt. His stick described the great arc of the bay. At its apex he inscribed a small circle, Coronnan City. Radiating outward from the capital, the boundaries of the twelve provinces took form. Then he added the mountains that nearly encircled the kingdom. At the southeastern corner he marked a large X.

"Crude, but accurate enough for our purposes." Jaylor examined the drawing. The sparkle in his eyes denoted the return of his good humor. He was still a little pale, and tight lines formed beside his mouth. But his muscles were firm, and his feet made restless patterns on the cave floor.

"Can you do better?" Darville stood from his crouch beside the map to his full height. He was defensive, yet easy with his old friend.

"Only with magic," Jaylor admitted. "And that I would rather conserve right now."

Brevelan watched the two men stare at each other, measuring and assessing. She was reminded of two dominant hunting dogs in the village kennels. Rivals as well as work mates. Rivals for what?

Jaylor's eyes caught her own and lingered. Darville too sought to capture her gaze. She raised her chin and stared out the cave entrance defiantly. She would not be the center of their contest. As soon as Shayla was restored, Brevelan would return to the privacy of her clearing. And the loneliness.

"Once the rogue gets out of the mountains, he can put his burden on a sledge." Darville avoided naming the nature of that burden. All three of them shivered. "He shouldn't be hard to track in these hills. We've lost part of a day. But we travel light, and we don't need to guard our backs."

"On the contrary, Darville." Jaylor added a few details to the map. "In the mountains he need only levitate the dragon. She's heavy, but then so is a wine cup to an apprentice. For a magician so practiced and grown so strong, his travel through here," he pointed to the southern mountains on the map, "will be easy. We have a better chance of catching him closer to other people, where he must travel surreptitiously." He surveyed the map which was now more complete, a few lines redrawn to make it more accurate.

"Which pass will he take out of here?" Darville crouched again to examine their handiwork.

"This one." Brevelan found herself pointing outside the cave toward a valley between two lines of peaks. She didn't need a map. She could follow Shayla without one, she realized. A faint glimmer of the dragon had reawakened in the back of her heart.

"Not likely," Darville contradicted. "This one is wider, easier." He pointed to a different valley.

"This one is more familiar and direct. It is where he left you to die, knowing no one would try to help an injured wolf when they sought a missing prince," Brevelan asserted.

"No one but you." Darville's gaze softened as he searched her eyes.

"I'm an outcast from my people because I do such things. Thorm couldn't know I was near enough for Shayla to call." She had to remember not to refer to the rogue by his true name.

"There is a lot this rogue doesn't know," Jaylor interrupted. "But he is so arrogant he won't admit there is anything about magic he can't master. That is our true advantage. He thinks my magic traditional and therefore damaged with the loss of Shayla. He will travel openly in the mountains because he thinks he frightened us into believing he is all-powerful."

"He's not all-powerful. He had to fight us to complete his spells," Brevelan added. She raised her eyes to the tall magician, who moved restlessly back and forth near the cave opening.

A raindrop landed on the rocks outside. It was fat and heavy, the prelude to more to come. A damp breeze found its way into the cave.

"Thorm had to draw magic away from Darville to finish his work with Shayla," Jaylor mused as he paced. "So we know his powers, great as they are, have limits."

"If we tax his strength every step of the way, perhaps he will have to drop the spell a little to deal with us." Darville's enthusiasm for the upcoming battle speeded up his own steps around the cave.

"First we have to find him. Let's go." Jaylor gathered his pack and staff.

"It's raining." Brevelan draped her thin, homespun cloak about her shoulders. They both looked at Darville in his borrowed, ill-fitting trews and cloak.

"I can't stop the rain. Only dragons are supposed to have power over the weather," Jaylor said.

"Without the dragons, the rains will be as heavy as they are in SeLenicca—so heavy they damage food crops. Only trees thrive in that amount of rain," Darville re-

minded them. "Spring will be delayed, crops will fail."
Some of his eagerness faded.

"And people will die," Brevelan said.

"I can't change the weather, but I can provide for us."
Jaylor set down his pack. He grabbed his staff with both
hands.

Brevelan felt the change in the energy pulsating from
Jaylor's body. A ball of sparkling lights flew into the
cave. Then a small puff of wind brought a new pack,
filled with journey foods, and deposited it tidily at her
feet. From its top spilled a new cloak, similar to Jaylor's,
but smaller, to fit her shorter height. She dipped her
hands into the folds of thick wool and snuggled it against
her face. It smelled new and fresh and clean. She felt
warmer already.

Beside her bundle, another appeared. More food and
clothes for Darville. "Raiding the University stores
again?" he asked Jaylor. A smile tugged at his lips. Had
Jaylor done this often to supply their boyhood pranks?

"They were intended for the use and comfort of students. I'm still a student, technically." Jaylor shrugged as
he reclaimed his own cloak from his prince. "Get
changed. We need to move."

"Just who is in command here?" Darville whirled to
face the magician. Brevelan held her breath, unsure of her
own reaction to this minor skirmish for authority.

She braced herself for the onslaught of strong emotions
that always accompanied this kind of confrontation. She
was so prepared she barely felt the slight whoosh that hit
her.

"I am," Jaylor replied. "We are dealing with magic, not
armies and soldiers. I am the better equipped to decided
our strategy."

He had tight control over his emotions. Darville bared
his teeth and growled deeply. The hair on the back of his
head began to bristle. She sent him enough peace of mind
to ease her own tensions.

"And I am your prince, possibly king already!"

"You are still partly wolf, and I can make you one

again if you push me." There was no malice in Jaylor's voice, only authority.

"Would you really?" Darville laughed at the obvious absurdity.

"If necessary." Jaylor smiled too.

"And I will make you both rabbits if we don't begin this quest," Brevelan replied. She looked back at them from the entrance. "Are you coming, boys?"

As they passed in front of her, Brevelan tugged at Jaylor's sleeve. "Jaylor, if it is this easy for you to transport food and clothing across the kingdom, what will prevent Thorm from sending Shayla to his castle by the same method?"

"I don't know. Unless she is still alive within the glass and transport will kill her."

CHAPTER 21

The sensation of being followed crawled up Jaylor's back like a swarm of hungry wood ticks. He shrugged his shoulders underneath his pack.

"Mrreww," Mica protested sleepily from her customary perch.

"Oh, hush, Mica." He reached up to scratch between her ears. She rubbed her head against his palm, and he felt her concern.

"Who follows us, Mica, when we know our enemy is ahead?" he whispered to the cat even as he checked Brevelan's position in front of him. Darville strode beside her. Jaylor could see in the unevenness of each step that the prince was having trouble matching his impatient stride to her short legs. The need to range ahead, then circle behind haunted Darville.

"What's wrong?" Brevelan swung around to face Jaylor.

Darville stopped, too. His hand reached for a sword that, under normal circumstances, should swing at his hip. At the same time his lips pulled back in a snarl. His nose twitched, testing the air.

"Mica thinks we're being followed." Jaylor continued to stroke the cat's ears.

"Are we?" Brevelan's eyes searched about her. She too was stretching her senses.

"I think so."

"Into the bushes." Darville pushed them off the path into the low shrubbery.

Around the smaller plants that verged on the path, taller, straighter trees cast sheltering shadows. Jaylor looked at each trunk until he realized he was searching for the distinctive mottled bark of the Tambootie. It was early spring, with little chance of finding any timboor to help hide them. On this, the uphill side of the path the trees were all long-needled everblues. Their pungent resin filled his nose and mouth with a healthy clean scent.

Across the path, on the downhill slope, nestled a clump of the trees he sought. His senses were so filled with everblue, he couldn't smell the Tambootie, nor could he see the bark in the deep shadows. However, the unmistakable flat tops of the trees lower down the hill were clearly visible.

"Stay down," Darville hissed at him.

Jaylor wasn't aware that he had half stood. He crouched down again. Tight muscles in his thighs and back reminded him of yesterday's exertions. Darville was as comfortable sitting on his haunches as he had been the day before—when he was still a wolf.

The hiss of Brevelan's deep, in-drawn breath alerted him to the presence of their followers. He desperately needed to ask what she felt from the intruders. Darville's glare warned him that absolute silence was essential.

"There's another dragon tree." One voice drifted to them from around a curve in the path.

"Ain't we got enough *s'murghin'* leaves for the master?" A second, gruffer voice responded. The timbre of the voice triggered a sour taste in Jaylor's mouth. Why?

"Master said two baskets full. Then meet him where the creek joins the river that flows to the bay."

Brevelan's eyes went wide. Shock stilled her features. She knew something.

From somewhere deep inside him, Jaylor found a thin line of magic. He strung it out in an umbilical to Brevelan.

The meeting place, it's close to the village, on the back path to my clearing. Her thoughts came to him clearly. But she held something back, as if she sensed his magical eavesdropping.

What, my sweet? What disturbs you? he prodded.

The barkeep.

The gruff-voiced man. The rancid taste of steed-piss ale. The man approaching them had been among the villagers who tried to burn Brevelan's home. He would acknowledge only one master—his legal lord, Krej.

The other man is a steward at Krej's castle. He, too, may be a magician. Brevelan's thoughts found him on their own.

"That one." The two men came into view. The steward pointed to a healthy tree, not quite as tall as its neighbors. The barkeep set down his two oversized baskets. One was full, nestled into the other, empty one. "Don't look big enough to climb to the top," the barkeep grumbled.

"You don't have to go to the top to get the new leaf shoots."

"Your master specified top leaves only."

"Because dragons eat from the top. That's the only part of the tree they can reach while they fly. I'm sure a dragon would nibble any part of a Tambootie tree it could get to. Just fill the basket so we can move on."

"Can't understand why," the barkeep whined as he stooped to separate the baskets. "Ain't good for nothin'. Can't even eat 'em. Almost as poison as the fruit. Poison to every livin' thing except *s'murghin'* dragons."

Almost as poison as timboor? Jaylor pondered the statement. He could eat timboor, so could Brevelan. He'd bet Darville couldn't, nor the barkeep or Krej's steward. But the master himself, Krej, Lord of Faciar, cousin to the king, and rogue magician, probably could. What was his use for the leaves of the same tree? And was this the evidence he sought to convict the rogue in the eyes of the Council?

"Just get to work. And stop grumbling," the steward ordered. "When Krej is king, you won't question his orders."

Darville growled. He reached for the absent sword even as he leaped onto the path to challenge the two men.

Mistake. Once again the wolf instincts to defend had taken over. Jaylor couldn't take a chance. If either of the men should recognize their prince, and escape, Krej would know that Darville was restored. That piece of information had to be kept secret for as long as possible.

Jaylor's magic caught up with Darville in mid-leap. From one eye-blink to the next, a bundle of clothes landed on the path as the angry prince grew shorter, hairier, meaner, and even more angry. Once more he was a menacing wolf determined to rip out the throats of his adversaries.

The shock of landing on all fours sent ripples of pain along Darville's back. The unnatural jarring did not disturb the momentum of his quest. The two men needed to die. He needed to do the deed. His eyes narrowed. From deep in his belly came the sound of blood lust. He leaped again before the men could react.

The first man, the one he'd never seen before, was his target. Familiarity with the other man made him divert his attack. But they were both evil. They both would die.

His weight carried both himself and the man to the ground. Triumph pounded through him as his mouth watered. Saliva dripped from his teeth. He could taste the hot blood even before he sank his fangs into the quivering, pale flesh of the hairless man.

This man would die easily. Then he would kill the other.

Screams erupted around him. He paid no heed.

Louder they came. And louder again. They were the screams of the man beneath him. He shouldn't be able to make a sound with his throat ripped and his blood in Darville's mouth.

A cry of distress penetrated his need to kill. The distress grew and became his own. Brevelan called him.

The death of this man would kill Brevelan as well.

Brevelan.

His other self.

He sat back on his haunches. The man rolled away and scrabbled up the slope. The other man was gone. His frantic cries echoed through the valley below as he slipped on the rough path.

"The witchwoman! The witchwoman lives. She has sent the wolf to kill us all."

Darville forgot the men and his need to kill. Brevelan was calling him.

He had defended Brevelan and sent the men fleeing. To show just how pleased he was with himself, he scooted downhill a few paces in mock pursuit. He stopped and bayed at his retreating quarry. The exercise burned some of the extra energy pounding through him. Then he bounded back to Brevelan's side, tail thumping.

Her foot invited him to sit on it. So he did. Her arm was within easy reach. He greeted her by taking her wrist, ever so gently, into his open mouth, even as he leaned his full weight into her.

Brevelan.

This was where he belonged.

Tears sprang to Brevelan's eyes. Darville's love and sense of belonging washed over her. She welcomed the familiarity of his wolfish greeting. She needed the warm contact of his body pressed against hers. For a few moments longer she cherished the bond that held him close.

"He is a man, Brevelan," Jaylor gently reminded her. "And a prince."

"I know." She choked out the words. A huge lump formed in her throat. Her body ached for the wolf to continue leaning into her. It was not to be.

"Step away, Brevelan. I need to change him back."

"I know." This time she couldn't watch. She pulled her long braid over her shoulder and played with the bark fastening. The tendrils of escaping hair took her concentration. She loosed them, ran her fingers through the long strands. Deftly she rebraided the distinctive red hair.

No matter where she went, its rare color stood out, identified her with Krej. She would always be known as a witchwoman, whether she had magic or not, just because of her hair.

"When you have finished, give me your knife." she commanded Jaylor.

"Why?" He sounded startled.

"I wish to cut off this braid. It's cumbersome, dirty. If we are to travel the length and breadth of the kingdom in search of Shayla, I do not wish to be burdened." She turned to stare at Jaylor, commanding him with her eyes.

"No," he returned flatly. Darville looked from one to the other, waiting for the magic that did not come.

"It is my hair, my choice."

"No." Jaylor took a step toward her.

She wanted to back away from his advance. His eyes held her in place. She remembered the thin coil of magic he had used to connect them. But once he had read her thoughts, once she had known the pattern of his mind in hers, she had returned the magic and spoken to him without words.

Something special bound her to him, just as she was bound to Darville.

She couldn't allow that to happen. She was destined to live her life alone. If she allowed herself to depend on these two men for comfort, companionship . . . love. . . .

"Give me your knife." She stiffened her resolve.

"Brevelan." He reached out an empty hand in entreaty. "Your hair is beautiful." His words were soft. She strained to hear them.

"Beautiful?"

"You are beautiful, unique, special. Please leave it."

Of its own volition her hand came up to touch his fingertips. It was like touching his mind again. As their hands joined, they were connected by that same something that had allowed her to send him words without speaking. A swirl of bright red and blue and copper magic encased them. She stepped into the circle of his arms. His lips touched the top of her hair.

The magic spun faster, tighter. He lifted her chin with one hand as the other held her against his broad chest. She raised up on tiptoe to be closer to him. Their lips touched. Jaylor deepened the kiss, merged with her, became one being with one mind, one idea, one goal.

Gently, Jaylor raised his head. A finger traced her lips. Wonder filled them both.

The magic died. As fast as it had sprung up, it faded.

Deep inside herself, Brevelan felt the emptiness of its absence. She looked into Jaylor's eyes and saw the same emotions. He looked deflated. She felt lonelier than ever.

"You will not cut your hair." Darville's deep voice penetrated her abstraction. He was once more a man and naked.

"Get dressed," Jaylor responded. He shook himself free of the lingering spell. She looked for the telltale signs of fatigue. They were absent. Jaylor didn't even look hungry.

"Those men got away. They'll talk. Our enemy will move faster, change his plans. We need to follow quickly." Darville moved briskly, efficiently, once more a prince and a soldier.

"I'll regather the scattered leaves." Jaylor made no move. Rather, he stood facing his old friend, spine rigid, eyes defiant.

"No. We haven't time," Darville decided.

"They were important to Krej's minions. I will find out why."

"No," Brevelan gasped. She stepped between the two tall men. "You mustn't. Tambootie is too dangerous!" She reached to touch his chest, to implore him not to experiment.

Darville took her other hand.

She gasped for air. Their jealousy was suffocating her.

"You seem to have lost weight, master magician."

Baamin looked a long way up to the man who broke the taboo and spoke to the Senior Magician before being addressed. Maarklin, the exceedingly tall magician to the court of Nunio, looked down his even longer nose toward Baamin. He still wore his blue master's cloak over his unadorned fire green robes. His height and natural bearing added elegance to the simplest garments. During their days as apprentices they had called the tallest of the class "Scrawny."

They'd called Baamin "Toad knees" then. No more. Now they called him "Master."

"The strain of the times," he replied with a dismissive

wave of his hand. There were reasons for his decrease in girth. Like a sudden revulsion for the taste of meat. Traditional magic required a magician to restore his body with animal protein. This rogue magic thrived on breads and roots. Meat now made him sluggish. But Scrawny didn't need to know that.

"Unusual summons, sir," commented Fraandalor, the member of the Commune posted to the court of Krej in Faciar. He too was tall, but slightly stooped, as if his blue cloak and shimmery gray robes were too heavy for his shoulders. Years ago he'd been known as "Slippy," like the sea snakes that washed up on the shores of the Great Bay every summer. Sea snakes provided a sweet nutritious meat when prepared properly. But the cook had to be careful lest careless cooking left a natural poison in the meal.

Baamin reminded himself that Slippy could very well have been corrupted by his lord's greed for power. Or by the temptations of rogue magic. Was Slippy the man wandering the southern mountains in the guise of Baamin's nightmares? Impossible. He couldn't have performed magic in Shayla's cave two days ago and be back in Coronnan City today.

"Unusual circumstances." Baamin perspired heavily under his formal court robes, blue cloak and trews, long gold tunic and fine cambric shirt that hung on his reducing belly. Responsibility and new powers lay uneasily on his shoulders.

"Gentlemen, please take your places." He waved them to the thirty-nine chairs placed around the formal table, made especially for the Commune of Magicians almost three hundred years ago. It was round, as tradition dictated, forged by dragon fire of solid black glass—perhaps the most valuable item in the entire kingdom.

Except for Shayla, Baamin thought. *A glass dragon is much more valuable.*

"Did you say something, sir?" The magician to his left raised a puzzled eyebrow.

"Just arranging my thoughts." Baamin took his own place farthest from the sealed door. The room was as round as the table, devoid of windows or decorative hangings. The only contents were the huge glass table and stone chairs. It was kept comfortably warm through a system of vents from the kitchen fires. Even so the perspiration turned cold on Baamin's back as he assumed his role as leader.

"A most inconvenient summons," Slippy reiterated.

"Most inconvenient circumstances." Baamin glared at the questioner. "Gentlemen, the king is gravely ill. He barely draws breath, his body does not move."

"That shouldn't make much difference," Scrawny snorted. "He hasn't done anything in years. By the time the kingdom realizes he's dead, we will have a smooth transition of power to Darville."

"There are . . . ah . . . complications." Baamin coughed.

All attention centered on him. His personal armor slid into place just before he felt their probes into his mind. Probes that were forbidden by traditional ethics. His armor was strong, fueled by his new inner powers. He easily absorbed the probes and turned them back to the senders.

The lines of magic honed into arrows of poison and sped back whence they came.

Seven of the twelve reared back in pain. Astonished at Baamin's individual power, they put all of their remaining magic back into their own armor. The slim traces of magic that had been in the room disappeared. The other five magicians slumped slightly from the attack, then straightened in respect. Their armor remained solid.

The five undoubtedly held rogue power. But did they know it? Had they practiced with it? Were they in league with other rogues?

"We are still a Commune," Baamin asserted. "And if we don't work together for a common good, the kingdom is in danger of collapsing."

"There isn't enough magic left," one of the seven protested. He was gray with fatigue from maintaining the little protection he could summon.

"Perhaps, perhaps not. But if we work together, we can overcome the problem without resorting to the jealousy and civil war that disrupted us once before. We may have to attract new dragons to the kingdom." The noise of their questions and protests assaulted his ears as painfully, but less dangerously, than their magic. Baamin reasserted his power over them without magic.

"I said together!" His voice boomed around the room. Silence.

"Shayla has been kidnapped and transformed into a glass statue by a rogue."

The silence became deeper, more profound.

"I have forces in the field seeking her location. We are the best-educated men in the kingdom. I need you here, searching for a solution to the divisions that threaten the Council." He speared each one with his gaze. The Commune had been built on interdependence, trust, and common goals. The Commune must continue with or without a king. With or without a dragon.

CHAPTER 22

Desperately, Baamin swam up through the folds of sleep. He had to awaken. He had to end these repetitive dreams.

Blackness closed over him, dragging him deeper into the world of his worst nightmares.

His own naked body pranced around and around a giant cave. His fuzzy sun and fog face sprouted long, long, longer teeth. Powerful muscles rippled beneath his sweating skin. A tune poured forth from his soul. Each note conveyed magic into the most massive spell of his life.

His magic swirled around an amorphous form of crystal.

Awe struck him nearly dumb. A dragon transformed into precious glass shimmered before him. He'd never seen a dragon before. Might never see one again.

At last the song died on his lips, and he fought for reality again.

Dawn glowed on the horizon outside his window. He sat up, panting for breath. Exhaustion still dragged at his muscles. Yet he feared to sleep again. If he closed his eyes, he would dream.

The same dream that had haunted him time and time again for the last four nights.

Was it all a dream, or had he actually transported himself to the southern mountains and wreaked havoc on the kingdom by kidnapping a glass dragon?

Darville sniffed the air for danger. The smell of smoke was old and wet. It permeated the clearing even now, some four or five days after the villagers had torched Brevelan's hut, probably only hours after she had left it.

His nose felt clogged. Then he remembered he was human again. His wolf senses were dulled.

"Let me scout around," he whispered.

Jaylor nodded in reply as he quietly set down his basket of salvaged Tambootie leaves.

Darville watched Brevelan's eyes fill with tears while her chin jutted forward. *Stargods!* but she was brave. Even though his memories of the moons he had lived here were dim, he knew this woman, knew all of her moods, her strengths, as well as her vulnerability. For her he vowed revenge. The prancing rogue and his *s'murghing* minions would pay for this destruction.

He scouted the perimeter of the clearing with care. No snapping twig or scuffling undergrowth betrayed presence. Every few steps he sniffed and tasted the air.

Maybe his senses were dulled. But he knew what danger should taste like. That combined with the soldier's skills he'd been taught since childhood should serve him well. But he'd feel a lot safer if his familiar sword hung from his belt, or if he could really smell again.

The clearing and its environs were empty. Had been for several days. He missed the rabbits and squirrels, the goat, and the nest of mice in the thatch. Only the partially destroyed hut and hints of memories remained.

Three-quarters of the way around the clearing his boots scuffed against something soft. Underneath a network of debris, he found the soft brown fur of a lop-eared rabbit. He recognized the small scar across the dead buck's nose. This had been one of Brevelan's pets. It had been trampled by heavy boots.

Darville's anger ran cold through the veins. The creature had probably returned to the clearing seeking shelter from the strangers who invaded this place, only to be caught in the melee.

Saying a silent farewell, he re-covered the rabbit with dead leaves and ferns. At least he could spare Brevelan the knowledge of this one small loss.

"They're gone. The area is completely empty," he informed his companions upon his return. "The thatch is gone, and part of one wall, but the hearth is undamaged."

"We'll stay the night," Brevelan decided for them. "I'll gather kindling. You two get to work on a roof of some kind."

Darville looked at Jaylor. A spark of animation hit his friend's eyes.

"Yes, Mother," they replied to her stiff back as she marched into her ruined home.

"Remember to wash when you're finished," she called back over her shoulder. "Little boys need to bathe every evening," she scolded them. A false note tinged her levity.

"Think she'll feed us real food if we behave?" Darville thought greedily of a thick haunch of venison. But he doubted he'd be able to eat rabbit again.

"Depends on how you define real." Jaylor avoided his eyes.

Darville felt his old friend's laughter. "I mean some meat. Roots and gruel can't fill an empty belly after a day's hard work."

"They will fill you if you let them." Jaylor finally looked at him.

This time Darville looked away. His belly felt slack. It protested constantly. He knew Jaylor had felt the same hungers many times in the last two days. Yet he had accepted Brevelan's meatless diet. "I don't think I can continue to work hard and walk all day without meat," he replied sheepishly.

"I could change you back into a wolf for a few hours, let you hunt." Jaylor's face looked bland, except for a tiny twitch at the corner of his mouth. The same twitch that had been a signal for a new mischief when they were children.

"Would it be for only a few hours?" Darville was skeptical. He knew his friend's penchant for practical jokes.

Once, when Jaylor was thirteen and he fifteen, their gang of wild and restless friends found sport in tormenting a stray dog. Sickened by the cur's pitiful squeals of pain and confusion, Darville had flung himself into the midst of the cruelty, fists flying. Jaylor wasn't far behind. When fighting the older and more numerous boys proved futile, Jaylor had used his waning strength to throw a spell. Each of the bullies sprouted a dog's tail.

And the tails were tied together with bits of devil's vine. A particularly thorny, choking, and pernicious weed.

Confused, the bullies had chased each other in circles, trying to unite their bonds, pricking their fingers, and unable to remove the thorns or the knots.

The stray dog had bounded free.

That memory reassured Darville. Jaylor wouldn't leave him in wolf form for long. And then he wouldn't have to eat another stew of roots and herbs.

"It's a deal. Do you want me to save you some of the kill?"

Jaylor's face fell. Darville felt chagrined. He'd used the wrong words.

Kill.

Brevelan could never forget that each bite of meat had once been a life.

"I guess not." Darville tried to smile. "After we fix the roof, we can take a dip in the pond."

"You splash too much," Jaylor replied, his own sense of humor returning.

"Only when you dunk me."

"Who, me?"

Darville slapped him roughly on the shoulder. "Of course, you. You've been doing it since we were babes in short britches. You never could resist rubbing it in that you were bigger than I."

"Younger, too."

"Not as smart."

"Stronger and more stubborn."

"That's for sure." They continued to wrestle as they crossed the clearing and began working on the thatch.

"It's too dangerous," Brevelan affirmed to Jaylor.

Jaylor tried to ignore her.

"I agree." Darville faced him, hands on hips, shoulders

back and chin thrust out. "We haven't time for you to experiment. Old Thorm, or whoever that rogue might be, is probably already out of the mountains."

Brevelan and the prince were joining forces against Jaylor's determination. He wasn't sure he could fight both of them. Darville was strong enough to knock him senseless. Brevelan had the power to persuade him of anything. Anything at all.

"Mbrrt!" Mica confirmed her own opinion of Jaylor's seeming foolishness. She paced in front of the warm hearth, round hazel eyes glowing, back arching.

"Not you, too, Mica?" Jaylor protested to the anxious cat. Her soft presence had always seemed supportive. Some of his determination slipped away when he raised his eyes from the basket full of Tambootie leaves.

The herbage had begun to wilt over the day and the night since it had been abandoned by Krej's steward and the barkeep. Still, the scent from the essential oils permeated Brevelan's partially repaired hut. A vacancy lingered behind his ears and his heart beat irregularly whenever he closed his eyes.

"This is too important to ignore. Krej and his pet rogue use the leaves in some way to increase magic powers. I have to understand how this works if I'm going to undo that very complicated, very powerful spell." Verbalizing helped define his motives. It also made sense of the floor that kept tilting toward the repaired roof.

"I'm sure he doesn't eat the poison. And even if he does, he'll wait until he's safely back at the castle." Brevelan grabbed a dented pot full of water and placed it over the flames to bring it to a simmer. The sputtering green flames lighted her face, highlighting her delicate features. The red of her hair took on a coppery glow, an elemental color firmly rooted in the soil of Coronnan.

Jaylor wanted to reach out and touch her gently, to reassure her and let her know he loved her. His fingers itched to bury themselves in her thick hair, separate each beautiful strand into a copper veil. The leaves called to him, begged him to forget the color that was grounded in the soil. Why not fly with the colors radiating from the wonderful leaves.

His hands continued to grip the basket on the floor in front of him.

"This is something I have to do." He returned his gaze to his study of the leaves. If only he could look into them, delve their secrets the way he looked into a spell book with his glass.

"I'm sure Krej uses an infusion. It's safer, easier to control the dosage." Brevelan continued her preparations for that procedure.

"Maybe he makes a salve of them and rubs it on his skin." Darville dipped his hands into the basket, then quickly withdrew them as if burned.

Jaylor ignored them. He sought the thin shard of glass in his pack. It was wrapped in a special oiled cloth, several layers thick. When he withdrew it, he felt for a tell-tale vibration out of habit. The glass was cold and lifeless. No one was summoning him.

With a special vision, used by all magicians when holding a glass, he sought the secrets of the leaves. Their image jumped at him, larger than life. He adjusted his hold on the glass, concentrating on the variegated green and white center vein of a particularly fat leaf that had not yet wilted. He forced his mind to look at the leaf as if it were just another spell cloaked in obscure language in a forgotten book.

"An infusion of sun-dried leaves is the logical answer. How could one man eat that many leaves? But it would take several basketsful to prepare a year's supply for an infusion," Brevelan chattered on.

Jaylor ignored her.

Mica climbed into his lap. She butted her head against his hand. He nearly dropped the glass.

Jaylor pushed the cat away. She protested and climbed back. Her almost human stare dared him to push her away again.

"Consult Baamin at the University. Maybe he knows what to do with Tambootie," Darville suggested.

Jaylor barely heard him. The continued comments of his friends no longer held import. There were only himself and the leaves of Tambootie enclosed within the walls of the hut.

A drop of thick oil on the spine of the leaf shimmered with green and gold, red and blue, purple and orange. All the colors that glowed through Shayla's fur were in that drop of all color/no color liquid. He touched the drop with his fingertip. It clung. He licked it off.

Sweet/bitter/cold/hot/bland/spicy.

All the flavors of the world burst forth on the tip of his tongue. He tasted all the colors, saw all the flavors. His soul expanded to find more colors, more tastes, new sensations.

Jaylor licked the spine of the leaf where he could see more drops. They exploded into his system, filling him with wisdom and knowledge.

Life was suddenly reduced to a simple equation.

Magic became natural and easy.

He licked the leaf again, chewed its green and white tip, needed more.

His mind soared upward, outward. His soul chose a different direction.

Dimly he knew he licked and chewed a second leaf, a purple one this time, then a third solid green and a fourth mottled pink and green. They gave him the power to merge his mind and body and soul. He chose to drift separately.

"Is he . . ." Brevelan gulped back her fear. "Is he . . . dead?" Fiery green ice sped through her rapidly numbing body. *Jaylor!* Her mind screamed. *Come back to me.*

Darville hunched over Jaylor's slumped form. He felt for life-sign at his friend's neck. He shook his head in puzzlement, then pushed his shaggy golden hair back out of his eyes and tried again. "I can't tell." He shook his head again, this time in despair.

"Let me." She shouldered him aside. Panic nearly choked her. Jaylor had eaten several leaves, perhaps six or seven, before she and Darville had noticed. They had pulled him away from the lethal basket of leaves, but not in time.

"Jaylor," she whispered.

Still no response.

Her mind called again in protest. *Come back to me!*

A faint vibration responded to her call, not from his body but from the void, above and beyond reality.

"Jaylor!" she demanded of the vibration.

It hummed and threatened to drift away, uninterested in her plea.

"Don't you dare leave me." She firmed her grasp on that thin thread of life.

It drifted no farther away but did not return.

When they had hidden in the bushes beside the path, Jaylor had used a thin umbilical of magic to touch her mind. Traces of that silver thread still trailed away from the faint vibration.

She searched her own soul for the other end of the fragile magic cord. It was buried deep, behind the tiny throbbing bit that was her connection with Shayla. Her end was copper, Shayla's was as transparent as glass. Color didn't matter. She had to splice or weave all the magic strands together.

I rode through the day and night for four days. Eight journey steeds died beneath me. I pressed them too hard with compulsions. They failed me. If only those fools hadn't lost the Tambootie, I could have flown to Coronnan City on the winds.

My magic is stretched too thin. My head aches. There are spots before my eyes. I had to abandon Shayla to my servants. They will transport her to the great hall by sledge. I must be in control of the Council before my agents lead the enemy army over the border. Coronnan will win the battle with them, but only if I am the one to lead our troops to victory. That is the arrangement made with Simeon of SeLenicca many moons ago.

I didn't have the strength to project my image onto

Marnak's body, nor through Scrawny's glass. The Council must not act without my "presence."

I must have my Tambootie to keep up this pace. Coronnan needs me even if the Council of Provinces doesn't know it yet.

CHAPTER 23

"**Y**ou and your cosseted Commune have failed, Baamin." Krej glowered at the magician who sat in the Council for the ailing king.

"In what way, Lord?" Baamin stalled. The Twelve—the lords of the Council—sat in a round room, larger and more luxuriously furnished than the one used by the Commune. The twelve windows boasted colored glass in the pattern of each lord's device. Their elaborately carved chairs bore the same designs. The thirteenth chair was specially carved with dragon heads curving over the top, dragon claws at the end of each arm and leg. It was empty now, reserved for the king.

Behind each lord and slightly to the right sat his magician. For three centuries, master magicians had been posted to the twelve courts as advisers and links to the king and Commune. For those same three centuries the magicians had owed first allegiance to the Commune, the combined body of all master magicians, rather than to any one lord—or king.

No one lord could gather power over another through his magician.

The system had been devised by the lords.

Now Krej was throwing doubt on the value of the Commune.

After the nightmares of the last week or more, Baamin questioned his own value within the Commune.

According to Jaylor, Krej had arranged the destruction of the dragon nimbus and therefore robbed the kingdom of Communal magic that could overpower any single rogue.

But how to prove it, when Baamin doubted Krej's guilt himself.

If the Commune was tightly knit, as protective of its individual members as they were of the whole, the Twelve were even more so. Krej's treason would have to be proved by concrete evidence, not magical observation.

"The western border is all but gone." Krej looked into the eyes of each lord in turn. "Raiders are infiltrating. I have pleas for help from six villages that have been sacked, burned, their men killed, and their women raped and kidnapped. Children wander hungry and homeless— vulnerable to the Rovers who also prowl our lands. Word of these tragedies will reach our jealous neighbors soon. They will mass their armies and attack, then they will take our unprotected resources rather than paying dearly for them. What do we have left to fight them with?"

Baamin felt a compulsion spell behind Krej's words as well as his magnetic gaze. Who dared throw such a spell? Outward magic was forbidden in Council. By law and tradition, a magician was allowed to communicate with his lord through magic but could throw no other spells.

Who had grown so strong that he defied this most valued of prohibitions?

"We have an army." Andrall, Lord of Nunio, Scrawny's affiliate lord, argued at the prodding of his magician. "We've kept them trained for just such an emergency."

"They've gone soft, fighting imaginary enemies," Krej returned. "And who is to lead them? King Darcine," he sneered the title, "is near death. His son is missing. Off dallying with his latest mistress, I presume."

"Don't you know where Darville secludes himself?" Baamin asked desperately. He tried to throw a truth spell over this domineering lord. The spell bounced back, neutralized and harmless.

Krej was armored. That spell was legal in Council, but it was usually thrown by a magician to include himself and his lord. Baamin couldn't detect the source of the spell.

"How should I know where our feckless prince has

wandered?" Krej stood and began pacing the room with calculated and controlled steps.

"Gentlemen," he addressed the room, "the kingdom is in crisis. Our protective border is disintegrating, our enemies are massing for attack. Rossemeyer on our southeastern border is demanding marriage to our prince or they will declare war. SeLenicca, to the west, claims such a marriage will be an act of war against them. And where are our beloved king and his son to sort out this nonsense? Darcine lies dying and Darville was last seen out hunting several moons ago. Neither is in a position to guide us. Even the Commune, which has protected us so long, has become ineffectual."

There were murmurs of anxious agreement around the room. No one questioned Krej's source of information. Baamin felt the five still strong magicians "nudge" their lords with reassurance. They were men he thought he could trust, men who had been close friends for many years.

The other magicians tried persuasion, without success. If they had powers beyond traditional magic, they didn't yet trust them enough to call upon them. These magicians were younger than himself. He knew them as masters but not as men. Could he trust them enough to teach them rogue magic?

"I have summoned Prince Darville home from his monastic retreat," Baamin stalled. He kept his shoulders straight, his face impassive. It would not do for Krej to penetrate his own armor and learn the extent of his magic as well as his doubts and fears. He couldn't forget that Krej's face had been beneath the mask of his nightmares at the ball.

"And how long will his return take? There are no monasteries within a week's hard ride." Krej answered his own question. "Gentlemen. We don't have that long. We need to take action now! We must show ourselves as strong enough to repulse all our enemies. Enemies that have been trying to penetrate our border for generations."

Krej's pacing ceased. He stood directly behind the king's chair, a copy of the throne in the Great Hall. His

position and posture effectively assumed control and
eliminated Baamin from view by the other Council members.
His handsome body and the high back of the throne
stood between the magician and the rest of the room.

"In the absence of the king, we, the Council of Provinces,
have the power to act for him," Andrall interjected.
"We can raise and provision an army, order the magicians
to summon the dragons, if necessary." His voice calmed
much of the turbulent emotion in the room. Scrawny was
prompting him.

Wasn't he? The "nudge" didn't feel right, didn't carry
Scrawny's signature. Baamin peered around Krej to get a
better view of his colleague. Andrall's magician was staring
at Krej as if enthralled. Slippy was actually prompting
the Lord of Nunio. Law specifically forbade a magician
to advise any but his own lord. And why was Krej's magician
prompting the one lord likely to stand up to Krej?

"What dragons?" Krej thundered. His voice echoed
about the room in ominous thunder rolls. All were
stunned into quiet.

"Have any of you ever seen a dragon?" Silence greeted
that question. "What good is a creature of myth? Where
is the magic they are supposed to give us? We must act
now, elect a leader." Himself no doubt. "And send what
is left of the army to fight the raiders. Let that be their
training ground for the conflict to come with the trained
troops and mercenaries our neighbors can summon."

"Our king still lives," Andrall reminded them. "We
don't need to elect a leader. As long as we are in accord,
we can function for him."

"Read your history, Lord Andrall," Krej sneered. "Do
you know what happens when you try to run a war by
committee?"

Several men in the room shuddered, including Baamin.
Stargods! Krej was right. The last time that had happened,
Coronnan had dissolved into fifty years of civil
war.

"In view of the circumstances," Lord Wendray from
the border city of Sambol stood and addressed the assembled
Council of Provinces, "very shortly I will be in dire

need of an army. The raiders grow stronger every hour. Even now I should be home organizing defenses. Gentlemen, I am a merchant, governing a merchant city on the western border, not a warrior. Give me an army to defend the vulnerable western reaches. But give me an army led by a capable general." He leaned heavily on his pudgy fists.

"There are several capable generals in our army," Lord Andrall argued.

"But none of them has ever seen real combat," Krej countered. "For that matter, no one within the kingdom has ever seen combat." He stood behind Scrawny for a moment.

Baamin watched their auras merge and grow. Scrawny! His oldest friend, the magician he trusted most, was in league with Krej. The joined aura of red and green magic expanded to include five lords and their magicians. All five men were linked to Krej by marriage or betrothal to one of his children. All five were weak, malleable men. None of their magicians—three of them old friends who had demonstrated rogue abilities—resisted the illegal magic persuasion.

Couldn't any of the other magicians see the magic? Why weren't they fighting it?

"You are the youngest, most fit and best educated of all of us." Lord Marnak, whose son was to marry Krej's fourteen-year-old daughter next moon, spoke in an enthralled monotone.

Hastily, Baamin summoned his own magic in a counter spell. Illegal though it might be, he had to break Krej's command over the Council.

Power rippled through his body. He massed it, allowed it to strengthen, then threw it at the buzzing aura of red and green haze. The power erupted from his mind in a silver-blue dart. He aimed it at Krej's heart. The illegal aura buckled a fraction under the assault. Krej closed his eyes in concentration. The red and green haze reformed around the shattered pieces of Baamin's magic.

Deep within the inviolate aura, Krej smiled. His eyes

narrowed, evilly. Baamin didn't have to hear his mocking laughter to know who had won this minor skirmish.

"Lord Krej is the best qualified to lead us out of this entanglement. He is the strongest and the closest relative to the king," Marnak mumbled on. "We must make him regent."

"I disagree!" Andrall stood in protest. The aura rippled around him but did not cover him. Who was protecting the Lord of Nunio if not his own magician?

"You have been outvoted, Andrall," Krej drawled. "I am now regent of Coronnan and I command you to be quiet while I make plans for our defense."

"You must rest, Brevelan." Darville's hands gently pressed her shoulders back against the thin pallet on her cot.

She shook her head in denial. "I can't." The words came out a croak. She swallowed deeply and spoke again. "If I let go, even for an instant, I will lose him."

As if in response to Darville's urging her to rest, her control over the thin copper and silver tendril of magic that held Jaylor to this reality came nearer to shredding. For three days she had maintained the contact. She had pulled on it, spliced it, rewoven it dozens of times, and still he resisted her tether.

A deep sadness threatened to engulf her. Could she continue to live without Jaylor? Yes, she could survive. But did she want to?

She'd known him less than a moon, and already his presence was as natural to her as breathing. She couldn't let him slip away.

She concentrated on splicing the bond that held them together. The scent of Tambootie floated through the hut.

"At what cost?" Darville sounded as cranky and impatient as she felt.

"How can you ask that?" she demanded. It had been so much easier when Darville was her favorite puppy. Now he was a man, a handsome man who filled the hut with his vibrant presence as much or more than Jaylor ever did.

They had cleared the hut of every trace of the cursed Tambootie leaves as soon as Jaylor's inert body failed to respond. But the drug was in his system. Removing it from the hut resulted in no change.

Then she had tried coaxing him back with more Tambootie. Still no change.

"He's my friend, too." Darville looked chastened. "For many years he was my only friend." He wandered to the open doorway where a thin shaft of sunlight tried to penetrate the interior. In the five days since Shayla's transformation, this was the first letup in the rain. "I learned early that the people at court befriended me because I represented power, glamour. Standing next to me made them feel bigger than they really were. Except Jaylor. And a few of the town boys who knew me only as Roy and not as a prince." He took a deep breath.

Brevelan felt his gentle memories. She had no energy left to strengthen his feeling of quiet nostalgia. She lay back upon the bed.

"It was easy for me to slip away from tutors and guardians. They were more interested in their own positions than in me. That's how I met Jaylor. He had slipped out, too. He likes being outdoors. He claims he can't think or study behind stone walls," he chuckled. "But when we were together, neither of us did much studying." His grin lifted with remembered mischief.

Brevelan drew Darville's emotions into herself. Carefully she allowed her body to relax while she wrapped Darville's pleasant reverie around her contact with Jaylor. Maybe this trip through childhood memories would encourage his spirit to return.

"We were constantly in trouble. No one had ever allowed either of us to play before. We gave each other that ability."

"I'm happy you found one true friend. It's important to someone in a position of power. Jaylor will always be someone you can trust."

"Because he loves me and not my position. He has his magic. That's stronger than any temporal power I could grant him."

They were quiet a moment. Brevelan used the time to check her tie to Jaylor. It was stronger and so was the Tambootie smell. She relaxed a little more, easing the tired strain on her neck and back.

"But it was you who rescued me, nurtured me, taught me to trust again." He whirled to face her. "I can't lose you, too!"

"His spirit has not drifted farther away. I must believe he means to return to us. When he can." She tried to let Darville feel her concern for both of them. It was a weak attempt. Too much of her energy was still channeled into her fragile contact with Jaylor.

"We need him to restore Shayla." Darville sounded defeated. "I sense the male dragons want to leave the kingdom if she and the litter she carries aren't returned soon." Despair tinged his posture as well as his voice.

"How are you linked to them?" Was it similar to her own awareness of Shayla, a link she held even now entwined and braided with her contact to Jaylor.

"They, the entire nimbus, are just there, somewhere in the back of my head, or my heart. I don't know which. I do know where each one is, when they mate, when they have disputes." His excitement turned to a deep sigh. "When they die."

Brevelan looked deeper into herself. Only Shayla was there. Her mates were missing.

"And your father?" she prompted.

"For three hundred years, there has been a special . . ." he reached for the right words. "A special link between a king and his dragons. The royals are aware from birth, but only the anointed and consecrated king is bound so tightly his very life is affected by the health of nimbus. I've never had the 'why' explained."

They both shivered. Shayla was encased in glass. What had that done to the king?

They had no way of knowing what was transpiring in Coronnan City. Jaylor had had no contact with Baamin since the night in Shayla's cave.

"So that's why your father has always been sickly," she stated flatly.

"Ten and twelve years ago several villages, not just the one here, went dragon hunting," Darville explained. "I was twelve the first time. Too young to lead the Council."

Mica came in from her scout of the clearing. She butted her head into Darville's ankle. He stooped to pick her up. With the purring cat on his shoulder, he continued his narrative. His words took on the cadence of the cat's purr. The rhythm drifted over Brevelan like a soothing song.

"Over the centuries, people have forgotten the wondrous things dragons did for the kingdom during the Great Wars of Disruption. Nimbulan lured the dragons to Coronnan—they were mostly very young dragons seeking nests of their own. I don't know how he gained their loyalty, but they went into battle for him, found a lord worthy of the crown, ended the long years of civil war."

"Why kill them? I really can't understand why our people went so far out of their way to murder such wondrous creatures."

"Not everyone can see the beauty, the majesty, the magic in our dragons. They have forgotten why we owe the dragons a debt of gratitude. Some know only that they raid cow pastures and scoop boatloads of fish out of the bay. The original pact with the dragons guaranteed them hunting rights and tithes of livestock. In normal years there is more than enough for both people and dragons. But in bad years, when people are living on the edge, just barely surviving, they look for a cause. Some found the dragons' natural feeding habits a good reason for their own failure." They both shivered at the implications.

The magic umbilical tugged from Jaylor's end. Some portion of him was aware of the conversation. He had something to add.

"Jaylor thinks Lord Krej deliberately impoverished his province to foster that notion. The Equinox Pylons have gone undecorated for over a dozen years." She felt lighter, less tired. Jaylor wasn't actively trying to escape his ties to Coronnan. He was interested. He would return.

But when?

Darville whirled about, his shaggy blond mane flying

in agitation. "Krej can't undermine the welfare of his own people! He took oaths when he assumed the lordship."

"Men can break oaths, can never mean to keep them even when swearing." Like a husband who vows to cherish a new wife and then abuses her.

"I have to remember my 'wonderful' cousin is really a traitor, capable of anything. Last year, when Jaylor was engrossed in his exams, I was very lonely. Krej became a constant companion. I thought he was a friend, too." He sighed. Mica butted her head against his chin in sympathy.

Brevelan felt his loneliness. It became her own. She reached a tentative hand to touch his cheek. The contact sent tingles through her body. She was reminded of the times Jaylor had kissed her. She needn't fear a man's touch, only certain men's. She spread her hand to cup his face. He leaned into the caress and kissed her palm.

"We'll work it out, Brevelan. But you must rest, even if you don't sleep." Gently he guided her shoulders back onto the bed. A deep warmth and contentment engulfed her.

She closed her eyes for just a second. The thin strands of copper, silver, and glass that held Jaylor to Coronnan dissolved.

CHAPTER 24

Quiet drifting. Light and shadow. Heat from the sun, cool from the moon. He slid upward until the colors and patterns of Coronnan melted together. A copper thread dangled from his hand.

He caught a purple updraft, found a dragon playing there. He grabbed hold of a silvery green wing and allowed the creature to guide him through the pink air.

Upward they soared. Blue wind rushed past them. The yellow-red-green-yellow sun came closer. Their speed slowed as they reached the ultimate height. They hovered a moment, cherishing the wild sense of life pumping through each of them. Their hearts beat as one, and the wind harmonized by thundering past them in an interesting counter rhythm.

Below, the green land divided itself into puzzle pieces with bluish-silver lines of magic. The lines resembled the fragile cord, sometimes copper, sometimes silver, bonding him to the body he had abandoned an eon ago. A few white cloud puffs obscured any other borders, the ones established by men but recognized by no one else. The magic border that should surround this insignificant patch of green had faded to nothing.

Sharply downward they plunged, so fast their breath was pushed back into their throats. Sharp cold air became a wall. They pushed it aside with the blink of an eye. A steep cliff of black granite rushed to greet them. At the last moment they flattened wings and pulled up to soar again over the top. Flushed and exhilarated, they leveled off.

Together they surveyed the snowcapped mountains.

Their bellies were numb. The game lurking in shadowed
ravines offered no interest or relief. But a Tambootie tree
needed cropping. Compulsively they snatched at the top
layer of new leaves as they skimmed past, away from the
sheltering mountains.

Over level ground again, a different dragon flew under
them. He switched from the green wing to the blue back.
A moment's unsteadiness. Then he found a new pulse and
he merged his identity with the older dragon.

This dragon flew more intricate patterns. They dipped
and soared, played with the wind, spun and reversed in a
tail's length.

A city squatted like an ugly beetle on the islands of the
Bay delta, enmeshed in an intricate web of bluish-silver
magic.

They spied on puny creatures below as they went about
incomprehensible tasks. Some battled, some coupled,
some slept.

Many men met in a closed room.

Time rolled forward and back, sometimes quickly,
sometimes drifting as lazily as he.

A familiar man, cloaked in a dirty aura, met two others
by a chattering stream in southern forests, just below the
clearing where six magic lines converged. They felt anger
in one man, fear radiated from the others. Beside them
stood Shayla, encased in magical glass. Sparkles of sunlight on her covering blinded them.

Or was it their tears?

He and all of the dragons shuddered. Heat built deep
within them. Flame touched their tongues and needed release. He dropped the slender thread that bound him to
his other life, his other love. Strands of copper drifted
away from him. *She* would not approve of their actions.

Another dive. Terror filled the faces of the men. They
should turn back. Men are not for killing.

No! Turn back!

What matter? *That one* had ensorcelled Shayla and the
litter she carried. *That one* had endangered all. That one
deserved to die by dragon fire.

He felt the contempt of the angry man who didn't fear

a flaming dragon anymore. Bits of an angry soul reflected from the glass that was Shayla. The two were intertwined. Kill the man and they would kill Shayla.

"Noooooo!" he screamed.

"Master?" The kitchen boy poked his head around the corner of Baamin's quarters.

"Yes?" he replied wearily. The boy moved closer. He seemed taller, more defined than just a few days ago. Adolescence must finally be catching up with him.

"Master, you haven't eaten in two days." Worry creased the boy's brow.

Baamin felt a small surge of gratitude before his worry and fatigue filled him again. No one else cared what happened to him. Krej had taken over the Council and the magicians. Since then no one had consulted him about anything. So he sat, alone, in the dark of his study with only his books and his nightmares for company. He brooded, he plotted and schemed.

And reached no conclusion.

He didn't trust Krej, Lord of Faciar, Regent of Coronnan. Yet, what else could they have done but elect him regent?

Stargods! There was no one else to lead this kingdom against its enemies. No one until Darville returned. Dragons only knew when that would be!

"I'm not hungry."

"You need food to replenish your magic." The boy placed a plate of soft cheese and bread on the desk, next to Baamin's elbow. The flowing sleeves of Baamin's robe spilled over a text, he didn't remember which one.

"What good is magic? Krej is solving our problems with armies and spears." And doing it very well, with energy and organization. Coronnan hadn't seen the like for more than ten generations.

"Armies destroy much more than just other armies. Nimbulan said so." The boy stared at the arc he drew on the stone floor with his bare toes.

Interest flowed through Baamin's veins again. "You

read the journal?" How was that possible? The boy was
so stupid no one had bothered giving him a name!

"Bits, sir." He still refused to look up.

"How many bits?" Baamin reached to lift the boy's
chin so he could see his eyes, see if intelligence glimmered there.

"Enough." There was a brief flash from the large
brown eyes, then they were lowered again.

"Enough to learn the principles of old magic?" Baamin
slid a little truth spell over the boy. At first it began to
glow with the green fire of truth, then abruptly died.

Armor would bounce the spell back. This one just
ended, as if absorbed and nullified.

Brevelan awoke from her nap feeling empty, deprived,
and utterly alone. Frantically she search for the slender
thread binding her to Jaylor. Shredded fragments of copper dangled uselessly from her soul. All traces of silver
and crystal were gone.

Jaylor was gone. While she slept, his spirit had slipped
away.

She bent her will to the magic thread, trying desperately to repair it, to build a new one. Anything to bring
him back! The silver hid from her. There wasn't enough
magic within her, within all of Coronnan to find it. She
was alone.

Never again would she listen for his steps as he explored her clearing. Mica would have to find a new
shoulder to ride on. Brevelan could go back to preparing
small, sparse meals for herself alone.

She would be without her faithful wolf familiar, too.
Darville needed to return to his own life in the capital.
Tears rolled down her cheeks. Tears of guilt and heart-
break. She didn't try to hide them from the golden-haired
man who whittled by the fire.

Darville came to her then. Crouched beside the bed, he
pushed a stray tendril of hair away from her face. She
leaned into his hand. His gentle caress cupped her face.
Strength and comfort flowed between them. Since that
first storm last winter, Darville had been with her con-

stantly. In her loneliness she had hugged him close many times.

Now it was his turn to hold her.

"What are we going to do now?" she whispered into his shoulder.

"Whsst, little one. When you are rested, we must go to the capital and find Baamin. He'll know how to help Shayla, if anyone can." He stroked her hair.

They both looked at the extra cot by the hearth where Jaylor's body lay. It was just an empty shell. Their friend was no longer there to give it life and animation.

Jaylor was gone! The emptiness washed over her, pulling her into cold despair.

Darville hugged her closer, sheltering her from the pain, making it his own. She yearned for his warmth. For a moment she allowed herself to sink into his embrace, to savor the feel of his arms encircling her. His lips brushed her hair and his beard tangled with it. She could almost pretend he was Jaylor. Then his scent filled her.

He smelled of trees freshened by a spring rain. He had picked a few wildflowers, and their pollen lingered. Mica had been in his lap. His hair was damp, as it had been so often after a playful splash in the pool when he was a golden wolf. She savored the comfortable familiarity of him. Her fingers reached and tangled with his thick, uncombed golden hair. When she tried to pull away, he held her tighter.

"Let me hold you, little one." He sat beside her, cradling her against his chest.

She needed to be this close. His heartbeat filled her mind. Her pulse quickened to match his rhythm. Their hearts entwined and beat as one. She felt her being merging with his. Wordless communication soothed them both, brought them to understanding. Her arms encircled his waist. This was Darville, not so different from the companion she had cherished for all those many moons.

Darville kissed her cheek and eyes. How many times had his wolfish tongue caressed her? He couldn't hurt her then. How could he hurt her now? She need not fear this man who was so much a part of her. But they were still two separate beings. She needed to join with him, to find the wholeness that Jaylor had taken with him.

Her mouth found Darville's lean, bearded cheek. He turned his head to capture her lips. Such a warm, undemanding kiss. Her heart swelled with tenderness. Her breasts were too small to contain her emotion. They tightened.

She deepened the kiss, demanding more of him, and herself. Her body nestled against the firm wall of his chest. His kisses fanned over her face, down to her neck. His tongue found the most sensitive delicate hollow, his hands sent flame through them both. His desire became hers. Her need filled him and grew stronger.

Heat built deep within her, expanded, surrounded him, and flowed back. Heat and need. There was so much they needed to share, to say to each other with voices and bodies.

There was a tug at her shoulder. She shrugged out of her kirtle and shift. The heat continued to build even as cool evening air washed over her sensitive skin. An ache built with the heat.

The roughness of his shirt teased her taut nipples. Impatiently she pulled the garment up over his head. His skin covered sleek muscles that rippled and molded under her touch. Their bodies melted together as if they had always belonged together. They needed to join their bodies to complete what their souls had already begun.

Colors burst forth. Bright splashes of copper and gold. Darts of the colors of their lives spread out across the heavens, into the void where only dragons and souls existed.

Passion and need rose and soared within them, pulling them higher, faster, ever farther. A distant blue blended with their elements and drew others into the vortex until they were all colors, no colors, swirling in the wind created by dragon flight, soaring with dragon ease on the currents above and around them.

They flew with dragons. A braided shaft of red and blue separated from the nimbus and twined around them, joining their union. It plaited and blended their copper

and gold within its unique twists of blue and red, binding
each part into a whole.

Time drifted in lazy circles. Brevelan did not, could not
fight it. She was complete. The lonely emptiness that had
driven her was filled to overflowing. Her need was temporarily sated. With a deep sigh of contentment she
closed her eyes and slept, wrapped in warmth and love.

Morning light crept through cracks in the walls of the
hut. Brevelan lazily opened her eyes. It was late. She
needed to be up and about. There were chores to be done.

The double cot was crowded as usual. When the nights
were cold, Darville and Mica joined her. Often several
squirrels and mice, a rabbit or three, and sometimes even
the bright yellow and gray jay bird, who scolded her so
frequently, cuddled close to keep her cozy. A better arrangement than sharing a narrow pallet with three
blanket-greedy sisters.

She shifted a little, surprised at just how crowded the
bed was this morning. A heavy arm, sprinkled with
golden hair, rested across her waist. A leg encircled
hers.

Awareness burst upon her. The arm belonged to
Darville. He was no longer a wolf, but a man. A strong,
and wonderfully gentle man at that. She touched the fine
swirls of hair on his chest. With her toes she caressed
the leg and felt a responding movement from behind
her.

She stilled her body and mind, as she did when secret-
ing herself in the forest. Darville was not the only person
in bed with her.

Cautiously she peeked over his broad shoulder, toward
the cot by the hearth.

It was empty!

"Jaylor?" she called softly, with her mind as well as
her voice.

"Hmmhph?" he murmured from behind her.

"Jaylor!"

"What?" he replied, a little more awake.

"What!" Darville responded.

Her eyes met Darville's, then they both looked to the other side of the bed, toward the wall, where their friend lay, relaxed and grinning, and as naked as they.

"Good morning," he greeted them.

CHAPTER 25

Jaylor examined the hut with new eyes. He leaned against the open door, surveying his surroundings. The circle of stones forming the hearth was the same as he last remembered, and yet not. When he looked at familiar objects straight on, they were covered with distorting mist. But a sideways glance revealed sharp outlines, clearer than he had ever experienced before. Sort of the way he had to tackle a difficult spell-unraveling.

He turned his attention to a reexamination of the objects he knew so very well. The oversized cot against the far wall definitely looked different. His experiences there colored his perceptions. The blankets had been straightened, just barely. The imprint of three tightly woven bodies still remained, while the smaller cot he had spirited from the University storerooms stood empty and barren.

He grinned. Life, as well as the air around him, had taken on a new clarity. He could almost see through solid objects in the familiar/odd room. Brevelan was more transparent than anything else. Perhaps her empathic abilities made her so easy to read. Or was it the intimate entwining they had experienced while he was in the Tambootie-induced coma?

She was embarrassed, puzzled, pleased, and appalled, all at the same time. He grinned again, felt his body stretch all over, including his manhood, and didn't bother to suppress the feeling.

Yesterday he had flown with dragons. Today he knew more about magic, and himself, than ever before. He was willing to bet even old Nimbulan didn't know what Jaylor knew now. Yesterday he had feared the power Brevelan had over his mind and body. Today knowledge had wiped away the fear.

But before he could explore that thought, turn it into action, there was a rogue to tend to.

For the safety of the kingdom and the well-being of the beloved dragons, Krej had to be removed from power—temporal and magical. Jaylor's Tambootie-induced vision of Krej screaming at his servants beside the glass statue of Shayla had ended all doubt of the rogue's true identity. Sooner or later the all-powerful lord would slip and expose his magical abilities. Jaylor intended to be present with other reliable witnesses when that happened.

"Someone comes." Brevelan raised her head from the pot of stewing grains she stirred. She refused to meet his eyes, or Darville's, for that matter. Her head remained lowered as she hastily exited. In a few moments, her thoughts would either open or close the path for the visitor.

"How does she know that?" the prince asked. He had been pacing the room, anxious for their simple meal to be finished so they could continue their pursuit of his cousin.

Restless energy had infused the prince since their early rising. Jaylor felt it pulsating against his own aura. He resisted the urge to pace alongside his friend.

"This clearing is in a focus of magic." He eased a soothing timbre into his voice. "It attunes itself to each of its tenants in turn."

Darville responded to the tiny spell of his voice and settled on the rickety three-legged stool beside the hearth.

"Don't manipulate me with your magic!" he demanded even as he fought the lethargy Jaylor imposed upon him.

Surprised he would notice, Jaylor drew back the slight control. He shouldn't be surprised. Last night Darville had been as active a participant as he and Brevelan. Henceforth the three were linked in a way he hadn't yet explored.

He continued with his tale. Darville needed to know what was involved with Brevelan and the clearing. His future might depend on that information.

"For three hundred years this small glade has protected, sheltered, and fed special witchwomen." Jaylor posted himself near the crack in the door to observe Brevelan's return, with or without company. "I believe Myrilandel was the first."

"Who?" Darville was only mildly interested. His arms and legs still twitched but his mind was calmer.

"Nimbulan's wife. He had to exile her, along with the other rogues, when he established dragon magic. But he provided for her and their children. That is why the cot is oversized, so he would have a place to sleep when he visited. That is why the hut wouldn't burn completely, only the thatch that has been renewed since he threw the protective spells."

"Explain this 'focus' of magic. Can it be used against Krej?" Darville asked. "I thought dragons were the source of magic, and they are dwindling. With Shayla's enchantment there shouldn't be much of anything left."

"For conventional magic. Nimbulan was what we call a rogue, or a solitary, long before he tapped the power of the dragons and the Tambootie, which could make magic communal. Ask yourself, what was his source of power? How did he entice the first dragons and enslave them to this kingdom and your royal line!"

"Maevra is near to birthing. You must come now. She needs you." A strange voice came from the edge of the trees.

"Yes, of course. Just let me gather my things," Brevelan replied.

"She can't go alone." Darville whispered. "Krej may have sent these women to entice her to a witch-burning."

The prince's anxiety wound through Jaylor, becoming his own.

"You can't be seen there. Krej's spies will report your restoration. They don't trust me either."

The door latch rattled in warning.

"I'll be but a minute." Brevelan eased through a narrow opening. It was pushed wider by her golden wolf. She raised her eyes in surprise.

From behind the door, Jaylor put his finger to his lips

to signal silence. He held Darville's discarded clothes close against his chest.

"They'll expect him to be by your side," he mouthed.

She nodded her acceptance. A smile tugged at the corners of her mouth. "You just wanted him to hunt for himself so you could have more breakfast." An infectious giggle threatened to erupt from her.

He smiled back at her. She was once more comfortable in his presence. The sun poked through the cloud cover and dispersed the rain. Jaylor's vision cleared.

Darville guarded the door of the carpenter's home. He blinked his eyes in the sunlight and stretched out across the doorway. Occasionally a person or two wandered past. They were curious. New pups always brought out the others. They had to inspect and sniff to make sure the newcomers were worthy of the pack.

He eyed them suspiciously. When one ventured too close he growled, low and deep so they would know he guarded the ones inside. Brevelan was with the woman.

His other-man-self knew Brevelan, his mate, needed protection. But she wasn't whelping. It was the other woman. Her cries of pain and the smell of her fear unsettled him.

Darville couldn't see Jaylor, secreted in the woods. But that was all right, as long as his scent was near.

His nose wiggled as he sorted the scents of each of the passersby. Some he knew. Some he didn't. There was no malice among the women, just curiosity. Only one man smelled of evil. He also smelled of rotten fish.

Then there was the man across the common. He had stationed himself in the opening of the cave. Every so often he drank from the long container in his hand. The container that men called a mug smelled of the foul water they drank in that cave. The man had no smell.

That warned Darville. He cocked his ears, allowed his neck ruff to stand in alertness. Men disguised their smell when they stalked prey. If the man-with-no-scent hunted Brevelan, he would have to get past one very protective wolf. And Jaylor, too.

A flicker of movement off to one side told where Jaylor hid. Darville crept forward a paw's length and growled again. The movement should signal to Jaylor that the man at the cave was trouble.

A thin wail of a human pup pierced the air. All movement in the village stopped. Darville sensed each person listening, leaning closer to the carpenter's home. The wail repeated, stronger this time. The pup lived. The carpenter emerged from the cave. He pushed the scentless man aside in his hurry. Darville let him pass into his home. He had no right to stop him now that the whelping was finished.

"A girl!" Disappointment hovered on the edge of the carpenter's voice.

"The child lives. She is healthy. And your wife will grow strong again to bear another," Brevelan reprimanded him. The birth was finally over. She and Darville and Jaylor could now get on with their journey. She hated to take the time away from their quest, but she was compelled to assist Maevra. Whether these people admitted it or not, this village needed her as much as she needed them.

The new father inspected the tiny scrap of life she held before him.

"You said it was a boy." He didn't reach to hold his daughter.

"I said the child was large enough and strong enough to be male." The child was also determined. She just might become the next witchwoman for this village.

Maevra roused from her exhaustion. "She's hungry, just like her father. Give her to me." She reached out for the now squalling infant.

Brevelan returned the babe to her mother. She wanted out of this dim, confining house. The dark emotions of the father, her own fatigue, and the smells of birthing threatened to choke her.

She needed Darville and Jaylor to dispel her loneliness again.

"We were promised a boy," the carpenter sulked. "Old

Thorm said you might substitute a changeling so you could keep the boy for yourself. Yourself and that meddling magician!" His tone turned menacing. A growl from the doorway stopped his words.

"Only the *Stargods* can promise the gender of a child. Take up your complaint with them," Brevelan spat back at him. She edged closer to the door and Darville's protection.

"You take the name of our gods in vain!" Clearly the man was drunk. Or under a spell. Otherwise he'd never dare risk the ill will of a witchwoman.

She looked to Maevra and the now nursing child. Once the man returned to normal, he wouldn't harm his wife and daughter. His malice was all directed toward Brevelan.

"I'll demand no fee for midwifing a live and healthy child, since the result displeases you." Brevelan allowed her disgust for the man to wash over him. Maybe if he saw himself as she saw him, he could shrug off whatever compelled him. He stepped toward her. Darville bared his teeth.

"Get out, witch." Fear palpitated around him. "Get out and take the *s'murghin'* familiar with you. No decent priest should tolerate you and your kind. You won't be welcome back." His arm pointed to the door, uncompromising. Darville stepped closer. His teeth dripped, the hair on his neck stood straight up.

"No, Darville," she commanded. The carpenter appeared a little startled at the princely name. "His blood isn't worth your time." She gripped the animal's fur and tugged him backward. "If I were indeed in league with the source of evil, I would curse you, and curse this village." She held in check the power she felt rising within her.

"This time I'll only leave a reminder with the men who condemn me."

From the doorway, the freedom and safety of the woods enticed her. Jaylor hovered there. He would hear and understand her need for the words that spilled from her lips.

"Until you forgive me in your heart, as well as with words, until you know for truth that I wish you and yours only health and happiness, and until you can come to your wife with gratitude for the gift of the child she has given you, you will not be able to bed any woman." The words came from someone else, somewhere else. She didn't really wish this village ill. Still the words flowed. "And no child will be conceived in this village until all the men here feel the same."

The carpenter blanched and looked as though he would faint. Brevelan ignored him and marched out of his house.

Moments later, from the shelter of the trees, beyond the sight of the village, Brevelan hugged each of her friends in turn.

"Remind me not to make either of you angry at me," Darville said with a chuckle.

"That was some curse you laid, Brevelan," Jaylor agreed as he handed Darville his clothes. Hen-bumps covered his back in the cool spring air as he bent to pull up his leather trews.

His legs were long and well muscled, straight now but still bristling with fine golden hair. His buttocks were tight . . . Brevelan spun to face in the other direction, embarrassed by her train of thought as well as her hungry appraisal of his body.

"I didn't intend to curse them." She studied the pile of packs and Mica washing a neat paw on top of them.

"And you didn't, Brevelan." Jaylor's hand was gentle and warm on her shoulder. "You held back the full blast of your anger. I felt little power behind your words."

She leaned her cheek against his caress, gathering comfort from him.

"Not much anyway," Darville muttered.

"I'm willing to bet that every man for miles around is going to spend the better part of the next nine months trying to prove you wrong. Some will even go so far as to drag their women beyond the village so the child will not be conceived within its limits." They all chuckled at that.

"But there was power," Brevelan murmured. She

glanced over her shoulder to make sure Darville was
clothed before confiding in them both. Since last night
she had been thinking of the three of them as one person,
bound together by duty, quest, and love. She needed both
of them to unravel the mess she had caused.

"What do you mean?" Jaylor's eyebrows raised.

"As my anger grew I could feel a tingling drawing up
from the ground below. It filled me to overflowing. I had
to release it. The word came from the power, not from
me."

"Stargods!" both men exclaimed.

"Sounds like old Nimbulan chose this place for his exiled wife with reason." Jaylor began pacing, hands out as
if testing the warmth, or the power, of the ground he
walked.

"Nimbulan?"

Briefly he explained the history of her clearing.

"So that is why the clearing called me. It chose me as
its next witchwoman." This truth troubled her. As a child
she had feared her magic, almost as much as her da had.
Gradually she had come to accept it as a part of her. But
if her magic came from the clearing and not herself, she
could never master it, never come to peace with it.

"Partly." Jaylor reached out for her again. She dodged
his hand. This was something she had to understand and
control on her own.

"Brevelan." This time it was Darville who captured her
shoulders. "Listen to him."

"The clearing chose you because your magic is
strong."

Had he been reading her mind? Of course he had. After
last night they had all three been communicating more
with thoughts than words.

"Your magic is your own. It was with you at birth. You
came by it naturally. The clearing needs someone as
strong as you. It doesn't give you magic, it gives you the
peace to explore and grow. Witchwomen of your caliber
need the clearing for protection. Otherwise, you would
have to face the prejudice and malice of villagers like
these every day."

"It's not their prejudice. They liked me and were learning to trust me until Old Thorm told them differently."

"Krej. Old Thorm is just one of his many disguises."

"Let's move." Darville thrust Mica onto Jaylor's shoulder as he organized the packs. "If that's the case, they'll follow soon with torches and stones. We've got to be halfway to the capital before dawn." He gathered Brevelan close in a brief hug of reassurance. "While Maevra was birthing, the barkeep was watching me. He had no smell."

"Krej must have given him magic armor. As well as instructions to sow distrust in the village."

Chills ran up Brevelan's spine. How could her own sire, blood of her blood, flesh of her flesh, hate her so much?

"No, he's just incapable of caring for anything other than his power. It's as addicting as the Tambootie," Jaylor confided as he, too, hugged her close.

She gathered them both to her side. "It will be a long journey." She sought the eyes of both men. "We will be together constantly. I want you both to know I will tolerate no jealousy." She tried to keep her voice stern, but the love she felt for them, and from them, lifted her mouth into a smile. "I will be owned by no man."

"Neither of us will do anything without your consent, Brevelan." Jaylor looked to Darville for confirmation. The prince nodded his agreement.

She loved them both, would cherish them both while she could. "I know that," she replied. "And when this business is finished, we will each go to our separate destinies."

They nodded in solemn agreement even as they pulled her closer.

CHAPTER 26

Baamin watched the rain wash the window shutters with a steady stream of cold water. The cobblestone courtyard of the University was totally deserted. Not so the market square. Everyone had a task, either preparing themselves or acquiring equipment and stores for the growing army. Increasingly heavy rains had to be ignored. Armies couldn't wait for the elements.

The shouts and clangs of mock battles deafened observers on the nearest mainland from dawn to dusk. Those not so occupied sought refuge from their numbing fear of invasion in prayer or charms. In living memory nothing had so threatened the peace of their mundane lives as the news of border raids that penetrated ever deeper into the provinces.

Coronnan was going to war. Troops had been mustered from every station of life in all twelve provinces. No one was exempt. Training took place near the capital, and then massed troops marched somewhere to the west.

Baamin sighed heavily. He was Senior Magician and king's councillor. But no one had told him the location of army headquarters. He knew, of course. But he wasn't supposed to know. He had been abandoned along with the king he had served well for so many years.

No one else bothered to remember the king who lingered near death. Lord Krej was their leader now. He infused the populace with the energy and knowledge to save them all. Something the magicians hadn't been able to do when crisis struck.

Baamin's own self-doubts heightened his lonely depression. Was he responsible for the terrible disasters that threatened his homeland? Or had he only dreamed those terrible moments in Shayla's cave.

"Aah ... aah ... aahchoo!" Seven students dived to protect feeble candle flames from the blast of the sneeze erupting from the eighth apprentice.

Inside the University, the few remaining apprentices shivered and sniffled in the damp classrooms. Fuel had been rationed for Lord Krej's grand defense of the kingdom.

"How are we supposed to learn a summons if you blow out our candles!" one frowning boy complained as he wiped rheumy eyes with the back of his sleeve. Greasy tallow candles gave off a lot of oily smoke and a weak flame. Spells became misdirected in the clouds of ugly smoke. The good beeswax tapers had all been confiscated by Lord Krej and his generals.

Apprentices, too, had been commandeered into the army. There was no magic left for them to work. Therefore the University had no right to reserve boys from service to their country. Of the thirty apprentices entrusted to Baamin a few weeks ago, only eight showed any rogue potential. He had lied and lied and lied again about the boys' ill health and weak constitutions so the recruiting officers would overlook them.

"Now, boys," Baamin soothed his irritable charges. "We'll try it one more time. Find a core of magic deep within you." He paused long enough to allow them to do this. "Close your eyes and keep a strong image of your receiver in your mind. Now send the magic through the flame into the glass and onto your partner."

Only the sound of an occasional raspy breath broke the silence of the room. Baamin's gaze wandered to the newest apprentice, sitting in the corner, away from the other boys and their contaminating colds. His concentration was absolute. The rest of the boys might not have existed. His candle burned steady, bright and clear, unlike the other boys', magnified by the glass he held in front of it.

The kitchen boy. Who would have thought the stupid drudge, who possessed only a charming smile and a will-

ingness to please, would turn out to be the most adept
rogue magician of the lot?

Baamin didn't know how else to explain this newest
phenomenon. The boy couldn't gather magic. So he had
been barred from the classrooms years ago. He could,
however, drag up enormous quantities of the stuff from
some other unknown source. They really should give him
a name. "Boy" just didn't seem to describe him anymore.

"Did anyone ever give you a name?" he asked under
his breath.

The boy shook his head. He was concentrating on
sending the flame through his precious shard of glass
across the room to his study partner.

Across the room, one of the boys sitting in a circle sat
up in surprise. The summons had reached him. No one
else was having the same success.

"Would you like a name?" Baamin prodded.

The boy nodded again as he prepared to receive his
partner's attempt.

"What name?" This was why the boy was considered
stupid. He was incapable of carrying on a conversation.

"Only when I'm concentrating on something else," he
replied to Baamin's thoughts.

"What?" The senior magician had to sit, hurriedly. The
boy was thought-reading, without a trace of a magic umbilical and while learning a new spell! This was unheard
of.

"Nimbulan could do it." The boy sat back in his chair
as his partner once more tried to direct enough magic to
send his flame through the glass and across the room.

"Did you read that in his journal, too?" Baamin felt
moisture on his brow. The room was frigid and he was
perspiring. What was he going to do with the boy?

"You're going to train me. That's what you're going to
do with me."

"*Stargods!*" Baamin kept his mind closed. The boy
looked up, puzzled.

"You shut me out."

"It's impolite to read another's thoughts without an express invitation."

"How else am I supposed to know what's happening around me?"

"How long have you had this ... er ... talent?"

"Don't you have it, too?"

Baamin's head threatened to separate from his body. All the blood rushed to his stomach and tried to turn that beleaguered organ upside down. The hot moisture on his brow turned icy.

"Lesson is over," he announced to the boys. "Pick new partners and practice going from one room to the next. We'll meet again after supper." The boys rushed from the room, eager for food and replenishment. Baamin snagged one collar before its owner could escape.

"Pick a name for yourself." His tone commanded the boy to obey without hesitation. He didn't try a compulsion spell; it wouldn't work. Like the truth spell, the boy would just absorb it, dissect it for any new knowledge, and likely turn it back on the throwing magician.

"Like what?" The boy's eyes opened wide, revealing dark brown windows that begged him to open his mind again.

The senior magician resolutely kept it closed. He knew too many secrets to allow this untried boy unrestrained access to them. But then the boy had probably been private to state secrets for years.

"Anything you like. You seem to have no family to please, and no traditions to fall back on. Choose something that describes yourself, or what you would like to be." He tried to resume the friendly father figure image that invited trust.

"I want to be like Nimbulan, or like you, sir." The eyes begged entrance again.

Baamin was falling deeper and deeper into those eyes. At the last moment he stepped away from the boy, shaking his head clear, his thoughts firmly shuttered. How much had this boy learned from people who didn't know of his telepathy?

"Quite a bit, sir. That's why I can do magic. I've been practicing what the boys think about when they study."

Stargods! He'd found a way into his mind anyway.

"And just where did you find the magic to practice

with? You were tested several times, and you can't gather magic."

"Why gather and store it? There's a never-ending supply at your feet."

"At my feet?"

"Yes, sir. In the ground, there's bluish-silver lines. They look kind'da like the dragon wing tips. Can't you see 'em, sir?"

Baamin shook his head in dismay. He couldn't see them yet, but before the boys had finished supper he'd find a way.

And where had Boy seen a dragon to know what the lines looked like?

"I don't think you should call yourself 'Nimbulan' or 'Baamin,' Boy. People would think you were giving yourself airs above your station in life." An inkling of a plan took shape in Baamin's tired brain.

"But I won't always be a kitchen drudge, or an apprentice."

"No, not always. But for now it's important that everyone else sees you as a kitchen drudge, perhaps in the palace where you could hear the court and army gossip." Again the boy's eyes widened. He saw what Baamin wanted.

"A name's important. I'll think about it while I'm listening to the regent's cook and steward."

"Lord Krej leaves for his own castle next week."

"I'll practice the summons spell tonight. I'll need you as a partner so I can find your special vibration anywhere."

"Uh ... Boy, have you ever read a man's dreams?"

"Only once, sir. Too boring and confusing." He shrugged his shoulders in a timeless gesture of dismissal.

"Do you think you could tell if a man's dreams originate within himself or are imposed upon him?"

"Never tried."

"Forget I asked." Baamin shooed the boy toward his dinner. He couldn't take the chance of anyone reading his current nightmares.

* * *

"Halfway to the capital by dawn?" Jaylor snorted sarcastically. Dusk was crawling across the countryside and they were barely two hours' walk from the village. Rain plagued every step.

Buckets of intense downpour flooded creeks already swollen with spring run-off. Hard-packed roads and newly plowed fields took on the cloying texture of the mile-wide mud flats in the Great Bay. Every step Jaylor took became an effort.

Rain such as this could only be the *Stargods* mourning the loss of their beloved dragons.

If he was tired, wet, and chilled from the ceaseless plodding, how did Brevelan feel?

"A figure of speech. We need to hurry. Who knows how much damage Krej has done already." Darville reached again for the missing sword at his hip. "Come on. We can't fly like dragons. We've got to reach Krej's castle between here and the capital as soon as possible." He lengthened his stride to emphasize his need.

"I think we'd best find shelter for the night," Jaylor voiced his own opinion. "We'll make better time in the morning when we're rested and fed."

Darville stopped short. Their eyes met each other's in defiance, over the top of Brevelan's head.

She shivered and they both reached an arm to draw her close. They shivered with her, feeling everything she felt.

The men's eyes met again in challenge. The rain dripped into silence, surrounding them with a wet curtain. The three of them might have been the only creatures alive.

"If you'd both loosen your hold a bit, I might be able to breathe." Brevelan pushed at both their chests.

Jaylor felt the heat from her hand. He wanted to take the time to absorb it, cherish it. Instead he eased his grip on her shoulder. He noticed Darville did the same.

"You're feverish, dear heart." The cause of the heat in her hand disturbed him. His own body flushed in sympathy. "We'd best find shelter." Even Darville, with his one-track, lumbird mind, should see the sense in that.

"Last summer, a charcoal burner gave me directions

and a meal. He moved back to the village and died last winter." Her eyes closed in momentary pain. Jaylor knew she had felt the man's death, probably nursed his last illness.

"Perhaps his hut is still standing. I'm not sure I could find it again from this direction." Brevelan shivered again. This time her arms encircled both men to bring them close again, as if she needed the heat of their bodies to chase away the chill of the rain as well as the chill of death.

Her sense of loss passed quickly. But not before it engulfed Jaylor and, from the look of him, Darville, too. They were becoming too sensitive to her uncontrolled emotions.

"We'll more likely find leaning walls and a collapsed roof," Darville grumbled as he kissed the top of her head. His lips lingered a moment. Jaylor felt their cherishing warmth almost as soon as Brevelan did. He clamped down on his instinctive jealousy. The three of them were too closely linked. They all knew/felt what the others did.

"I'll scout ahead." Darville broke the empathic link. "If I were a charcoal burner, I'd want my hut sheltered from the weather, close to the burner but protected from a chance flame." He scanned the woods around them. "Over that way." He dropped his pack and moved off in an easy lope. Even in man form, his stride resembled that of a golden wolf.

Jaylor snuggled Brevelan close against him within the folds of his cloak. His chin rested on top of her head so that her breath fanned his chest. "He won't be long," he reassured her.

"He will probably find the place by smell." Her tone was light, almost a giggle.

Smiling, he, too, kissed her hair. "There seems to be some advantage to changing him back and forth. He's a wolf with a man's intelligence and a man with the keen senses of a wolf."

"And what of you. What have you retained from your flight with the dragons?" She looked up into his eyes.

"I don't crave meat if that is what bothers you." Instead he craved the Tambootie, just as the dragons did. The giant winged creatures required the herbage as part of their balanced diet. It also gave them invisibility. He didn't need it for health or protection, yet he still felt compelled to eat it.

Jaylor allowed Brevelan to probe and absorb his emotions. "What I remember is a tremendous sense of wonder. They are such magnificent creatures, yet so sad. Without Shayla, their need for Tambootie is all that keeps them in Coronnan. Their anger at Krej may be strong enough to break that one chain. If they can find Tambootie elsewhere, even a different variety that doesn't make them invisible, they'll leave, taking their gatherable magic with them."

Some of the sadness engulfed them both. They gulped back sobs together.

"We have to save Shayla." Brevelan stepped away from the embrace. Her determination surrounded her like an aura.

"We have to get you warm and dry," Darville broke into their private thoughts. He grabbed his own pack and Brevelan's as well. "The hut still has a roof and a stash of dry firewood. There's a stream nearby for clean water." He marched off, leaving the others to follow.

A fresh torrent of rain strengthened the existing downpour, sending icy runnels down Jaylor's neck. "That's all we need, more water!" he called after his friends and lovers.

Love. It was their love, for each other and theirs for him, that had brought him back from the ecstatic flight with dragons. Only an emotion so powerful could break his addiction to the herb that fed the dragons and created their magic. But would it last? Would their love be enough to fill the aching emptiness left behind when the evil herbage wore off?

No wonder Tambootie was considered the essence of evil. Even now he hungered for it, wondered if he could work any magic at all without it.

* * *

The raiders have gone too far. I paid them to harass the farmers and steal a few cows. Instead they have burned everything in their path.

The merchant city of Sambol on the border is in danger. No traders have dared pass through the region because of the raiders.

Simurgh take them all! I only needed an excuse to raise the army and discredit the Commune. I don't need a full-scale war and a disruption of trade.

All my generals and lords keep running to their priests and shrines to pray for guidance and deliverance. Stargods, indeed! We must rely on ingenuity, perseverance, and cunning, not on feeble prayers to nonexistent deliverers. Simurgh helps only those who fight for themselves and for him. If my head didn't ache so badly, I could convince them with a snap of my fingers.

CHAPTER 27

Baamin crept softly around the islands of Coronnan City. The cloying mist of midnight saturated and chilled his plain brown cloak. His boots made soft squishing sounds in the mud. Only this late were the streets free of milling crowds, soldiers, and priests. He needed privacy to trace out and memorize each of the elusive silvery-blue lines Boy had brought to his attention.

His path took him across a series of city bridges east to west, the same direction as the sun.

The line he was following wavered and fled from beneath his feet. He paused and squinted. It eluded him.

"*Stargods,* help me," he pleaded. This wasn't the first time he had lost track of the power. His body cried for sleep. The blankness of fatigue covered his mind. And yet the need to know more gnawed at his soul.

He hadn't been this tired since his apprentice days, learning to gather magic and throw it back out again. No wonder Jaylor wielded this rogue magic with ease. He was big, with powerful shoulders and a horrendous appetite. He could probably lift a sledge steed without magic.

Out of long habit, Baamin reached within himself for some magic to guide him and to restore his aching muscles. The well was empty. He hadn't even tried to gather any magic in several days. Deliberately he stepped back onto the silver-blue line, at least where it had been the last time he could see one. From the depths of Coronnan he pulled some magic into his tired body. He allowed it to feed and restore him, more so than a meal and a nap could.

Had he done this in his dreams and traveled to the far

corners of Coronnan, wreaking havoc? He'd always been taught that the very essence of rogue magic was evil. The idea surfaced that his untapped rogue talent had finally eaten away at his University-trained ethics.

He tried to banish the idea and failed. If only Lord Krej were not a constant reminder of how the greed for power corrupted.

Krej had to have lost his magic talents when he left the University fifteen years ago. But his addiction to power could have developed during his magical training. Since assuming the Lordship of Faciar, he must have nurtured the insatiable need to the point of seeking out a rogue to do his dirty work.

Baamin could never accept Jaylor's assumption that Krej was the rogue himself. The lord's presence in the capital while the rogue was operating in the southern mountains was too well documented.

If Krej were deposed or killed, would the rogue return whence he came and leave Coronnan in peace?

Sounds from one of the small cottages sent Baamin slinking into the shadows. "*S'murghin'* hound!" A disgruntled voice drifted across this quiet corner of the city. A door opened. Another muffled curse and the thud of a foot catching the cur in the ribs. "Stay out all night. I'll not disturb my sleep just so's you can pant after that bitch in heat." The door slammed.

The dog wuffled and snorted through his nose. Baamin continued to press his back against a cold stone wall, willing invisibility.

The dog found him anyway. He sniffed at the magician's feet and hands, lifted his leg, and sauntered off. Baamin watched him go before slipping out of his hiding place back onto the path of magic he thought he had been following. It was the same route the dog had taken.

A silver glint off to his left winked at him. He whirled to catch a better glimpse of it. The lovely trail wandered back the way he had come, west to east, the path of the moon.

He stepped onto the line and squinted his eyes. The old, old planetary magic filled him, climbing through his tingling feet and legs into his hungry belly. It rested there a moment and then climbed higher into his sight.

Blue, silver, white, palest green, the colors burst through him. An entire web of power lay at his feet. He continued his tracing, following wherever the web led him, along the path of the invisible moon. He no longer needed the cloud-shrouded orb to guide his steps.

Now that he knew how to look for the web of power, he found the old magic had a luminescence of its own. How had he missed it all these years?

Because he hadn't looked. Nimbulan had gone out of his way to eliminate all knowledge of the old magic when he discovered the power generated by the dragons. There was too much danger from magicians using magic for their own gain rather than for the good of the kingdom.

Only when the Commune could combine their magic against all others had magic become "safe."

Krej had found a way to break the Commune. If there was no magic to gather, they couldn't combine against him. Doubts gnawed at him again. Suppose Lord Krej had only capitalized on the work of another traitor?

Baamin would never know unless he mastered rogue magic and understood his own soul better. So he continued his cold lonely march around the city, weaving in and out of old alleys, through small houses and shops.

The city sat in the middle of a vast network of power. Its ancient location commanded more than the head of the Bay. It commanded the beginning and the end of the magic. No wonder the University had been situated here. Those buildings were older, much older than the central keep of Palace Reveta Tristile, which boasted a fair number of secret passages and subterranean tunnels. More secrets might yet be hidden within the ancient halls and cellars of the University, like Nimbulan's library.

The courtyard between the University and the palace contained an outpouring of blue, so tightly wound together it appeared as a large column coming straight up from the center of the world. Here was where the kings were consecrated. Here was where the nimbus of dragons confirmed a man's right to rule the kingdom and themselves.

He'd never seen an entire nimbus of dragons gathered for such a ritual. He'd never seen a single live dragon—unless his dreams were more memory than imagination. There hadn't been a need in the past ten generations for a dragon to consecrate a new king. The crown had passed easily from father to son in smooth order since the end of the Great Wars of Disruption. Was that why the dragons had begun slipping away from Coronnan? Because they weren't needed anymore?

But they were needed. Now more than ever. They needed to confirm Darville as rightful ruler and provide enough traditional magic to oust the usurping Krej. To control a rogue.

Baamin envied Jaylor, who had touched Shayla, talked to her, seen her fly. He just hoped the boy had had time to give her that tiny vial of medicine. Just two drops of the ensorcelled water would increase her litters and speed the maturation of her young to insure a healthy nimbus once and for all.

Jaylor had to find Shayla and break the magic hold over her.

Until then, Baamin would make use of whatever magic he could find. It was his duty to protect the kingdom and its rightful rulers any way he could.

Even if he discovered himself to be the villain of the piece.

If only he could see a dragon, he could happily die.

They are lost again. Such a simple trick. They are too stupid to learn that I am in control and will remain so. The journeyman is stronger than I thought. But he'll never break the spell—even if he is smart enough to realize just how important the wolf is.

My spies tell me all. They can do nothing less. The wolf is still a wolf. I am in control of Council and Commune.

I don't need the crown—though that token would be nice—for I have power. As long as I have my Tambootie, I need nothing more.

*The weakling Darcine will die soon. Without Darville
the Council will have no choice but to follow me.*

"*S'murgh* it!" Darville cursed behind the hand he used
to wipe rain from his face. "The charcoal burner's hut."
Three days of plowing through rain and mud and they
were right back where they'd started. Three days of wandering in circles, sleeping under hedges and getting wet-
ter and more miserable by the minute.

At least Brevelan wasn't really sick. The last time they
were at this hut she had merely been suffering from exhaustion, physical and emotional.

"Jaylor," he grabbed his friend's arm. "You've got to
do something. Krej has enchanted the pathway."

"Like what?" Jaylor blinked back at him. He looked
too innocent. Darville knew that look from their childhood years. Underneath the wide-eyed gullibility a plan
was forming.

"You could summon up some of your legendary magic
and break the enchantment." They didn't have time for
these games.

"You could be less lumbird-brained and blaze a new
path," Brevelan accused.

"The existing pathway is most direct, easier walking,
and level!" he asserted.

"The path is enchanted to draw travelers away from the
capital." Jaylor studied the twisted wood of his staff. His
eyes squinted along its length back the way they had
come. He was using some kind of magic to discern the
nature of the problem. "I expect it's part of Krej's defense. If we can't find Coronnan City, invading armies
can't either."

"So, do something. You're the one who broke his other
spell."

"First we're going to get dry and have a meal,"
Brevelan insisted. She turned and began trudging through
the gray trees toward the gray shadow that was the hut.
The rain was gray, too, as was the mud beneath their feet.
Even their clothes and faces looked gray.

Coronnan was losing its vibrant colors. The life of his

kingdom was draining away in the incessant rain. Darville had to get back to the capital before Krej destroyed everything.

"We don't have time," Darville returned.

"Don't argue with her." Jaylor grabbed his arm.

Darville shook off the restraint, anger and frustration feeding his normal restless impatience.

"Haven't you yet learned that she's the strongest of us all?" Jaylor reclaimed the sleeve. His powerful fingers threatened to rend the cloth.

Darville stared at the restraining hand. Jaylor stared at his staff. Brevelan stared at them both.

"I suppose we should take one more night to dry out before we try again." Darville surrendered to their superior advice. "There's a farm about another hour further along."

"The farmer is one of Krej's spies." Jaylor pointed his long staff at Darville's chest. "Do you really want to be a wolf again tonight? You make a very handsome pet."

"Don't start that, Jaylor. I have very little patience left. Why don't you call someone at that University of yours and find out what's happening in my capital?"

"I can't waste my magic on a summons if I'm going to break another of Krej's spells in the morning."

"You're stalling! Why?" Darville accused. He reached once again for the sword that should hang at his hip. He felt empty, off balance without the weapon.

"I'm conserving my magic for important spells."

"And what's more important than getting me back to the capital?"

Just then Mica chose to slash his shoulder with her claws. Pain jolted him back to the reality of their circumstances. The little cat arched her back and hissed at both of them. Her claws continued to dig into his flesh, through several layers of heavy cloth.

Stop it!

Darville wasn't sure if the cat or Brevelan shouted in his ear. The voice that halted his next verbal assault sounded like both of them combined.

"Stop this childish bickering," Brevelan commanded.

Her delicately shaped hands rested on her hips, her lower lip quivered. Her eyes, slitted just like the cat's, held him captive. Beside him he felt Jaylor also squirm under her gaze. Perhaps he was right. Perhaps Brevelan was the strongest of them all.

Silence settled over them. Mica broke her defensive stance by cleaning her front paws while still atop his shoulder. Darville felt just a little weak-kneed when Brevelan finally looked away. He stiffened his spine to correct for the weakness.

"Now," Brevelan took command once more, "we need more dry wood and clean water."

Darville stomped off the path in search of any bit of old wood hidden beneath something that would have kept off the worst of the rains. He needed to move quickly and strongly to shake off the lingering effects of Brevelan's control. A control that came from her own strength and his love for her, not from any magic.

He kicked himself for allowing her that much power over him. As prince of the realm, he had to learn to be independent of outside influences. A strong king listened to his advisers, weighed the merit of their words, and then made his own decisions. Something his father had never learned.

And he, Darville, would never, ever, be as weak as his father.

But Brevelan had been right. He and Jaylor, and Brevelan, too, couldn't afford any petty bickering. But *he* should have been the one to make that decision. *He* should have noticed the enchanted pathway would not only lead travelers astray but disrupt their unity as well.

It was classic military strategy. He'd learned it from ancient textbooks before he was ten.

Divert. Disrupt. Demoralize. Destroy.

This was a lesson he would remember when the time came to rescue Shayla. Krej was proving to be a sound strategist. Darville would just have to be smarter.

"Master?" Boy poked his head into Baamin's study as dawn crept across his windowsill.

"Yes, Boy?" He propped one eye open from his brief doze at his desk. He had spent another long night tracing lines of magic power. The hours of extremely hard work were taking their toll on his aging body. He'd had to have several robes altered to fit his decreasing girth.

But when he finally slept, he slept soundly and dream-lessly.

"I heard somethin' in the palace last night."

Baamin sat up straighter. If the boy risked coming to his study, even at this very early hour, the news must have import.

"Lord Krej, he's expecting some 'bassadors."

"Ambassadors," Baamin automatically corrected the boy. "Speak properly, Boy." He spoke more curtly than he'd intended. With a great show, he unscrewed the cap from his flask and took a swig. Would Boy read his thoughts again and know the restorative in the metal bottle was only sugar water?

"Ambassadors, sir. From Rosie Mire. Something about an alliance."

"Rossemeyer?" Rossemeyer, a poor desert kingdom with an abundance of nomadic mercenaries, the treacle beta, and not much else. The warriors they bred preferred real wars instead of training exercises to keep up their legendary strength. They were coming to enforce their ultimatum. Darville as bridegroom to their beloved princess, or war.

Which natural resource did Rossemeyer covet—black fire rock, gemstones, the lush flood plains of Coronnan River? Perhaps they knew Prince Darville was missing and the entire charade of alliance was an excuse for invasion.

Then again, Rossemeyer could be searching for an abundant supply of the Tambootie.

Baamin didn't know why he thought of the aromatic wood as a natural resource. Once the idea took root, he began to see it as the answer to many questions.

CHAPTER 28

Jaylor sighted along his staff. He pointed it straight down the main north-south road. Or rather, he pointed it where the road should be. Due north. But the road appeared to be coming from the northeast. The edges of the road wavered with more than just the distortion of rain on mud.

He changed position, aiming the staff and his concentration along the new sighting. *Stargods!* The road shifted, too. Now it appeared to be more to the northwest.

"Where is the road now?" he asked of Brevelan and Darville who stood directly behind him, far enough away not to interfere with his concentration.

"Looks like it runs due west, straight into the Bay," Darville replied. "But it shouldn't."

"No, it shouldn't. Which means we are fighting a delusion. A very strong delusion." Frustration gnawed at Jaylor's concentration. With all this strange magic bouncing around him, he couldn't think or see straight.

"If we followed the sun, rather than the road?" Brevelan's voice was tentative.

He gathered her hand into his own to reassure her, and himself. "The time has come to start breaking down some of Krej's spells. By the time we reach his castle, I want his magic in tatters. The more energy he spends repairing what I have torn apart, the less he'll have to throw at us."

She gulped and nodded. He did the same and knew that Darville mimicked their actions.

"What about those blue lines of power you described?" Darville asked. He, too, was squinting, trying to see where they should be going. "Can you tap into them, or use them as a guide?"

"Lines of power," Jaylor mused. "The dragons showed me lines of power, running through Coronnan, like so many irrigation ditches, emanating from the very depths of this world." His vision focused backward to his flight with the dragons.

Blue-silver webs encasing the world far below him. Tambootie trees seeking them out. Veins of copper ore filling the hollow paths of burned out power.

When he'd come out of the Tambootie-induced vision of dragons, he hadn't been able to focus his eyes if he looked at something head on. Only when he inspected individual items from the side could he maintain a clear view.

The trap in Darville's transformation spell had been laid for a direct attack. Breaking the spell had required a roundabout route. Jaylor turned his body due west. He looked sideways at the road running north, moving only his eyes

There! The thoroughfare ran true to form with no evidence of magic glamour distorting the edges.

"The Tambootie has caused Krej to approach everything sideways," he announced.

"So?" Darville cocked his head in a very wolfish way. Jaylor grinned at his friend.

"So all I have to do is decide which direction he faced when he threw the spell. Then I face opposite to unravel it." Jaylor nearly danced in front of his friends. Impulsively, triumphantly, he gathered them in a massive hug. His warmth and joy spilled over to include them all. "I know his secret now!"

"Mrrew," Mica informed him that he was a little late of coming to this knowledge. She poked her head out of the folds of Brevelan's cape. "Mbbbrrrt!" *Beware the tricky magician.*

"Of course, Mica. We should have known Krej would never do anything directly." Brevelan scratched behind the cat's ears. "You daren't take any more Tambootie, Jaylor. Can you reverse his spell without it?"

"If I let the web beneath my feet power the spell . . ." His thoughts tumbled out of order. "Lines of power run straight. Tambootie twists."

Jaylor sought the bluesilver lines. His eyes squinted nearly shut. Colors blended together, grass and sky, trees and road. A bright spring flower faded to nothing in the kaleidoscope he created with his vision.

He isolated the traces of yellow and banished them from his sight. Red, too, he eliminated. Shades of purple and brown were easy. The greens were prevalent. They took more concentration. But finally they, too, fled from the swirl of colors.

Only the blue was left. A strand of the single color danced about, twined, and braided back on itself. Elusive, lovely, powerful. It strung itself forward and back, into a delicate tracery of magical lines. Some ran up the trees into the sky. Some danced around his feet. But one line. One long, straight, and thick line ran directly beneath his feet, from south to north.

He needed to make his spell twist though he drew power from a straight line. Six paces back, the road bent unnaturally around no natural barrier. He looked closer at the bend. Two power lines joined at an oblique angle. If he traced one line into the junction and the other line out, he almost saw a curve. The original road builders had left the junction clear. Remnants of an ancient Equinox Pylon lay crumbling there.

He moved back and stepped directly onto the joint.

"Just twist the magic around and get us out of here," Darville grumbled. "We aren't getting any drier standing around waiting for the road to straighten itself out."

"Easier said than done, my prince. But I'll see what I can do." Jaylor turned to face east. Krej's castle lay to the west. His Great Hall filled with unnatural statues gave him inspiration.

The road bounced within his vision again. He ignored it, seeing only the true direction of the blue lines. Slowly he drew power through his feet, up his legs to his belly and chest, then out along his outstretched arm and staff. The road aligned with his vision. "Got it!"

Slowly, he pulled more magic up further into his heart. It resisted, humming a discordant note. He pulled harder. The magic fled from his body, leaving a sour sound in his ears.

"Tricky bastard! He should have faced west, so he didn't." He shook his head to clear it of the lingering noise.

"Give me a moment to clear my head." He faced west.

Brevelan's small hand touched Jaylor's shoulder. He leaned his cheek against it. Warmth and reassurance filled him.

He clasped Brevelan's trembling hand with his own.

The magic vibrated in answer.

"Hum something, Brevelan," he suggested. Excitement filled him once more. "Something sweet and lyrical." The exact opposite of the jarring notes that lingered in Krej's magic.

A soothing little tune came from her throat. The magic within him sang it back.

"Sing with her, Darville," he commanded with strength and new courage.

"What!"

"Don't argue, just hum, the same thing she sings." His heart beat in counterpoint. He lifted his own voice and wove a deep harmony to their higher tones. Each musical line blended and twisted around the corner. He had his curve of music around the straight line of power.

The magic filled him, spread through all their limbs, climbed to new heights. The three of them were one being, sharing thoughts, emotions, power. One body vibrated with pulsing magic. They took off and soared together once more. He leveled his staff along the line of blue—right where the road should be, while his body looked toward the Great Bay.

Blue. Silver. Green. Red. Purple. Copper. More blue. The colors of Coronnan braided themselves along the staff and shot forth in a line, straight and true.

The road found its direction, wavered and shimmered, then settled along its original route.

"I believe we have a journey to make, my friends."

Jaylor smiled as he lowered the staff and took his first step on the road to Castle Krej. He kept Brevelan's hand tucked into the crook of his elbow. Darville's hand rested on his shoulder. None of them was willing to break the unity they had found while flying with the dragons.

Mica purred. The soaking rain gave way to broken shafts of sunlight.

They are coming closer. I can feel their presence. The journeyman is more clever than I thought. He has broken one spell. There are many more traps along the way. I shall twist and twist again the magic that will delay him. He'll never break through my defenses. No man can defeat me. I have accomplished too much.

If only this headache would go away. The pain throbs constantly, demands my attention when I need all my concentration to maintain my spells and save the bumbling army from their own mistakes. I can't allow the minor inconvenience of a lost battle to destroy my schedule of conquest.

A little more Tambootie. I must have a little more to ease the pain, increase my concentration, strengthen my spells.

Baamin stood outside the door to the king's study, uneasy, undecided. Only it wasn't the king's anymore. Krej's ambition had gone too far. The Lord Regent's inflated conceit needed to be curtailed before he managed to destroy Coronnan and the Commune with it. But was Baamin, Senior Magician, the man to stop the king's cousin?

He couldn't delay any longer. Someone had to take action and he seemed to be the only one capable of seeing what needed to be done.

With a flourish of his staff and a flash of harmless blue powder, he stepped through the doorway, into the king's study.

"The border city of Sambol has fallen," Baamin announced.

"What!" Krej shouted, half rising from the thronelike chair behind the desk.

"The border city of Sambol fell to a series of attacks by a well-organized army, disguised as raiders," he repeated. "Raiders who carried purses of gold drageens from the mint in your province of Faciar." The news wasn't pleasant. Krej's surprise at the news was. "How did they obtain uncirculated coins that only you could have provided, Lord Regent?"

"Sambol can't have fallen. I had messages from Lord Wendray last night. He assured me that his troops had beaten back the men who breached his walls." Krej waved his hand in dismissal, totally ignoring the implied accusation that he had paid the raiders to attack Sambol. "How did you get in here, old man? I gave orders banning you from my presence."

"I'm a magician. I have my ways." Baamin shrugged. He was enjoying Krej's discomfort. Krej had spent his boyhood either in his mother's isolated care or in the University. So he'd never learned about the existence of the myriad secret tunnels that ran through and beneath Palace Reveta Tristile. But Baamin knew them and could enter nearly any room in the palace. He'd explored them numerous times when he and Darcine were young.

"The dragons have deserted the kingdom. There is no more magic to make you a magician," Krej asserted. The Lord Regent settled back into his chair but continued staring at Baamin as if he were vermin.

"Are you sure about that?" Baamin refused to move from his place just inside the door. He allowed his eyes to squint just a little. There was the faintest trace of a silver-blue web at his feet. It faded into nothing where Krej sat.

Either Krej couldn't find the lines, didn't know they were a power source, or he'd been unable to move the desk and chair to a stronger location.

"I'm very sure, Baamin." Krej, too, was squinting now. What did he see—the lines or Baamin's aura? Swiftly, Baamin drew in his thoughts and energies. His mission would be for naught if Krej saw either the vial of deadly powder in Baamin's pocket or his intent to use it. If Baamin found the courage to kill Krej tonight, problems would surely follow. If he allowed Krej to live, the red-haired lord would continue to wreak havoc on them all.

A knock on the door behind him did not disrupt the locked gazes of the two men.

"I . . . ah . . . brung yer . . . ah . . . wine, sor." A slurred, juvenile voice stammered shyly.

The kitchen boy slid between Baamin and the door-jamb. He seemed shorter, younger, more ragged, and more stupid than he had just last night. His shoulders were slumped in a posture of humility and defeat. In the classroom he stood straight and proud. The master re-sisted the urge to examine his pupil for signs of magic disguise.

"Put down the tray." Krej barely registered the boy's presence.

Boy did as he was told with a clatter, and more than a few drops of wine splattered across the desk and Krej himself. A quick picture of Krej gasping for air, his face purple, tongue swollen, life fading, flashed into Baamin's mind. He nearly gagged at the thought of a man dying in such a horrible manner, by his poisonous hand.

Still, the deed needed to be done. He was resolved. The only way to save the kingdom from Krej's manipulations was to eliminate Krej.

"Clumsy oaf! Who had the audacity to send such a stu-pid, filthy, miserable idiot to serve me?" The Lord Regent pushed away the boy's attempts to mop the spill. Each swipe of Boy's less-than-clean cloth resulted in more wine spreading across the documents on the desk and Lord Krej.

"Go. Now, before you do any more damage," Krej bel-lowed as he cuffed the boy's ear.

Boy ducked quickly. Almost too quickly, as if he had seen the blow coming before it was sent.

Baamin saw a document disappear into Boy's filthy, oversized tunic. His only acknowledgment of the theft was to close his eyes slowly as Boy scuttled past him out the door.

Baamin breathed deeply and recaptured Krej's attention. "If you doubt my information, then send a messenger on your fastest steeds to intercept the wounded rider Wendray dispatched before dawn. The city has fallen. What's left of the defending army is in well-organized retreat." Baamin paused to allow the news to penetrate.

He fingered the vial in his pocket. If he started murmuring the proper spell now as he stood over the line of power, the magic would be at its most potent as he slipped the powder into Krej's wine.

"Or perhaps messages would travel more quickly if you allow your pet rogue to summon Master Haskell who's stationed there. He knows as much or more than your own spies," Baamin goaded as he took two steps toward the desk and the glass of wine. The words of the death spell were firmly fixed in his mind. He need only utter them.

"Your imagination runs wild, old man,' Krej sneered. "Leave me." He drank deeply of the wine, pointedly offering Baamin none. "Go pester someone more gullible with your dangerous maundering." The regent's eyes narrowed as he once more scanned the senior magician. "You belong in a monastery with the rest of the failed magicians who become false priests of the mythical *Stargods*. Priests are the only people willing to put up with you." He waved a hand in dismissal.

"Check your sources again, Lord Krej." Baamin damped his temper and his forward movements at the slur against the official religion of the Three Kingdoms. "You might also make sure you have taken into account all that I know about you and about the king's dragons."

The information to convict Krej was at hand. Baamin need only find all the bits and pieces and present them to the Council. Forfeiture, humiliation, and death were the penalty for treason. Horrible, painful death.

"You haven't heard the last of me, my lord." With a smile, Baamin threw a handful of green powder that exploded into blue fire. The poison remained firmly in his pocket.

Tricks and sleight of hand.

But Krej's temporary flash-blindness gave Baamin the opportunity to disappear quite dramatically.

And left the Lord Regent alive and well, for now. Considering the death that awaited a treasonous lord, Baamin wasn't doing Krej a favor by allowing him to live tonight.

"*Simurgh* take your dragons and your magic. I am the only one who can save this country from three centuries of mismanagement. Not you, not your dragons, and certainly not some ancient legends about saving angels descending from the stars to wipe out a nonexistent plague." Krej's words echoed down the halls.

"You'll learn, Lord Krej," Baamin muttered from his hidden alcove. "You'll live and learn not to question legends and certainly not to tamper with the Senior Magician!" He touched the vial again. "I couldn't bring myself to kill another man tonight. I don't think I ever could." Perhaps his nightmares were only the product of his overactive imagination. Now he knew deep in his soul he could never kill another man, never transform him into anything less than a man.

The road curved west to avoid a rampaging stream. Jaylor considered the obstacle carefully. It was too wide and fast to ford. They must follow the road and hope for a bridge.

Darville threw a rock into the frothing water. "Is there any place in the kingdom that is dry?" He looked up to the heavy clouds. The rain washed some of the travel dirt from his face and beard.

"It's possible this bad weather is caused by a lack of dragons." Jaylor slumped. He was tired. They were all tired. They'd been on the road for more than a week and had traveled only a little over two leagues.

"Do you hear voices?" Brevelan reached a hand in front of her, testing it, weighing it for emotions carried on the wind.

"I don't remember a village in this vicinity on my journey south." Jaylor pointed his staff along the road, focusing on its vibrations.

Darville took several cautious steps. "I don't think we

should be seen." He sniffed the air. The hair on the back of his neck stiffened. He bared his teeth. "Into the bushes." He dragged Brevelan with him, expecting Jaylor to follow.

"That won't be necessary." A strange voice spoke behind them.

As one, they whirled to face the hidden speaker. "Zolltarn!" Jaylor cried in alarm. He stepped in front of Brevelan, putting a barrier between her and the stranger.

The Rover looked older than he had a few weeks ago. But the wings of silver slashing through his blacker-than-black-hair and the whipcord lean strength of him were the same. Though worn and threadbare, his garish red shirt, his trews and boots as black as his hair, were carefully mended and clean. Around his lean waist was wrapped a brilliant sash of purple.

Brevelan peeked around Jaylor's broad back for a better look at the man's face. Jaylor felt her curiosity but sensed no fear.

"Ah! my young magician friend." Zolltarn narrowed his eyes as if assessing Jaylor and his companions. His wary stance belied the amiable voice.

"I haven't time to linger in your camp, Zolltarn." Jaylor was equally on guard.

"Perhaps your friend would be willing to aid us as you could not?" The Rover's black eyes scanned Darville.

"My friend is needed elsewhere as well." A new hardness came into Jaylor's voice. He clutched his staff tighter, prepared to aim a paralyzing spell at the Rover.

"What kind of aid should I give to people exiled from Coronnan?" Darville sounded wary. As he should.

"You don't want to know, Roy." There was a time when they would have laughed at the kind of aid needed by the Rovers. Since they had shared Brevelan's bed, assisting Zolltarn in rebuilding his clan seemed betrayal.

"But he is young and strong. My tribe could benefit greatly from his services." Zolltarn smiled with a wicked leer. "And I am sure he would draw great pleasure from the duty."

"Does he mean what I think he means?" Darville asked.

"He does." Jaylor didn't need to share his friend's thoughts to know he had guessed Zolltarn's purpose. "Not this time, Zolltarn. We must be on our way."

"When we reach the capital, we will find you, maybe continue this discussion." The Rover stepped closer.

"You go to the capital?" Brevelan sounded apprehensive.

"We were invited by the new Lord Regent. He needs many men. We need to search for one of our own who was stolen from us."

"You won't like Krej's idea of duty, Zolltarn." Darville finally spoke. "He needs men for an army to fight raiders and invaders on the western border. Some of those he asks you to fight might be your own kin. You won't be allowed to search for anyone, least of all one of your own who is lost."

Alarm spread across the older man's face. "Then perhaps we will find a different road to follow." He placed one friendly hand on Jaylor's shoulder; with the other he firmly grasped the staff. "Can we at least offer you a night's hospitality?"

"Zolltarn?" Brevelan dared address the man. He turned to her, releasing his grasp on Jaylor's shoulder but not on the staff.

"You have questions, little beauty?"

She blushed under his admiring appraisal.

"Why are you being so kind? Legends of your people tell us to be wary of your thieving."

The Rover threw back his head in laughter. The movement caused his arm to jerk at the staff. Jaylor held tight.

"Ah, little beauty, your legends were created by old women to frighten children. We are merely passing each other in journey. Though I could use the men," his eyebrows lifted in a knowing leer, "I have found they will serve me better if they come to me willingly."

"You won't find many willing in Coronnan. We have been taught to avoid you, lest you steal our goods, our children, and our souls." Darville tried to step between Zolltarn and Jaylor.

Seven other Rovers jumped from concealment in the woods. Darville still pushed forward. The others grappled him. He swung his fist and connected with one jaw before being wrestled to the ground. Arms and legs flying, he brought his opponents down with him

The blood lust of his youth swelled through Jaylor's body. He and his gang of town boys had learned to fight in the streets and alleys of Coronnan City. They could hold their own with the dirtiest fighters in the capital.

He flung one knotted fist upward to connect with Zolltarn's perpetual grin. His staff blocked a kick from behind.

A third Rover caught Jaylor with a blow to his middle. He doubled over and turned around, one booted foot kicking out behind, into the center of Zolltarn's chest.

Brevelan screamed behind him. His blood froze. She didn't have the clearing to protect her. How would she fight off strong men?

New fury impelled him into the fray. He swung his staff right and left, knocking Rovers aside. One after another they fell with bruises and breaks as he fought his way to Brevelan's side. Only one man remained between him and his beloved. He brought the staff down on the man's head. The bold young Rover with broken teeth and a malicious smile slumped to the ground as the twisted wood broke into three ragged pieces.

"Enough!" Zolltarn cried to his men. "The magician has broken his staff, we have no need to steal it." The Rovers melted into the woods, carrying their wounded with them.

CHAPTER 29

"My staff!" Jaylor yelled as he took off after the retreating Rovers. "You *s'murghin'* bastards broke my staff!"

Dense woods closed around him within a few steps of the path. Heavy underbrush tangled every footstep. Thick vines reached out from low hanging tree limbs and encircled his ankles. He was flat on his face in the middle of a saber fern.

Desperately he hacked at the vine with his knife. The pithy plant oozed a corrosive sap that dulled and discolored the blade.

"Give it up, Jaylor." Darville limped over to his prostrate friend. "We'll never catch them now. They melted into the shadows like so many ghosts."

"They broke my staff, Roy." Jaylor resorted to the adolescent name for the prince.

"I know, Jay. I know and I'm sorry."

"The staff was my only hope of reversing Krej's spell on Shayla."

Disappointed silence hovered over them.

"We'll cut you another staff, Jaylor." Brevelan picked her way through the overgrown ferns and downed trees to his side.

"That won't help much. I have to be matched to the staff. The wood grain has to be used to my brand of magic to channel it, focus it. The more I use it, the stronger becomes the partnership. We just don't have enough time to break in a new one."

"Could we mend the old one?" Darville suggested.

"The fibers would be too weak."

"Then we'll have to find another way." Brevelan reached out a hand to help him up.

He just stared at her.

"There is no other way." He cradled the broken pieces of wood against his chest.

"We just can't walk through there." Brevelan stared at the jumble of cottages nestled together. The back of each cottage, hut, and prosperous farmhouse faced away from the looming fortress. Sheets of rain set up a further barrier between Castle Krej and the village, between herself and the people who lived here.

Each step became heavier and more reluctant than the last.

"This is the most direct way to the castle . . . and Shayla," Darville complained about her slower pace. He tried to take her arm and urge her forward.

Brevelan recoiled from his touch. "You don't understand," she nearly sobbed, retreating into the haven of Jaylor's shoulder. His arm encircled her, but she felt no strength, no support from him.

She knew these two men so well she expected to feel every emotion they felt as soon as they did. Now they were closed off, consulting each other over the top of her head.

They had been on the road for weeks. Every meal, bed, and thought had been shared equally. They had no secrets from each other. Except this.

"I can't let them see me! And Jaylor doesn't have a staff to grant us invisibility." This time she stepped away from them both, backward, the way they had come.

"Brevelan, my sweet, no one who knows you could believe you killed that man," Jaylor reassured her. "Even Krej didn't really believe it when he taunted you in Shayla's cave. He was only trying to feed your fearful memories to negate your magic." He reached for her hand.

She stood firm. "But I did kill him." She lifted her face to the rain. The water couldn't wash away her memories of that awful night. . . .

* * *

In the bridal chamber, the village women had bathed Brevelan. Combed her hair until it shone. Fussed over the fresh bedding and finally slipped a clean shift of fine linen and embroidery over Brevelan's head. They had winked and remarked on that fineness and how the new husband would appreciate it—for a few moments anyway. And what a shame to leave the garment on the bride since it would only be torn away so quickly.

They had left, giggling. But a few had looked back over their shoulders with a trace of concern. This was considered a good marriage. Brevelan was young and healthy. The bridegroom was as old as her da but prosperous and had sired several sons on each of his first three wives.

Brevelan shuddered with a chill born of more than the evening dampness. Before the exquisite coverlet could warm her, *he* came in.

He was drunk, of course, as were his ribald companions. Good-naturedly he blocked the doorway with his squat body. Barred from their fun, the other men, and a few women, shouted their displeasure.

Brevelan didn't have to understand the exact words, or her husband's crude reply, to know they expected to watch the proceedings. It was a part of close-knit village life for the celebration of a wedding ceremony to extend to the bedroom. They all wanted to make sure the groom was capable of siring any child the bride produced months down the road.

The blood drained from her face and hands. Her trembling become more violent as her husband shoved the door closed and barred it. The pounding on the mismatched slats of wood became louder. He slid Brevelan's carved wooden clothes chest in front of it. The intruder's entrance would be delayed, should they manage to break though the buckling wood.

"We'd best hurry or they'll think they have a right to be part of this." His smile showed no mirth or joy.

She couldn't reply.

His good woolen tunic fell atop the chest. The straw

mattress shifted under his weight and his boots landed on the floor with a thud that echoed through her mind with menacing force. The mattress shifted again as he stood long enough to shed his trews. Only his knee-length shirt covered his bulging need for her.

She shrank away to the far edge of the bed.

"Come here, wife," he demanded. His eyes narrowed to slits.

She couldn't obey, though she'd vowed to before the priest and village. Instead she pulled the covers higher.

"Don't play shy with me." He climbed closer on his knees, braced with one heavy hand. The other yanked the blanket from her grasp. There was the sound of rending cloth as the embroidered edge tore through her fingers.

Someone outside the door laughed at the sound. So did her husband.

"We all know there's no such thing as a virgin in this village. Lord Krej makes sure of that." Spittle foamed at one corner of his mouth. His excitement mounted. He grabbed her breasts and squeezed until she cried out in pain. "If his brat isn't already growing inside you, mine will be soon enough."

That shocked her. Hadn't he heard the rumors? Didn't he know Lord Krej was probably her father? Their lord might be cruel and lustful, but he wasn't so evil as to rape his own daughter!

"Doesn't matter whose brat." He belched. The foul smell of too much ale combined with too much meat in his body assaulted her. She wanted to retch. "One of his bastards brings favors to the family. I could use a few favors." This time his mouth came down on her in a punishing, openmouthed kiss.

She gagged.

He laughed. Then he hit her, backhanded across the face. Once, twice, then a third time for good measure. With each blow his hand tightened until it was a fist that connected with her eye. Her lip split, too. She tasted the copper of blood and fear. She tried to push him away.

"No. Please, no," she begged.

"Got to teach you who'll be master in my house," he

laughed and belched again. "Can't have you thinkin' you know anything but what I tell you."

Without another word he captured her small useless fists in his free hand. His grip was as punishing as his kiss. His leer traced every inch of her barely shrouded body. Once again he crushed her mouth.

She could feel bruises forming. The small pain in her face and hands built and traveled to her shoulders. Her chest and stomach cramped in fear. Instinctively she drew her knees up in protection.

Still forcing her hands above her head, he used his weight to wedge her legs down and apart.

He was heavy. She couldn't breathe, couldn't think. Her pain and fear mounted and spread. She sensed her emotions swelling into an empathic cloud that formed outside her body, filled the room, and echoed from floor to ceiling. A scream escaped her lips as her fear magnified itself again. The listeners laughed. Her husband shuddered, breath burst from his mouth in a soundless explosion. He collapsed across her.

Her imprisoned hands didn't respond to the sudden slackness of his once too-tight grip. His inert weight across her body hindered any movement. When she finally levered away, her vision was transfixed by his protruding, staring eyes, the spittle and blood on his lips, the ugly black blotches on his face.

Deep within her the healing instinct demanded she reach out and dissolve the blockage to his brain. Her fear of him overrode that instinct. He was dead already. She could do many things to help him, if he still lived. But no pulse fluttered against her tentative touch, no breath stirred his graying beard.

The sounds of the people waiting at the door retreated. They must have believed the deed done and so lost interest.

Brevelan was alone with the man her radiating emotions had killed. . . .

"Is that why you ran, little one?" Darville chuckled as he enveloped her in one of his possessive and protective hugs.

Even Jaylor was smiling.

"You didn't kill the man. He killed himself." Jaylor added his own strong arm to the embrace. Mica was there, too, butting her wet, bedraggled head against Brevelan's chin.

"You're wrong, both of you." There was still one thing Brevelan needed clarified. "Part of my healing talent is to take a person's fear and pain into myself and give them back the strength to fight their ailment." She swallowed hard and looked away. "On that night," her voice dropped in shame, "I couldn't take away his need for anger. I felt it and it terrified me. Instead of giving him peace and gentleness, I gave him fear—agonizing, paralyzing terror. I was like Jaylor's glass. I took my small emotions and made them bigger. So big his mind couldn't handle it and forced his body to die."

"Perhaps," Jaylor mused. "More likely there was a weakness in his body that would have killed him the next time he felt any violent emotion. He sounds like a man who couldn't live without anger and couldn't live with it."

"Remember the spotted saber cat, Brevelan," Darville interjected. "It refused all contact with your mind. That man was so filled with anger and hate he wouldn't have accepted your gentling even if you could have broken down his barriers."

Love from all of them poured over her.

Brevelan stood straighter and stronger for that love. She hadn't realized how strong was their bond. While she thought she had only relived that fateful night in her mind, they had shared the entire experience. Just as they had shared the magic when they broke Krej's diverting spell. Just as they had shared the flight of dragons the night Jaylor had returned to them.

Baamin continued to mull over the alliance the kingdom of Rossemeyer wanted with Coronnan. The promise of trade and mutual military aid hinged on the marriage of their princess, Rossemikka, to Prince Darville.

He read again the document Boy had purloined from

Krej's desk. Though couched in pleasantries, the language of the missive clearly outlined the consequences if the alliance failed.

How would the Lord Regent respond to this offer and the impending arrival of two ambassadors? He didn't have a prince to exchange for the much needed armies. He had only a golden wolf wandering the kingdom with a journeyman magician and a witchwoman of uncertain power.

But Baamin had access to the prince. If Darville ever arrived back at the capital.

"Boy?" He summoned the boy's image through his glass and his candle. He was so easy to find, even across the miles, as if Boy's mind were tuned especially to Baamin's thoughts.

"Call me Yaakke, sir." The boy's image was clearer than most master magicians'.

"Yaakke?" Son of Yaacob, the usurper. Now why would Boy choose that name? And who did he plan to supplant.

"That is the name I have chosen, sir." Behind the boy were the noises of Castle Krej's busy kitchen.

"We'll explore that later, B . . . Yaakke. Have you seen my journeyman yet?"

Yaakke closed his eyes briefly before responding. "They approached this village, sir, then turned back."

"Keep track of them. I need to speak to Jaylor as soon as you can contact him. And see if you can keep them out of trouble." He'd given up trying to summon Jaylor himself. His journeyman had either ignored the spell or cut him off. What was he hiding? Or was Krej's rogue interfering and interrupting the communication?

So his beloved Brevelan was like his glass, Jaylor thought. She magnified magic. What if, instead of using his glass on a flame, he summoned Old Baamin by holding her hand and staring into her eyes? She'd have to sing to amplify the natural resonance of the land. He was impatient to experiment.

The rain drizzled down his forehead to drop from the

tip of his nose. This was neither the time, nor the place
to play with new magic techniques. He needed to be
warm and dry, comfortable, before he tried something so
outrageously new.

He'd have enough problems when he finally encountered Krej. Without a staff, he'd need every bit of concentration and familiarity with the spells before he freed a
dragon from a glass prison. He'd kept his senses alerted
to every tree he passed, hoping against hope to find a new
staff. So far nothing had called to him.

"I think we'd best find a place to hole up until dark."
Darville scanned the dreary village once more.

"There's an inn several miles north." Brevelan pointed
the way. "The landlord caters to traveling merchants. Krej
likes the luxuries strangers bring to his market. He
doesn't like to house and feed them. Nor does he like his
villagers talking to outsiders. We might get the idea that
other lords are not so harsh or demanding. No one will
question the presence of strangers at the inn."

"Are they all legitimate merchants, or does Krej trade
with magicians and mercenaries from afar, as well?"
Darville stared murderously back at the castle.

"There have been rumors of covens and sacrifices to
pagan gods for years. They started with Lady Janessa,
Krej's mother." Jaylor thought back to his early years at
the University when court gossip couldn't say anything
good about the foreign wife of King Darcine's uncle.

"That's one lady I don't care to meet again." Darville
turned away from the lair of their enemy. "Her eyes are
eerie, uncanny—always fully dilated. She looks at people
like a slippy eel devouring a nomad Bay crawler."

They trudged along the wide path. The mud, churned
by the huge feet of sledge steeds, made walking difficult.
Twice they were forced off the track by swearing farmers
prodding their beasts with loads of produce in the direction of the inn.

"Darville," Jaylor spoke quietly to his friend. "We are
on Krej's home territory. He must not see you." He sym-
pathized with the prince's distaste for the coming
transformation.

The broken pieces of his staff were in his pack. Fortunately he'd thrown this spell often enough not to need the focus the wood provided.

"Everyone here will gladly spy for Lord Krej," Brevelan added. "Some say they owe their souls as well as their livelihood to him. He'd know of your presence and our purpose within moments.

"I know, I know," Darville groused. He turned his back as he shed his cloak and warm tunic. "Try and keep my clothes out of the mud." He handed his outer garments to Brevelan, his pack to Jaylor. His fingers lingered on Mica's wet fur as he set her down on the path.

"Be gentle with me when we share a meal this time, Mica." He rubbed the side of his nose where she was in the habit of swatting him away from his kill. "At least I'll be warm and less likely to feel the rain."

He shrugged his shoulders in preparation for the spell that would hit him square in the back if Jaylor used the staff. Without the focus, the magic engulfed him in a cloud. He didn't even flinch as his form shifted into that of an oversized golden wolf.

CHAPTER 30

The inn smelled wrong. Too many strangers here. Darville couldn't sort their scents. He sensed fear and greed. Illness, too, but he didn't know which smell belonged to which person.

He paced beside Brevelan, keeping her between himself and Jaylor, pressing closer to her with each step. His neck bristled with disquiet. A growl boiled just below his throat, not quite ready to emerge. He was prepared for anyone, anything that might attack her.

Thwack! a water jug shattered on the beaten ground beside the well. A woman stood hunted still, her silent stare jerked between them and her broken jug. Then she ran back toward the inn. Brevelan took a step toward the woman. Darville followed, keeping his place between Brevelan and the inn.

He showed his teeth and allowed the growl to travel up his throat. The woman had smelled of fear and betrayal. He could almost taste her emotions on his tongue.

"Mama?" Brevelan sounded strangled. Jaylor held her close. Darville growled again.

"Go away." The woman looked over her shoulder from the doorway of the inn. "Go quickly. You killed him. The *Stargods* have cursed us because his death went unpunished. The elders will burn you." She bent her head and turned to flee. "Only when you are dead will this rain stop and crops grow." This time she looked Brevelan in the eye.

There was sadness dwelling in her as well as a burning anger.

Don't be ridiculous." Jaylor pushed Brevelan behind

him. "The entire kingdom is cursed with too much rain, not enough sunlight. It's part of a natural weather cycle."

His words were brave, his actions wary. Darville growled again.

"They will burn you." The woman stepped away from them.

"Why are you here, Mama? The wife of the headman should be at home." Brevelan reached a hand to stay the woman's retreat.

"Because you killed a man and went unpunished, there is no bread, no crops, nothing to feed my family. I'm here to earn a bit a bread so the babies won't cry all night and the men will have enough strength to wrestle some kind of crop from the ground." Her bitterness poured out of her. Brevelan stepped back from it.

A tear trickled across Brevelan's cheek. Darville pushed his head against her leg, offering her comfort.

"Yikiiii!" A stone hit Darville's flank. It was weakly thrown and dropped without damage. But it hurt. He spun in his tracks looking for his attacker. No stone must be allowed to penetrate his guard and reach Brevelan.

Angry men streamed out of the inn. They were all around them now. Some with stones. Some with torches.

Brevelan was frightened. Jaylor was, too. They were all in danger. Darville kept his guard.

"The witch and her lover have returned to taunt us with our misery. She's bastard born, no get of mine. See how she consorts with familiars." A man at the front of the pack shouted.

"Da, please listen and understand!" Brevelan pleaded. The crowd moved closer.

"Kill them! Burn them all. It's the only way to stop this cursed rain." Another man waved his torch, beckoning the others forward.

Darville sprang at the man. His teeth sank into the arm that carried a torch. Another man kicked him. He bit that one on the leg.

Shouts and kicks from every direction. His teeth sank into flesh here and there, front and back. He tasted blood and knew satisfaction.

Part of him knew that Jaylor struck out with fists and the pieces of his staff, even as he backed away from the crowd. They both worked to keep the angry men away from Brevelan.

Then a chance stone struck her. Blood trickled from her temple. Jaylor caught her. Darville spun to find the throat of her attacker. Brevelan was down and he had to rip out the man's throat.

A torch followed the stone. He smelled burning cloth. "Back, Puppy, back." Jaylor's words penetrated his battle-maddened mind. He knew they had to retreat.

Still he fought the people who pressed him. There were fewer now. He lusted for the blood of one of them, any one of them.

Suddenly he was flung backward. A flash of light blinded him. He landed with a thud on his side and knew only blackness.

Jaylor ran with the unconscious Brevelan over his shoulder. The backlash from the magic nearly blinded him. He wasn't aware that he'd thrown the spell. It must have emerged from the depths of his need to protect Brevelan and Darville.

When his eyes cleared, he saw the wolf collapse under a stony attack. His breath nearly stopped until the wolf staggered to his feet and followed him.

From somewhere he found enough strength and magic to drop a barrier between the angry men and himself and his companions. He'd been thinking about throwing magic since the first attack but hadn't had time to think a defense through.

His steps grew heavier, the path dim. Sweat poured into his eyes and fear clouded his judgment. Then he was into the woods and beneath a dense cover of brush.

Darville limped in a few moments later. He lay panting where he dropped.

Brevelan stirred a little and moaned. Blood still trickled from the darkening spot on her temple. Jaylor touched the spot as gingerly as he could. She moaned again and dropped back into the darkness that held her mind.

Helplessly he held her close against his chest. His stomach turned cold when he touched her pale face. She was so still! He was almost too tired to search for her mind or her aura. Somewhere he found enough magic to examine her more closely. She lived, but her mind had retreated from the raw emotions of the villagers. She was hurt more within herself than without.

And he was untouched. Guilt cramped his gut. His personal armor had protected him. It had risen so fast, so instinctively, he was barely aware of its presence; he hadn't thought to extend it to her and Darville. His thoughts had been only to fight, and anger at the cruel superstition that moved strangers to attack an innocent woman.

Darville's ear pricked at a rustling nearby. The hair on his back and neck stood up in warning. No sound issued from his throat as he prepared to spring at any intruder.

The noise stopped. Jaylor reached for the pieces of his staff again even as he extended his personal armor to include his companions. His favorite tool might be useless for magic, but it had proved an effective club.

"Journeyman?" A small voice whispered from the bushes to their left. "Journeyman, Master Baamin sent me to help."

Jaylor relaxed his grip a little as he recognized the kitchen boy who so cheerfully washed the wine cups.

Darville remained alert.

The boy emerged from his cover, a leading rein in each hand. Behind him two steeds plodded. They were handsome beasts, well fed and curried. Jaylor couldn't say the boy was equally well cared for. He was skinny, ragged, and dirty, but older and taller than when he'd last seen him. Boy stood straighter with more confidence, too.

"Here, sir. It's the best steed I could steal from Krej's stables."

Jaylor squinted at the ragged lad huddled before him. Why had Baamin sent this boy? Wasn't there anyone else at the University more intelligent, more reliable?

"I'll take the wolf across my saddle. We'll follow quick as we can." The boy urged the mounts forward.

Jaylor tried to capture the boy's eyes with his own and

failed. Boy looked everywhere but directly at him. Mostly his gaze hugged the ground.

"The wolf will be fine." He reached to scratch the ears of the exhausted Darville. The wolf returned his gesture with a weak lick across his hand. He was tired and sore but recovering. "It's the lady I'm concerned about. The steed must carry us both swiftly. There's a monastery in the inland hills, several hours from here. Do you know it?" Few were aware of the existence of that retreat. The inhabitants were mostly older magicians who no longer had the strength to gather magic and throw spells. They spent their days mapping the heavens for an omen of the *Stargods* return and painting wonderful images of miracles. These respected elders had one of the best healers in the kingdom at their disposal.

Jaylor pulled Brevelan's limp form closer. A large purple swelling was already appearing on the side of her face. No rain penetrated his thick copse to wash her pale face clean of the blood and mud of their attack.

"I don't know the place. But I can follow. May I hold her while you mount, sir? You've got to leave quickly. The steed will be missed and they'll chase you." Finally, the boy looked up. His dark eyes were wide and innocent. They begged Jaylor for understanding and. . . . He didn't know what the boy wanted from him.

Jaylor shook his head clear of the need to open his soul to those eyes. Even if this was the kitchen boy, Jaylor had learned too much to entrust his secrets to anyone.

"No." Distrust filled him. The boy had arrived too soon, before the fight was truly begun. He couldn't possibly have run all the way from the castle in the amount of time the inn patrons took to gather and launch their assault.

The boy had to have stolen the two mounts and headed for the inn about the time Jaylor was throwing his transformation spell onto Darville. Before any of them knew trouble was brewing.

Instead of speaking further, Jaylor lay Brevelan across the steed's back. With one hand he steadied her inert body and tangled the other in the coarse mane of the fidgeting beast. He vaulted up. Once settled, he shifted Brevelan to cradle her against his chest.

"The wolf is not damaged. He can run beside us to the monastery."

"My master, Baamin, bade me to watch out for you three. I'll follow with the wolf." Grim determination stretched across the boy's face as well as ... disappointment?

Jaylor wasn't sure what to make of the boy. Better to keep him in sight than risk his spreading mischief elsewhere. They still had a long ride to safety.

"Very well. Follow as best you can."

The first of the wounded from the battle of Sambol limped into the capital. Of one mind, they headed for the market square beneath the walls of Palace Reveta Tristile. Shocked and benumbed citizenry followed in their wake.

As the crowd grew, so did their anger and bewilderment. Lord Krej had promised victory. They had put their trust in the man who promised safety and protection.

Emotions ran high, surging ahead of the exhausted soldiers to the gates of the palace. Shouts awakened the dozing guards. Pounding fists on the closed gates alarmed the Council.

Baamin inched his way through the crowd. Everywhere there were cries and wails of anguish as news of death and mayhem followed in the wake of the retreating army.

Most of the capital citizenry ignored the magician's progress toward the palace walls. They were too caught up in their own misery to notice anything. The rest of the people were either openly hostile or avoided contact with him with disdain. They recognized his blue robes if not his face.

Baamin nearly wept at the disrepute fallen on magicians as much as at the anguish of the people around him. There had been a time when he could prowl the market and no one looked twice at his magician's robes. Magicians were commonplace in the capital. University-trained healers and priests were sought after frequently.

He forced his way toward a stricken soldier who stood

swaying, barely standing with the support of a plain walking staff. A bloody bandage wrapped his head, another barely covered a gaping wound along one arm. Gently Baamin touched the man, lending him strength as he sought a rudimentary healing spell.

"Get away from him, ye murderin' sorcerer!" An unkempt woman pushed Baamin away from the man he sought to help.

"Keep your treacherous 'ands to yerself, sorcerer!" another woman spat at him.

"We'll take care of our own. If it weren't for the pampered magicians, we wouldn't be in this war. My Johnny wouldn't be dead!"

"Kill the magicians and stop the war!"

Baamin backed away, doing his best to fade into the crowd. Fortunately they were so caught up in the press toward the palace that the malcontents didn't have time to carry through any threats to his person.

At a shop entrance he discarded the blue robe, and was clad in only a simple shirt and trews—like everyone else. Only then did he press forward through the crowd.

He stopped short before a dry fountain. It had been twenty, possibly thirty years since he had wandered through the capital city alone. As soon as he had received his master's cloak he had been assigned to a court. After ten years he had returned to the University to teach and do research. Most of his time in those days was taken up with his duties. There were servants to run into the market for him, deliver messages and so forth. Excursions outside the University walls were limited to trips into the countryside with his students.

And in the last fifteen years, since becoming Senior Magician and adviser to the king, he rarely left the University except to go to court. Those trips were usually in the company of soldiers, servants, courtiers, scribes, and other hangers on.

Baamin had not truly come in contact with the people of Coronnan since his journeyman days.

Carefully he watched the people around him. Those who continued to go about their daily business had no use for magic. Those who bewailed the losses in the battle sought their own, unlicensed healers and priests—not those who were University trained and magicians of the Commune first.

In the last thirty years, magic had been confined to the realm of politics.

No wonder the people sneered at him, avoided him, made the sign of protection against evil behind his back. Magicians, like politicians had become dirty and evil in their minds.

And Krej exploited those fears in his public attempt to discredit and strip the Commune and the University of talent and authority.

But Krej's promises had backfired. Distraught women pelted the formal balcony with sewage and rotten vegetables. With new resolve, Baamin faced the protected window where royals were accustomed to appear before their people.

Krej emerged from behind drawn shutters. The disgusting missiles ceased to reach as far as the balcony. The Lord Regent looked weary, strained. He licked his lips frequently, as if thirsting for something unattainable. Finally, Krej lifted a benevolent hand to silence the jeering crowd.

Baamin, ever sensitive to the presence of magic, nearly recoiled from the soothing power emanating from that hand. No, not directly from that hand, from someone hidden behind the shutters, or possibly standing at a further distance. Anger boiled up in him. Never in the history of Coronnan had magic been allowed to sway the will of the people—at least not since the Great Wars of Disruption.

Now Krej was authorizing illegal magic openly, because he thought there was no one to notice or counter the spell. Baamin fought the urge to throw his own spell over the crowd. That action would put him on the same level of deceit as Krej. He couldn't live with himself if he sank to such a level. And in that moment he had proved to himself that he had not been the prancing rogue who stole the last dragon from the kingdom.

He raised his own hands. For the first time in his life

he was grateful for his short stature. Krej could not see the raised arms above the crowd.

A tiny silver-blue spiderweb appeared between his fingers. Baamin concentrated all his will into maintaining the filaments of magic light.

Like any good spiderweb, the magic became sticky, attracting flies. Krej's spell was the fly lured and trapped into the web.

The angry noise of the crowd rose to a new crescendo. No longer lulled and persuaded by Krej's magic, they pelted the Lord Regent anew with filth and rotting garbage.

Krej raised both hands and the spell increased. Baamin continued to draw power into his hands. His arms ached with the strain of holding them up under the onslaught of new magic. Still he trapped Krej's power.

This couldn't be the Lord Regent! Yaakke was still at Castle Krej reporting on the regent's activities. Who, then, wore the mask and glamour of the king's cousin? And who maintained that glamour? Pieces of Jaylor's puzzle began to fall into place.

"People of Coronnan!" image-Krej addressed the crowd. His voice boomed over the populace. The people shouted angry curses back. "Listen to me. We have won a great victory."

"Lies! All lies. Our wounded say different," an angry tradesman shouted back.

"Count the dead. They are more than the living!" cried a woman with a black shawl of mourning over her hair.

A rotten apple smashed into image-Krej's chest. It splattered against the plush nap of his overtunic. His outline wavered, revealing a slimmer, shorter man than the Lord Regent. The bloody mess of a spoiled egg followed the apple. It missed the target as magic armor finally surrounded image-Krej. More proof that the man on the balcony had no control over the magic flying into Baamin's trap.

Stones appeared among the flying missiles. An overripe pear penetrated image-Krej's armor, followed by a jagged piece of paving.

Image-Krej retreated to the safety of the room behind
him as guards moved out into the crowd. With cudgels
and staffs they pushed the crowd back from the palace
courtyard, back from the market square, almost into the
surging Coronnan River.

At last Baamin lowered his trembling arms. His knees
sagged. He barely had the strength to stand, but he forced
himself to melt back with the crowd rather than be discovered by the guards.

No more would he allow magicians to be merely politicians, isolated from the people, oblivious to their needs.
Magic needed to be for the good of the general populace
and not just the lords and leaders.

"You can't bring her in here!" a stooped old man with
wispy gray hair and beard whispered to Jaylor from the
safety of the monastery gate. "No woman may pass
through that door."

"I'm a journeyman on quest. I demand a healer for myself and my companions in order to complete my quest.
It is my right." Jaylor pushed the gate with his booted
foot a little harder than he meant. It flung out of the old
man's grasp to crash against the stone walls of the outer
court.

"There hasn't been a woman inside these walls for
three hundred years. Just her presence could disrupt the
entire flow of magic among the brothers."

"*S'murghing* nonsense." Jaylor stomped into the
courtyard, surveying the place. Darville, followed by
Boy and the horses, stayed close on Jaylor's heels. Like
a castle, the monastic retreat was built with tall crenellated outer walls, a courtyard with stables and kitchens,
carpenter shop and smithy housed in sheds around the
yard, backs against the defensive walls. The heart of the
monastery was the stone tower in the center, right next
to the impressive chapel. Both edifices butted up against
the eastern wall.

The guest hall to the far right stirred with more activity
than the main building. Three men, coarsely dressed in
homespun, sat on stools before the entrance. Their boots

were new and clean. Stacks of armor and weapons surrounded them. A grizzled, gap-toothed man, dunked a
soiled rag in a bucket of grease, then applied it to a
sword. A very long and sharp sword.

"Lord Krej is gathering mercenaries," the gatekeeper
continued to whisper. "They have stopped here to rest
and gather new supplies."

Rude male voices erupted from within the guest hall in
bawdy song. The smell of stale beer, urine, and unwashed
bodies followed the obscene lyrics out the window.

"Show us to a room away from the dormitory. We'd
rather not disturb them." Jaylor stepped forward again.

A fold of his cloak drooped to reveal more of
Brevelan's face and head. The gatekeeper gasped at the
sight of her University red hair.

Jaylor could almost read the man's thoughts. Hair that
bright indicated a rare and special magical talent in
males. What, then, was this woman capable of?

"In Masters' Hall there are many empty quarters."
There were hardly any masters left to inhabit the spacious
suites.

"Fine. The wolf will stay with me. The boy must return
to his duties with the horses." Jaylor beckoned Darville
forward.

A servant ran out from the stable to catch the steeds.
He ran an admiring hand along the neck of Jaylor's
mount as he looked to the old man for confirmation that
these magnificent steeds would really be entrusted to
such as he. The boy yanked the reins away from him.

"I'll keep watch for your return," he called to Jaylor as
he vaulted into his saddle. With the clatter of shod hooves
against stone, Boy disappeared through the center gate.

Jaylor mounted an outside staircase that led to the isolated third story of the main building. No soldier poked
his head outside the guest hall into the gathering darkness. Only the three cleaning armor were in a position to
see him, or the burden he carried, and they appeared too
involved in their work to notice.

Darville's nose brushed his leg with each step, unwilling to be separated from Jaylor and Brevelan.

With the scuttling gatekeeper in the lead they slipped down a dark corridor toward the wing reserved for masters.

They stopped before a massive doorway. The portal was sealed by magic. The old man touched the lock with his staff. The door remained firmly closed.

Jaylor heaved against the resistant wood with his shoulder and a muttered spell. The door sprang open.

"How did you do that? You're only a journeyman!" The old man gasped in wonderment.

"This has been a long quest." He buried his face in Brevelan's hair. "Too long and dangerous a quest."

"I'll send the healer." The old man backed away in awe.

"Puppy?" Brevelan roused from her stupor.

"He is safe," Jaylor assured her.

But he didn't hold her any closer, didn't caress her hair. Her first waking thought had been for Darville.

CHAPTER 31

A warmly furred, wet muzzle pushed at Brevelan's hand. She scratched his ears.

"Yes, Puppy, I know it's time to get up," she murmured. Her eyes were so heavy it couldn't possibly be morning yet. She lifted reluctant eyelids. Pain slashed through her head from the light of a single candle. Memory followed the pain with equal ferocity. She and Darville weren't back in her safe clearing anymore.

"Where are we?" She curled into a tight ball, burying her painful head in her arms.

No verbal answer, only Darville nudging her. She opened her right eye, the one that didn't hurt as much as the other. Threadbare tapestries, which had once been rich, covered the walls of a very large room. A real candle lit the space beside the bed, while a gentle fire in a fireplace, not a central hearth, added warmth as well as cheery light. Sturdy shutters covered long narrow windows barring the cold and rain from these opulent furnishings.

Cautiously she stretched to explore the bed where she rested. It was too wide and comfortable. More than wide enough to accommodate herself and two others who had grown used to sleeping rough, drawing warmth from each other. They'd never get used to these luxurious surroundings designed for the wealthy and privileged who lived in the capital. Was she in the palace?

Somehow she doubted that. Darville was still a wolf and Jaylor was not present. She suspected they had been brought to the University. But everything was bigger, richer than Jaylor had described his meager journeyman's quarters.

"Are you all right?" She petted Darville with questing fingers. She sought injuries, despite the growing pain in her head with each movement, each thought.

For answer, she received a sloppy kiss across her hand and cheek. He took her wrist gently into his mouth in loving greeting. She returned the gesture with a scratch behind his ears. The wolf took her response as permission to climb into the high bed with her. Once beside her he urged her into quiet repose again. Mica roused from a sleeping ball at her feet and scooted to her other side.

As if they were back in her own clearing she nestled between them, drawing comfort from their nearness and protective concern. She was no longer embarrassed that her beloved wolf was really her cherished prince. Jaylor must return soon and restore him to his natural form. Then all would be well. Jaylor would see to that.

She fell into a light doze.

A sound roused her. Men's voices spoke softly on the other side of the door. Her fingers curled into Darville's fur. Her mind groped for the identity of the men. A familiar step on the floor of the outer room. Then the door was pushed open a crack.

"Dear heart, I've brought the healer. He'll take away your pain." Jaylor smoothed her brow with the gentlest of hands.

Deep inside herself she found a small soothing tune. She tried to hum it, but her head hurt too much. Jaylor's hand continued to caress her forehead. She allowed his love to fill her and chase out the other, hurtful memory of men with stones and torches, the painful rejection by her mother and her da.

The tune followed his love into her mind.

"The swelling has stopped. But the bruise is painful." Jaylor informed the other man.

Brevelan peered at the small man who wore the robes of a master magician. Jaylor, still in his travel clothes of trews and tunic over a homespun shirt, appeared so much more wholesome and masculine than the little man who scuttled like a beetle toward her. She cringed away from his barely washed hand. Dirt and something that smelled of blood clung to his broken fingernails.

She clung to Jaylor's hand. The bond between them healed her more than the potions and powders the healer pulled from a pouch at his overfed waist ever could.

The smell of meat on an unwashed body assaulted her senses when the healer reached to touch her wound. She felt the death of the animal the man had eaten for his supper. Had he killed it himself?

Then the man's own emotions engulfed her, pressing her back into the bed like the walls of a dungeon. Precious air became scarce. She didn't need to hear his thoughts to know his intent.

Desperately she tugged at Jaylor's hand until he looked directly into her eyes. She had to communicate to him the man's evil intent.

"Grrrowwwwl." Darville's teeth threatened the man's approach. He must have understood her silent communication.

Jaylor's eyes finally locked with hers. She fed him as much information as she could through her own. His deep brown eyes widened in surprise, then slitted in thought.

"You may return to your master." Jaylor didn't look at the healer.

"The lady is in pain. It is my duty to ease it as best I can." The healer's voice was squeakily high, almost effeminate.

"She is not used to strangers. Your presence will hinder any healing," Jaylor asserted. Brevelan continued to cling to him.

"Nonsense. I'll bathe the wound in this salve and give her a dose of this powder in a cup of wine. Red wine, I think, 'tis rich and will restore her blood faster." The man continued to fuss with his pouch near the candle.

Red wine to mask flavors not intended for healing! "No." Brevelan found her voice stronger than she thought. "Your true master bade you to use witchbane and adderroot."

The man gasped. He stepped away from the proximity

of the bed as his hands crossed at the wrist and flapped away any evil. "What witchcraft is this?" His voice sounded strangled.

"It's true, then. You serve a different master than the *Stargods* and the elder of this monastery!" Jaylor rose to tower over the man. The breadth of his shoulders shielded Brevelan from the little man, but not from the emotions of hate that beat back and forth between them.

Once more she sank into the oblivion of black sleep.

The thick book landed with a thud on top of the growing pile at Jaylor's elbow. "Useless," he muttered and reached for yet another tome.

"Not useless, just not containing what you sought." The Elder Librarian straightened the pile of books that threatened to topple. He caressed each volume as if it were a beloved child.

"Precisely." Jaylor flung another of the volumes at the library wall. It struck the neat rows of other books and brought them to the floor with it. Elder Librarian dashed—as fast as his years allowed—to rescue the abused books. "How do I find a counterspell to a spell created by a man with complete disdain for traditional magic?" Jaylor muttered to himself. "A spell that will work without a staff."

The noise created by the fall didn't ease the growing sense of time wasted. "I'm supposed to be more stubborn than smart, if you believe my master. So why can't I find some answers by sheer perseverance?" He looked to the old man. All the members of this community were older than time. Worn out old men with no other place in Coronnan. He shuddered when he remembered the time one of his teachers had suggested Jaylor, along with his poorly aimed spells, remove himself from the hallowed halls of the University to this very monastery.

"Perhaps, because you are smarter than your master thought, you will find the answer with your mind or your heart before your impatience wins." Only a very old man could have the patience of this librarian. " 'Tis not the nature of the spell you must unravel that troubles you. You know that answer already, but not until the other problem leaves your mind clear."

Jaylor looked the man over with new insight. He'd been using his magic vision so much lately he hardly realized what he was doing. There was a small web of power just beneath his feet, feeding his enhanced vision. The librarian's aura showed worry and fortitude and patience.

And there was no smell of meat about him.

"You've given up eating meat," Jaylor stated flatly.

"I've lost my taste for it." The elder shrugged.

"Since when?" Suddenly he needed to know the answer, as if trusting this man depended upon it.

"Since there was no magic left to gather." The old magician's eyes avoided his.

"Most people of Coronnan don't gather magic and they still eat meat."

"True."

"Brevelan forced me to lose my taste for meat. I find my magic different, but stronger, since then." He clued the old man to speak of his own change. He had noticed the elder choosing his place to stand in the room, right over another power spot.

"It occurred to me that there must be another source of magic, older than man himself, used by the magicians we now call rogues." Elder Librarian raised his eyes and allowed them to meet Jaylor's for the first time since the journeyman entered the library. "Traditional magic has only been available for three hundred years."

Jaylor felt the older man's probe, turned it aside, and sent one of his own. It, in turn, was pushed back toward him. This was no failed magician put out to pasture! But for whom did he use his power?

"Adderroot is a poison I know of. Which is witchbane?" Jaylor decided to test this man for reaction. If he showed suspicion at the combination, then he knew of the healer's attempt to poison Brevelan.

"Witchbane?" The librarian moved to one of the long lines of his beloved books. "Witchbane? I've heard the name but not in a very long time." He rummaged behind a few books and withdrew a very old one. "This might tell us." He blew dust from the spine and cover reverently.

"The healer sent by the gatekeeper tried to give some to Brevelan last night." Suddenly Jaylor had to trust the old man who counted books as dearer friends than his fellow elders.

"Oh, dear!" Elder Librarian paled. "I suspected our enemy had placed spies within our midst. I had no idea it was someone so highly respected."

"Or so trusted by all. Isn't he the same healer who was consulted when the king's heart fluttered and nearly failed a few years ago?" Suddenly Krej's master plan fell into place. "Has he been slowly killing the king?"

"Possibly," Elder Librarian whispered, as if afraid to utter such treason. "I thought the destruction of the dragon nimbus was responsible."

So this old man was aware of the loss of the dragons, too.

"But only Darcine's health is in question. His son is hale and hearty, strong and determined." Jaylor began pacing, making sure his steps stayed close to the lines of power he sensed beneath the stone floors.

"Darville was never consecrated. His tie is not as tight to the dragons."

Jaylor began talking to himself, straightening his thoughts with each word. "The bond is tight enough for one dragon to risk everything to protect him." He stopped by the window. In spite of the chill rain outside he had opened the shutters earlier. As always, the confines of a building destroyed his ability to think creatively. He leaned out to look down onto the massive courtyard. Cool rain pelted his face and cleared the fog from his thought processes more than mere words could.

"But that, too, was part of his plan. Our enemy had no hope of finding and snaring the last dragon without the prince. That was why he lured him into the mountains, then tried to kill him. It was a trap for the dragon!" He paced to the next window and threw those shutters open also.

"A trap delayed by the intervention of a witchwoman." His words came out loud enough for the old man to hear. Silence pulsated between them as they thought, trying to find the logic in one so warped as Krej.

"Where does her magic come from?" Elder Librarian's eyes looked innocent. His questions seemed to be just to satisfy the insatiable curiosity of a man dedicated to books and knowledge.

"She believes Krej to be her true father. You noted the hair color. Krej's mother is from another land. Who knows what kind of magic talent, or lack of ethics, she passed on to her son."

"Krej! It can't be. Why, Brevelan must be at least eighteen, maybe older. If Krej were truly her father . . . he was barely sixteen himself, just a new journeyman when she was born. I knew him then. His powers increased until the day he left the University at twenty. He was married within the moon. Since then he could have no magic!"

Jaylor couldn't help grinning. "Sex and magic have very little to do with each other." He knew that for certain, now.

If anything, his powers had increased, or was that the Tambootie he still craved.

"We have not yet found witchbane in the book." Elder Librarian looked away first.

Jaylor grinned at his embarrassment. Magic, old and new, he could discuss with this respected elder, sex he couldn't. "No, we haven't found a reference to witchbane."

Jaylor tried to comb his hair with his fingers. It was neatly tied back into a courtly queue. He scraped his jaw with his hand instead. That, too, felt strange without the beard he'd grown used to. Now he was groomed as a magician should be. Even before he was bathed, shaved, and combed to look like a master magician, he felt that he was a master. He just didn't have a cloak to prove it.

And there wasn't much of a Commune left to grant him that honor.

"But what you really need is a book on unraveling

spells when you don't know how they've been thrown."
Elder Librarian climbed up a sliding ladder searching for
a different volume. Like a bay crawler he pulled himself
along the shelves sideways.

"I know who threw it and how he did it. But there are
pieces of his soul wrapped up in the spell."

"An evil soul within the spell?" The old man gasped as
he stumbled to the chair opposite Jaylor. Elder Librarian
breathed deeply, searched the shadowed corners for answers, and finally looked back to Jaylor. "There is a book
in my quarters. A very old book that was forbidden three
hundred years ago. No book should be destroyed, so,
when I stumbled across it, I hid it rather than cast it into
a fire. I will fetch it for you. But you will not like the information contained there."

"Why not?" Jaylor probed the man. The spell shattered
when it hit armor.

"During the Great Wars of Disruption, such spells were
common. They hold traps of great magnitude for other
magicians. The only way to break the spell is to die."

CHAPTER 32

Elder Librarian was not entirely correct, Jaylor mused as he carefully closed the ancient book and set it aside. He didn't have to die in order to break Krej's enchantment of Shayla. If, and that was a very big if, he could capture the pieces of Krej's soul entwined in the spell and encase them with his own ephemeral spirit, then he might survive. But his own soul would be doomed to wander with Krej's throughout the firmament or writhe in hell for all eternity. It all depended on just how nasty Krej really was and if he had allowed any of his good qualities to form the spell.

Was Shayla's freedom and the safety of the kingdom worth the cost?

Without a staff the question was moot.

He shook his head and paced the outer room of the suite he and his companions occupied. Mica sat in the middle of the hearth rug bathing an already immaculate paw. Brevelan and Darville slept in the inner chamber. He should join them. The moon had set hours ago. The night was far advanced.

This was a decision only he could make, and his resolve still wavered.

Brevelan and Darville had helped him before when he broke the spell of diversion on the road. He couldn't allow them to help him again at the risk of their lives and their souls. Mica purred her agreement.

"I've found a way around Krej's traps twice," he quietly told the darkness in the corners of the room. "I've got to try. For Darville and Coronnan, I've got to try."

Darville stirred in his sleep as Jaylor quietly rustled

among the packs. At the first indication of his friend's wakefulness, he stilled his hand on the three pieces of his staff, now tied into a bundle like so much kindling. Regret for the lost tool—an extension of himself clouded his vision.

"What keeps you awake old friend?" Darville whispered. Brevelan slept soundly on.

"I must finish my quest," Jaylor replied tersely.

"Let me find my trews and boots." Darville yawned as he too searched the packs.

"No, Roy. I have other chores for you." Jaylor stared directly into Darville's sleepy eyes.

The golden-brown pools glimmered in the reflected light of a shielded candle. He didn't blink as Jaylor wove his next words deeply into the prince's thoughts.

"Brevelan will need witchbane from the healers' quarters. She must throw it in Krej's face, make sure he breathes it. Or she can mix it with his wine, but he must drink the full cup. It will negate his powers. But she must be careful how she handles the drug. Not one single drop must touch her skin.

"You, Darville, must face the Council with a sword on your hip to defend against assassins. Elder Librarian will see you transformed back into a prince if I do not return. And if I fail, Darville, you will protect Brevelan. As long as I know she is safe, I am free to risk everything."

The words washed over Darville's furred back. He understood each and every sentence. He would follow the directions until each command was completed.

Darville scouted the crowded courtyard of the monastery. Mercenaries sat in the weak sunshine, mending and polishing their gear. Few, if any of them, paid heed to a scruffy golden dog or a multicolored cat on the prowl. Darville knew that Brevelan was hiding somewhere near the piles of war materials. It was dangerous for her to be seen by any of the foreign men. She had her task and Darville had his. As soon as they were all certain the healer was entrenched with a mug of ale and a long tale to tell a bawdy crew, the companions moved.

The healer's scent was strong in his rooms. Darville found the things he had touched, learned the individual scents, minus the healer's. Somewhere in these two rooms was the potion Brevelan needed. He searched his memory for the scent the man had carried when Brevelan was hurt.

Mica leaped onto a sturdy table. Her nose was as busy as his own. He nudged open the lower cupboards. While his nose worked, his ears were alert. No sound of steps outside the door. Darville was sure he would smell the approach of the healer before he heard him, so distinctive and strong was his odor.

There was nothing of interest in the cupboards, nothing that reminded him of the first time he had seen the healer.

A jar rocked on the table as Mica sought the shelves. Darville growled a warning to her. They didn't have much time. She had to be careful. She hissed her arrogant response.

He sought the boxes under the bed.

"Meroower?" Mica questioned him.

He bounded closer, nose questing. She had found what they sought, wrapped in leather and tied with rawhide.

"Grriipe," he yipped instructions.

Carefully the little cat grasped the bundle in her mouth. It was too big.

Footsteps echoed in the hall. Someone was coming!

Darville whined as quietly as he could. The cat spat at him.

The person stopped with a hand on the latch, lifted it. They froze.

The door began to open. Then the latch dropped. The person moved away, as if he had changed his mind.

Impatiently Mica batted the bundle to the table with her paw. She followed in a graceful leap. Darville stood against the table, happy to stretch his back. The bundle fit easily in his mouth.

From her position on the table Mica swatted the latch until it opened. Then they both slipped out and away. Brevelan should be back in their rooms by now with the weapon she was to steal from the watchtower.

* * *

They have evaded me. The staff is broken and useless but still they find magic to counter my plots. They must have been helped. But who? Who would dare defy me?

Baamin. The old meddler must have found a way. He is dangerous, not as weak as I thought.

I'm not sure I have time to neutralize him.

The Council comes.

I will inform them of the battles my armies have won. No one will dare question my information. If I say the battle was won, then we won.

They will be forced to see that only I can save Coronnan. Only I can be their king. The University must be terminated. Only I can control the magic.

I'll need more Tambootie.

Night had come round again. Alone, wrapped in his nearly invisible dark cloak, Jaylor studied the village behind him and the castle above him on the hill. It was a huge castle. One of the oldest in the kingdom, dating back to before the Great Wars of Disruption, possibly even to the time of the Stargods. It stood on a strong defensive point overlooking the bay on one side, the capital valley on the other.

From the crenellated outer wall, a single sentry commanded a full view of the narrow but fertile valley. The back of the citadel was dug into a cliff. Five tall towers soared upward, imitating the sheer, unscalable walls of the cliff face. As tall as those towers reached, the rock barrier behind was higher—so high no enemy could scale downward or drop into the stronghold and live. Neither could they approach unseen.

There, displayed in the grand hall, protected by Tambootie wood paneling, he hoped to find and free a glass dragon.

If he was strong enough.

If he knew how.

If he could manipulate any magic without the aid of his staff.

Once again he saw in his mind the clouds of colored

magic, heard Krej's chanting voice, close to the music his
daughter used as a channel, but not quite. Jaylor had always used his staff to control the raw power he drew
upon. His magic was tightly focused. Krej's was just as
powerful in final effect but spread over a broader surface.

It was the difference between a widely spread drizzle
and a short intense squall. They both dumped the same
amount of rain with entirely different intensity. Great
bursts of energy opposing a slow, smooth dispersion.
Would his magic be strong enough to blast through Krej's
before his strength was gone?

He rubbed his hands along the short pieces of his staff.
Zolltarn had set out to steal or destroy it, probably on
Krej's orders. They had succeeded.

"It was only a focus, not a part of the magic," he reminded himself. Still, he felt naked without the length of
twisted wood.

But the staff was gone and he was alone. Jaylor had
only himself to count on, or blame, for this night's work.

The small gate by the kitchen midden was easy to find,
since he knew where to look. Elder Librarian had done
his work well in providing the original building plans for
the castle.

The sky was black; no moon showed through the
clouds during this bleak hour after midnight. The cooks
and drudges would all be asleep. He must work his magic
and leave before they arose for their morning baking.

He slid through the dark halls, one hand on the cold
stone walls, counting his steps, memorizing his path. The
great hall was at the top of a narrow stair. A tapestry to
his left was the entrance to the banquet hall, formerly a
soldiers barracks. Opposite that opening was a thick,
locked door.

The lock snapped under his mental probe. The door to
the wine cellar at the University had been harder to open.
Krej must not fear intrusion. The lock was merely for
show.

The smell of the Tambootie wood paneling assaulted
Jaylor's senses. It filled his head and made the constant

craving for the leaves of the tree deepen. But there was no change in the amount of magic he controlled.

Cautiously he moved toward the menacing figures on display. He recognized the great tusker and gray bear from Brevelan's descriptions. There was an empty pedestal that must have held the spotted saber cat—the one Krej had released to entice Darville into the mountains. Other figures loomed about him, but he didn't take the time to investigate.

And there, in the center, rearing up on hind legs, wings half unfurled, was Shayla. Starlight from a dozen open windows glistened through the glass dragon. She shimmered as if alive, just waiting to pounce on her prey.

Jaylor swallowed. His quest was nearly ended. He just had to break this one last spell!

He turned away from Shayla so that he saw her only by sliding his eyes far to the left. The bundle of his staff in both upraised hands, he counted his breaths. In—one, two, three. Hold—one, two, three. Out—one, two, three. In again, hold it three. Out for three counts. His heart beat matched his breathing. His mind and body stilled and prepared.

Blue lines of power slipped before his vision. He found one that pulsed in tune with his heart and lungs. It flowed through him with ease.

Vibrations of magic trembled in his hands and along the pieces of wood. He aimed the jagged ends of them at the glass sculpture slightly behind and to his left. Silver-blue webs encircled his fingers and reached out to every corner of the room until they found the glass dragon.

The magic encircling Shayla hummed and wavered. The dragon blinked in surprise. She fought the spells woven around her.

Jaylor pushed more power through his body. He felt himself rising to the heavens with the magic that was all around him.

The humming grew louder, shriller. His ears hurt, his mind reeled as his heart beat faster and faster until it would no longer be contained within his frail body.

Shayla fought him, fought all the magic. Her eyes grew larger, her mouth tried to open.

With one last, mighty shriek Jaylor crashed to the ground and Shayla froze.

"Jaylor!" Brevelan wrapped her arms around the staggering magician. Dawn crept through the windows as she led him to the nearest chair. "Where have you been for two days and nights?" Her fingers checked his pulse as she pushed aside his soggy cloak.

His breathing was ragged and his heart irregular. Exhaustion left his skin gray and tight.

"I failed. I'm sorry." Tears flowed down his cheeks in the dried path of others that had been shed earlier.

"Shayla. You've been to Krej's castle, alone?" Darville marched into the sitting room from the sleeping chamber. He hadn't slept anymore than Brevelan had these past two nights.

Brevelan eased a lock of hair off Jaylor's forehead, checking for fever. His eyes were too bright, his pulse too rapid. "You need food and rest," she commanded as she beckoned Darville to help their companion into bed.

"I'll not sleep. If I do, I'll dream of Shayla, trapped within the glass forever. She tried so hard to be free it nearly broke my heart." Jaylor dropped his head into his hands, his body racked with sobs.

"What went wrong?" Darville began to pace along the same path he had nearly worn into the hearth carpet since Jaylor's midnight departure. His boots trampled a garden of faded woven flowers.

"Nothing, everything. I couldn't use my staff. There were traps in the magic, more traps than I'd planned for."

Jaylor didn't resist Brevelan's attempts at comfort. He was too preoccupied to notice the tune she hummed. She forced strength and peace through her fingers into his scalp as she massaged his temples and brow.

"We've overcome his traps before." Darville stopped his pacing.

"Not like this one. Trapping Shayla in glass was probably the greatest piece of magic ever thrown. Breaking that spell would be even greater. I'm not even a master yet, how could I be so arrogant as to think I could accomplish anything close to Krej's power."

"Stop that, Jaylor!" Brevelan ordered. "You're tired and temporarily defeated. But you've already accomplished great things. You'll break the spell. You just need more time and a little help." She drew him up to stand beside her. "Now off to bed while I fix a hot meal. When you've slept, we'll try something new." She couldn't allow him to see the worry she felt for him. He'd never been this self-doubting. Many ailments of the spirit she could heal. This one was deeply rooted, feeding itself with memories of every failure from his youth.

"You don't understand, beloved. If I don't manage to break the spell, Shayla will die, the nimbus will be broken, and Coronnan will be at the mercy of Krej and all the outland kingdoms. If I do manage to break the spell, I'll die. I'm not sure my mind will allow that."

"Would some Tambootie help?" Darville looked hopeful.

Jaylor stopped to think a moment.

Brevelan hid her fear. The last time he had eaten of the Tambootie his mind had been lost, nearly forever. What would a repeat dosage do?

"I don't think so. Krej seems to have found a way to feed his powers with the drug. I just separate from my body when I use it."

Good. He had dismissed the dangerous idea.

"A new staff, then?" Darville prompted.

Jaylor just shook his head and wandered toward the sleeping room.

"A new staff, indeed." Brevelan glared at Darville. "A magician's focus is highly personal. Not just any piece of wood will do."

"I was only trying to help."

"You did. We'll mend the old staff while he sleeps."

"Mend the wood? You can't do that."

"I think I can, with a little help." The tune was already forming in her head. After all, a broken staff couldn't be so much different from a broken bone or the dislocated shoulder of a golden wolf.

CHAPTER 33

Stupid, stupid, STUPID! Ambassadors all the way from Rossemeyer to offer an alliance and now they want to withdraw. Can't they see how much I need their armies, their wealth. With their support I could win the war in a week and conquer all of my enemies in a moon.

But they insist the alliance is dependent on our prince marrying their princess. News that Darville is missing caused them to retreat into private counsel. They wouldn't even consider marrying the chit to me. Of course, I'd have to eliminate the current wife. About time anyway. The only brats she can whelp are girls and I need sons.

Seems the King of Rossemeyer has moral reservations against such a move. S'murghing fools. Why be squeamish about breaking marriage vows of fealty and honor taken before the Stargods—gods that no longer exist—*when an entire kingdom, nay empire, is at stake!*

I'll take some Tambootie. Then I will be strong enough to convince the drooling imbeciles of the rightness of my course. Perhaps I should feed the ambassadors some Tambootie as well.

From his outpost in a fisherman's hut, Baamin closely monitored the activities in Krej's castle. Yaakke had placed a piece of glass near a candlestick in Krej's chosen meeting place. Through his own glass and a hearth fire Baamin "saw" the family solar above the banquet hall. Seven of the Twelve sat on benches, chairs and window sills, wherever there was a place to rest their ample bottoms. Some were weary from a long journey. Others were fearful of Krej. One, Lord Andrall, was downright worried about the course of the war.

The border city of Sambol had fallen to SeLenicca three days ago. Krej's army had been routed. The enemy was marching up the Coronnan River unhindered.

Clearly, Queen Miranda of SeLenicca and her consort, King Simeon, would not allow the proposed marriage alliance with Rossemeyer to take place.

"We do not have the resources to fight the square beards." Andrall's weariness showed in the planes of his face. "There is no prince to receive the ambassadors from Rossemeyer. They are leaving at dawn. How long before their army joins that of SeLenicca? They both want our copper and our gold, not to mention our crop lands and protected fishing."

"You must find a way to call the dragons, Lord Regent!" Lord Jonnias urged. "If only one dragon flew over the enemy encampment, they would run back to their own lands in cowardly fear."

"There are no dragons left, fool!" Krej nearly screamed. That is why King Darcine is so near death."

Apparently only Baamin knew that Darcine had indeed died yesterday morning at dawn. The messenger bearing those dire tidings would arrive at the castle within hours. If Darville were not present when the news reached the Council, they would be forced to name a new king.

Krej was the only candidate.

Unless there was a live dragon present. Shayla could refuse to consecrate Krej as king. She could choose Darville as the next ruler.

Not even the Council of Provinces could argue with a dragon.

Baamin closed his observations of Krej's castle. He had to summon Jaylor. They were nearly out of time.

Lights winked from the arrow-slit windows of Krej's forbidding castle. It loomed over the valley, massive, black, unapproachable in its cliffside isolation. The sun hovered a hand's width above the great expanse of the bay. A gloomy twilight hovered in the sheltered valley below the home of the Lord of Faciar, Regent of Coronnan.

Darville tugged the coarse woolen peasant's hood closer about his face. The sword strapped to his back made it impossible to humbly slump his shoulders in imitation of the other men around him. Still, it was surprisingly easy to blend in with the crowd of villagers trooping into the castle to prepare for the evening's festivities.

He almost wished for his familiar wolf form and senses. His tall human body just couldn't hear and smell as well. He had to be more alert than ever. Grief for his father had to be pushed aside until a later time.

A sensation of being watched prickled along his spine. He bent over from the waist, back still straight, to catch a runaway apple. Using his position, he looked about. No one seemed overly curious. He straightened up cautiously.

He noticed Jaylor's eyes dart anxiously about as he bent to heft a bulky sack to his shoulder. There was a weariness in his stance, as if he carried a burden heavier than the sack and the mended staff secreted within it. If his posture were merely an act to blend in with the peasants, Darville would applaud Jaylor. But it wasn't. The magician had been depressed for days. When the summons came from Baamin, his mood had become worse.

Darville couldn't read Brevelan's feelings at all. Sometimes she seemed to have absorbed Jaylor's onerous worries. Other times she was bright and cheerful. Right now, she just kept her face buried in the basket of cabbages she carried. Earlier, Darville had combed a great deal of flour through her hair to mask its bright color. Now it was tightly braided and coiled at the nape of her neck, like that of any respectable matron.

The length of her slender neck tantalized him. He suppressed the need for her that filled him day and night. Not until this adventure was finished could he indulge in the luxury of thinking of Brevelan as his own. When he ruled the kingdom, then and only then could he make Brevelan his queen.

Torches flared at the kitchen entry. A guard, in Krej's

colors of green and dark red, scanned each face. Doubt-
less the Lord Regent had passed orders to watch for the
trio.

Darville only hoped Krej still believed him to be a wolf
so the guards would not be on the lookout for a tall blond
prince as well as an equally tall magician and their delicate witchwoman companion.

The guard grabbed Jaylor's shoulder, spinning him to
face the light. Darville's breath caught in his throat.

Before his eyes Jaylor's shoulders drooped, his profile
blurred and shifted. Fascinated, Darville watched the
spell of delusion transform his friend from youthful magician to stooped and wizened old man who needed the
suddenly visible twisted staff of wood to support his
body.

The guard shrugged and allowed him to pass.

Darville let loose the air he'd trapped in his lungs. Several more people passed through the inspection point
without question. Brevelan was next.

A heavy hand came down on her shoulder. She looked
up with frightened eyes, like a startled doe. Her face was
very pale in the torch light. The guard fingered a tendril
of hair that had escaped the thick coil. His words dropped
to a whisper.

Darville saw the heat rise in her face. He kept his eyes
on the guard while his free hand sought the dagger at his
belt.

Killing the guard would only draw more attention to
himself. He slid the long knife back into its sheath. He
had to control his emotions.

Even as he berated himself he watched Brevelan's eyes
turn cold. She raked the man's body with her gaze and it
was obvious he came up lacking. This time the guard's
face turned red. He dropped his hand and allowed her to
pass.

Once again Darville breathed deeply in relief. Just a
few more people and he, too, would be into the castle.

The guard stopped another woman. She seemed more
receptive to his proposition. They lingered in the doorway
blocking the passage of the other peasant helpers.

"Hey! What's the hold up?" Darville heard himself shout in the rough estimation of a peasant accent. "We've got work to do. Let's get this *s'murghin'* inspection over with. Lord Krej don't like his dinner bein' late!"

"Yeah. Don't want the lord angry with us for your dallying!" Another man called.

"Stop pesterin' our women and get on wi' yer job."

"Stop yer yammerin'." The guard cursed the mob surrounding him. Embarrassed he passed them all through with only a brief glance at their faces.

Sometimes the best way to avoid detection was to call attention to oneself.

The kitchen was hot. An entire side of beef roasted in the giant fireplace on the central wall. Darville sniffed deeply of the belly-warming aroma. Game birds turned on smaller spits at side hearths. Long tables down the center of the huge room were crowded with men and women chopping vegetables, sifting flour into cavernous bowls and doing all the other noisy, busy work necessary to preparing a banquet. Small boys darted about fetching supplies while smaller girls swept up discarded peelings and other residue.

Heat and savory smells washed over the prince. The noise of a hundred people filled his head. It was like coming home. The kitchen in his own palace was much the same. As a small, lonely boy he had sought refuge there when his parents and tutors were too busy to entertain him.

There was always at least one cook or drudge willing to let him taste and experiment.

Before the nostalgia could blind him, he sought his companions in the throng. Jaylor was already edging toward the staircase leading to the upper floors. Brevelan had just deposited her cabbages near the scrub sink. As she straightened, her face lost all color. Her eyes began to roll upward in faint. He was beside her before the others noticed her odd behavior.

Meat. The smell alone would make her ill. The sight of it roasting, plus the churning emotions and frantic activity of all these people, had caused her to seek refuge in unconsciousness.

He grasped her around the waist just as her knees buckled. "Not here, love." Again he used the rough syntax of the people around him.

A woman with a huge chopping knife glared at him.

"Like as not it's her first child, eh?" The woman opened her mouth in a near toothless grin. He tried to smile back at her. "Well, get her out of here. We don't need another body underfoot," the woman commanded.

Darville didn't argue. The woman was too occupied with her turnips to notice he led the wilted Brevelan toward the interior of the castle rather than back outside into the fresh night air.

"The main hall is there." Brevelan pointed to the archway to their left. "That is where the banquet will take place." She peeked through the draperies masking the servants' staircase from the huge central room.

Pain throbbed behind her eyes, the pain of Jaylor's coming ordeal and the press of too many people. She gulped back the flood of emotions. If only there were a tiny tune somewhere in her soul that she could summon to counteract the rising panic within her.

But there were no tunes left in her. Grief for Jaylor overwhelmed all else.

Jaylor seemed calm since reaching a decision that freed his emotions from fear. The wild mood swings he had suffered since he'd failed to transform Shayla the first time were gone. But, she sensed, he was shutting her out of his mind as well as his feelings.

Darville, on the other hand, was fairly bouncing with excitement, despite his suppressed grief for his father. He tried to hide it from her, but she knew him too well. When this night was over, Darville would be king, duly consecrated by a dragon.

"I'll need a place to hide until the assembly is gathered and you are prepared to . . . to do what ever it is you're going to do," Darville said. His eyes scanned the hall with a soldier's eye to strategy.

"Take Mica." Brevelan pulled the dozing cat out of Jaylor's pocket. "She'll find you a place." Briefly she nuzzled the cat's head. Mica's eyes opened round and hazel, and for once she didn't shift to a vertical amber slit as she looked into Brevelan's heart. Understanding passed between them.

"I guess this pesky cat can be of some use," Darville growled, though his voice held the same tone as a puppy's whine for attention. He pulled Brevelan close and kissed her hard. "For luck," he whispered for her ears alone. One gentle finger caressed her cheek.

"You have the witchbane?" Jaylor interrupted.

"Right here." Darville patted his breast pocket. "I won't hesitate to throw it at Krej at the first sign of magic." He looked once more into the hall and slipped through the draperies.

Alone with Jaylor, Brevelan turned her attention to the next task.

"I can smell the Tambootie paneling." Jaylor's nostrils pinched in distaste.

"All of the walls in this room are covered with the wood, even the floor and ceiling. Krej used to keep a Tambootie wood fire burning in the hearth, until it made the servants so ill they couldn't continue their duties." She had to breathe through her mouth to keep the acrid odors away.

The staircase landing seemed to grow smaller as Jaylor's magic filled it. Brevelan touched his arm and felt much of what he saw.

The animals were still there. A gray bear, a wild tusker as large as a hut, a snow-white stag with fifteen points on his rack and several others she could not name. The spotted saber cat was gone, she hoped never to return. No animal, no matter how ferocious, deserved the living death of Krej's sculpture cages.

In the center of the room on a low, wide dais stood Shayla. All of her intense beauty was captured in the glass. Each transparent hair of her fine fur was crystallized to reflect back the light of a thousand torches.

Along her spine, horns, and wing ridges, a rainbow of colors swirled, daring the eye to look anywhere but at her.

Brevelan tugged at Jaylor's arm. "Shayla said that dragons eat of the Tambootie to become the source of magic, yet they have none of their own! Krej eats Tambootie like a dragon. How can he throw magic and be a source as well?"

"That I don't know. Unless his body reacts with the Tambootie differently. When he is near, I can sense no gatherable magic anywhere near him." He shook his head, puzzled. "There is no time to worry about that now. I must find the strongest point to stand. There are precious few lines of power running through this castle."

"No one is in the room." She felt all the emotions in the castle, but they were behind her and above her. "No one except Krej can stand to be in this room for more than a few minutes."

"Where is he right now?"

"Above." His emotions were easiest to separate from the others. "He is very upset about something." Too upset. She had to block him out before his anger became her own.

"Good. Maybe he'll be so preoccupied he won't notice us." Jaylor pulled her tight against his chest and kissed her with fierce passion. "For luck," he grinned.

Deep in his eyes she saw another sentiment. The kiss was for farewell.

CHAPTER 34

A myriad of servants scurried among the trestle tables below the dais. Plain white cloths covered the boards; pewter platters and plain iron knives marked each place. The head table, on the dais, where Krej and his special guests would sit, was covered with the finest white damask and set with plates of gold and cutlery of fabulously expensive and incredibly rare steel, forged in secret half a world away.

Spring flowers sweetened the rushes underfoot and tasteful arrangements of greens and dried plants adorned baskets about the room. A grouping of three such tall baskets shielded a tiny alcove where Darville crouched unseen, with the pesky cat, Mica.

He shifted his weight for the umpteenth time. Mica hissed at him to be still. He felt like swatting her. His legs and back ached from the unnatural position. Mica was perfectly content to curl her small body into a tight ball and doze until action was needed.

But the image of Mica transformed into a lovely nude woman, with hair as bright and multicolored as the cat's shimmered before Darville's mind. Had he dreamed the true nature of the cat or had he really seen her in Shayla's cave? He shook his head clear of the image.

He couldn't nap and he couldn't dwell on dreams. He needed to stay alert. He half-wished for his wolf form. The four-legged creature would be much more comfortable hunkered down in this cold corner.

He shifted again just to spite the cat. This time his purloined sword clanked against the stone wall at his back.

A servitor in green and red tunic and trews whirled to

seek the source of the noise. Darville froze, hardly daring to breathe. The blacker than black hair with wings of silver at the servant's temples looked familiar.

The man scanned the room with wary eyes. They rested on Darville's hiding place then moved on. So did his hands. One moment the table was fully set. The next, two of the knives were missing.

Zolltarn the Rover! Of course. Darville knew he'd seen the man before. Like as not, more than two of the metal knives would be missing before the guests were seated.

Darville tried to blend in with the stones at his back. It didn't work. As soon as the other servitors were gone from the room, Zolltarn began searching the flower arrangements.

Silently Darville stood and eased his dagger from his sheath. When the Rover was close enough, he dragged the thief back into the shielded alcove.

A sound and your throat is slit," he hissed. His right arm encircled the man's chest. His left held the wicked dagger across the bobbing apple in the middle of Zolltarn's throat.

"Probably not, companion to the magician and the little beauty with red hair." Zolltarn almost chuckled, as much as any man in such a position could chuckle.

Darville raised an eyebrow but kept silence.

"A knife in a throat is a messy way to die and you have not the time or patience to clean up."

Mica hissed her agreement.

"A knife in the back is just as easy and cleaner. So answer my queries instead." Darville swallowed deeply. Though trained for combat since early childhood, this was the first time he had held a man's life in his hands.

"I can but try. Krej pays well for information. Can you pay more?"

"You payment will be your life if you answer truly. How much does Krej know about me and my companions?"

The man laughed, but not loudly. It was an evil kind of sound. That made it easier to prick the stretched skin of the Rover's neck. Zolltarn stopped abruptly as a tiny drop of blood oozed from the cut. Darville swallowed deeply again at the sight of the blood he had inflicted.

"The Lord Regent asked if I had stolen a wooden staff from the magician and his lady who were traveling with a great golden wolf."

"And if you saw such people in your journeys, did you steal the staff?"

"Ay, yes, we did. A shattered piece of wood is as good as stolen. I report everything to Lord Krej when he pays. But I did not know then that his description of you meant a real wolf. He would give much to know the wolf now walks on two legs instead of four."

Darville breathed a little easier. He didn't release the pressure on the man's neck. "What will buy your silence?"

"The promise of your seed for my people after this night's adventure. Your sons would be kings."

"My sons will be kings anyway. I do not waste my seed on temporary alliances." At least not since he'd met Brevelan. She was the only woman he wanted now.

"There is a boy, Yaakke, in the kitchens. He could grow to be very powerful if guided by me." The man's voice becoming seductively smooth. Fortunately, Darville had spent enough time with Jaylor and Brevelan to resist this attempt at compulsion.

"I am not like my cousin. I do not trade in lives. If the boy wishes to go, he may. It is his decision, not mine."

"Then I do not know what to ask for. You do not look as if you could pay more than Lord Krej. After all, he is Lord Regent with the wealth of a kingdom at his disposal."

Anger burned deep within Darville's gut. Mica hissed again. It sounded like she was commanding him to kill the evil Rover. He was very tempted. But the man might be useful yet.

"I can tell you where my cousin keeps his prettiest baubles. It will take you most of the night to break the seal on the lock."

"I am a Rover. I can smell such hiding places."

"Not in this castle, home to a rogue magician." The

Rover made a hasty (if halfhearted) gesture against evil at that comment. His eyes went wide, but there was no struggle to wiggle free of the very sharp dagger at this throat. "In a moon or more of searching you might find it. Do you have that kind of patience?" Darville felt more than a little satisfaction at the visible signs of the Rover's fear.

Zolltarn started to shrug, but the knife blade scraped his neck once more. Another drop of blood oozed from a cut.

"Tell me and you have my silence."

Baamin pushed aside intruding servitors and guards with a regal gesture of his staff. He allowed his armor to glow in his signature colors of yellow and green. No man tried to interfere with him twice.

A tap of his staff against the wide double doors to the banquet hall gained him entrance to the private feast. Eerily silent wind preceded him down the center of the room.

Shocked silence followed.

"What are you doing here?" Krej half rose from his thronelike chair in the center of the dais. His voice sounded unnatural in the increasingly heavy hush.

The senior magician stopped his progress toward the high table. All around him the noble men and women of the kingdom gasped at Krej's impropriety. One should never be this rude in public, and certainly not in front of foreigners. The ambassadors from Rossemeyer made frowns of disapproval toward their host.

Baamin suppressed a small smile. He needed the support of all these people. Very shortly he would ask the nobles to turn against the man they had elected regent. But that was only a small portion of his duties tonight.

If Jaylor failed, then he, Baamin, Senior Magician, had to follow through with Shayla's rescue.

"It is my right to sit at Council," Baamin stated simply.

"The Commune is broken. You have no more rights, old man, just as you have no more magic," Krej sneered.

He must be very certain of his position to risk such a public display. It was time to upset some of his security.

"Are you sure about that?" Baamin raised his right hand. It held a ball of unnatural red fire. He pointed at the ball with his left hand. One finger wiggled. The ball raised and bounced about the room. It landed in the headdress of one highborn lady but did not ignite it. The red flames split into a myriad of stars cloaking the lady in flattering sparkles of blue, red and gold.

"Oh, how lovely." She caught a few of the cold sparks in her hand and blew them to her husband, like a lover's kiss sent across the room. As each morsel of light landed in the man's palm it spread and grew into a delicate flower.

More smiles and exclamations of pleasure.

"I have arranged my own entertainment for tonight." Krej reseated himself. "Pay him no mind, gentlemen." He spoke more casually to the ambassadors at the high table. "An old man, feeble in the brain."

"So feeble I can not do this anymore," Baamin taunted as he brought forth thunder and lightning. This time the crowds cowered in anticipation of rain. It came, but Baamin evaporated it before it could drench the guests. It did, however, douse some of the torches. Select portions of the hall plunged into darkness. Shadows crept outward in imitation of uncertainty and evil. One small and insignificant drudge nodded to him from one of those shadows.

Tricks and sleight of hand to alter the mood of the assembled guests. Baamin had to make them vulnerable to his suggestion when he denounced Krej.

"Enough of this play, Baamin. You were not invited because the kingdom has no more use for you or the Commune. My armies are now our source of protection. Return to your University and pack your belongings. Three mornings hence, my soldiers will take possession of the buildings as barracks and storage and training ground." Krej dismissed him with a wave of his hand.

"I think not, my Lord Krej. By morning our rightful ruler will command the army." The time had come to finish this game. He could sense Jaylor's readiness. He need only be sure Krej's attention was fully engaged.

"I am the rightful ruler of Coronnan. Need I explain to you once more that during this last, and most likely final, illness of our king and in the absence of his heir I have been elected regent?" Krej's face was heated, growing nearly as red as his hair.

"But I am missing no longer, cousin." Darville stepped from his hiding place. His strong left hand rested on the hilt of his sword. His other hand lingered near a pocket as he moved close to the dais. Though not richly made, his clothes were respectable, and the prince's very regal bearing left no doubt as to his identity.

The ambassadors shifted uneasily. They looked from their host to the newcomer, unsure of where to place their allegiance.

"You might as well be." Krej was standing now. "You've been away for several moons with no explanation, no regard for the welfare of Coronnan. You've allowed your father's health to fail through your unconcern. And now that I have things under control, you've decided to return." His hand waved to the guards who lined the walls. They began to move slowly forward.

"You should know precisely where I was, cousin. For 'twas you who lured me away, and you who allowed a rogue magician to entrap me into the guise of a golden wolf." Baamin and Jaylor had agreed beforehand that they could not accuse Krej of rogue magic without visible proof. Hopefully Krej would supply that proof before the night was over.

Noble guests looked carefully around for signs of any rogue. Some made the cross of the Stargods, others crossed their wrists and flapped their hands in an older gesture against evil. Three cowering women did both. Baamin could hardly think over the babble of frightened whispers. That suited him fine. The prince was handling the situation quite nicely.

"The last time I saw you, Lord Krej, I was ensorcelled in the guise of a golden wolf, familiar to a witchwoman,

who just happens to be your illegitimate daughter."
Stunned and superstitious silence met that announcement.

Baamin silently applauded the young prince for linking
his recent captor with Krej. The witchwoman probably
kept the enchanted wolf in hiding on her father's orders.

At that moment a small bundle of multi-colored fur
chose to race and bound through the great hall. Baamin
recognized the cat from Yaakke's report. He called her
Mica. A suitable name considering her nearly iridescent
fur.

Mica made a show of circling Darville's legs, while
yowling her displeasure over something. The prince ignored her.

"Get that cat out of here!" Krej jerked back from the
edge of the table just as Mica leaped from the dais to the
table. She spat at him with incredible disdain but did not
linger near the Lord Regent. Instead she sauntered to the
ambassador, sniffed his hand, licked it and began to purr
so loud Baamin could hear it half a room away.

"This cat," the ambassador's face lit with a mighty
grin, "where did she come from?" He stroked her fur with
lingering affection.

Krej continued to lean away from the cat's presence.
"It's just a cat. There are numerous ones about to catch
mice." Not likely, judging from Krej's dislike, or fear, of
this one.

"The cat came with me," Darville interrupted.

"She is near duplicate of our princess's pet, such unusual fur. The cat was much beloved but disappeared
some time ago. Princess Rossemikka has mourned the
loss ever since." The ambassador's attention was now on
the prince.

Baamin continued to watch Krej for signs of trickery.

"A gift of this cat to the Princess Rossemikka would be
a suitable token for one who seeks alliance," the second
ambassador suggested.

"NO!" Krej bellowed, but not at this suggestion. His
eyes narrowed to angry slits, his face paled to the color
of the table cover. "He can't. I won't let him rob me of

my treasure!" The Lord Regent jerked to his feet unsteadily. "Guards, into the great hall. Kill the intruders!"

Hastily, Baamin threw a magic barrier across the archway. No one must interfere with Jaylor.

But Darville was faster. His right hand flung something into Krej's face. "Poison! The prince has poisoned me," the Lord Regent screamed in pain. He clawed at his face with desperate hands. His breath rattled and gasped.

"Go to Jaylor, quickly!" Darville commanded Baamin as he drew his sword. "I'll hold off the guards as long as I can." Already the prince's sword slashed and grappled with the soldiers seeking to defend their lord.

"Is Shayla still alive?" Jaylor whispered.

Brevelan nodded. "Just barely."

Jaylor began deep breathing in preparation for the ordeal before him. From Brevelan's raspy tone he guessed his time was limited. Shayla's imprisonment would kill the dragon very soon. Her freedom would see his own death.

He was resigned to it now, after days of worry and depression. There was a lightness in his mind and body. His life, and death, had a purpose.

The magic beneath his feet vibrated through his being in rhythm with his respiration. He nurtured the flow for several counts until he felt full to exploding with raw power. He raised the mended staff over his head until the magic pulsed within it too. With luck, Brevelan's splice would last through this one last spell.

He didn't want the magic and the power raw. It needed to be refined and fine-tuned to imitate Krej's original spell. In his mind Jaylor relived the scene in Shayla's cave.

Once again he saw the beast-headed rogue capering to his own chanted spell. He had used the chant very much as Brevelan, his daughter, used her music.

The magic vibrated again, in time with the remembered chant.

There had been words, too. Words describing the desired result of the spell. Jaylor didn't like words. They tended to be imprecise, ambiguous, compared to the very vivid pictures he created in his mind. But this spell had been created with words, so it must end with words.

> "Precious dragon from glass.
> Precious glass from sand."

The magic hummed louder within him. He felt the pressure of people at his back, anger, fear and the clash of steel. He didn't care. Nothing mattered but the power of the music inside him.

> "Ordinary sand from the sea.
> Nurturing sea from creator air."

Brevelan sang the tune beside him. It filled him to overflowing. The staff glowed. With great effort he contained the magic within him. The spell was not yet complete.

> "Blessed wind from air.
> Purifying air for freedom.
> Freedom for dragon made of glass,
> sand,
> seA,
> aIR,
> WIND!"

With the final words he pictured that glorious flight with the dragons playing with the wind, soaring above Coronnan in an exquisite cherishing of the ultimate freedom. There were no chains to the ground, no compulsions to eat of the Tambootie, no restrictions and no pain.

Colors burst forth from his staff in a glowing storm, red and blue and copper in a braided shaft arrowed toward the back corner of the room, bounced and fled straight into the heart of the dragon, green and red and the elemental copper flowing in a hazy halo about the sculpture. Blue and red balls bounced about the room, landing on each of the other sculptures, himself and

Brevelan. All the colors of Coronnan split into a bright haze that filled the huge hall. Then they wove back into braids of magic that twined with each of the sculptures.

The sound of wild gusts of air pushed the magic into the directed targets.

Bits of copper broke loose from the braids of bright colors. The element sought and surrounded tiny morsels of emerald and dark ruby encased in the glass.

Krej's life spirit contained in the spell faded and fled to the far reaches of the hall.

Freed from the restrictive traps, Jaylor's magic burst loose. Just barely, he kept it within his control.

His overworked lungs and heart stuttered. And still he drew more power up from the bowels of the planet, fed more and yet more magic into the spell.

The magic of Coronnan pulsed through his veins, tore through his body mercilessly. With a mighty effort he turned the staff to the dragon's tail. It twitched. With the tiny movement, glass broke and tinkled to the floor. That small amount of freedom generated a greater swipe of the mighty tail.

Farther and farther up the dragon's spine the glass fractured, splintered, shattered. With each release, Shayla's tail slashed further and further. It beat at the glass on her hind legs and belly. It flogged the metals encasing the other animals nearest her. Those, too, began to shatter. Then her front legs shook free of the ensorcellment.

Jaylor heaved his staff forward to Shayla's broad chest and neck.

He was the power, the *Power* was Jaylor. He mastered the *Power* and was mastered by it. Nothing existed except the *Power.*

He saw the dragon as she had been; he was with her, in her, her mate and herself all at the same time. Through her eyes he saw himself and the quaking Brevelan, who touched the dragon's mind. He saw Darville fighting for his life with a purloined sword against three hefty guards, and Baamin's feeble attempts to contain the fight and their enemy Krej as they all spilled into the great hall. He felt Shayla's pain and loneliness, cherished the freedom that was creeping up her back and neck.

With a mighty twist, the last shower of glass cascaded from her head and horn.

"Grrooowerrrrrrrrrrrrrrrr!" Shayla roared, once more herself. The other animals echoed the triumph of Jaylor's magic over their enchantment.

Jaylor slumped to the floor, deflated at the separation from Shayla's and Brevelan's mind.

The magic ceased to flow. Jaylor ceased to breathe.

CHAPTER 35

"Seize him! Seize him you fools," Krej ordered his burly guards.

Three men advanced on Darville, swords drawn and at the ready. The prince moved to stand between them and the doorway to the Great Hall. He had to give Jaylor and Baamin time.

Slash and parry, duck and dive under the man's guard. He pushed all of his concentration, anger and strength into maintaining his position. He'd fought three men on the training field. Three bored soldiers who were afraid to be too aggressive with a prince.

These three men in red and green surcoats were well trained and eager to please a ruthless lord. They pushed Darville back, closer and closer to the door. One man distracted him with a flourish of fancy blade work.

Darville answered him stroke for stroke. A second man slipped in under his guard. Blood trickled down Darville's arm. His mind registered the fact that he was wounded. His body had yet to feel it.

He clenched his free hand into a fist and slammed it into the face of the man with the flourishing sword. He staggered backward into the arms of the third man. That left only one to deal with.

Then the cut began to burn and so did his mind. With renewed fury and bared teeth Darville slashed and lunged until the bigger man and his partner were pinned against one of the long tables. The third man seemed to be out cold on the floor.

A woman screamed and overturned her chair as she backed away from the fight. Servitors and nobles alike ran or scurried into dark corners for protection. Strong men cowered and weak women stared at the blood on his arm and the blood on the throat of the guard in fascination. The other guards hesitated in a semicircle around him. Darville didn't know what kept them back. Had Baamin thrown some kind of armor? A little late if he had.

"Swear your loyalty to me!" he commanded the man pinned beneath his sword. "I am your prince, soon to be your king. Swear your loyalty or die."

The guard gulped loudly. The sword point scratched his throat as the words worked their way up. "I swear," he croaked.

"And you, all of you as well will swear." Darville swung around to face the crowd. A few of the nobles were already on their knees murmuring the words of fealty.

"Forget this puny princeling. I am your rightful lord!" Krej screeched, half blinded by the witchbane.

No one answered him. Hands covering his face, the Lord Regent turned and ran toward the Great Hall.

Darville saw the move and lunged to capture his cousin in a cruel grip. "Call off your men, Krej!" he commanded.

Krej continued to hold one hand over his eyes but said nothing. Darville realized his cousin's magic was neutralized, or he would never have been able to touch the man. The witchbane had worked.

"Very good, your grace," one of the ambassadors applauded with voice and hands.

"We believed your people weak. You have just proven yourself a warrior worthy of our princess," the other ambassador bowed low. He still cradled Mica in his arms. The traitorous cat looked all too content to stay with him.

"Look at him, you traitors!" Krej bellowed. "Look at how he bares his teeth and his hair stands up, just like a wolf. He is still part wolf and can never be trusted. Is this the man you wish to be your ruler?" With a mighty jerk, Krej pulled away from Darville and lunged once more for

the tapestry that masked access to the Great Hall and
Shayla.

Darville bounded after him, sword at the ready. The entire crowed followed.

The woven drapery tore down the middle and slipped
to the ground in limp folds.

No one noticed a weary royal messenger, spurs
clanking on the stone floor, limp into the banquet hall.

"SHAYLA!" Brevelan commanded with voice and
mind. The great dragon head swung back and forth in anger, mouth agape, sparks dripping from her teeth. Her
gaze pinned Krej and Darville to the wall near the entrance.

He must pay for his evil. Shayla's voice once more
filled Brevelan, after weeks of absence. Even with the anger, Brevelan felt a little more complete now that her
dragon was with her.

"Not here, not now, and not by you." She fought for
control.

I am the one wronged.

"But restored."

My young?

Brevelan pushed her awareness to the tiny life forms
within Shayla. Eleven of them, where before there had
been twelve. Sadness at the one lump of inanimate flesh
filled them both. But the others were fully formed and
nearer readiness than they should be.

It is too soon! Shayla wailed with a spittle of flame
from her gaping muzzle. *They will be born out of cycle.*

Brevelan sought to contain the fire. "They will live.
And so must you. Kill my father now and this crowd will
gladly watch you die. Your brood with you."

Another morsel of flame ripped toward the growing
crowd huddled against the interior wall.

"No, Shayla. If you kill my father, you kill me as
well." Brevelan knew it in her heart. She was tied by
blood and magic to the one man in the entire kingdom
she wished she could disown. Blood of her blood, flesh of
her flesh. She would feel his death, share his pain more

fully than any but Mama. If the death of an unknown squirrel in the meadow pained her, Krej's death in the same room as she would kill her.

"Grrrooowerrrrrr!" Shayla belched forth one more burst of defiant fire. She whirled about the room, seeking escape. Her tail lashed back and forth, sweeping a pathway. Yet it kept free of the recumbent form of Jaylor, her deliverer. The one time she came close to his body she almost curled her tail around him in a protective coil.

The magician loves you. The words came to Brevelan with typical dragon abruptness. Then there was only silence.

Darville sagged with Shayla's silence There was a momentary hole where his heart used to be. He pulled Brevelan tight against him to fill the void. The world righted for him again.

As long as Brevelan was at his side, he was complete. He was in command.

"A live dragon, ensorcelled in your own Great Hall, Lord Regent?" Darville almost spat his question. He whirled to face his cousin, pointing his sword at Krej's throat. He wished he could murder the rogue magician on the spot and get away with it.

"You are in no position to question anything, wolf-man." Krej eyed him levelly. Though shorter and older than himself, Krej was still a commanding presence.

"Rogue magic was outlawed three hundred years ago for precisely these reasons," Baamin reminded them all. "Magic cannot be allowed if it is used for the sake of greed and power. It must be controlled by the Commune and used solely for the good of the kingdom."

"The statues were present in my hall, yes. But you will never prove that I am a magician, nor that I did anything more than accept great art from a stranger. No one in his right mind will want to prove anything else," Krej reiterated. "I was the only one capable of organizing a fragmented kingdom. I brought forth the army. I defended our borders. Even as we speak, Lord Wendray is retaking the border city of Sambol." He paused long enough to look his fellow councilors in the eye. "You will all stand with me because I am the most able to continue to rule."

Shayla roared her disapproval of that. Her wings flapped and she prepared to exit, but her tail still encircled Jaylor's body.

Darville wondered if he should go to his friend, see if he still lived. Why else would the dragon protect him, as she had protected Darville last winter.

But Darville couldn't afford to remove his attention from the Council members just yet. Krej was so very sure of himself, so very compelling in his belief that he was in the right. How could the Council disagree?

"And what happens when the war is over or when my father dies?" Darville forced himself to think like a king, plan for the years to come and not just for the moment's need and the grief he continually thrust aside. His spine took on the formal posture and regal bearing he had been taught as a child. It came naturally now despite his longing to bare his teeth and growl his frustration.

He hardly noticed when Brevelan turned away from him, skirts kilted to her knees as she ran to Jaylor's side. She would be back when he needed her. Of that he was sure.

"We will address that issue after the war or when Darcine finally dies. He should be recovering now that Shayla is flying." Krej gestured his dismissal of the matter.

"We will address that issue now, since you created the war." Darville's mouth lifted in an involuntarily growl. He needed to sink his teeth into Krej's neck and taste the hot blood. He needed to kill!

With great effort he mastered his bestial urges.

"My lords," a tired voice whispered. A man in the royal livery looked to both Darville and Krej, not knowing who should receive the message. "My lords," he spoke a little louder to the entire company. "King Darcine is dead. He passed into the dimensions beyond at dawn yesterday."

Silence descended over the room with a crash. Then a hubbub of questioning voices arose like a roar. The noise was no louder than Shayla's own cry of mourning. She let forth one mighty blast of dragon fire against the outside wall. Wood and stone exploded outward. The stench of burning Tambootie engulfed the room.

Heavily, clumsily, Shayla lumbered toward the gateway she had made. Her wings flapped in the limited space, gathering speed.

The wind created by her laboring pinions pushed Darville back into the crowd. He reached out a protective arm toward the dragon. Only Jaylor, still lying on the floor in the boneless heap where he had collapsed, and Brevelan kneeling at his side, remained in the center of the room.

With one last mighty sweep of wings and tail, Shayla bellowed forth her anger and launched herself into the dark night. The other animals shook free of the last traces of magic and followed her.

"Shayla, come back to me," Brevelan whispered through her tears.

Not while the evil one lives. He has killed my king.

Darville gave the assembly a moment to think about the awesome sight of a dragon in their midst.

"My father is dead. I am the next legal heir," Darville announced to one and all.

If only life were that simple, Baamin wailed to himself. "The king is dead," he bowed his head in a moment of grief for his old friend. "There are two claimants to the throne, Darville as prince and Krej as duly elected Lord Regent. Shayla has flown away without naming her enemy and without consecrating the next king. She has gone and has taken her mates with her." He faced the crowd and allowed the gravity of the situation to sink into their minds.

"Who now decides how we should be governed? Council and Commune must come to an agreement." The old magician was suddenly weary and doubtful of the outcome of that agreement.

"Without dragons, there can be no legal magic and therefore no Commune," Krej reminded them all.

Baamin has witnessed the tremendous power working through Jaylor, tonight. Boy—Yaakke, as he preferred to be called—possessed power as well. With a few more like them he could play watchdog over individual magicians to keep them ethical and controlled. The Commune could still serve a purpose.

But the throne was in contention. Baamin's Commune would support Darville, give him the edge to control the Twelve.

"I've lost ten farms, two dozen people, and more, to the raids across the border in the last few weeks," one lord spoke up at last. "I have to support Lord Krej as regent if not king. He's shown what he can do for this kingdom. Darville's young yet. Untried and still showing signs of his ordeal with wolves."

Lord Andrall from the extreme north stepped forward to stand beside Darville. "What has Krej done for this country? The army is routed, the battles have all been lost. He's lied to us repeatedly. And how does he know what is happening on the field of battle if he isn't using magic?" Andrall swung his gaze back to the regent with malice. "I've never trusted you, Krej. I didn't vote for your regency. Now I stand by my lawful prince. I think once we've heard his adventures, we'll all agree he's had enough experience to launch the next campaign against our enemies."

Baamin looked about in distress. This was what he feared most. The Great Wars of Disruption had begun under similar circumstances. He had to reconvene the Commune immediately.

"While the king was so ill, it was our right to elect a regent. The dragon didn't approve Darville as king. How do we know he's not the 'evil one' she mentioned? I stand by Lord Krej." Lord Jonnias moved to stand beside the regent.

One by one the lords moved to the side of their chosen commander. Against the wall their ladies separated equally. Baamin felt powerless. This was one time he could use no magic. Decisions like these had to be made freely; if made under magic compulsion they would break apart eventually.

Finally Kevinrosse, the chief ambassador from Rossemeyer, moved forward. "We came to seek alliance with Coronnan. Our offer was for marriage between Prince Darville and our beloved Princess, Rossemikka. Lord Krej tried to offer himself in the marriage. We found that dishonorable in that he is already wed." He continued to caress the small cat he carried in his arms. "If he is willing to behave with such disregard for morality in the matter of an alliance, we believe he will do so in every other matter." He swallowed and looked around at the divided company. "Therefore, Rossemeyer extends the offer of marriage, alliance, armies, and wealth to Prince Darville."

"Mere promises from a poor kingdom that has always been our enemy. Promises that our neighbor SeLenicca have vowed will lead to war. Which war do we choose? In either case, Coronnan needs a strong leader, experienced in battle." Krej dismissed the ambassador with complete contempt.

"Then we will war among ourselves as much as with our enemies," Baamin muttered. He felt utterly defeated. The kingdom he had dedicated his life to preserving was divided. But he had seen a dragon this night. He had heard some of her words. There was nothing left to live for.

"Jaylor?" Brevelan whispered. She knelt beside him, ignoring the arguments of the politicians behind her. Jaylor's eyes remained closed. Gingerly she felt for a pulse at his neck. At first she despaired of finding any flutter of life.

But her healing sense pulled outward, demanding to be used. He must be alive. He must. She hadn't felt his death, only his pain and the utter blankness of his retreat from that pain.

She flattened her palm against his chest. Energy pulsed through her into his heart. Push, retreat, push and retreat again, forcing Jaylor's organ of life to pump blood. Push and retreat.

One beat of response. Barely.

His lungs shuddered and strained for air. She gave it to him.

She sought his mind, fearing it had flown away with the dragon, as it had once before. No, it was there, deep within, hiding from the pain. Best to leave it there a while.

A lilting tune of peace and love came into her head. She sang it to him with crooning care. The notes rose in a haunting cry for her lover to return to her. Her song soared and filled the room with her love for the dying magician.

"The clearing will be so empty without you, dear heart," she finally whispered through her tears. "I will be so empty without you."

A little life stirred under her hand. The tune came out louder, stronger. She wept with the poignancy of her music and relief that he was fighting to join her once more. His heart stammered in its rhythm, caught her song and found its proper cadence. She felt her own heart join his in the battle to retain life.

With a tremendous shudder his lungs fought the paralysis of his pain. She took some of the pain away, allowed it to dissipate in her stronger body. Air left her lungs and filled his body and left him again and filled her until he was breathing in the natural course.

His eyes struggled open, glazed with pain. She tried to take it away, but it was too powerful. Her body and mind recoiled from the task. She had to protect the new life within her as well as his.

"Shayla?" Jaylor croaked past parched lips and tortured lungs.

"She is safe," Brevelan reassured him. Her own lungs were beginning to ache with the force of maintaining his life.

"There is no magic left within me. I used it all up. There is nothing left of me." His sadness nearly overwhelmed her. But with it was resignation as well.

"Your magic will come back." It had to. She knew he would never be complete without it.

"No. There is only so much a man can do. This night I used a lifetime of power. There is no more." His eyes closed. The blackness nearly swept over her, too.

"Jaylor!" she called. "Jaylor, come back." Her mind screamed for him, but he was hiding from the pain of loss as well as the pain the magic had ripped through his body.

"Brevelan." Darville stooped beside her. "Brevelan, it is important you hear what I have to say."

She looked up. Tears blurred her eyes. She blinked them back. There was time yet to think of Jaylor. He needed rest more than her healing touch.

"Yes, Your Grace, I'm listening." She had to remember now to address him as her prince and not her friend or her puppy.

"These men," he pointed to the richly dressed one who carried Mica and his equally resplendent companion, "have offered an alliance. They want me to marry their princess."

Her heart felt stabbed. Darville marry? It would be the end of their companionship, the end of the love that had sustained them through so many weeks of hardship. She clutched Jaylor's cold hand along with Darville's, reforging the bond.

"I told them I cannot. My heart is already committed to you."

She sagged with relief. Still she clung to them both, as she had since Jaylor had invaded her clearing.

"The Council is divided. To reunite them I think it wise for me to marry Lord Krej's oldest daughter." He didn't give her time to feel pain over that. "Though born out of wedlock, you are Krej's daughter. Royal blood runs strong through you. You have spoken with dragons, that is proof of your birth."

Jaylor's hand twitched in hers. His eyes opened and he stared directly into her soul. Mica hissed and leaped from the ambassador's arms and into her lap. Her purr spoke volumes.

Brevelan's decision was made. "I could never be your

princess, Darville." A tremendous ache surround her heart. Though she loved him, they could not be together. "I can never live in a city, can never preside over a table filled with meat. The numbers of people your princess would need to see everyday would cripple me with their uncontrolled emotions."

She sought his eyes for understanding. He, too, was filled with the pain of the separation that must come. "I love you dearly, but Jaylor needs me, and I love him, too. You need someone stronger, better educated, lovelier than I."

"But it is you I love. You are more than just my princess, Brevelan. I need you, as much or more now than I did when you rescued a wounded wolf from a killer storm. Coronnan needs your sensitivity and compassion. Only you can guide me as I rule them," Darville argued.

"You need a woman bred to politics, educated and sophisticated, who can share your life in the capital. I cannot. Now if Master Baamin will order a litter, I will return to the monastery with Jaylor. He needs me." *But I love you. I love you both.*

"Jaylor, did you give the dragon the vial of medicine before she was enchanted?" Baamin asked urgently from directly behind Darville. There was no answer, only a few labored breaths.

Almost reverently the old magician removed his own blue cloak with white stars on the collar and spread it over Jaylor.

Brevelan continued to hold Darville's gaze with the love they no longer had the right to express.

"Master, is everything gonna be all right now that the dragons're gone?" A filthy boy tugged at Baamin's robes in anxious query.

Brevelan watched the urchin rather than be tempted by Darville's pleas.

"Yes, Yaakke. We will work to make everything right. We know our enemy; we can find a way to defeat him."

"What about him?" He pointed a grubby hand toward Jaylor. "Will he be all right, master?"

Brevelan longed to take the child and dunk him into

the nearest bathing pool. But she didn't have the time or energy to spare. Jaylor continued to breathe by force of her will alone.

"The best healers in Coronnan will be summoned to make sure Jaylor gets well," Baamin reassured the boy. "But he has wielded a great deal of power this night at tremendous cost to himself. He needs time to rest and solitude to meditate."

"No other healers will be necessary, Master Baamin." Brevelan stood to face the senior magician and the gathered assembly. "As soon as we are both rested, I will take Jaylor back to the clearing. The clearing Nimbulan created to protect Myrilandel and their children and generations of dragon guardians who followed them. Jaylor and I must be there when the dragons come home."

EPILOGUE

They think they have defeated me. I still have a few surprises up my sleeve. They shall not deprive me of my treasures or of the power. The Tambootie has made me one with Simurgh. We will not be denied.

It will take a little time and much planning, but the fools will learn. Somewhere there is an antidote to witchbane. Perhaps I shall take a little retreat and find the answer in an ancient book dedicated to Simurgh. A book whose pages are pressed from the Tambootie. Then I shall start again. Maman will help, she is the high priestess of Simurgh.

I cannot allow another weakling to rule Coronnan. Only I can wield the power concealed within her depths.

Only I can have a glass dragon for a pet.

IRENE RADFORD

THE DRAGON NIMBUS HISTORY

☐ **THE DRAGON'S TOUCHSTONE (Book One)**
0-88677-744-5—$6.99

☐ **THE LAST BATTLEMAGE (Book Two)** 0-88677-774-7—$6.99

☐ **THE RENEGADE DRAGON (Book Three)** 0-88677-855-7—$6.99
The great magical wars have come to an end. But in bringing peace, Nimbulan, the last Battlemage, has lost his powers. Dragon magic is the only magic legal to practice. And the kingdom's only hope against dangerous technology lies in the one place to which no dragon will fly . . .

THE DRAGON NIMBUS TRILOGY

☐ **THE GLASS DRAGON (Book One)** 0-88677-634-1—$6.99

☐ **THE PERFECT PRINCESS (Book Two)** 0-88677-678-3—$6.99

☐ **THE LONELIEST MAGICIAN (Book Three)**
0-88677-709-7—$6.99

Irene Radford
Merlin's Descendants